DEADLY
OUTCOME

EL PASO MYSTERIES SERIES

BERRY HAWKINS

Layout design by Ink Lion Publishing

First Edition March 2017

DEDICATION

To my wife, La Rue, our son, Berry III, and our daughter, Dr. Lisa Fraga, for their encouragement, support and love.

To the Keller Writer's Association and Lamb of God Writer's for their help and direction.

To Pam Kemp, Kay Dykes, and Kathleen for proofing, cover design and formatting the book.

Chapter 1

2:48 a.m.
3 December 2012
Beasley residence
Mountain Land Subdivision
El Paso, Texas

OSCAR BEASLEY PULLED HIS PILLOW over his head, and reached to find the phone, tipping over his water in the process.

"Oscar! Answer the phone. It's always for you anyway," Jackie moaned, as she leg-pushed him out of bed.

"I'm trying. Get a towel, will you? I spilled water on the rug."

He found the phone. Fell out of bed reaching for the lamp. "Hold a second," he muttered. Sweeping his arm out, he found the lamp. "I'm tangled in a sheet." He caught his fall with his other arm, leaving one leg free, and the other wrapped in covers. He worked his way out of the tangle. "Sorry. Who's calling?"

An outraged voice shouted, "You manage the Better Deal on Central?"

"Indirectly. I'm the district manager. Who's this? Do I know you? Why are you calling me in the middle of the night?"

The man didn't offer his name, but he claimed a sign in our window offered this number. Unaware of the sign, Oscar stammered a confused response, "I see."

"I'll tell you who I am, you idiot. I live behind your store." As the man yelled, Oscar could hear an alarm going off in the background. "Your damned alarm is screaming so loud I can't sleep! My wife is crying. Lights are flashing. Do something before I put a torch to the place."

Oscar stammered, "Something's not working. Our alarm system is programmed to call the police. They're supposed to turn off the alarm remotely after they get the call."

"Your problem! I've got to work tomorrow. Get the damned thing turned off."

Hoping to move to a less emotional confrontation, Oscar consumed some humble pie. "I'm sorry this is a problem for you. I appreciate the call. Can you tell me if the police are on the scene?"

"I checked. No one's there. Front window's busted."

"Sorry you had to go to so much trouble." Oscar paced, trying to make sense of what the guy was saying. "Did you call the police?"

"No. Didn't want to call you either. Someone might figure I'm the one who broke in and took stuff."

"Thank you for doing the right thing. I'll call the police and get someone over there to shut down the alarm as soon as possible. It would be helpful if you gave me your name. The police may have some questions."

"No! Not gonna get involved. You handle it." The receiver clicked.

"Turn out the lights, and come back to bed," said Jackie.

"Can't. I've got to go to work."

"At this hour? Don't be ridiculous."

"Oh yeah! I've gotta go. There was a break-in on Central. I'll just go on to the office from there."

"Oscar, who was that on the phone?"

"A guy who lives behind the store reported a break in. He was complaining about our alarm and lights. His wife gave him hell, so he gave me a piece of his mind. Said we're keeping the whole neighborhood awake."

"Oscar," scolded Jackie, "You're making too much noise, banging stuff around, slamming doors and talking too loud. The kids need their sleep."

"Sure, okay, sorry. Would you call the police? I need to go. Tell them about the break-in—that I'm on my way. I don't want them to mistake me for a burglar. Have you seen my blue blazer? I had it hanging on the chair by the lamp."

"Did you look in the closet?" she fussed, "I put it there, where it's supposed to go. Do you want something to eat before you go?"

"No. I'll grab a bite after I get this sorted out. "

"Oscar. Next time you answer the phone, try to be more careful."

"I will. Sorry about the mess."

"Fix your tie. It's crooked."

Oscar straightened his tie, laid a quick kiss on Jackie's lips, and made his exit through the mudroom and into the garage.

Jackie followed him into the garage. "Promise me you'll be careful."

"I promise. Don't forget to call the police. Hug the kids for me."

The drive time presented an opportunity to think things through. Dan Coleman, the store manager, needed to know. He dialed Dan's number.

"Dan here. Who's calling? You know what time it is?"

"Dan, it's Oscar. No, it can't wait. Your store had a break-in; a front window's broken. The police haven't responded."

Dan asked, "No police? Have you called them? Who called you?"

"No. I asked Jackie's to make the call. A neighbor called me. I'll fill you in when we get there. We need to get to the store, see what's going on. I don't know the code, so you'll need to turn off the alarm."

"Oscar, you're going to get there first. The code is 4119. Oh! That won't work. You don't have a key. You want me to call my assistant? He lives just five or ten minutes away."

"No," he reflected, "We don't need him or a key. I'll step through the window frame. No window, remember? Besides, the company expects you and me to handle these kinds of situations."

By the way," Oscar inquired, "When did the company put the sign in the window with instructions to call me in the event of an emergency?"

"Came in company mail maybe three-four months ago. I thought it came from you," said Dan.

"Didn't come from me. Caught me by surprise," said Oscar, "I usually get a call from the security people. The neighbor who called was upset about the racket and the lights. Bet he's not the only one. You need to get going. Be careful on the way."

Chapter 2

2:30 a.m.
3 December 2012
El Paso, Texas

GLENN BERGMANN WAS DRIVING and in a surly mood. It was Leo's fault. If he'd set the alarm clock right they'd be on their 1:00 a.m. target time, not half past two. Leo knew he was going to catch hell when this was done.

Things aren't right. It's too wet, too cold, and too damned foggy, this truck is a piece of garbage. We ought to abort. Can't. We need the money.

Besides all that, Bergmann's monsters, the reminders of his fear of the dark and his love/hate relationship with his father, had come roaring back. A childhood legacy caused by locked closets and brutal whooping's intended to alter his behavior, causing instead, an inability to face the night.

He'd loved his father; at least until the night his dad pounded and stabbed his mom to death. Glenn had been twelve, small for his age, but strong enough. He'd evened the score with his baseball bat, only to spend his remaining youth in juvenile detention.

He was shivering, not from the cold, nor one of his crack induced muscle spasms. He could handle cold and even cocaine shivers, it was the monsters. The monsters, he knew, were his father reincarnated, unreasoning, angry and out of control, trying again, to throw him into scary isolation.

The others could see he was struggling and looked away, but they knew his history, had seen his bruises and marveled that neither Glenn nor his mother had ever told. To others they appeared normal, middle-class and happy. Behind closed doors, he'd experienced a living hell.

Glenn wrestled with his wretched memories, compartmentalized his fears and decided to get on with his life. Sometimes that worked, too often, he lost. Those times he used a needle for soothing relief. Tonight he had to decide, were his concerns about this heist springing legitimately from his instincts for survival or had the ghosts of his past taken control?

His Texas license said he was twenty-three, it showed a man who appeared fifty, revealing to those who'd seen it before, the effects of addiction to drugs. Crack cocaine and meth had been sources of courage and strength, now they induced coughing, sleep deprivation, loss of appetite, aggressive and often paranoid behavior, as well as an unquenchable need.

The booming muffler and the angry scrape of worn-out wipers made him cringe as though a razor blade had taken a swipe down his back. *Damn it all! How am I supposed to concentrate with this racket?*

"Leo, I ought to kick your butt," he snarled. "This bucket of bolts is a disaster. It's too small. I can't turn the steering wheel without hitting you in the face with my elbow. Why steal a truck with one bench seat for three people, when there're more two-seaters out there than bench seats? It makes way the hell too much noise. We're going to wake up the whole neighborhood, not to mention the fact that I can't see. Next time I tell you to swipe some wheels, use some sense, or you'll be singing soprano. Understand?"

"Hey, man, I'm sorry! It looked pretty cool. Thought you'd like it," said Leo.

"Next time, pick one that doesn't stick out. This thing draws attention like a house on fire."

Bergmann was straddling a fence of indecision. He decided to make another drive-by. He tiptoed the stolen black low-rider Chevy pickup in front of the closed supermarket, made a slow U-turn, rolled to a stop, raised his arm to command silence, lowered the window, killed the engine and listened. He heard the patter of rain on his jacket and the metallic crack of a cooling engine, nothing more.

He re-started the truck, idled it around to the back, where a light atop a telephone pole and another above the receiving door were fitted with mercury vapor bulbs casting pale blue light and creating dark shadows down the back of the building.

"I thought I saw something move back here on our first pass," said Bergmann. "Help me look."

He stopped again, put a finger to his lips, and shook his shaved head to indicate no talking. He listened and looked; saw poorly stacked wooden pallets, bales of cardboard and a row of damaged shopping carts, plus two over-filled dumpsters surrounded by trash they couldn't contain.

Not satisfied, he got out of the truck, looked for movement. Nothing! Then he saw it. A flash of black fur, a cat startled by their intrusion, jumped out of and off the edge of one of the dumpsters.

Damn! He got back in the truck, twisted on the bench seat and faced his cohorts. "Would you believe it? A cat! Now we know. Let's vote. Do we go or not?"

Hearing no response Bergmann bit his lower lip and drew blood. His face turned red. He hunched his shoulders, doubled his fist and crashed it down on the steering wheel. His face contorted from the excruciating pain. "Aw, shit!" he exclaimed.

It took a moment for the pain to subside. "Dammit!" he said. "Listen up. We're out of hooch and about out of money. You guys want to do this job or not? If you want to work with me, you'd better pay attention."

Jolted to responsiveness, Juan stammered, "Sorry. Looks good to me. I'm ready. I was thinking about that redhead we met last night at the Loco Luna. Man, she had a pair."

"Juan, you dumbass! You'd better get your pea-brain in gear and focus on what's happening here. I need to be able to count on you."

"Why you coming down so hard on us," asked Juan? "Seems like you're mad at everything."

"Why? How about I don't want to wind up back in the slammer? That's why!"

"Sorry, man, me either. I apologize. I'm good to go."

"Leo? How about you?"

"Me? I'm ready. Looks cool. Let's get it on."

"That makes it unanimous," said Bergmann.

Wordlessly, as was their routine, the burglars donned their black baklavas and sought divine protection and forgiveness, by making the sign of the cross.

Bergmann circled back to the front street, stopped, doused the headlights, took one last pull from a hand-rolled joint, smothered the stub in the ashtray, then backed the truck into a space near the left-side entrance. It bottomed out, and then bumped the curb.

"Damn it, Leo! See why I wanted a regular truck? This thing is for show, not utility."

There were no outside lights illuminating the front of the store. Inside, three distant fluorescents wrestled with the dark.

Bergmann turned to face the others. "Okay. Showtime. Listen up. If we don't have the smokes on time, we leave anyway. Juan, you get the empty boxes out of the back. We won't need the sledges. This time we've got something better. We'll use one of their concrete garbage containers. Leo, help me move one over by the window. It'll take all of us to heave it through."

They'd found a way to beat the system. It was all a matter of timing, of getting in and out in four minutes flat. They'd rehearsed it and used the system so often they felt comfortable they'd never get caught. All they ever took were cigarettes cartons. They loaded three boxes apiece and left the rest. It'd worked like a charm for ten of the past twelve weeks. On only two occasions had unexpected interventions screwed up their plans.

The selling price for most brands of cigarettes was about fifty bucks per carton. Stolen, they fenced for half that amount, enough to cover their habits.

This store had been carefully researched and on their schedule for two weeks. The building had a sophisticated alarm system programed to notify the police if a contact was broken. Not a problem. Their truck would be loaded and gone before law enforcement could respond.

They hoisted the two hundred pound garbage container and used it as a missile to take out a window. Bergmann started his stopwatch. The break, as expected, set off a loud, screeching alarm and some red and blue strobe lights. The flashing lights were unexpected and panicked both Leo and Juan. They dropped their cartons and turned to run.

Bergmann saw they were about to make for the woods and shouted a firm command, "Cool it!" Remarkably, he got their attention, avoided panic and regained control. They were in and out in less than four minutes.

Chapter 3

3:51 a.m.
December 2012
Residence behind the store

IT'D BEEN A TOUGH DAY at the Stanton Street Bridge. Border patrolman Ted Furnish was drained. He'd showered, skipped dinner and gone to bed. His slumber was interrupted by a poke in the ribs.

He poked back, "Eve, what the hell? I'm trying to get some sleep."

"Don't get mad at me. How can you sleep through that noise and the flashing lights? Do something."

"What do you expect?" muttered Ted. "They'll leave when they're through."

"You need to get over there and ask them to turn off the alarm and the lights."

"No way. It's cold and drizzling rain."

Eve jumped out of bed, switched on a lamp, slipped on her housecoat, "Well, if you won't go, I'm going. I need some rest."

"Whoa! Hold on," moaned Ted, "You're not going out there. I'll go, but under protest. I don't see this as being necessary."

"Ted, I hate to ask you to do this, I really do, but please, do it for me. You love me, don't you?"

"Sure, you know I do," he replied. "But sometimes you press your luck."

"Honey, take your gun."

"No way. Cop sees a gun; he'll shoot first ask questions later."

Two steps out the back door, Ted encountered rain, cold and fog. He retraced his way back, looked for and located his cap, windbreaker and flashlight. "Ought to own an umbrella," he mumbled. "Then again, no one in El Paso owns an umbrella. Why should we? Rains twice a year, if we're lucky."

Two canines disrupted his walk down the alley. A pit bull named Brut, snapped at his legs. The other, a Doberman named Horse, was trying to jump his six-foot fence. "You sorry mutts. If I catch you on this side, you're history."

When he rounded the corner of the building, he confronted an empty parking lot. *What the heck?*

Glass littered the front sidewalk. Just inside the lobby a concrete garbage container was lying like a dead body among the shards of crystal.

No cops, no cars, no one around. *Wonder why no response to the alarm?* He should call 9-1-1. If he called, he'd be up half the night. He'd worked a long day, was tired, and wanted to get some sleep. *Damn the luck!*

Ted spotted a sign. "Call this number in the event of an emergency." *Good! That's better than messing with 9-1-1.* He committed the number to memory and made his way home.

Eve had made coffee, wanted a full report. He explained what he'd found. It hit him. He'd forgotten the number.

"Dammit!" He said, "Give me something to write on. I've got to go back and write down that number."

Chapter 4

4:00 a.m.

TWO BLOCKS OUT OSCAR could already see the flashing alarm lights. The rain was at it again, complete with lightning overhead. The scene had the feel of a movie war in progress. Something was odd. There wasn't a single person in sight, no lights on up or down the street.

You'd think everyone would be out of bed. Maybe Mr. Unknown Identity isn't the only neighbor who doesn't want to get involved.

The siren of a patrol car pierced the night. The noise and flashing lights added yet another layer to the uproar of the night. Oscar shook his head in disbelief. *I don't need this! I'll get another phone call.*

The patrol car skidded to a stop adjacent to Oscar's Crown Victoria. Oscar stepped out and waited as two officers got out of their vehicle. Both officers had their side arms drawn and pointed in his direction.

Geez! Oscar raised both arms above his head with mouth agape in wide-eyed disbelief. His blood pressure spiked.

The Hispanic police officer addressed Oscar politely and firmly, "Sir, this is a crime scene. Please explain why you are at this location?"

"Take it easy, officer. Guns scare me. I'm not going to give you any trouble."

Oscar continued, "The call to nine one-one that brought you here came from my wife. I'm supposed to be here. I'm Oscar Beasley. I manage these stores. I need to go inside and turn off the alarm."

The sergeant's facial expression remained deadly serious. "We'll need to see some identification. Don't move until I tell you."

Oscar replied, "I have ID. It's in my billfold, right rear pocket."

"Keep your hands up. I'll get the billfold."

After checking the contents and returning the billfold to its original location, the officer said, "Put your hands down. I see you're who you say you are." The officers pointed their guns away from Oscar who sighed in relief.

"Mr. Beasley, we can't let you enter the store. At least not until we ascertain that it's safe. Even then, you'll have to enter under supervision. You might unwittingly contaminate the scene. We're going inside. You stay here. We won't be long." Flashlights and revolvers in hand, they stepped through the window opening carefully avoiding the remaining glass.

Oscar's relief was temporary. Two additional vehicles with sirens screaming were headed in the direction of the store. Oscar's peripheral vision picked up their flashing lights. As they came into view, he saw one was a police cruiser, the other a similar, but unmarked sedan.

They parked next to Oscar's car. Two uniformed officers got out of the black and white. A man and woman in civilian clothing from the unmarked car were hard on their heels. The ununiformed woman, an attractive redhead wearing a dark brown suit, approached Oscar. In her raised hand were a police badge and her ID.

"Good evening, Sir. I'm Detective Lieutenant Kathy Smith. Can you tell us what's going on here?"

After a brief hesitation he responded, "Actually, no. I haven't been inside. I'm Oscar Beasley. I supervise this store. A couple of policemen got here about the time I did. They're inside."

Feeling a need to further explain his presence, Oscar continued with his explanation, "A neighbor called me to complain about the noise and lights. I need to turn off the alarm and flashing lights before we make more customers angry. Your guys said no. They seem to think I would contaminate the crime scene."

"Good. Exactly what they're supposed to say. They also have to make sure no perpetrators are still in the building," said the Lieutenant. "Mr. Beasley, I'm going to ask you to continue to wait while we see what we're dealing with. I suggest that you ratchet down your anxiety level a few notches. We have a job to do and we're aware of your presence. Stay here. We're going to go in and see what's what. Shouldn't take long."

"Lieutenant," said Oscar, "Be careful. The officers inside have their guns drawn. No lights are on in most of the store. They're liable to shoot you."

"Not going to happen," said the officer. "We have radio communications, but thanks for the warning. See you shortly." The Lieutenant assigned one officer to remain outside the store. She and her two accompanying officers drew their weapons, turned on flashlights and entered the store via the missing window opening.

While he waited, Oscar took in the scene. There were two front entrances with eight-foot by twelve-foot glass panels between. The panel to the right of the left side entrance was almost entirely missing; a few pieces of glass hung to the window frame, most of the glass was missing from the frame.

A glance into the front lobby revealed a heavy concrete cover from one of the store's garbage receptacles resting on its side. The lobby and the sidewalk outside were littered with hundreds of shards of glass. Candy from an over-turned rack was scattered across an aisle. Cartons of cigarettes were scattered about the lobby, which led Oscar to rule out vandalism and think it was most likely another cigarette burglary. While his stores have had only two, he was aware that a dozen or so had occurred in recent weeks in the city.

Looking beyond the investigation, He decided it was time to figure out a way to put cigarette storage in all his stores under lock and key. In the meantime, he had limited knowledge of what would have to be done between now and the store's eight a.m. opening time to get the facility in shape to serve customers. He had a huge sense of frustration at not being allowed to go inside.

Chapter 5

4:30 a.m.

STANDING AROUND WAITING was making Oscar impatient. Finally, after fifteen minutes he noticed someone in a uniform climbing over the windowsill and headed in his direction. The half-light shielded the officer's identity until he was directly in front of Beasley.

"Sir, I'm Sergeant Eli Sanchez. Detective Smith asked me to bring you inside to turn off the alarm and to turn on more lights."

Did you find anyone in the store?"

"No sir, no intruders. I apologize, There wasn't a way to know if you were a perpetrator or not. Lieutenant Smith sent me out here to let you know the scene is clear. Be careful as we step inside. There's glass still attached to the window frame and the lobby floor is like skating on marbles."

Headlights interrupted their conversation. As the vehicle moved closer, Oscar recognized the van. "Perfect timing! That van belongs to our store manager, Dan Coleman. We aren't going to be climbing over the windowsill. We're going in the front door. Dan has a key."

"I'm for that."

"Sergeant Sanchez. Before we go inside I need a favor. Would you turn off the lights on the patrol cars? A neighbor complained that he couldn't sleep."

"Not a problem. It'll take just a second."

Coleman parked and walked up to Oscar, who remarked, "Hi, Dan, meet Sergeant Sanchez. We're both more than a little glad to see you. I'm in a holding pattern waiting to turn off the alarm and light switches. The officers inside the store just made sure the burglars were gone."

Dan responded, "I'm glad I got here before you realized that I'd given you misinformation. The switch for the alarm system is in my office, to which you have no key. I also failed to tell you the overhead lights panel is in the hall by the receiving door. I drove like a bat out of hell, hoping you wouldn't fire me."

"I'm cool. No need to fall on your sword. By the way, Lieutenant Kathy Smith, asked us not to contaminate her crime scene. Sergeant Sanchez, here, is our escort and baby sitter. His marching orders are to arrest us if we touch anything without permission. Is that not so, Sergeant?"

"Reasonably accurate, sir," said Sanchez. "If you're ready, we can take this conversation inside now."

Dan unlocked the front door. The three men went inside. Dan silenced the alarm and turned on the inside lights.

Oscar turned to Sergeant Sanchez, "Mr. Coleman and I need to do a little walk about to assess our losses, check for damage and see what's going to be required to put our ship back in the water. Do you have a problem with that?"

"Yes, sir. You need Lieutenant Smith's permission."

"Can we get that now?" asked Beasley.

Sanchez said, "Sure," They made a quick swing of the store, located Kathy Smith.

Oscar approached Lieutenant Smith, "Lieutenant, Mr. Coleman and I need to get some things going in order to have the store open by eight o'clock. That is, with your permission, of course."

Turning to the other detective, Lieutenant Smith said, "Excuse us, I need to have a little conversation with Mr. Coleman and Mr. Beasley. When you wrap this up, work that little room where the checkers verify their tills and the small office next to it. Dust the safe for prints first, because we'll be having it opened shortly."

Revolving to face Coleman and Beasley she squared her shoulders, and carefully articulated a request clearly not to be questioned, "Gentlemen, we need to talk. Mr. Coleman, may we use your office?"

Puzzled and concerned, Dan responded, "Sure. Follow me."

Neither Dan nor Oscar had a clue, both are aware something was wrong. Detective Smith's attitude was just a couple of degrees short of a boil, her complexion flushed to the shade of her red hair. Following the closure of his office door, Dan, who wished to be elsewhere, sought refuge in making a pot of coffee. Oscar took a seat and waited for the poop to hit the fan.

"Before the two of you go charging ahead with your own agenda we need to get some things straight."

Oscar, turned and muttered to Coleman, "Sweet Jesus, what did we do to piss her off?"

"Damned if I know," he whispered.

"I think, Gentlemen, you don't understand what's going down here. This is a crime scene. You don't decide when to open the store. I'll decide. We have a hell of a lot of work to do. You need to relax. It'll get done. The store will get open and life will go on. When we open these doors, it'll be my decision."

In the meantime, we'll determine if your safe was violated, if merchandise is missing, look for evidence of who made unauthorized entry and determine to what extent this property and its contents were damaged.

In time, your penny counters will be filing insurance claims for losses. Those losses must be discovered, quantified and documented by my people. Our report is the validation for your company's claims. It can't be rushed?"

Oscar was getting a bit hot under the collar. "We understand and appreciate what you are doing. There are, however, some things we could be doing simultaneously with your investigation that will expedite our ability to serve our customers. Surely you can appreciate our expenses continue even when we are not generating sales. We also have employees paid hourly who are earning no income unless they work. Is there a middle ground wherein we can work together to satisfy our separate goals?"

"Probably not. I think you'll just get in our way. It's not like this is the only thing happening in El Paso. We need to wrap this up. It's going to take me another hour or two to write all this up after we complete the investigation."

Beasley said, "Lieutenant, I really wish you would give this some more thought. We have a job to do as well. We can't just let customers inside and do business. We have to get ready first."

Kathy mulled this over and said, "Okay, we can work together. Let's do it this way: don't get in our way or screw up our investigation. For now, I want you to sit down and make a list of what you want to do, and then I'll do what I can to make it possible. I'm going to make my own list, because you need to do some things for me. I will have mine in fifteen minutes. Will you?"

Oscar considered the question briefly, "Yes, we'll have it ready and meet you here in fifteen minutes. Dan, let's get this show on the road."

Chapter 6

6:02 a.m.

THE DISRUPTION TO ROUTINE caused by the burglary put the store's opening preparations seriously behind schedule. Putting together a priority list for Lieutenant Smith forced them to decide which activities had to take place.

They set five priorities: clean up the mess, be certain that it was safe to shop in the store, check shelves to make sure items the customers need are in stock, that they would have sufficient staff, and adequate cash on hand for cashing checks and making change.

Dan and Oscar completed their list and made copies for themselves. They returned to rendezvous with Lieutenant Smith. She was ready and waiting for them with her list in hand.

"Sergeant Sanchez and I have our agenda with copies for each of you." stated Lieutenant Smith. "I see you have yours as well. If I may have a copy, I'll see if we can juggle things around so we get all items accomplished as quickly as possible. For convenience sake, I'm going to call my priorities the "A" list and yours list "B". You won't like this, but we'll be dealing with my stuff first."

Oscar's hand went into the air, "I'm not sure you understand. Some of the things on our list take considerable time. Our perishables departments require preparation and set-up time.

We'd like to get some things going now, or those departments will be very late in being ready."

"Then I suggest," said Kathy, "That we get started on my list right away. Our first item is to make a log of missing items, the approximate value of these items, as well as any damage. I'll want a rough estimate of cost to repair the damage."

Their conversation was going nowhere unless they bought into the Lieutenant's agenda, so Oscar said, "Dan can give you a better ballpark figure for missing merchandise than me. I'm a better resource for damage cost estimates, because I work with those numbers. I'll be making some notes, since I'm required to submit an estimate of losses and damages."

Kathy replied, "Fine with me. Let's start from the front entry and work our way to the rear. Sergeant Sanchez will be my scribe. He'll provide you with copies of his notes."

Directing her assembly to the front lobby, Lieutenant Smith asked Dan, "What appears out of place in this area of the store?"

Dan replied, "Almost all of our carton cigarettes are missing. It appears to me nothing else has been removed."

Officer Sanchez remarked, "Cash, or something they can convert to cash quickly, is what thieves are after. Drug users often use cigarettes to purchase drugs."

"Dan, give me a dollar estimate of what's missing," said Kathy.

"Between fifteen and twenty thousand dollars at retail. However, I can do better than an estimate. Our computer system maintains a running inventory. All I have to do is subtract the cartons they left behind to give you exact dollar information."

"Is that a time-consuming process?" Lieutenant Smith inquired.

"No, fifteen minutes at the most."

"Impressive! Oscar, how about this broken window? What's the replacement cost?"

"Lieutenant, I'd like to get Dan to call our window supplier. They work 24/7. They can be on site, install a new window and provide an invoice with the exact cost in less than an hour."

"Mr. Beasley, I told you we were going to handle my priorities first. That is a "B" List item. However, I'll make this one exception.

Mr. Coleman, you may make your call."

"Yes, Ma'am, I'll be right back."

"No! Meet us at the store safe. There's a good chance it's been cracked," commented the Lieutenant.

It was located in a small space adjacent to the "count-down" room, where checkers verify their beginning tills. At the end of their shift they use the same location to reconcile till's contents to their transactions.

Sanchez, Smith, Beasley and Coleman, crowded into the tiny office. The safe appeared not to have been disturbed.

"I'd like for you to open the safe to be sure it hasn't been opened," said Kathy.

Dan got to his knees, found he was resting on a piece of broken glass, picked up the glass and tossed it into the wastebasket. He placed his right hand on the dial and used his left to shield the view of the dial from the others. He spun the dial the necessary four sequences and levered the door open.

He reported the contents of the safe: two open-top boxes containing rolls of pennies, fourteen empty cashier tills. Missing was all the office cash, cash from the setup tills, a large bag of rolled coins, the previous day's sales deposit, all blank money orders and a check writing machine.

"Mr. Coleman," questioned the Lieutenant, "Is it possible a store employee might have touched or opened this safe between last night and this moment?"

"Not to my knowledge."

"Do you see anything obviously out of place or missing that you failed to mention?"

"I don't think so. Wait a minute! They got my coins. I'm a coin collector. My coins are missing!" exclaimed Coleman, "I keep a quart jar in the safe. When the jar's full, I buy the coins and take the coins home. It was nearly full. There was one piece of glass in the safe and one on the floor. They broke my jar."

The Lieutenant said, "That's exactly the kind of thing we're looking for. Did you touch the glass?"

"I'm afraid I did, then tossed it in the trash."

"Don't throw the trash out. I'll get someone to see if your

fingerprints are the only ones on the glass. I was watching you and didn't see the glass or see you throw it away. That was a big oversight on my part. Were there any unusual coins in the jar that we might tie back to the burglary?"

"No. The coins were wheat pennies and some Indianhead nickels. None of them were unusual."

Oscar added, as he crossed his arms, "Looks like they did a number on us. They got everything of value that they could easily carry. These guys have probably done this before. I wonder how they got in the safe without blowing off the door."

Sanchez suggested, "Someone used the combination. This is really stupid, but sometimes an employee who is afraid they'll forget the combination writes it down near the safe. I've found combinations on the wall next to a safe."

The Lieutenant said, "Let's get back on track. We're just about done in here. The lab crew dusted the safe, but they aren't through. Don't touch anything in this office. We need to get out of their way, so they can wrap this up."

The "A" List was made up of three parts: securing evidence that might be used in getting convictions, documenting damaged and missing items and making estimates of the value of missing items and repairs.

It took much less time than Dan or Oscar expected, about thirty-five minutes. Dan indicated he was reasonably certain only the safe and tobacco department had been violated. Lieutenant Smith allowed Dan and Oscar to start the cleanup and opening preparations.

Lieutenant Smith asked, "Dan, I need one last thing from you. Can you provide me an exact accounting of the amount of the missing contents from the safe?"

"Absolutely. I'll get our bookkeeper to reconcile what was left untouched to the total reported to be on hand. The difference will be the total missing."

"For now, I'd appreciate an estimate. Do you have any idea how much that is likely to be?"

"I can come close. Yesterday was a slow day, probably seventy to eighty thousand dollars in the sales deposit, add the missing office funds, which we call the bank, normally thirty or forty thousand dollars, possibly more, and the total will be well over a hundred thousand dollars."

"How long until you can get me the exact number?"

"Less than an hour. The bookkeeper is on the other side of the yellow tape. Her first priority will be to order money from the bank, which will require about twenty minutes. Afterwards she can get on it."

"That'll work. We're about ready to take down the tape. Holler at me when she has it for me please."

Oscar addressed both Dan Coleman and Lieutenant Smith, "I hate to interrupt, but I have a responsibility to call Willard Rhodes, our company's director of security. It's seven a.m. I think this would be a good time for me to make the call, Lieutenant, if you are through with me.

"Sure, go ahead," answered Lieutenant Smith.

"Dan," said Oscar, "I'd like for you to call the alarm people while I make the call to Rhodes. Give them hell about that damned alarm. Help me to remember to suggest to Rhodes that he get our company attorney to consider going after the alarm company for recovery of our losses."

Chapter 7

7:00 a.m.

EMPLOYEES BEHIND THE YELLOW TAPE were wondering when their bosses would get the show back on the road. Sergeant Sanchez conveyed a few words to the officer assigned as gatekeeper at the tape and hustled back into drier confines. The officer motioned to employees and vendors to pass around the barricades.

Store employees put their collective shoulders to the wheel and accomplished what normally required twice the time. Vendors still on hand made deliveries and departed. Companies whose vendors had given up were contacted and asked to return.

Extra staffing was called in to clean up glass, litter and merchandise left askew. The bookkeeper arranged for a special "hot-shot" armored car delivery of cash. For the most part, the store was prepared to serve customers.

At 8:00 a.m. the barrier of yellow crime scene tape came down and the store opened its doors, one hour behind schedule.

At the request of Oscar Beasley, Detective Smith was conducting a debriefing meeting in the store's conference room. In attendance were Police Lab Chief Sylvester Biscayne, Beasley, Coleman and Lt. Smith.

Lt. Smith began, "Gentlemen, our on-sight investigation is complete. Later today I'll send you an e-mail summary you can use to provide to your insurance carrier as documentation for claims. If you have additional undiscovered losses, please call me. I'll add them to my report. Sylvester Biscayne will lead this discussion."

Biscayne paced to the front, and adjusted his glasses. "The primary function of our lab crew is to search for physical evidence to aid in determining the identity of perpetrators and other evidence vital to their apprehension and prosecution. Mostly, we search for fingerprints criminals leave behind. I'm sorry to report that the safe had been wiped. We've dusted and found some prints in the area of your tobacco storage. We plan to run those prints through the FBI database. We'll let you know if we get any hits.

We determined how the safe was opened. We found a combination of numbers written on the underside of a mail slot. It's not uncommon for employees who fear they'll forget a combination to hide the numbers nearby. Unfortunately, criminals know to look for the numbers.

If anyone has questions or comments, I'll field your questions. If not, Lieutenant, I'll turn the meeting back to you."

The meeting was interrupted by the arrival of Better Deal Regional Security Director Willard Rhodes. Oscar made the introductions, Rhodes was seated and Oscar suggested, "Lieutenant Smith, the meeting was about to be turned back to you. You can proceed."

Lieutenant Smith thanked Sylvester for his report. "We recognize there is a remote possibility that one or more of your employees may be involved in the theft. While I view this as unlikely, we want to leave no stone unturned to find who robbed your store. Before I leave today I need a list of all employees who had the combination to the safe, the names of the employees who prepared the deposit and put the cash away. I'll be calling and asking for these people to come in for lie detector tests. If any information pertinent to the burglary comes to light, I'll let you know."

Dan Coleman raised his hand; "I'll step out and arrange for someone to get that information for you. I'll be right back."

Willard Rhodes rose and addressed Lieutenant Smith, "Lieutenant, we appreciate your diligence. I plan to drop a note to Police Chief Rector, to let him know that you're doing a commendable job. It's my intention to proceed with our own internal investigation. I happen to agree with you that it's likely this was an inside job."

Smith furrowed her brow and turned to Rhodes, "Mr. Rhodes, I think you misunderstood my comments. Frankly, I view it highly unlikely this was an inside job. However, it's my job to consider all possibilities."

Clearly annoyed at her response, Rhodes replied, "Obviously we're in disagreement. In my experience over many years of dealing with employee theft and other security issues, it's most often been our own employees, not outsiders, who steal.

Chapter 8

KATHY SMITH MADE A QUICK TOUR of the store to make sure they had not over-looked any of their equipment. Oscar Beasley asked if she was about to leave.

"I am. We'll do our best to catch your intruders. I annoyed your security officer, but there's no logic to his inside job theory. I'm concerned our investigations may get tangled up, but I can see he's not at all inclined to work together."

"Kathy, I'm embarrassed he's such a cowboy. He has a history of being heavy-handed, but manages to keep his job because he has a close friend in a key position protecting him. Other than him, the management of this company is people-oriented."

"Let's keep in touch. I'm going to see your guy Coleman and leave. You have an idea where I'll find him?"

"Try his office, he was there a couple of minutes ago."

It was now late morning and the store was full of customers. When she arrived outside the office, she could see through a window that Coleman was inside. She tapped on the door. "May I come in?"

"Sure."

"No time to visit. Got to go. Wanted to see if you have the list I requested?"

"I do. It's short. I'm concerned there may be persons unknown with the combination. It was pretty embarrassing to hear the combination was available to anyone in that mailbox. Here's your list. Need anything else?"

"Yes, I do. If you don't mind, I need for you to schedule them to meet with me at City Hall. They may need to take a polygraph test. Schedule one hour sessions and leave a thirty minute gap between individuals."

Dan responded, "Is it necessary to have them going all the way downtown? I'd rather you meet with them here, 'cause they'll be on the clock. We have to pay their travel time and mileage."

"Dan, do you want to get a bunch of rumors started? If we have interviews or polygraph tests here, the rumors will fly. Let's not embarrass these folks any more than necessary."

"Makes sense. I'll do it your way. Will you be giving me feedback?"

"If it pertains to the burglary. This is not a witch hunt."

"I appreciate your consideration of my people. How soon do you need the schedule?"

"ASAP, if you can get to it."

"It'll take a couple of hours, maybe more. It's tricky to plug something extra into their work schedules. I'll send it to your e-mail address."

As she walked away, Dan was wishing all police officers had the sensitivity, empathy and good judgment he saw in Kathy Smith. She was definitely one of a kind. A third generation street cop, who swore she'd never be one, valedictorian of her high school class, a Bachelor of Science from UTEP, and a Masters in Math from UT-Austin, no marriage on the horizon, a gal who competed in a guy's world and beat them at their game. She could shoot and work under a basket, catch and throw a pass, steal a base, long-distance run and drive off the tee with the best. When she served her country, she chose the Marine Corps, where she excelled in hand-to-hand combat and weapons skills.

When she conceded that police work was in her genes, she blew away test scores, was first in her class at the Academy. Not only was she the best shot in the Police Department; she could take any cop to the mat.

Her first interview was with Tim Sullivan, who prepared the sales deposit on the night of the burglary. When asked to account for his whereabouts, Tim responded that he was at home the entire evening and through the night. His wife, Claire, would confirm they were together from thirty minutes after store closing to this morning, when he was asked to return to the store.

"Will you take a polygraph test?"

"Absolutely! I want to be tested. I'm anxious to remove all doubt about my integrity."

Sullivan's openness and willingness to take a test are hardly the behavior of someone with something to hide.

"You say your wife will confirm your whereabouts? Would she mind coming in to talk with me? Or I can meet her or drop by your home."

"I think she'd rather you come by the house. I'll give you her cell phone number, so the two of you can work out the details."

"Thanks."

Per Tim's request, Kathy set up his polygraph time for the next afternoon.

Later, she contacted Claire Sullivan to arrange a meeting to take place about the same time Tim was meeting with the polygraph operator at City Hall.

Their meeting went well. Claire was bright, attractive and seemed entirely honest about Tim being with her all night. She volunteered to take a polygraph test if needed. Kathy told her that wouldn't be necessary.

A phone call from the polygraph operator reported that Tim had passed his test with flying colors.

Meanwhile at the store, the separate investigation mounted by Willard Rhodes, was being conducted in a much less professional manner. A licensed polygraph operator, Rhodes had set up his polygraph machine in Dan Coleman's office. His approach was rude, accusatory and heavy-handed, often reducing his subjects to tears.

In the course of the interviews, a cashier mentioned she knew something of importance. Another cashier, her friend Ruth Downs, related to her that she had seen Tim Sullivan take money from a cash register.

Rhodes thought this information might help validate his conspiracy theory, so he arranged to interview Ruth Downs.

Ruth Downs was an attractive and nicely bosomed divorcee. She affirmed she had seen Tim take money from a till and put it in his pocket. She failed to mention Sullivan had asked her to observe he was opening the till to exchange a dollar of his own currency for four quarters to use in a coffee vending machine.

Opening a cash drawer for anything other than a customer transaction is a violation of company policy. Having a witness to clarify his intentions might have mitigated the violation, but he had broken the rules. Without the complete explanation, Tim was subject to termination for the infraction.

Had Rhodes pursued his questioning, he would have discovered malice in Ruth Downs' allegations. She had been pursuing Tim for weeks without reciprocation, that in a final attempt to break up his home and marriage, she had offered him sex. Sullivan rejected her offer, gave her a lecture on virtue and suggested she should get some professional help.

Ruth Downs had been rejected and angered. Tim had suggested that she needed psychological help. She found this very insulting. She couldn't resist the opportunity to lash back at Tim. To her, it mattered little that Tim had never encouraged her advances. She was emotionally sick with a fantasy romantic fixation on Tim.

Rhodes would use the poison pill planted by Ruth Downs as an additional nail in the coffin of guilt he was building for Tim Sullivan. He didn't care about the truth or Tim Sullivan. His agenda was about his future, his ego and in confirming the burglary was an inside job.

Psychologically, Willard Rhodes was not quite as serious a basket case as Ruth Downs, but he too, had some issues.

Rhodes set his next interview to be with Sullivan. Sullivan, having just hours before passed a polygraph test administered by the EPPD, was confident he would pass this one as well.

Polygraph operators are trained to know interviews should be private and discrete. The glass wall of Dan's office provided visibility for everyone who passed from the stock room to the sales area; hardly an appropriate setting for interviews.

Prior to the meeting with Sullivan, Rhodes checked to see if Sullivan had a police record. To his surprise, Tim had been arrested at age seventeen for unauthorized entry with no conviction or punishment.

When Sullivan arrived for his interview with Rhodes, he made an attempt to initiate a low-key interview and to build a bond of trust with Tim:

"Tim, I want to you to know that you have not in any way been singled out as a suspect. Our purpose is to talk with employees to clear the air of any possibility of collusion by an employee of the store with the individuals who burglarized the store. Do you have any problem with this line of questioning?"

Tim responded, "No, Sir. I'll do whatever I have to do to remove suspicion I might have been involved, but I do have a question before we get started."

"What's your question?" asked Rhodes.

"Are you going to ask any personal life questions unrelated to the burglary or my job?"

Rhodes couldn't help thinking, *strange question.*

"I don't plan to. If any questions seem intrusive, just tell me. Now, if you don't mind, I need to attach some contacts from the machine to you and put a cuff on your arm?"

"Sure, go ahead."

After he had the contacts connected, Rhodes went on with his explanation, "Tim, I'm going to ask you some questions that we call the pre-test. The purpose is to set a base line of your responses to know when you're telling the truth and when you're not. I'm ready to begin. You should just relax and answer my questions truthfully. You ready?"

"Yes, Sir."

"Is your name, Tim Sullivan? Answer yes or no."

"Yes."

"Do you reside at 999 Obama Street, El Paso Texas?"

"Yes."

"Have you ever told a lie?"

"Yes, of course, all children tell a fib at one time or another."

"Just answer all questions yes or no. I'll ask the question again. Have you ever told a lie?"

"Yes."

"Your wife's name is, Claire?"

"Yes."

Between each question Rhodes had been making notes on the response tape being generated by the machine. He turned to Tim and said, "Okay, I have a base line and I'm ready to start the test. This time I want you to respond to my statements as being either true or false."

"Your name is Tim Sullivan?"

"True."

"Your wife's name is, Claire?"

"True."

"You took money out of a cash drawer at the Best Deal Super Market."

Tim was very much taken aback by this question. He decided he had no choice, but to answer the question as true, "True, but it wasn't a dishonest act."

"I instructed you to answer true or false. I'm going to ask the question again. Did you take money out of a cash drawer and put it in your pocket?"

"True."

Tim was frustrated and furious that he was given no opportunity to explain the circumstances when he took money out of the till.

Rhodes asked the next question in a tone of voice that could only be taken as an accusation, "You cannot live within your income."

Tim responded, "False." Even though this was a correct answer, the machine indicated an untrue response.

Rhodes moved aggressively to his next question. "You and others planned the burglary of the Better Deal Super Market."

"I did not!"

"Answer true of false."

"False, then, because it's not true."

"Answer only true or false. You planned the burglary."

"False." The answer was another false positive. Tim was too nervous and upset to give accurate readings.

"You provided the combination to the safe to the burglars."

Tim, secure in the knowledge of his innocence, was totally frustrated at the inaccurate polygraph readings and began to get very angry at Rhode's accusations. He clinched his fists and narrowed his eyes at Rhodes and said, "No, I didn't, my answer is false."

At the top of his voice Rhodes shouted at Sullivan, "Your answers are not truthful. You lied about the money from the cash drawer, you lied about the burglary and sharing the combination. I want the names of your cohorts. Who else was in on this burglary?"

"No one! Not me. Not anyone from the store. If that machine says I'm guilty it doesn't work. You probably don't know how to operate the thing." Tim yanked the contacts from his body and removed the cuff.

Rhodes shouted back, "I know you're guilty and I'm going to prove it! As of this moment you're on suspension without pay."

"You can't suspend me, I quit." Sullivan shouted as he raised his arm as if to strike Rhodes. "Someday you'll have to answer for what you did today. It'll be to an authority higher than me." He stormed out of the office pushing his way through the crowd of employees and vendors who had been eavesdropping on the encounter through the glass wall.

Chapter 9

SEVERAL EMPLOYEES DECIDED not to take their scheduled polygraph tests because they were afraid they'd be accused of being involved in the burglary. Dan did his best to persuade them to reconsider. They said they'd quit before they'd take a polygraph.

Dan was caught in the middle. He didn't blame his employees for not wanting to be interrogated with Gestapo technics by Willard Rhodes. On the other hand, he sure didn't want to tell Rhodes to jump in the creek.

He knew Oscar Beasley was still in the store. He called him on his cellphone and said, "We've got a problem."

"What's up?" inquired Oscar.

"Meet me in the produce room."

"I'm on my way."

Dan was pacing the floor like a dad waiting for his first-born to arrive.

"What's the problem?"

"Rhodes with a capital R," said Dan. "My people are walking off their jobs and refusing to take his polygraph tests."

"Tell them everyone has to do it. That it's painless."

"Tried that! Didn't work! I haven't had a chance to tell you, but Rhodes has lost it. He got into a shouting match with Sullivan, accused him of being part of the gang that robbed the store.

Sullivan quit and walked out. You've got to do something."

"Okay. I'll talk to him; see if I can get him to settle down. If I can't, I'll cancel the interviews."

At noon Rhodes invited Coleman and Beasley to join him for lunch. Both accepted, because it presented an opportunity to persuade him to moderate his style of questioning.

Their destination was Jose's Mexican Café. Jose's was packed, the result of offering great food at moderate prices. When seated, their table was close to others, creating a sense of being seated at several tables simultaneously, not a good place for a discussion.

After they had ordered, Rhodes proceeded to recount Tim's interview within earshot of others.

Oscar was shocked at Rhodes' bad judgment. He mouthed a silent instruction to Coleman, "Do something."

"Hey," said Dan, "Did you see what happened when we finally opened for business? It was like a grand opening day."

Clearly annoyed at being interrupted, Rhodes said, "I was busy dealing with a crook. I discovered Sullivan has a history of arrest for breaking and entering, plus an accusation of till tapping. He failed his polygraph on questions about the burglary. Instead of facing the consequences, he lost his cool, threatened to cold-cock me and tried to quit. He was too late for that. I fired him before he said he quit."

"Mr. Rhodes, your termination won't stand. Hiring and firing is a store operations responsibility. You can make recommendations, but that decision falls in the area of my responsibility."

Rhodes dismissed this argument with a wave of his hand. "I'm sure your boss, Jake Early, will support my decision."

Tongues were wagging at nearby tables. Rhodes seemed unaware that his comments were to blame. Oscar and Dan avoided any further mention of store business.

On the way back to the store, Oscar brought up the feedback from employees not wanting to take polygraph tests and made a suggestion that Rhodes moderate his interview style.

"Makes no difference," said Rhodes. "I've decided to discontinue the tests, because I've got my man. When I share Sullivan's polygraph results with the police, they'll use that information to break the case."

On their return, they were surprised to see Tim Sullivan waiting in the front lobby. "Mr. Rhodes," said Tim, "I went from here to the public library, where I researched everything they had about polygraph testing. My results should be considered inconclusive."

Sullivan was adamant about his innocence and said he had confidence he would pass a second test, insisting the previous test results are wrong and blamed Rhodes' outbursts for causing false positive reactions. He insisted that he be given another test.

To the surprise of both Beasley and Coleman, Rhodes agreed to retest Sullivan.

Given the outcome of Sullivan's morning test, Oscar and Dan decided they should station themselves near the interview location.

Rhodes reconnected Tim to his machine and repeated the pre-test routine he had used in the morning. Sullivan retained his composure and confidence.

Rhodes began to push harder, "Who else was involved in this burglary? Were you involved in this burglary?"

A tornado of thoughts race through Sullivan's mind, *he asked who else is involved? His question implies I'm guilty. I can't answer that! What's he mean? Am I involved? No! Well, maybe, sort of, I prepared the deposit, I was the last one to handle the money; is that going to make me out as guilty?*

The needles switched sharply to reactions associated with lying and guilt, another false positive reaction.

"I knew it. Got you! Now I want the whole story and names of the others involved," said Rhodes.

"I'm not guilty. You're wrong; you don't want to know the truth. I don't have to put up with this. I'm out of here," said Tim as he once again yanked the monitor cuff and electrodes from his body.

Oscar, who had seen the whole episode through the office window, spoke his mind, "Mr. Rhodes, you're out of line. I've known, Tim Sullivan, for ten years. No way is he connected to this burglary!"

"You tend to your knitting and I'll tend to mine," said Willard. "Sullivan's dirty. His test nails him to the cross. Make sure he doesn't get another paycheck. I'm going to put some heat on the police to identify and round up Sullivan's buddies."

Oscar pulled Dan aside, "Let's get out of here and get some coffee. I need your help to find a way out of this quagmire."

They made their way to a nearby doughnut shop. "Rhodes is out of control," said Oscar. "He's destroying an innocent man's life and reputation.

The problem here is that we're dealing with company politics. Willard outranks us both. His buddy, Jake, is our boss. We can't get justice for Sullivan without cutting our own throats," said Oscar.

"About the only one I'd trust to hear us out is Peterson," said Oscar. "He's seldom in El Paso. We'd have to go to Dallas to talk with him. Besides that, it'd be a huge risk to go over Jake's head. Jake's almost certain to find out."

"If we don't take the risk, an innocent guy is going take a fall and the company is going to look like a bunch of dodos," said Dan.

I'll make the call, set up a meeting. In the meantime, you're going to have to write up termination paperwork on Sullivan. He quit. We heard him. The sad thing about this is everyone is going to assume Sullivan is guilty," said Oscar.

Chapter 10

DAN AND OSCAR RETURNED TO THE STORE and found that Rhodes had removed his polygraph machine from Dan's office and left instructions to cancel all remaining scheduled interviews.

Oscar remarked, "He left without confronting the issue. That works for me, but we've still got to do something about the damage he's done. I'd like to use your office to call Mr. Peterson's office, see if I can get an appointment to see the man face to face."

"When you get through, you probably ought to head home if you're going to Dallas. You've already put in a twelve-hour day."

Oscar's call to Better Deal in Dallas was directed to Charles Peterson's administrative assistant, Ann Edwards.

"Oscar," Ann replied, "he's going to ask. Why do you need to see him?"

"Tell him a situation is being mishandled. That it's about to become a media circus that could do serious damage to the company's good reputation."

"Oscar, I hope you've thought this through carefully. I'm concerned it may not be well received. You do know Mr. Peterson is ex-military and has strong feelings about using the chain of command?"

"So I've heard. Hope I'm not ripping my britches. I've considered the potential consequences. The situation justifies the risks."

"Is Mr. Early aware you're asking to see Mr. Peterson?" asked Ann.

"A definite no."

"I'll see what I can do. His calendar is tight. I'll press him to squeeze you in and get back to you with a time and place."

Fifteen anxious minutes later, the meeting was a go; lunch tomorrow, Town Club, downtown Dallas.

"Ann, I hate to show my ignorance, but where's the Town Club?"

"It's on the rotating top floor of the Dallas Walker-House Hotel, has a 360-degree view of the city. I'll fax the street address along with Mr. Peterson's cell number in case you don't connect," said Ann.

"I owe you. Thanks," said Oscar.

"Oscar," said Ann, "there's free parking in the garage under the hotel. He'll meet you in the lobby. Do yourself a favor. Don't be late. What else may I do for you?"

"How about wishing me luck?" asked Oscar.

Oscar left his house at two a.m., which allowed an extra hour for the time zone differential. He stopped only for coffee, fuel and nature's calls.

Ten hours down a straight four-lane Interstate provided time to mull things over. He rehearsed his comments for Mr. Peterson and tried to forecast an outcome.

This trip was likely to be a career-changing event. He decided it didn't matter if it cost him his job. What mattered was right and wrong. A good and decent man was getting shafted. Oscar realized he was the only one to possibly set things right.

With just seconds to spare, Oscar charged into the Walker-House lobby, careened into his boss, Jake Early, knocked him onto the marble floor. Charles Peterson saw him coming, sidestepped the assault.

Peterson chuckled, "Great way to start a meeting, Oscar. Welcome to Dallas, I hope you don't mind. I asked Jake to fly in this morning. I believe he should be here. Help me get him back on his feet."

Before Oscar could offer an apology, Jake Early growled at

Peterson, "Charlie, I don't see what you find so humorous. He hit me like a Cowboy linebacker. You wouldn't think it was so funny if it was you on your ass."

"Come on, Jake, it was an accident. You'll survive. Besides, I imagine Oscar sees less humor in the situation than you."

Jake waved away Oscar's hand and shot him a hostile glare. It occurred to Oscar: *maybe this isn't such a good idea.*

To mitigate matters, Peterson intervened, suggested they take the elevator to the Town Club.

The club sits atop Dallas' second tallest building, its exclusive requisites are highlighted by "Members Only" signing and a greeter doubling as gatekeeper.

The headwaiter steered them to a table marked "Reserved," and motioned to an attendant to see to their needs.

The sixty-six-story steel and glass edifice had high ceilings, deep Berber carpets, leather and hardwood furniture accented by modern art and floral arrangements. The view through floor to ceiling glass walls was a breathtaking panorama of Dallas.

From their table out of earshot from other patrons, Peterson, explained, "I asked for privacy. Are you comfortable with this location?"

"Yes. The setting is fine," Oscar said.

Peterson offered a suggestion, "Let's order and enjoy our lunch before we get down to business?"

Their waiter, a young Taiwanese, suggested oriental chicken salad, Peterson added a bottle of Texas Merlot and blueberry cheesecake. The food was delicious.

"So," asked Peterson, "Oscar, how did you make the trip? I was a little concerned you and Jake might be on the same flight."

"In my personal car. It seemed inappropriate to make the trip at company expense when I'd initiated the meeting," said Oscar.

"Mm," considered Peterson, "An interesting perspective. I think Better Deal won't mind if you turn in mileage expense. We do, however, appreciate the thought."

The chitchat during lunch moved from comments about the club, the view, inquiries about family and health and finally to a contentious political encounter between the Palestinians and the

Israelis in the Middle East. Sensing that tensions had subsided sufficiently, Peterson moved stealthily to the crux of their meeting. "Oscar, you called this meeting. Something must be important for you to make an end run around Jake and drive all the way to Dallas. Tell us what's going on."

Oscar took a big breath, and put his napkin back on his plate. "Yes, Sir. Night before last we had a break-in at number nine on Central. The store's cigarette inventory was taken and the safe robbed. Willard Rhodes took an interest in the burglary and believes it had internal assistance.

Police investigators didn't buy into Willard's theory. They polygraphed our cash handlers, with no negative results. They told us burglars know employees hide combinations. They look for, find and use them.

The EPPD conclusions didn't discourage Rhodes. He's convinced himself that Tim Sullivan, our assistant manager is complicit to the burglary."

Jake interrupted, "The man is paid to look out for our interests."

"Jake, let Oscar finish," said Peterson.

"What's really disturbing is the heavy-handed way Rhodes has been conducting his investigation. He's shooting first, asking questions later, making accusations in front of customers and employees and has exercised no discretion in his interviews and polygraph testing.

I personally witnessed Rhodes administer a vicious and unprofessional lie-detector test on Sullivan. No one could have passed a test in those circumstances.

Later, Sullivan came back, insisting on another test. Rhodes accommodated him, but used trick questions that again netted false positive reactions. Instead of rephrasing questions, he insisted he had his perpetrator. Sullivan told him to go butt a stump and resigned."

Oscar paused briefly to see how his remarks were impacting his two-man audience. Mr. Peterson showed interest and concern. Jake's countenance reflected continuing anger and displeasure.

Oscar resumed, "It appeared to me that Rhodes was

grandstanding to draw attention to himself as he saves the company. Maybe he's ambitious, wants to be promoted. Whatever his motives, he's made a public spectacle of a private and confidential situation. Other employees saw what happened to Sullivan; they're afraid it could happen to them.

We spend thousands of dollars every week convincing the public that we're good corporate citizens, that our people are trained to serve them, that our stores are a special place to go. The entire cost of our losses associated with the burglary doesn't compare to the negative impact of Rhode's black boot investigation. He's got his priorities all screwed up. That's why I'm here. I had to do something.

I apologize to you, Mr. Early, for going directly to Mr. Peterson. I should have gone to you with my concerns, but I know you have a very close relationship with Willard. I thought it would be hard for you to deal with this situation objectively. The stakes are too high here to risk a possible bias reaction."

Chapter 11

CHARLES PETERSON LOOKED DIRECTLY at Beasley, "Oscar, you're offering a pretty flimsy excuse for not taking this matter up with your immediate supervisor. He's in his position because he's fair, not bias in his judgment."

"Maybe I've made a mistake," said Oscar. "But I know Tim Sullivan. There's no way he's involved in this burglary."

Jake interrupted, "Darn right, you made a mistake. I'm not going to put up with you going around me."

Peterson raised a hand, "Hold on Jake. You know I believe in following protocol, but I'm not ready to nail Oscar to the cross. I respect his intent, though I don't agree with his avenue of approach. He's raised some questions about Willard that beg investigation."

Peterson turned to face Oscar, "Oscar, would you excuse us for just a few minutes. I have something I need to discuss with Jake. Come back when I nod."

"Yes sir, whenever you wish."

"Good. See you shortly."

After Oscar was out of earshot Peterson turned to Jake, "What was that about? You've been out of character. I know you're ticked because Oscar called me. I'm beginning to think he's right about you being unapproachable. You need to listen to what your people

44

have to say."

Jake fired back, "This guy has been bad-mouthing Willard Rhodes, a damned good man, and he's been insubordinate to me. I thought you brought me here to fire this guy."

"Jake, if that's what you think, you're badly mistaken. For the moment, forget the chain of command issue. Do you think you can keep your temper in check, or do I listen to Beasley by myself?"

"I'll keep my cool."

"Fine. See you do."

Peterson signaled for Beasley to come back to the table.

When he was seated Peterson said, "Oscar, we want to hear why you hold this man Sullivan in such high regard and your recommendations for damage control."

Maybe I didn't make a mistake after all.

"Mr. Peterson, it seems to me that managers have an obligation to speak up on behalf of subordinates. We worry about our image and reputation with customers. Shouldn't we be equally concerned about how we're perceived as employers? Personally, I won't work for a company that doesn't treat employees fairly."

Peterson looked offended, letting Oscar know he was not happy at his remark about fair treatment, "I don't know where you are going with this, but if you're insinuating we mistreat our people, you're wrong. We have a long history for having the best industry workplace practices."

"I know, that's what attracted me to Better Deal, but a reputation has to be earned every day. I'm here because one man's actions are about to trash our goodwill."

"You asked that I tell you what I know about Tim Sullivan. My history with Tim Sullivan began ten years ago. I was a store manager for another grocery chain. He was my assistant. Tim's performance was better than any assistant I've had before or since. Ironically, he consistently turned down opportunities for promotion because he had other goals in life.

Tim was five years old and the eldest of the three Sullivan children when his father disappeared. His mother was a proud and independent woman. She raised him and two younger siblings with no child support or public assistance.

Tim has no education beyond high school. Irene Sullivan was a devout Christian who provided for her family by cleaning houses and taking in ironing. Tim became the man of the house and helped raise the younger siblings. As he got older, he became the second breadwinner.

At age sixteen he was six foot six inches tall. He didn't play sports. He helped his Mom make ends meet.

Once, when there was no food in the house, he broke into a house and stole food. He was arrested, not convicted, because the homeowner withdrew the charges. Tim swore he would never break a law again.

He was academically gifted, but he knew his Mom couldn't provide for his brother and sister if he pursued an education. He became interested in Bible teachings, particularly in the life of Jesus. He decided to follow Christ's example and minister to others.

I met Tim when he was twenty-three years old with a wife and a couple of toddlers. He had seven years' experience working in grocery stores, knew his way around every department. His peers liked and respected him for his work ethic, his dependability, his gentle nature and how his judgment was consistently fair and impartial.

In addition to working in the store, Tim was a lay-minister in a very small Baptist church. His longer-term goal was to become an ordained Baptist minister.

Tim and I worked together in Roswell for a year. I left to come to work for Better Deal. I recommended him to take my place. He was offered the position, but turned it down because it wasn't compatible with his plan to become a minister."

Six years passed with no contact with Tim. Last year, he came by my office, asked to speak to me.

After the good-to-see-you-again banter, he told me that he had continued to work in the same store until two years ago. He gave up that position when he was ordained and became an associate pastor in Roswell."

Two years ago, Tim was called to be Senior Pastor for New Hope Baptist Church here in El Paso. The church is located just a few blocks west of our number nine location. He's paid a salary, plus modest living and car allowances.

The church is a small start-up mission church. They rent a building, are looking for a building site and plan to construct a church with volunteer labor, but lack funds for materials. Tim hit me up for a job; saying he would work any hours except Sunday's and Wednesday evenings. His objective was to use his earnings to purchase building materials.

We had just lost an assistant manager at number nine, so I hired him on the spot. He's been doing a great job, is involved in the community and seems to know everyone. He's a huge asset for the store.

I know Tim as well or better than anyone who works in my district. Willard Rhodes is wrong about this man. He's treating him unfairly, and he lost all objectivity in how the conduct of his investigation is impacting customers, our business and the company's reputation. If you place any weight at all on my opinion, I urge you to take immediate action to curtail Rhode's conduct.

I appreciate you listening to what I've had to say. I'm ready to accept whatever reprisals you feel are appropriate for going around Mr. Early."

Jake Early had been looking for an opportunity to refute Oscar's allegations about his friend. "Oscar, I'm not able to accept what you say as factual. Your allegations don't match my history and experience with Willard. Maybe you have a personal history with Willard that has escaped my attention. Personally, I'm going to have to reject your report, because I don't believe it's accurate."

"Gentlemen," suggested Peterson, "This is not a Kangaroo Court. All the charges made here will have to be checked and confirmed. We'll not make any decisions until that's been done. In the meantime, this matter is confidential and I don't want to hear of either of you making remarks to the press. I think this meeting is over. I'll handle the bill. I suggest both of you get home ASAP because you will need to be in place to act as decisions are made. Good day."

Chapter 12

Ten a.m.
11 December 2012
Home of Al and Carol Landry
Lebanon Street
El Paso

THE WOMEN OF FAITH BIBLE STUDY Group was having its second meeting. Their meeting locations rotated each week. Carol Landry was hostess.

Their leader, Marie Pierson's recent affiliation with New Hope Church and agreement to teach women's Bible studies was helping the church to grow. The woman was a "hoot." She saw humor in everything, whatever she had on her mind, she blurted out.

Marie was in the process of wrapping up the meeting, "Thank you all for coming. Your involvement tells me you're interested, which makes my job easier and more fun. The Study of David is considered the best of all of Betty Monroe's Bible studies. Every time I teach this study I discover new meaning, inspiration and direction in the scriptures. There's a lesson in this discovery. We should never cease our search for understanding of God's Word."

Mary Pat, a first time visitor to the class, raised her hand. "I've got a question. You said God considered David a man after his own heart? In today's lesson David was a sinner."

"Great question! David was a sinner of the first magnitude. There were lots of things wrong about the way he lived his life, but he had an unwavering faith in God. God rewarded David for his faith with forgiveness. The central message of our study is though we are all sinners, if we have faith we will be forgiven," said Marie.

"In this study you're going to learn just how far David pushed the boundaries of God's forgiveness. He was a liar, a murderer and an adulterer whose just rewards should have been to eternally stoke the flames of hell. Yet he begged for God's mercy and was forgiven."

Marie continued, "I'm not suggesting that we can get away with the stunts David pulled. We probably can't, but there's hope for you and I, if we embrace the Lord and accept his love.

Okay, enough for now. Before we leave, be sure to spend a minute or so with Lisa and Mary Pat. We're blessed by having these two ladies come to attend our group. Please encourage them to come back," said Marie.

"We planned to have a study for twelve members. We have ten, so we have two more study guides available. Please reach out and invite your friends to come and join us. This is a wonderful opportunity to get to know others and to help them to come to know the Lord," said Marie.

"Next week we'll be meeting at Michelle Glover's house. We need two volunteers to bring cookies."

Four hands were raised, "I appreciate your willingness to help," said Marie. "We need just two. Lisa, I'll count on you and Marcia to bring the cookies next week. Mary Jo and Dolores, if you don't mind I'll ask you to bring them the following week. Will that work for everyone?"

"I see four nods of approval, so I assume the cookie bases are covered," said Marie. "Cathy, would you please dismiss us?"

Cathy rose and said, "Please bow your heads. Thank you; Lord, for this opportunity to study your word, to become better acquainted with fellow believers. We ask you please watch over our families and keep us safe. Guide us and direct us in all that we do and send us two more members. Amen."

Carol Landry helped all to find their coats and purses, reminding those who brought cookies to retrieve their plates. Departure was a ritual of its' own. One did not leave without hugging everyone.

Carol's friend and next-door neighbor, Lisa Hoskins, remained to help her put the house back in order. Afterwards, Carol suggested they have a cup of coffee and chat a spell.

"So how did you like the study?" asked Carol.

"Glad I came. Marie Pierson is a great teacher. Since I don't go to your church, I only know a couple of the ladies," said Lisa. "The ones I met today seem very nice. By the way, did you happen to hear the conversation about your preacher?"

"No," said Carol. "What did you hear?"

"The lady sitting to my right, Judy Stone said she was shopping at Better Deal. She over-heard a conversation between two men. The older of the two told the other to put Tim Sullivan on suspension, that Sullivan had stolen money from the store's safe. Isn't Tim Sullivan your Pastor?" asked Lisa.

Carol's jaw dropped in disbelief, her eyes filled with tears. "Tim's our pastor. He does work at Better Deal. Surely you must be mistaken."

Lisa said, "Carol, I'm just repeating what I heard."

"If this is true," she sobbed, "Tim is in serious trouble with the church. Please keep this quiet until we find out more about it. Who were the others who heard this gossip? I'm going to try to keep the rumor from spreading until we find out the truth."

"You'll have to ask Judy who she's told," responded Lisa.

"I will," said Carol as she took Lisa's arm and escorted her to the door, "I'm going to ask you to excuse me. I've got to find Al and get him involved. My husband's a deacon. He has an obligation to deal with this. In the meantime, pray for our pastor and our church. I'll see you at the next meeting,"

Lisa went home, put her dirty cookie tray in the dishwasher, and returned her Bible and study guide to her bedside table. *That was fun. There's nothing like a little juicy gossip to keep things interesting.*

Chapter 13

One p.m.
11 December 2012

CAROL LANDRY ENTERED THE WORKSHOP attached to their garage. "Al, I know you're busy, but we need to talk."

"I need to finish what I'm doing, don't want to clean these brushes twice. Can it wait?"

"I guess so. You're not going to like what I have to say."

He narrowed his eyes, stick out his lower lip and looked up, "Carol, what'd you want me to do? Mess up this finish and ruin this brush. Five minutes. That's all I need. Okay?"

"I'm sorry. After you finish, let's have a cup of coffee," said Carol.

Eight minutes later, Al walked into the kitchen. "So what's going on?'

Carol shared the rumor, "Judy Stone, one of the ladies in our bible study told Lisa Hoskins and others, she was at the grocery store and overheard a big shot tell the manager to terminate Tim Sullivan because he'd been stealing."

Tears streaming, she looked at Al, "Will the deacons fire him?"

"Sounds like malicious gossip," said Al. Tim wouldn't take a nickel from anyone. He's been asking us to reduce his salary so we'll have more money for the building fund."

"Judy Stone wouldn't tell anything unless it was true. New Hope is going to lose members if people find out we have a dishonest pastor," said Carol.

"All right, no need for you to get upset about this."

"That's better," she says, as she used her apron to wipe her tears.

Al grabbed his hat, opened the door to the garage and turned back, "I'm going down to the store and talk to Bill Taylor. I hope you're wrong."

Al got into his rebuilt '55 Chevy pickup and cranked the V-8 engine. It purred like a kitten. The only non-standard feature on the truck was the glass-pack muffler on the exhaust. It was music to his ears.

Al's friend, Bill Taylor was a fellow postal retiree who re-entered the work force as a part time produce clerk at Better Deal and loved his job. It got him out of the house twenty hours a week, allowed him to work on the sales floor and visit with old friends.

On the way to the store Al was nauseous; his stomach was churning. He admired Tim Sullivan. *How in the world could he get himself into such a mess?*

Al parked at the street curb rather than the parking lot to avoid getting body dings. He locked the truck and stood in place on the sidewalk for a few moments.

He meandered into the store hoping to find Bill on duty. He was seated in the deli, on a break and involved in a heavy discussion over a cup of black coffee with another of their long-time Post Office buddies, Joe "Speedy" Gonzales.

Addressing both friends, Al interrupted, "Hi guys! I see you're solving the world's problems. Got room for another old has-been?"

Speedy quirked back, "Yeah, but watch your mouth. We can do at least as good as the dummies you Democrats send to Washington."

"Smart Ass! You know I'd give away my Chevy before I'd vote for those jackasses."

"Now, Al. Did I hit a nerve? Aren't you Christians supposed to turn your cheeks and forgive others?"

"God will forgive my attitude toward Democrats. So what are you guys haggling about, our old alma mater?"

"We are. They're in a world of hurt. What did they lose last year? A billon bucks?" remarked Speedy.

Al replied, "Good thing we retired when we did. I hear there's talk about shutting it down and letting all the mail go by private carrier. No way did I ever think this could happen."

"Me either! So, Al, what's going on in your life? You and Carol staying healthy and out of trouble?"

He responded with a report that they were both in good health, other than having the same aches and pains as their friends. They were still mobile, doing their best to stay out of the hospital and spend as much time as their kids will allow with grandkids.

Al brought the discussion around to the issue and how it might affect their church. How he, as a church elder, had an obligation to track down the truth.

"Bill, I know you're wired in around here. I need to know what's going on."

"We've been told not to talk about it, but I think it's already pretty much out of control. I'll tell you what I know, just don't say where you heard it."

"Sure, my lips are sealed. Now what the heck's happening?"

"Last night someone broke into the front of the store, took all the carton cigarettes. The brass thinks it was just to make the police think it was druggies."

"They got into the safe and got away with over a hundred thousand bucks and other stuff like checks and money orders. The safe was opened with a combination. There must be some kind of evidence to make them think it was an in-side job."

"Everyone was asked to take a lie-detector test. I heard Sullivan's first test was inconclusive. He came back, insisted on a second test, which he must not have passed, because some big shot was trying to get him to sign a confession and give him the names of the other people involved."

"I heard that Sullivan has been suspended or fired. Is that true," asked Al.

"I've heard that too. All I know for sure is that he's normally on the schedule for today. He's not working, so something's wrong," responded Bill. "Sullivan's a good man. I'm having trouble believing all this crap."

Al got out of his seat. "Fellas, I've got to get back to the house. I appreciate the info about Tim. I'm going to call a board of deacons meeting together and let them decide what they want to about the preacher. Looks like he's dug a pretty deep hole for himself."

6:00 P.M., home of Al and Carol Landry

The five church deacons of New Hope Church and their church elder, convened for a meeting at Al's request. All but one had heard the rumor. Their church pastor was normally in attendance to these meetings. He was not invited.

Carol made a pot of coffee and told Al, "I'm not supposed to be part of your meeting. I'll be back in the bedroom reading next week's bible study."

Before Carol went to the bedroom she said, "Al, I please ask the deacons to be considerate of Tim's family. He's got a sweet wife and cute kids. I don't know why he did this, but I'm concerned they might be put out on the street to go hungry."

Her instructions matched his intentions, so he replied, "I can't guarantee what will happen, I've only got one vote, but I'll do my best."

Chapter 14

6:00 p.m.
11 December 2012
Landry Home

FOUR OF THE FIVE New Hope Deacons had guessed why Al Landry called the meeting. They'd heard the rumors.

There are always people who can't wait to share stuff about someone else. Perhaps they need attention, or to improve a poor self-image by defiling another's.

One teenager, who went home for lunch at noon, heard it from her mom. By the end of her last class, she had shared it in hundreds of text messages. By evening, the buzz was in countless texts, e-mails and even a post on more than one blogger page. Most recounts had been enhanced. In one contorted version it had become an armed robbery with blazing guns.

The most unfortunate event of the day was a text message forwarded to Mary Sullivan, Tim's daughter. That evening Mary confronted her father with the text. He was devastated, because the situation had embarrassed his daughter and broken her heart.

"Daddy," she had asked, "How could you do this to me?" She bolted to her room and locked the door.

At the Landry home, the stage had been set for a tragic outcome. Elder Thompson called the meeting to order and said,

"Someone is going to have to fill me in. I have no idea what this meeting is about."

"Troy," said Al. "You're aware that Tim Sullivan has a part-time job at a grocery store. He's been implicated as an accomplice to a burglary that occurred last night at the store. Burglars got away with a large amount of cash. Pastor Sullivan took two lie detector tests; then some big shot with the corporation fired him. His arrest is eminent."

At first there was a heated discussion leaning toward giving Tim a chance to explain. Then the discussion moved to the potential consequences of delay in disassociating the Church from the bad publicity swirling around Pastor Sullivan.

A deacon made a motion that their best course was to fire Tim Sullivan immediately. It quickly got a second.

Elder Thompson spoke, "A motion has been made and seconded we fire Tim Sullivan. Does anyone see a need for further discussion?" He looked around.

He was about to call for a vote. Al raised his hand, "Troy, my wife made me promise we'd take care of Tim's family. I think we ought to give him some severance."

"Give severance pay to a crook who robbed a store? I wouldn't. I think we need to fire him and be done with it. What do the rest of you think?"

No one raised a hand. Al shook his head and muttered, "God forgive you."

"The motion stands as stated," said Thompson. "All in favor of firing Tim Sullivan with no severance pay raise your hands."

Four of the deacons lifted their arms.

"Those opposed same sign."

Al raised his arm as he continued to shake his head. Then he spoke, "I need for you to show in the minutes of this meeting that I voted against this proposal, otherwise Carol will never forgive me."

"It'll be in the minutes," stated Elder Thompson as he looked at Al harshly. "I believe you called this meeting. Why the sudden change of heart?"

"Oh, I think he ought to be fired. It's the way it's being handled that bothers me. Your lack of compassion is hardly Christian."

"You're entitled to your opinion. Who's going to give Sullivan the bad news?" asked Thompson.

"You're the pastor's advisor," said Al. Seems to me that's your responsibility."

"Okay, I'll take care of it. No point waiting. I'll have him meet me at the church tonight, get his keys and cut him loose."

Someone asked, "How are we going to fill the pulpit until we can appoint a pastor search committee?"

"Why don't we ask Mike Jones to preach this Sunday? I believe he's available?" said Otis.

"You know him," said Thompson. "Line him up and get back to me to confirm that Sunday is covered."

"Any more business? If not, I need a motion to adjourn."

"So move," said Al.

"All in favor show of hands. Carried. Meeting adjourned."

"Al, would you dismiss us?"

"Father, thank you for the way you bless this church, help us through these difficult times and have mercy on Tim Sullivan and his family. Amen."

Chapter 15

7:30 p.m.
11 December 2012
Sullivan residence

"TIM," SAID CLAIRE, "Mary didn't come to dinner. I knocked, she was crying, told me to go away. What in the world is going on?"

"She's upset about a text message she received during school."

"She's said nothing to me. Why is she crying?"

"She's upset about rumors of me being involved in the burglary at the store," said Tim.

"Did you tell her you had nothing to do with the break-in?"

"She wouldn't listen." Tim responded.

The phone rang. It was ignored. Moments later, Tim's cellular phone rang. It was Troy Thompson, the church elder.

"I have to take this call," said Tim.

Tim reflected upon everything he knew about Troy Thompson. How he was now at the helm at a local meat packing plant after coming up through the ranks. How, in his role as church elder and mentor to Tim, Thompson had consistently been a source of good advice. It was Tim's view that the two of them had bonded to have a father and son relationship.

Tim picked up the call. "Hello Troy, This is Tim."

"Tim, the deacons and I just met. They've asked me to talk with you. Can you meet me at the Church?"

"I'd rather not leave the house right now. I will if it's truly important, but I have issues here I need to resolve. What this is about? I knew nothing about a deacon's meeting."

"Sorry about the timing. I'd rather discuss matters at the Church. Meet me there at eight o'clock."

"Okay, but I can't stay long."

A thought raced through Tim Sullivan's mind. *Is there a connection with this meeting and what is going on at the store?*

Tim told Claire there was a problem at the church. "Don't wait up for me, Tell Mary all this will go away, ask her to trust me."

"Tim, I'm scared."

"Me, too. We'll get through this. Remember I love you."

Claire was uneasy. Something in his choice of words had a ring of finality.

Troy was at the Church. Tim keyed the door open, noticing in the porch light the dour expression on Troy's face.

"Troy I can tell by the look on your face that something is troubling you."

"I've got a job to do. I hate it, but I have no choice."

"Sounds bad. What could possibly be so serious?"

"I'm going to get right to it. The deacons have voted to fire you. They've instructed me to take your keys."

"Why in the world would they do that? Has it got something to do with what is going on at the store?"

"It's got everything to do with what is going on at the store. The Church can't be associated with the mess you've gotten yourself into."

"I haven't done anything wrong. They're just doing an investigation. This is unfair and unjust. Surely there's some way to get the deacons to reconsider?"

"No, it's done. They have voted you out. I need your keys."

"I can't just give you the keys. I have books and belongings to gather. Can I bring you the keys in the morning?"

"No, I need them tonight. Pack up your stuff. I'll trust you to set the latch to lock behind you. Tim, I'm sorry. I hope you work your way out of this mess."

"Troy, how are we going to live? Did they vote to allow me severance pay?"

"No severance pay. They want you gone before morning. Good luck, you're going to need it. Good night."

Tim didn't go home after Troy left, nor did he pack any of his belongings. He was confused and depressed. *How could God allow this travesty? Mary is devastated. We're about to be outcasts in the community, with no resources, no hope.*

He became light-headed and nauseous, had to throw up. He made a dash for the restroom, narrowly avoided making a mess. He wet a paper towel to wipe his face and noticed he had a nosebleed. His hands were itchy and his ability to think diminished. He was a heartbeat away from a nervous breakdown.

Tim's purpose in life had been erased in seconds. He felt it had been hijacked. How could his friends desert him, condemn him, so quickly, unfairly and without compassion? His head began to spin. He was confused, ashamed and over-loaded with depression. He plunged into a state of unhappiness he couldn't endure.

Tim paced the floor for what seemed an eternity. He was unaware that his pulse rate and blood pressure were dangerously low, or that his heart beat had become irregular. His skin was now clammy and cool to the touch, his breathing, shallow and rapid. He was in life-threatening shock. Now unable to think clearly, he became dominated by absolute hopelessness.

He began talking aloud. "Oh, my God. I've tried so hard to please you. Where did I go wrong? Everyone has deserted me. I've ruined the lives of the people I love."

He fell to his knees sobbing in great heaves. "Life is so unfair. You denied me a father, sent Troy to fill the void. I loved that man. He cast me aside like garbage. There's nothing to live for."

Thoughts of taking his own life began to cross his mind. Near midnight he wrote a brief note proclaiming his innocence, searched for and found a length of rope and a ladder and carried them to the sanctuary. He fashioned the rope into a hangman's knot, climbed the ladder and hung the rope over a rafter.

Shortly after midnight the phone began to ring. Tim knew it was Claire calling because he hadn't come home. He didn't answer.

He knew the Bible said it was wrong to take his own life, but God had deserted him. He was exhausted, despondent and completely irrational. He climbed the ladder; and put the noose around his neck. His last words were, "God forgive me."

Chapter 16

7:00 a.m.
December 12, 2012
El Paso, Texas

THERE'D BEEN A SUICIDE, possibly a homicide; Detectives Kathy Smith and "Andy" Anderson got the call. A church custodian had found the body, called the preacher's wife and 911. Their unmarked cruiser laid rubber as it careened into the morning traffic.

"Sorry about the coffee. We'll get some later. Put the light on the roof. Let's get there before someone contaminates the scene."

An EPPD black and white and an Emergency Medical Response Ambulance were on scene, plus a beat up Chevy pickup, a Buick Regal and a Honda Civic. Kathy parked, didn't get out.

"What's the hold up?"

"Me. I hate this, tears me up. A preacher. That sucks." She picked up her note pad and took a deep breath. "Guess I'm ready. How about you?"

Andy gave her a brusque nod. "Yeah, I'm ready. Let's get rolling."

A horn beeped. It was Dr. Hamilton, the El Paso County Coroner. They waited.

"Morning, Doc. Hell of a way to start the day," said Kathy.

"Tell me about it. Two calls already. The other one's over at Five Points."

The body was hanging from a rope next to a twelve-foot ladder. Two kids in pajamas, maybe four and six, were huddled in a pew bawling. Their mother and two EMS responders were trying to console the kids. Two uniformed patrolmen were interviewing a man in a corner.

What a circus! Sweet Jesus! Help me get control of this mess.

It seemed to Kathy the most important thing was to get the body down and out of the way. She interrupted the patrolmen and reassigned priorities. She asked them to take over with the mom and kids. She wanted the Coroner to make a ruling, so the EMS people would be free to remove the body. She said she'd pick up where they left off with their interview.

"I'm Detective Smith. You the janitor?"

"That's right. I'm Robert Brown."

"Okay, Robert. Don't know what you've told the patrolmen, so this may be redundant. What's the name of the deceased," she asked.

"Fella's name was Tim Sullivan. He was the pastor here."

"The same Tim Sullivan from the store that got burglarized last week?"

"The same," he said, wiping away a tear.

Kathy glanced at the mother, shook her head and took another deep breath.

She turned back to Brown. "At what time did you discover the body?"

"At six, when I came in. I opened the door, found him hanging there," he said.

"Sure he was dead?" she asked.

"I checked, no pulse. Figured he'd been there half the night."

"Did he leave a note?" asked Kathy.

"Might of. Could be. I didn't look," he said.

"You find one, you get it to me. Okay?"

"Sure. You might ask them other fellas. Could be they found one. Okay if I finish my cleaning? Got to get to my other job."

Hold up just a bit. Doc Hamilton's got to take some pictures and such. One more question. Somebody reported they thought this might be a homicide. Was that you?"

"Wasn't me. Looked to me the man did it to himself. You might ask his wife. She made a call or two."

"I'm done for now. Wait until Doc is through, then check with me before you leave."

Kathy moved to the pew where the two patrolmen were talking with Mrs. Sullivan. "Fellas, I need for you to keep an eye on Mrs. Sullivan's children while I ask her some questions." She motioned to Mrs. Sullivan to join her in a corner of the room.

"Mrs. Sullivan," she asked, "Did you by any chance suggest to our dispatcher that you have reason to believe your husband's death might not be of his own doing?"

"Yes. I did," said Claire Sullivan.

"Would you explain to me why you said that?"

"Sure. We Baptists believe it's a sin to take one's own life. Tim would never commit suicide. But the main reason is because I think there's a possibility his death may have been connected to his part time job. Tim seemed to think there was a conspiracy to blame him for a burglary. God has always provided. Tim wasn't dishonest," said Claire.

"Just a couple more questions. Why was your husband at the Church last night and why didn't you do something when he didn't come home?"

"We'd had a very serious disagreement. Tim left the house in a huff, saying he was going to a meeting at the Church. He didn't come home. I thought he'd decided to spend the night at the Church because he was mad at me. I tried to call him to get him to come home. He didn't answer my calls."

"Mrs. Sullivan, I see that EMS has your husband on a gurney about to transport him out of here. Let's find out where they're taking him and what you need to do next."

"Dr. Hamilton. Would you fill Mrs. Sullivan in on what's taking place?"

"Sure. Mrs. Sullivan, I'm James Hamilton, the County Coroner. I'm sorry about your husband. You have my deepest sympathy. I'm through here. There's no evidence this was anything other than a suicide. I've ruled it as such. EMS will take his body to the County Morgue. You may have it picked up after you make arrangements. We're open to the public eight to five Monday thru Friday. Do you have any questions for me?"

All the woman could do was shake her head.

Chapter 17

September 1, 1989
Dallas, Texas

BACK ON HIS SIXTEENTH BIRTHDAY in September of nineteen eighty-nine, Everett O'Kelly would have told you it was the most important day of his life. In anticipation, he had enrolled in driver's education, studied hard, passed the written portion of the Texas Department of Public Safety's driver's test and earned his learner's permit.

The permit allowed him to drive under the supervision of a licensed adult. He made an "A" in the class and had a summer of driving the family car under the supervision of his mother.

He aced his test in spite of his concerns about parallel parking. His mom told him she was proud of him, but the big moment would be that evening when he showed his license to his dad and asked if he might have a car of his own.

Everett assumed the answer would be yes, because his parents were rich. They owned the Better Deal food chain of some three hundred and fifty-three super food/drug stores and had a net worth in excess of twenty billion dollars.

The all-important conversation began with encouraging possibilities. His father was very complimentary. Smiling broadly,

Everett piggybacked on the feedback by posing his question. He turned to his mom for support. She pointed back at her husband, indicating it was his decision.

His dad said, "Everett, your mother and I think you should find a part time job and earn your own money to buy a car, your gasoline, and auto insurance. We'll continue to give you an allowance, but the amount won't be sufficient to own and maintain an automobile."

"None of my friends had to buy their cars! Their parents gave them cars when they got their licenses."

"We know that, but we think it's important you know the relationship between what you earn and what you can afford. We think you'll take better care of a car if you earn it and be more sensible about running around when you're buying the fuel."

"What good is all our money, if we don't spend a little?" asked Everett.

"We've made our decision, it's not negotiable. If you want a car, you find a job; we'll help you determine what you can afford. You have to save money for a down payment. We'll co-sign a note to help you establish credit. If you fail to make payments on time, the car gets sold."

Everett was on the verge of tears. His facial expression revealed his bitter disappointment. He was thinking about the jeers to come from his peers. He told his folks, "I'd like to think about it."

Overnight Everett thought through his situation: *I have to have a car. I'm between a rock and a hard space. Guess I'll have to get a job.*

He wanted a BMW convertible like Chuck's, his next-door buddy. *Saving a down payment would take months. Maybe Dad will let me drive one of his.*

The next day Everett was too embarrassed to mention he'd passed his test, because his friends would ask if he was getting a car. He considered where he might apply for a job. There was a Better Deal store near their home that met his criteria of being within walking distance and paid above the minimum wage.

When school let out, Everett changed to a white shirt and tie, and told his mom he was headed to the store to apply. Helen called

Walter, who called the store and asked the manager to hire his son, but added, "If he doesn't do his job, fire him like you would anyone else."

The caveat was unnecessary. Everett did an outstanding job as a bagger and carryout resulting in promotion to checker. The extra earnings put the down payment sooner in reach.

In the meantime, Everett and his friends began smoking a little pot, just enough to put a crimp in his budget. This presented a lot of problems, not the least of which was that his dad would want to know where his earnings had fled.

About this time, Everett got a promotion to evening bookkeeper. One piece of his new assignment was to gather the money and report sales from beverage machines.

Everett incorrectly assumed there was no other way than his report to reconcile beverage machine sales. There were meters on the machines, but no record was kept of beginning and ending readings of these sales.

What Everett didn't know was that receiving clerks require beverage deliverymen to show sales for vending machines separately on their invoices. The accounting department periodically reconciles these invoices to vending machine sales.

Not foreseeing a day of reckoning, Everett began to siphon off a portion of vending revenues, part of which he put in a savings account.

Several months later, a junior accountant named Willard Rhodes was auditing invoices and noticed a disparity between the store's vending purchases and reported revenue. He decided to visit the store to investigate this anomaly.

Willard discovered that Everett O'Kelly, the older of the two sons of the owners of the company, was the bookkeeper who routinely made the report. Catching the owner's family member in an act of dishonesty was not a win-win situation.

Nonetheless, Willard arranged to have a chat with Everett. Early in their conversation Everett confessed, including his use of drugs and pleaded with Willard not to expose him. Ever the opportunist, Willard saw an opportunity to assure his long-term career success.

Willard was in a position to cover up the whole incident, so he made Everett a proposition. He'd look the other way on three conditions: Everett had to quit using marijuana, promise never to steal again and later, when he was in a position to help, he would aid Willard in reaching his goal to be Vice President of Corporate Security.

Everett agreed to all of Willard's conditions.

Chapter 18

8:00 a.m.
Division Headquarters
Better Deal Super Markets
El Paso, TX

WILLARD RHODES PICKED UP on the first ring, "Good morning, this is Willard."

"Willard, Jake Early. I got a call from Peterson. He had me catch a plane to Dallas yesterday. Oscar Beasley had an appointment to talk with him about your investigation. He was irritated because Beasley went around me. I thought he wanted me to fire him, I was wrong."

"What did Beasley tell Peterson?" inquired Willard.

"The first thing Beasley did was knock me on my butt."

"Did he slug you or something?"

"No, it was an accident," said Jake.

"What happened afterwards?" asked Willard.

"Beasley stood up for Sullivan and bad-mouthed you. I supported you, but Beasley's a smooth talker. Peterson shut me down, says he's going to check into Beasley's allegations. Thought I'd better give you a head's up. You may get a call from Peterson."

Rhodes responded, "You think he's about to fire me?"

"No, but he may ask you to back off from Sullivan. Got to go. I'll let you know if anything new develops. Let me know if Peterson calls."

8:20 a.m.

Willard's phone rang again.

He picked up. "Rhodes here."

"Mr. Rhodes, this is Kathy Smith with the Police Department. You asked me for a heads up about developments connected to the burglary. We got the fingerprint ID report from the F.B.I. They found nothing of interest. The prints were those of your employees, most of them, Sullivan's."

There's more, "Last night our dispatcher got a call from the janitor at New Hope Church. He found Sullivan hanging from a rafter next to a folding ladder. He called EMS. They tried heart shock and CPR. Nothing worked. The Coroner estimates time of death at midnight."

Rhodes interrupted, "Did he leave a note? He wouldn't have killed himself if he were innocent.

"I heard the janitor called Chief Rector about a note, but I haven't seen it. I don't think we'll know for sure if Sullivan was involved until we apprehend the people who took the money. I've got to take another call. Let me know if I may be of further service. You have a good day."

Rhodes considered Kathy's remarks. *I never dreamed the man would commit suicide.*

Rhodes knew his heart wasn't pure. The truth was, he'd been manipulating the situation to make himself appear competent and promotable. *I wish Sullivan had confessed. Now I've got to do some damage control, otherwise it's going to appear to be my fault Sullivan committed suicide.*

8:45 a.m.

"Jake, this is Willard. You asked me to call you if there were any new developments. That redheaded police lieutenant just called me. She said Sullivan hanged himself last night, left a note, but she hasn't seen it.

"For crying out loud, it's going to look like you pushed him over the brink. Most likely, you did. That exposes the company to liability and puts you and me in a lot of stink. You still think it was an inside job?"

"I do, but there's no way to know for sure. Maybe it was, maybe not."

"Well, you better find a way to prove it was, because if it wasn't, you and I are going to be hung out to dry."

"A lot depends on how this plays out in the media. I think I can put a lid on it. I've got some leverage with Everett O'Kelly. He pulled a dumb stunt when he was a kid. I covered his ass. He owes me. The company has leverage with the papers. The bigger problem is the note. If there's no note, it'll appear Sullivan did himself in because he was guilty. I'm wired pretty tight with Chief Rector. I'll find out what it would take to make that note go away."

"Might work. Are there any other loose ends that need attention?"

Willard thought about that a minute and said, "Yeah. Maybe. Say we make the note disappear, what can we do about the janitor who knows about the note? It would help if he up and left the country."

"Let me think about it and see if I can come up with something," replied Jake. "You've got a lot on your plate. Let me know how it goes with Everett and Chief Rector."

10:00 a.m.
Office of the Editor
El Paso Times-Herald Post

An article written by El Paso Times reporter, Marisol Chavez, crossed her editor's desk. It occurred to him the article might ruffle the feathers of a very important customer. At 10:15 a.m. he made a call from El Paso to Dallas.

Robert Norton, editor of the El Paso Times was a long-time friend and former Southern Methodist University roommate of

Everett O'Kelly the corporate attorney, board member and heir apparent to succeed his father as chairman of Better Deal.

"Everett, one of my reporters just submitted an article putting your company in an awkward position. As editor, I have an obligation to see we report the news. On the other hand, you're our largest customer. That buys you some discretion, so long as we have an understanding we keep it among ourselves."

Robert continued, "If you like, I'll fax the article to you."

"Bob, why don't you give me the condensed version, so I'll have a sense of what we're talking about?"

"Sure, but understand there's no way the article is going to press the way it's written."

"I still want to hear your condensed version," replied Everett.

"One of your managers just killed himself after being accused by your security director of being the inside man for a burglary of one of your stores. Our reporter thinks it's likely he was falsely accused. In addition to working for you, the guy was pastor of a Baptist church."

"You're kidding."

Robert continued, "I'm not. There's more. The man was well known and well liked. If it turns out he wasn't dirty, your company is going to look like it's been swimming in a commode.

It may be we can put a spin on the story to point less in your direction. I suggest you get your public relations folks to look at the article and get back to me with suggestions."

"How much time," asked Everett?

"Not much. We need to run some version of this story in tomorrow's paper. Our presses roll at 8:00 p.m. I can't change anything after 5:00 p.m. I need to wrap the story between 4:00 and 5:00 p.m., call me when you decide what to do."

11:02 a.m.

Everett was pacing the floor as he considered ways to deal with the issues raised by the suicide when his phone rang. "Everett, Willard Rhodes. Do you have a minute?"

"Yes. I assume you're calling about the Sullivan suicide. I've had a call from the El Paso Times. They're about to run an article that puts the blame for Sullivan's death on you."

"There's a way to make this go away, but I need your help."

"Willard, you need a lot more than my help. It appears you've dug a deep hole," said O'Kelly.

"It's not that complicated. The problem is the suicide note. If there were no note, it would appear Sullivan killed himself in shame and remorse. All we have to do is make the note disappear."

Everett replied, "That's easier said than done. Just how would you propose to make the note go away?"

"Easy enough. Not many people know there was a note. I'm tight with the Chief of Police. It might cost a few bucks, but I'm pretty sure he can be persuaded to make the note disappear."

"You're suggesting we bribe a public official? I don't think so. You need to come up with something better than that."

"Okay, smart guy, how about I go to your dad and tell him about a thieving, dope smoking son of his. How do you like this plan? Is it better?" Willard responded.

"Are you threatening me? That was a long time ago," said Everett.

"Call it whatever you want. You owe me. I'm calling in my marker. You need to help me bury that note or I'm telling all. Do we have an understanding?"

Willard had him by the short hairs. "What do you want me to do?"

Willard was clearly relieved. "That's better. Here's the plan: you deal with the newspaper. The company has the leverage. Make sure there's no mention of a note. Their article has to make Sullivan look guilty. I'll find out what it will take to make the note disappear and get back to you."

Chapter 19

11:42 a.m.
Dallas, Texas

EVERETT READ THE MARISOL CHAVEZ account of Sullivan's suicide. He could see why Bob had run up the red flag. If it made the paper as originally written, they'd have a lot of explaining to do.

According to the article, Sullivan left a note denying any connection to the burglary. Everett re-typed the article omitting any reference to a suicide note or heavy-handed interrogation. He added a comment implying authorities suspected Sullivan had committed suicide rather than face charges.

Copies for pre-reading were sent as e-mail attachments to Everett's dad, Charles Peterson and other members of the executive committee asked to attend an emergency meeting.

1:45 a.m.
Office of Herman Rector
Chief of Police
El Paso Police Department

(Phone rings) "Good morning, Chief Rector."

"Hi, Chuck, it's Willard Rhodes. Something has come up. I need to see you right away. I'd prefer somewhere confidential."

"You have a place in mind?"

Willard did have a place in mind. "How about I pick up a couple burgers and shakes and we meet in Memorial Park? There're some picnic tables around the curve behind the library."

"I know the spot. What time do you want to meet?"

"How about twelve-fifteen?"

"I can be there."

"Good. Mustard or mayo and what flavor shake?"

Chief Rector didn't take long to answer, "Mustard. Vanilla's fine. Bring some fries and catsup. See you shortly."

12:15 p.m.
Memorial Park

The Chief, a small man with a big paunch and wearing a cattleman Stetson, was waiting at a table under an eighty-foot pecan tree behind the library puffing on a stogie.

"Hi, Chuck, still a bit on the cool side out here. I'm ready for spring. All they had were home fries. Hope you don't mind the peels."

"I like them that way. So what's so important we've got to sneak around to talk?" asked Rector.

Willard took a bite and a swig, swallowed, wiped his mouth with a napkin and said, "You hear about the preacher?"

"I did. Good chance it's going to bite you in the ass," responded Rector.

"Could, but maybe not. We just need a little help from our friends down at EPPD."

Rector looked Willard in the eyes, "Are you speaking on behalf of the O'Kelly organization?"

"Of course, but unofficially."

"You must have something in mind. What is it," responded Rector?

"You have a note we'd like to disappear."

"Willard, you're out of your mind. You're asking me to break the law. I appreciate all the financial help from the O'Kelly's, but the answer is no."

"Hold on! We don't want to offend you, but I have a suggestion that might change your mind," offered Willard.

"I doubt it," said Rector.

"You may be surprised."

"I'm listening, but this conversation never happened," cautioned Rector.

"What conversation? May I go on?"

"For all the good it's going to do you."

"The last time we talked you were salivating over a cabin in Ruidoso. Did you buy it?"

"Couldn't afford it."

"How much cabin?"

Rector squinted his eyes in amazement, "Three hundred and sixty-five thousand worth of cabin."

"What if you could buy that cabin for say, fifty thousand instead of three sixty-five? Would the note go away?"

"You got that kind of money to throw around?"

"Let's say that I might be able to arrange so you could buy it at that price," promised Rhodes.

"For that kind of deal, I'd make ten notes disappear," confessed Rector.

"It's do-able if we've got a deal," said Rhodes.

"You've got a deal," he confirmed. *Wonder what's so important about that note?*

"I'll get approvals and get back to you in an hour."

Rector and Rhodes shook hands and went their separate ways.

1:00 p.m.
Executive Conference Room
Better Deal Supermarkets
Dallas, Texas

Walter O'Kelly's reaction to the article was as Everett expected. The initial discussion focused on the Sullivan family and making sure the company responded to their needs.

Everett intervened and pointed out that legally, helping the Sullivan's posed problems for the company. It would appear like admitting complicity and increase their liability exposure. He recommended they do nothing.

The committee, with the exception of Walter O'Kelly, approved Everett's plan. His dad preferred to risk the exposure to look after the needs of the Sullivan family.

Walter could have over-ruled his executives, but decided instead to use this situation as a test of Everett's potential to ultimately run the Company.

1:30 p.m.

From his office in the executive wing of Better Deal's El Paso offices, Jake Early dialed another office.

Willard Rhodes answered, "Hello, this is Willard."

"Willard, this is Jake. Just wanted to let you know, I've taken care of the custodian at New Hope."

"How'd you pull it off?" asked Willard.

"Piece of cake! Found a spot for him in Abilene with a big pay bump. I told him he has to report for work tomorrow, so he quit the church, no notice. He's already on his way down there. I told him we'd pay for a motel. A mover is going to pack up his stuff for his wife and move it tomorrow. We'll fly her to Abilene after the stuff is packed and on its way."

"I appreciate the help."

"No problem. Did you talk to Rector," inquired Jake?

"Yeah. We made a deal. I'm about to call Everett to find out if he dealt with the media and to let him know what it's going to cost him to make the note go away. Expensive deal, but that's his problem."

"Sounds like it's coming together. Keep me informed," said Jake.

1:40 p.m.
El Paso, Texas

Willard Rhodes was still in his office when he called Everett. His secretary Nina, answered.

"Nina, Willard Rhodes. Is Everett available to talk?"

"Yes, sir. I'll ask if he can take your call."

"Willard, Nina said you needed to talk to me. What's up?"

"I talked with Rector. He'll make the note go away, but it's going to cost you. There's a three hundred and sixty-five thousand dollar cabin he wants in Ruidoso. If we let him buy the cabin for fifty thousand, he'll burn the note. Your cost is three hundred and fifteen thousand."

"That's a lot of money. How the hell am I going to hide a transaction like that?"

"Your problem, Everett. You need to put the deal together today, because the note needs to go away now. Call me when it's a done deal. Did you get the media squared away?"

"Everything but sending the edited copy back to the newspaper."

"Good! I'll let you get to it. You need to jump on this real estate deal. I don't think Rector is going to do a thing until he knows the deal is done.

2:00 p.m.
Fax to Robert Norton
Editor
El Paso Times/Herald Post

Dear Bob,

My father extends his sincere appreciation for your sensitivity to our interests. The favor will not be forgotten. The El Paso marketplace is one of our most rewarding investments. We have twenty-two super stores there generating weekly sales in excess of nineteen million dollars a week. That's a 69% share of market. Our reputation and good image in El Paso is priceless. We will protect it at all costs."

Our executive committee reviewed the text of your reporter's article and incorporated some minor suggestions for change. I have attached the edited copy. The committee considers it crucial that you delete any mention of a suicide note in your article. We have more current information from the El Paso Police Department that there was not, nor has there ever been, a suicide note."

Should your reporter insist that her information about a suicide note was correct, we suggest that you have her re-visit her police contacts to validate and confirm this more current and accurate information. I suggest you wait until late in the day to pass along this information.

Our advertising department has been advised that the executive committee has voted to increase our El Paso advertising budget for your paper by $25,000.00 per week for the remainder of this calendar year. We trust this modest show of appreciation will be sufficient to assure your continuing scrutiny of our best interests.

Sincerely,
Everett O'Kelly

2:15 p.m.
Dallas Corporate Headquarters

Charles Davis, Better Deal Director of Corporate Real Estate had been summoned to the office of Everett O'Kelly.

"Charlie," said Everett, "We need for you to put together a very confidential real estate transaction. There are facets of this matter we would prefer not to get public scrutiny. I need for you to keep this matter between you and me until such time as it may become appropriate for discussion. This includes not mentioning it to any of the executive committee. May I count on you to keep it between us?"

Obviously not wanting to be put on a spot, Davis asked, "Mr. O'Kelly is a member of that committee. What if he asks me about the transaction?"

"If he asks," replied Everett, "tell him the truth. But I don't think he'll be asking, because for the moment at least, he doesn't know about it. I just don't want you talking about it out of school."

"As long as I don't have to lie about it, I can assure you I won't be bringing it up for discussion."

Having gotten the assurances required, Everett explained, "Okay, here's the deal: there is a sales representative for Mountain Properties of Ruidoso, Inc. named Alice Taylor, who has a listing for a log cabin on the Ruidoso River priced at three hundred and sixty-five thousand dollars. She recently showed it to Herman Rector, the El Paso Chief of Police. I want you to buy that property and close on the deal today. I'll sign the voucher authorizing payment. Is that possible?"

"We can put the money in escrow assuring payment, but we can't close on a property that fast. It'll take two-three days at the earliest to get the title company to have the paperwork ready," responded Davis.

"Can you provide me paperwork showing we have the money in escrow?"

"Sure."

"Okay. That'll work," said Everett, "but there's more. We're going to turn around and sell that property to Chief Rector for fifty thousand dollars. I'd prefer the deal doesn't have the company name on the contract. Don't we buy and sell some property through a shell company to keep sellers from milking us for big bucks?"

"Quite a deal for Rector. You must owe him big time."

Everett narrowed his eyes and glared at Davis. *Charlie you're being very stupid. Your job is to do what I say, not to question why I want to do it.*

"Damn it Charlie! I told you this was a confidential matter. I can't respond to that, and you shouldn't be bringing it up. Now how about the shell company?"

"Yes sir, sorry. Sometimes we buy and sell properties through Southwest Properties, LLC, a company owned subsidiary. We let Southwest Properties make the deal. Later we transfer the property to Better Deal. Saves us lots of money."

"What can I show Rector to assure him we have a deal in progress?"

Davis thought about that a minute or so, "I can prepare a bill of sale for the property showing we are selling the property to him for the fifty thousand dollars, contingent upon the close of the initial purchase. It takes my signature and an officer of the company to validate the sales agreement. You and I can do that."

"Can you have that for me today by four?"

"Sure."

"Do it."

4:00 p.m.

"Charlie. Your document looks good. You can start putting the deal together. Thanks for doing this on the rush," said Everett."

After Charlie shut the door, Everett called Rhodes.

"Willard, this is Everett. You got a minute?"

"Yes."

"I've got people working on the cabin deal. We can't close on the deal today, but I'm about to fax you a copy of a sales contract. It'll serve as proof the money for purchase of the cabin is in escrow and a signed copy of our agreement to sell the place to Rector for fifty thousand. The media has been handled.

Now I want you and I to have an agreement. Your burglary investigation bungles have caused way too much damage control. There's been no time to plan or double check anything. It could all come back to haunt us. There isn't going to be a next time. Our account is settled. You understand?"

"Yeah, I hear you."

"It occurs to me there's one loose end we haven't dealt with, that's the witness, the janitor who found Sullivan's suicide note. If that man says anything about that note to anyone, we are totally undone. What can we do to make sure this man doesn't go telling his story?"

"Jake Early hired him away from the Church. Found a place for him in Abilene, paid him more money and gave him six months' rent and utility re-imbursement, plus moving costs, provided he moved immediately. He's on his way. His wife and furniture follow tomorrow."

"Jake Early knows about all this? How many other people are in on this with you?"

"I had to tell Jake. He's not going to be a problem."

"You know what else bothers me, Willard? You. Eventually I'm going to run this company. You make me feel insecure. I don't like your behavior or your grandstanding. You bungled the investigation of the El Paso burglary. I want it shut down now."

4:10 p.m.

Willard was seated in his car across the street from EPPD Headquarters. He dialed Chief Rector's number.

"Chuck, it's Willard. I'm across from your office. You got a minute?"

"Sure. Come on up."

Willard looked around the front seat, took a single sheet of paper from a folder and put it in an envelope. He got out of his car, locked up and crossed the street.

As Willard was entering Rector's office, Kathy Smith happened to look up. *What's Rhodes doing here? He said he was going to tell Rector I did a good job, but that's not going to happen after I disagreed with him about his inside job theory.*

Kathy continued to sneak glances in Rector's direction for the next several minutes. The Chief's office was a soundproof glass enclosure, so she could only speculate as to what was being said.

Rhodes handed Rector an envelope from which he removed a single paper. After looking at the paper, Rector made a call and had a manila folder brought to his office.

He shuffled through the papers and removed a single sheet of paper. He showed the paper to Willard. Both men seemed to be agreeing on something about the paper. Rector took the piece of paper they'd been discussing, turned in the direction of his credenza and shredded the document.

Kathy's mind raced as she considered the possible implications of their meeting and their actions. *I wonder what the hell these guys are up to?*

Now they're all smiles and shaking hands. Rector picked up his phone and made another call. The same clerk returned and picked up the folder they'd been discussing. Rhodes left.

Kathy's upper lip tightened contemptuously and curled to one side. *Something here stinks to high heaven. I believe I just saw our Chief of Police take a bribe.*

Chapter 20

Saturday
El Paso, Texas

TIM'S SULLIVAN'S SUICIDE occurred in the earliest hour of Friday morning, too late to be reported in that day's newspaper. Saturday morning the story hit the street.

That morning, as Oscar Beasley was having his coffee and biscotti, he was startled to see a large photo of Tim Sullivan on the front page of the El Paso Times newspaper below a headline that read, "Suspected Accomplice Commits Suicide." The article written by reporter Marisol Chavez inferred that Sullivan was connected to the burglary at number nine. Moreover, it suggested that the reason for his suicide was an overload of guilt and remorse. The more he read, the angrier Oscar became.

He had been standing with Lieutenant Smith and Marisol when she asked the Lieutenant if there were any suspects in the burglary. He'd heard the detective tell Marisol there were none. Why then, would her article suggest Sullivan was involved?

He searched for and found the phonebook, looked up the number for the El Paso Times, glanced at the clock and thought it might be too early to find a reporter at work, but dialed the number anyway. He calmed himself, knowing that people hear the emotion, not the message. He wanted to be sure she heard his message.

"El Paso Times, how may I direct your call?"

"I'd like to speak to, Marisol Chavez, please."

"Good morning, this is Marisol."

"Marisol, it's Oscar Beasley, I'm surprised to catch you at work this early."

"You've heard the early bird gets the worm. Guess I'm the early bird," said Marisol. "You're the district manager I spoke with at Better Deal. How can I help you?"

"I have some concerns about your article in The Times as it relates to Tim Sullivan. I was there when Lieutenant Smith told you there were no suspects. Why do you imply Sullivan was a suspect in the burglary," complained Beasley?

"Mr. Beasley, I recall from our interview you defended your people, but the police and a number within your organization believe Sullivan was involved, that his guilt and remorse induced his suicide."

"You're wrong, the police never suggested that any of our employees were involved in the burglary. They cleared them all, including Sullivan, to their satisfaction," accused Beasley. You're right about one thing, there's someone in our company who blames Sullivan. He's wrong. I suggest you keep a more open mind about this," exclaimed Oscar.

"I'm sorry, Mr. Beasley," said Marisol, "We report the news as it unfolds. If something happens to establish Sullivan wasn't involved, I'll do all in my power to see it's reported."

"Thank you for that," said Oscar, as he ended the call. *The newspaper is more interested in making the pot boil than in reporting the facts.*

Jackie Beasley had been standing outside the open doorway to their sunroom holding a cup. Her delay in entering was out of respect. She didn't want to be a distraction to Oscar.

"Oscar, there you are. I found your coffee cup, but I couldn't find you. I thought you were going to punch out and wind down after a stressful week. I brought you more coffee. Who was that on the phone?" inquired Jackie.

"I was just ventilating a little frustration at a newspaper reporter. Tim Sullivan committed suicide Friday morning. The reporter took some liberties in her story."

"I hope you were nice about it," said Jackie.

"It's hard to be mad and nice at the same time, but I tried. Hope you don't mind, but I'm going to renege on my promise to take the day off. I'm going down to the police station."

"Of course I mind, but I know you're going to go anyway," she replied. Then her eyes twinkled and her lips became a smile. "I'll survive and try to understand."

"I appreciate you being a good sport. Let's drink our coffee before I get dressed."

Downtown El Paso

The desk sergeant repeatedly paged Detective Smith with no response. She was on duty, but apparently out of the building. Oscar gave up, returned to his car.

As he was cranking up the Ford, he glanced toward the donut shop nearby. Unbelievably, Detective Smith was seated next to the window.

"I'd just given up looking for you. Mind if I join you?"

"Not at all," she replied. "I decided to take a break. This is my regular spot. Want some coffee? The donuts are terrific."

"No thanks. I've had my limit and I'm not hungry, but I'd like to talk." he asked.

"Have a seat. What's on your mind?" asked the Lieutenant.

"Did you see the article about Sullivan's suicide?"

"I did."

"It didn't bother you?"

"Sure it bothered me. What bothered me most was what wasn't in the article. That really stirred my stew," revealed Kathy. "I called the reporter and gave her hell. Her article was inaccurate. I never suggested the burglary was an inside job. It also perturbed me she made no mention of Sullivan's suicide note."

"There was a suicide note?" asked Oscar.

"I didn't see one. I heard there was one. Marisol said that she'd been told at the scene there was a note, but she didn't actually see it. Her editor said she needed to confirm the note and what it said or take the reference out of her article. When she went to the EPPD, she was told there was no note."

"You think there was a note?"

"I do," replied the Lieutenant.

"Did they lose it or what?"

"I think it may have been trashed."

"Why would anyone want to do that?"

"Maybe you should ask your employer. They're the more obvious benefactor," snarled Kathy.

"Hey, be nice. Don't you think I'd know about it if we did something like that?"

Lieutenant Smith suggested, "Maybe you're not as smart as you think. Me either. You have a boss, I have a boss, stuff happens. We're too far down the pecking order to know everything that goes on."

Maybe I have my head in the sand, but I'm not going to stand around and watch a good family get shafted for what Tim didn't do.

When I saw that a couple of big shots in my company, one of them my boss, were trying to pin this burglary on Sullivan, I went around them. I don't know if that's going to backfire on me or not. I know I'm skating on thin ice, but I'm not going to back off," confessed Beasley.

"Oscar, I admire your attitude and I'm wanting to do something to set this situation right myself, but there's something you need to know before you get more involved," said Kathy.

"You make it sound like I'm about to cut my own throat. Don't worry! I'm a very careful guy," responded Oscar.

"I can see you think you're on top of the situation, Oscar. But I saw something yesterday that leads me to think there's more at stake and going on here than we imagine. It's possible bigger fish than Rhodes are guilty of trying to pin something on Tim Sullivan."

"That's a pretty serious accusation. What you are implying," asked Oscar?

"If you ask me to repeat what I'm about to tell you, I'll deny having uttered these words," said Kathy.

"Understood."

"Yesterday I was working at my desk and looked up. Chief Rector was greeting a visitor. His guest was none other than your friend and mine, Willard Rhodes. He handed over an envelope to Rector. The Chief was all smiles after he read the note. He and Rhodes shook hands like they'd come to some kind of agreement.

"Do you have any idea what they were discussing?" queried Oscar.

"Maybe. The exchange didn't raise any red flags, but that wasn't the end of it. Rector made a phone call. A clerk showed up with a folder. The Chief dismissed the clerk, removed a page from the folder and discussed it with Rhodes.

Rhodes read it; they nodded like they'd come to an agreement. Rector shredded the damned thing. They shook hands and Willard left. Rector made another call. The clerk reappeared and took back the folder."

"Something's not right. Before I give you my opinion, I'd like to hear what you think I saw?"

"Me? I believe you saw a public official accept a bribe. I also believe we now know what happened to Tim Sullivan's suicide note."

"We're of the same opinion. Unfortunately, we can't prove a thing. So what do we do next?" asked Kathy.

Oscar rose both hands, palm up and said, "Kathy, I don't have a clue. But I can tell you this: I can't just stand by and let a woman who loved and trusted a man think he let her down. Nor am I going to let two little kids who have lost their daddy think he was a dishonorable man. I don't have a clue how I'm going to do it, but I've got to figure out how to clear Sullivan's name and keep my job in the process. I have no right to ask you to risk yours, but I could sure use your help," proclaimed Oscar. "Think about it. If you don't want to take the risks, I understand."

"You're asking a lot. I can't see this being a win-win for either of us. I'll get back to you."

"Good enough. In the meantime, you need to be very discrete

about sharing what you saw with anyone. It might cost you your job, or put you in harm's way."

Chapter 21

Mountain Land Subdivision
El Paso

FOLLOWING HIS CONVERSATION with Detective Smith, Oscar went home intending to spend the balance of the weekend as he'd promised, with Jackie.

"Do I smell chocolate fudge?"

"You do, but don't get your hopes up. This is for a snack for Cub Scouts. You may have one piece. If there's any left after the meeting, they're yours."

Jackie looked up, saw he was pouting. "Oh, all right, take two."

"My sad look works every time," confessed Oscar.

"And I'm a pushover, but I'm on to you now," she said. "Short trip downtown. Did you find some answers to your questions?

"Actually, I found more questions, but it was worth the trip."

"That's good, because you were on my time. You realize you're talking in riddles and avoiding telling me what's going on?"

"Hard to answer because I haven't figured it out myself. When the fog lifts, you'll be the first to know."

"Okay, I'll quit meddling. What are our plans for the rest of the weekend?" asked Jackie.

"On the way home I had an inspiration. We need is some time

off, just you and me away from all this."

"Does this plan of yours include a baby sitter and taxi service? We're kind of tied down with school, piano lessons, brownies and cub scouts."

"Depends on your Mom. You think she'd cover for us?"

"In a heartbeat. Where're we going?" she asked.

"Sounds like you're ready."

"Born ready. Where we going?"

"I'm thinking Cloudcroft. It's between summer and ski season. The trees should be showing color. Maybe we can stay at The Lodge."

"I'd love to stay there. You've always said it was too expensive."

"They have off-season prices this time of year. Maybe we'll see Rebecca, the ghost they say walks the halls. I'll call Jake and see if I can take the week off."

Sunday morning
Ten minutes out from Alamogordo
Thirty minutes from Cloudcroft

"Your Mom must have had a bag packed," said Oscar.

"She loves our kids," said Jackie. "If you didn't notice, our kids weren't upset we're going away."

The drive up the mountain was beautiful. They stopped at a lookout point near the High Rolls tunnel to check out the view. Behind them, across the Tularosa Basin, they could see all the way to the White Sands National Monument and the majestic Organ Mountains.

Past the tunnel, the landscape changed from pinion pine and cottonwoods, to quaking aspens, Douglas fir, ponderosa pines and Colorado blue spruce.

There'd been a freeze Saturday night, causing the leaves to turn brilliant shades of red and gold. Golden aspen leaves were shimmering in the breeze.

They skipped lunch because they planned to splurge that evening at Rebecca's Famous Bar and Grill in the Lodge. Rebecca's signature entrée was Chateaubriand for two at an immodest $100, not counting appetizer, drinks or dessert.

The Beasley's were familiar with the exterior of the lodge from previous visits to the area. They assumed the interior would be rustic appointment.

When they entered the lobby and saw the elegant trappings, the deep carpeting and the beautiful paintings and statuary, they turned to one another with eyebrows raised and mouths open in surprise.

Their room proved to be equally astonishing. The furniture and appointment was stylish and expensive early American. After settling in, they decided to walk a nearby nature trail, then spent thirty minutes in the hotel spa. Back at the room, they cuddled, which led to a test of the springs of their king size bed.

Dinner dress for Rebecca's was casual, in spite of the upscale menu. At six p.m. they appropriately adorned themselves and arrived precisely at six-thirty for their dinner reservation.

They were shown to a table with an expansive window view showcasing the sunset that was highlighting the Tularosa Basin. At the opposite end of the room was a roaring rock fireplace, above which was mounted a painting of a beautiful woman.

Jackie inquired of their waiter, "Who is the subject of the painting?"

He replied, "That's Rebecca, our ghost."

The sirloin was all they'd been promised; the bananas foster dessert was superb. Oscar asked if they might have a moment with the Chef, intending to be lavish with their praise. He came to their table, but stepped back exclaiming, "Oh my God! Oscar Beasley, I haven't seen you since you moved away from Roswell; Lord knows how long ago."

Oscar was instantly in a bear hug with his long-time friend. "Jackie, you remember, Pierre LeBlanc. He was the Chef at the Roaring Twenties Hotel in Portales. We used to go over there Friday evenings when we lived in Roswell. Great rib eyes with sautéed mushrooms. Remember?"

"I remember Pierre," offering her hand. "How could I forget? He's responsible for all ten of my extra pounds. It's nice to see you again. Roaring Twenties was such an elegant old hotel. Is Mrs.

Bergmann still living?"

"She is! I talk to her every week. She's ninety-eight, sharp as a tack and still drives that old black Cadillac. She bought a huge ranch house out in the middle of no-where. She lives out there alone in a big house, which she keeps neat as a pin without help. Her cowboys tell me she runs a tight ship. The ranch makes money."

Oscar asked, "How long has it been since you worked at the Roaring Twenties?"

"A couple of years. Mrs. Bergmann sold the Roaring Twenties Hotel when she was ninety-five to some investors. When they discovered the dining room operated in the red, they cut me loose and closed the dining room. What they didn't realize was that the dining room was the attraction that kept the hotel full. In short order, they had to close the hotel as well."

"How did you wind up here?" asked Jackie.

"Buddy Gentry, the owner of the Lodge here in Cloudcroft, has been trying to hire me away from Mrs. Bergmann for years. He has long tempted me with a standing offer to be the Chef here at Rebecca's. It was an attractive offer, but I didn't have the heart to leave Mrs. Bergmann. When she got out, I had no reason to stay. I'd already called Gentry and accepted his offer before I got fired. Things have a way of working out.

Jeanie and I have been here two years and love it. The restaurant does very well, and the Lodge furnishes us a free cabin. Jeanie manages the golf course. I don't have to pay green fees. Life is good. I apologize, but I'm going to have to ask you to excuse me, I have to get back to the kitchen. I hope we can visit more before you leave."

"We'll be here an additional four days. Our plan is to leave on Friday morning. We'd love to get together with you and Jeanie before we leave."

Following Pierre's departure, Oscar signed their $180 meal check and added a forty-dollar tip. As they exited the dining room, Oscar suggested they duck into the Shaggy Dog Saloon for a nightcap.

"Oscar, you've had four glasses of wine, I'll have to have you carried to our room."

"Spoilsport," said Oscar. "Okay, let's call it a night. This has been a full day. I haven't even thought about Better Deal or any of the issues we left behind."

On their way down the hall toward their room it occurred to Jackie, "We forgot to tell Pierre how much we enjoyed the food. Remember to tell him when we get together. I'm looking forward to seeing Jeanie again. She's a hoot."

Chapter 22

Monday
6:00 a.m.

OSCAR SLIPPED CAT-LIKE from his side of the bed. He dressed in the dark, then opened and softly closed the door and headed for the hotel lobby.

"Good morning. These complementary?" he asked, pointing to a stack of Cloudcroft Monthly.

"Yes, sir. Help yourself."

He spotted the coffee bar and asked. "Where's the closest place to buy the El Paso Times?"

"Vendor box down that hall. May I help you with something else?"

"You got change for a dollar?"

"Yes sir. Here you go. Anything else?"

"No. I see the coffee. I'm good."

He found the cluster of four welded-wire vending boxes. *How the hell do they manage to have current daily papers from El Paso, Albuquerque, Alamogordo and Roswell in a small remote community like Cloudcroft?*

The logistics puzzle filed mentally away, he popped four quarters in the vending box, withdrew the Times and found his way to the lobby's coffee bar.

He drained a brew into a ceramic cup, looked for his favored hazelnut creamer, found instead thick cream in a silver pitcher and unrefined natural sugar. He passed the cup beneath his nose, savored the whiff. *Has a hint of chicory, nice. Now I need a place to park my butt.*

The long west porch beckoned, he tried it, found it bitter cold. In the lobby, he had his choice of seats and spotted a nice chair in a corner. Beside it stood a black bear in a threatening stanch. *No way Jose!* Looking further down the wall, there was a roaring fireplace toasting two plush leather chairs.

That's more like it.

He set down the coffee and papers and gave a chair a try. *Comfy,* he thought, as he squirmed to find the sweet spot.

Finally settled, he sipped his coffee and reached to sample the local news. It flunked his interest test. He reached for the other paper.

Someone settled into the adjacent chair, turned and spoke, "I thought that was you. Jeanie is sleeping in. This is where I have my morning coffee. Did you enjoy the meal last night?" asked Pierre.

"Great meal, but running into you was the high point. Oh, Jackie wanted me to see if you and Jeanie would like to play forty-two one evening?"

"Sure, if we can work it out. Jeanie works days. I work evenings. I'm off this Wednesday. Would Wednesday work?"

"Sure. How about dinner at six, dominos in our cabin afterwards?"

"If dinner may be my treat. Our sirloin is good, but I want you to try our Australian Lobster. It's to die for."

"Looking forward to it," said Oscar.

"So, are you still working for Better Deal?"

"I'm district manager for them in El Paso. It's a great job, but not as much fun as managing a store. I deal primarily with numbers, managers and problems. Right now I'm dealing with a hell of a problem. That's why we're here. I had to get away from it for a few days."

"Has it helped to get away," questioned Pierre?"

"Some, but the problem is hanging out there. If I mishandle it, I could lose my job," answered Oscar.

"Have you decided what to do?"

"I have some ideas, but I'm not yet sure how to proceed. The situation is complicated."

"What happened?"

"One of my stores was burglarized. Our security people think it was an inside job. Their finger pointing was too visible, caused some gossip. The rumors got out of hand and dominos started to fall, our man lost his job, his church, his relationships with his family fell apart and the poor guy hanged himself.

I don't think he was involved at all, nor does the investigating police officer. Unfortunately, my job doesn't allow me time to spend on fact-finding, nor am I much of a detective," explained Oscar.

"Sounds like it's a company problem," remarked Pierre. "Why are you letting it weigh you down?"

"The man had a wife and a couple of kids. It doesn't set well with me to let them think a husband and a father was a bad guy when I'm pretty sure he wasn't."

Pierre asked, "Makes sense! How's the family getting by?"

"That's another concern, they were left high and dry. I see the company as being culpable. I'm between a rock and a hard place."

"What a bizarre situation! What options have you considered?" queried Pierre.

"Right now my best hope," said Oscar, "is a police detective who may step up and help. She's on the fence, I don't know if she's going to help me or not. There are some politics involved, so it's about as risky for her as for me. What I need is a good investigator who can find out who broke into the store and establish that my guy didn't have anything to do with the crime."

Pierre decided to offer a suggestion, "It's none of my business, but if you don't mind, I have a possible solution."

"I'm grasping at straws." Replied Oscar, "What do you suggest?"

"Well, there's this guy," offered Pierre, "who comes up here a lot. He's retired from the F.B.I., used to be the Special Agent in Charge of the New Orleans office of the bureau. Now he's a private investigator, lives north of Roswell, has an office in Portales. His name is Lee Perkins."

"That's a familiar name. Isn't he the guy that took on the New Orleans mob that was shaking down all the merchants, providing killers for hire and controlling the gambling in New Orleans and Louisiana?" asked Oscar.

"That's the man," responded Pierre.

"Wow!" said Oscar, "that guy's famous. He got a lot of notoriety for taking down old "Fat Frank" Gigliano's organization. I read somewhere he's been consulting for moviemakers and TV shows. Is he still doing that?"

"No." responded Pierre, "he did consult for a TV series after he left the FBI and even played some minor parts in the movies, doesn't do it anymore. He enjoys being an investigator and he's good at it."

"How is it you know so much about him?" asked Oscar.

"I've known him a long time. Remember, I was a New Orleans chef most of my work life. I met him there.

"What makes you think he's the solution to my problems?"

"After Lee retired from the FBI," said Pierre. "He did a lot of things that made him money, including co-writing a couple of books. He backed away from all that high profile stuff when he got independent enough to do what he wanted."

He did some hunting and fishing, played a little golf. None of that was very fulfilling, so he got a P.I. license and went in business in Portales because it's close to his retirement home," explained Pierre.

"Portales is a small pond for such a big fish," stated Oscar. "Is he doing any business?"

Pierre paused to consider the question, "He's seventy years old and doesn't want to work too hard or stray very far from home. He knows a lot of important people and gets referrals, is picky about cases he takes. Doesn't do divorces or other slimy cases."

"Pierre, I can't afford to hire a private investigator even though that might seem the best thing to do. How do you figure he fits in with clearing my man?"

"What I'm thinking is Lee is probably the best investigator in this state, maybe the whole country. He ought to have some ideas and advice for you, might even tell you you're wasting your time. It's probably worth a trip to Portales and the cost of one office visit to get some first class advice," advised Pierre.

"That makes more sense to me than killing time around here for three or four more days. Tell you what, since you know him, would you call him and see if he is interested in seeing me? If he is, let's forget about dinner and the forty-two game."

"I've got his number in my cell phone, I'll call him right now."

Chapter 23

8:00 a.m.
The Lodge
Cloudcroft, New Mexico

LEE PERKINS WAS AVAILABLE for a two-thirty appointment. Oscar disappointed Jackie with the news they were checking out. Ever the supportive wife, she said that she understood. It took an hour to pack, check out and gas up. They were on the road by nine a.m.

The first leg of their trip to Portales was to take Route 244, a high mountain shortcut from Cloudcroft through the Chiricahua Apache Indian Reservation to a point just north of Mescalero, where it connects with US 70 to Ruidoso. The forty-four mile trip took one hour and forty minutes.

They took a short rest stop in Ruidoso, because Jackie wanted to take some photos of White Mountain, Ruidoso's ten thousand foot ski mountain. Hwy 70 from there to Roswell was an improvement over route 244.

At twelve-thirty they stopped at a Sonic in Roswell for burgers and drinks to go. The ninety-mile stretch of Hwy 70 from Roswell to Portales is the most boring stretch of road in the West. They could have driven the distance in an hour, had it not been so well patrolled.

They arrived with thirty minutes to spare. Oscar picked the first decent-looking motel, rented a room and carried in their bags. As soon as he was certain that he'd seen to all Jackie's needs, he went looking for Lee Perkins' office on Main Street.

2:30 p.m.
Portales, New Mexico

Downtown Portales was a robust business district built around a town square. Carefully restored, maintained and revitalized, all the buildings retained the charm of the original Spanish-style construction.

The arrow on the twenty-inch brass Perkins Investigations sign pointed upward. It was mounted on a brick facade next to a set of stairs facing the Roosevelt County Courthouse. Lee's office was the first off a hall over the Tower Theater. Its windows faced the courthouse.

Lee Perkins invited Oscar to take a seat. As he moved to the chair, he surveyed the beautiful paintings and trophies then remarked, "I'm impressed. You have some remarkable trophies. I particularly admire the full curve horns on that big horn sheep. Those sheep are hard to find because they hang out in really hard to get to locations. It's an exceptional mount. Where did you find it?"

"You're right, that was the hardest hunt I ever made. That damned thing led me a merry chase. I spotted him at about fourteen thousand feet on one of those straight up and down peaks near Creed in South Central Colorado. We had forty-mile an hour winds, lots of snow and ice. I thought I'd never get close enough to get a shot. It turned out that the shooting was the easy part."

"I was afraid when I shot him; he'd wind up two thousand feet below," said Lee. "Luckily, he fell where he stood, but the carcass was hanging by a thread. Getting to it and getting it down that mountain was torturous. I about froze. You really have to want one of those things."

Colorado only issues three big horn permits a year these days.

They issued one hundred a year when I got mine. I'd been on a waiting list for three years. Some people have been on that list for years and never gotten a permit. A big horn sheep mount is worth about $50,000. One like this one is worth twice that or more. I've had some ridiculous offers, but I don't think I'll ever part with it," explained Perkins.

"The three western oil paintings are beautiful. I especially like all the action shown in the one depicting a stagecoach robbery," said Oscar. "Are they prints?"

"No," said Perkins, "they're Jim Stewart originals. The one you like is called Robbery at Old Eagle Pass."

"I've seen the Jim Stewart collection at the Witte Museum in San Antonio, your paintings must be worth a fortune. How did you come to have these?"

"I could never have afforded even one of Stewart's paintings. He's a friend. He gave me these," confessed Lee.

"You must be some friend. They're incredible," responded Oscar.

"I met Jim Stewart on a hunt on the Tom Horn Ranch near Carrizo Springs years ago," said Perkins. "Tom knows Jim Stewart well; he commissioned a number of his paintings.

I gutted Stewart's first and last buck. We've been hunting together many times since, but he doesn't shoot anything, he just likes to go, carries a camera."

"That's quite a story and you're lucky to be his friend. Your paintings are better than some in the Witte collection," said Oscar.

"Thank you," said Perkins, "and yes, I am fortunate to be his friend. I've tried to balance his generosity. Jim Stewart has, or rather he had, one of the finest western gun collections in the world. I helped him locate and acquire a number of his handguns. He recently donated his collection to the Witte Museum.

I'm sure you didn't come here to suffer through my life story. What can I do for you?" asked Lee.

"We need to have an understanding about money. What I need is advice rather than investigative work. I'm not in a position to fund an investigation," said Oscar. "How do you charge for services?"

"I charge $700 a day or $85 an hour plus expenses. Initial consultation is $100, unless we're here all day. Then I'll be charging more. That okay?"

"Absolutely," said Oscar, "I just like to know what I'm getting into. I feel like I'm wasting your time," said Oscar.

Perkins smiled, "Why not let me be the judge of that? I'll tell you if I can't help you."

"I'm concerned about confidentiality," continued Oscar. "Just talking with you could cost me my job."

"Oscar, I wouldn't last long in this business if I couldn't keep secrets. Why don't you tell me your story and we'll see where it takes us," said Perkins.

"Sure. All this began for me in the middle of the night a week ago. A burglar alarm was tripped at a store I supervise on the East side of El Paso. I had my wife call the law and got there about the same time as the police.

Broken glass was scattered across the front end. They got away with our carton cigarettes and got into the safe and took a hundred thousand dollars in checks and cash, plus our American Express money order machine and four bundles of blank money orders.

They didn't damage the safe. The investigating detectives think the burglars found the combination to the safe hidden on the inside of a mail slot. They conducted a very thorough investigation and had all the key carriers and employees with access to the combination scheduled for polygraph tests. I was told all our people passed their tests.

Our company Director of Security, Willard Rhodes, believes the burglars had an inside accomplice, so he mounted his own investigation and began polygraph testing all employees," said Oscar.

"A female employee," said Oscar, "told Rhodes she had seen Tim Sullivan, an assistant manager who had closed the store, take and pocket money out of a till. Rhodes jumped to a conclusion. He decided he'd found his collaborator, so polygraphed Tim next.

He was heavy-handed with Tim, so he got inconclusive false-positive results. Rhodes stuck to his position anyway, thinking he'd nailed his culprit. Sullivan quit and walked out on him, but came back after lunch insisting he was innocent and wanted another test.

Rhodes agreed, to a second test, which I observed from a distance. He badgered Tim again and got more inconclusive readings. They had a shouting match in front of employees and vendors. Tim quit, walked out a second time.

It was impossible to keep a lid on Rhodes's investigation. People, who overheard, repeated it, the gossip multiplied exponentially, and the facts were contorted," said Oscar. Then he added, "I've seen Rhodes in action before. He's a damned bully, who should have been fired long ago, but he has friends in high places and he's clever at covering his tracks.

This is the worst part the story," said Oscar. "In addition to working part time at the store, Tim Sullivan was a Baptist minister. The story got to Sullivan's church Board of Deacons. The board didn't want to see their church tainted by having a criminal in the pulpit, so they fired him."

They took his keys, told him to get his stuff out of the church and left him. It was brutal. He hung himself."

Perkins spoke, "You'd think a church would show some compassion. What happened to do unto others?"

"It gets worse," said Oscar. My detective friend she told me she had reason to believe Sullivan left a suicide note denying he had been involved with the burglary. The Police Chief denies there was a note."

"Let me guess, you think somebody took a bribe," said Perkins.

"My friend," said Oscar, "believes she may have observed the actual transaction. After which the investigation of the burglary was called to a halt at both the Police Department and Better Deal's corporate security. Nobody's talking.

An article slanted to lead folks to believe that Sullivan's suicide validated his complicity was the lead story in the El Paso Times. There was no mention of a suicide note. The reporter admitted to me she had to rewrite her story because the Chief of Police said there was no note."

"Let's see if I'm reading you right," said Perkins, "You're suggesting your company knows negative publicity influences customer loyalty, affects a reputation worth millions. Not all that unusual. Corporations have power and influence. They're inclined to use it."

"That's exactly what I'm saying," said Oscar. "We're the largest advertiser in the newspaper. A single page ad costs twenty-five thousand dollars. We buy four to six pages a week of newspaper ad copy. That's leverage to influence what does or doesn't get in the paper. They have the leverage to make a note disappear."

"I know Sullivan didn't have anything to do with the burglary. That's total baloney. I feel really sorry for his family. Somehow I've got to prove he wasn't involved in the burglary. Pierre told me he thought you might have some suggestions."

Perkins spent about thirty minutes asking questions and making notes on a pad. He picked up on some missing details, like the quart jar of coins, how it had been broken, the results of fingerprint taken from the scene, pin pointing everything in chronological order.

Perkins said, "You're right about Rhodes. Someone should have dealt with his behavior issues a long time ago. I have no patience with people like him who abuse decent folks and place themselves above the law."

"Oscar, you said you don't have enough resources to pay for my time?"

"Lee, I wish I did, but I don't."

"I thought you probably didn't. Tell you what; I might just poke around a little anyway. Can you afford to pay my expenses?"

"I think so, at least for awhile. Would you want some money up front?"

"Write me a check for a thousand dollars, I'll let you know if I need more."

"You could stay with us at the house. We have a guest room."

"That would help. Why don't you write down your address for me? I can't leave today or tomorrow; I'll show up sometime day after tomorrow, probably late afternoon. I'll need an Internet connect for my laptop?"

Chapter 24

Beasley Residence
El Paso, Texas

THERE WAS KNOCK at the front door. Jackie looked through the peephole; saw a tall lean man wearing boots and a Stetson hat. He fit Oscar's description of Lee Perkins. She opened the door.

"You must be Jackie. I'm Lee Perkins. Did Oscar tell you I'd be coming along?"

"He did. I've been expecting you. Your room is ready. Oscar moved in a desk and phone, so you'd have a place to work. It has a private bath. Extra towels and washcloths are in the cabinet. The sign-on and password for our Internet are on the desk. May I help you with your things?"

"No. I've got it all right here. If you'll show me my room, I'll get settled."

Lee brought in a medium size suitcase, a shaving kit, his laptop, a portable ink-jet printer, his briefcase containing his single action Rugger 44 magnum and his Sig Sauer P220 automatic, plus a tote bag containing some reference books, contact information and ammunition for the pistols, his jogging gear and a pair of house slippers.

"Oscar won't be home for a couple of hours. After you get your things organized I have some hot tea."

"Thank you. I'll skip the tea. I've put together a list of folks I want to meet. If they'll see me, I may go out this evening. I might be late getting in. Might I have a key?"

"Yes," she replied, "We have a key for you. You can come and go as you please. You're welcome to eat with us or feel free to raid the refrigerator and fix for yourself. There's lunchmeat and cheese, TV dinners and leftovers. There are homemade cookies in the cookie jar and a pound cake on the cabinet. We keep beer and soft drinks in a second refrigerator in the garage."

Lee said, "You've gone to a lot of trouble. I appreciate it. I'll try not to be an imposition. If you'll excuse me, I'll bring my things in and get to work."

He switched on the laptop and checked his list. The first name on the list was Claire Sullivan. Lee wanted to find out if Claire had been telling the truth when she told the police that Tim was home with her the night of the burglary. Finding her wasn't easy.

Claire didn't know where to turn when Tim committed suicide. Events had distanced her from her church family. They had no savings and the timing of his suicide had been especially bad, catching her with only a couple of dollars in her purse and a near zero balance in checking.

Her folks still lived in New Mexico. She called her Dad who wired her a hundred dollars to buy gas. She packed the few belongings she could get in her old car, gathered up her kids and drove to Alamogordo.

Chester and Gloria Shipley lived in a small two-bedroom house with one bathroom. They had a bed for her, but no beds for her kids. They made a pallet on the floor for her children and arranged that the children would stay with her brother later. Bill and Olivia would keep the kids until Claire found a job and got her own apartment.

Her father and Bill said they would go after her furniture and other belongings when she found an apartment.

Lee located Claire's El Paso residence only to discover Claire wasn't there. Neighbors told him they had seen her pack a car, load up her kids and leave. The neighbor's kid said they were going to their grandmother's house. Lee could see through the front window that furnishings were still there, so he figured she'd be back.

Lee put his plans to see Claire on hold. In the meantime, he decided to see Detective Smith, who had led the police investigation of the burglary. He hoped to find out more about the missing note.

Lee missed her by minutes at her office. He asked the desk sergeant where Kathy lived. He wouldn't release the information. Her phone number turned out to be unlisted. He showed his retired FBI credentials and explained that he had some business to discuss with Kathy. The desk sergeant finally agreed to call her on her cell phone to see if she'd talk with him.

He handed Lee the phone, "Kathy, I'm Lee Perkins. I'm doing some work associated with a case you investigated. I know better than to bother you on your personal time, but this is time-sensitive and I'd rather discuss it away from other ears. Is there a chance we could talk this evening?"

"Perkins, Smerkins, whatever you call yourself, I'm off duty. I want to get out of this stinky uniform and soak my bones in some hot water. So no. Not a chance this evening. Call me tomorrow."

I'm ragged out too. I promise not to take long. I just can't go forward with what I'm doing without a little info from you. Please, just a couple of minutes."

"You're a persistent bastard! All right, five minutes and you're done. You know where I live?"

"I don't," he lied, thinking. *It might upset her if she knows I know.*

She gave him her apartment number. It was thirty minute drive away.

Kathy answered his knock; her greeting was cool and formal, her voice almost a snarl. The sour expression on her face screamed she was not a happy camper. Her hair was wet. She was wearing a terrycloth robe. She held what appeared to be a Bloody Mary.

Not offering Lee a drink was her unspoken statement of resentment to his intrusion. *My only hope*, he thought, *is that the Bloody Mary will mellow her mood.*

"Kathy," Perkins said, "I apologize for bothering you. I'm a private investigator; I used to do work similar to what you do for the FBI. I've been hired to clear Tim Sullivan's name. My employer believes Tim had no part in the burglary.

Kathy continued to look annoyed and said, "Just exactly whom <u>are</u> you working for?"

"Oscar Beasley told me he trusts and confides in you. He hired me to do two things: find out who burglarized the store and clear Sullivan's name. You can appreciate why he wants his involvement kept confidential."

"He's more serious than I realized," exclaimed Kathy.

"I wanted to meet you," said Lee, "to ask for your help. I need to know: did Tim Sullivan leave a suicide note? And what was in it?"

Kathy posed a question, "Let's say I tell you what I know. What are you going to do with it?"

"Fair question. If Sullivan left a note insisting he wasn't involved in the burglary" Lee said, "I'm inclined to believe him and discard the insider theory. If there was no note, that possibility stays on the table. I need to either implicate Sullivan or cross him off the list. Was there a note?

Kathy narrowed her lips. "Damned right, there was a note. One of my guys saw it, picked it up, took it downtown and gave it to the Chief. The Chief denies having seen the note.

I didn't see a note. Didn't have to because I knew Sullivan wasn't involved. I knew it after talking with his wife and I confirmed it when he passed our polygraph.

Better Deal has my boss in their pocket, I don't know how, but I think he's their puppet. If I could prove it, I would. I can't; it hurts like hell."

Lee was stunned. "There's some seriously bad stuff going down here!"

Lee took a moment to digest all he'd learned. *Why Rector would take such a risk?* "I can see you're between a rock and a hard place. I won't do anything that'll reflect on you. Is there a chance that you'll help me get other information I need?"

"I will," said Kathy, "on the strict condition you keep me as an unknown. I'm not ready to risk my job for the ghost of Tim

Sullivan."

"You have my word."

"Good. You want a beer or a Bloody Mary?"

Chapter 25

8:00 p.m.

WHEN LEE PERKINS GOT back to the Beasley residence, Oscar was at home. He and Jackie had already eaten and were relaxing in their den. Jackie made him a plate of the beef roast and vegetables they'd had for dinner and put it in the microwave.

At the table Oscar initiated the conversation. "We're glad you're here. If you need anything just let us know. Jackie told me you went looking for Kathy Smith. Did you connect," asked Oscar?

"We did, but she wasn't happy about the intrusion," said Lee.

"Sounds like you drew a blank."

"Actually, the time was interesting and well-spent. Once she got over being mad at me, she was helpful," said Lee.

"What did you find interesting," asked Oscar?

"She confirmed that Sullivan left a suicide note," said Lee. "She didn't see it, so she can't prove it existed. She has reason to believe Better Deal somehow persuaded Rector to shred the note."

"Is she willing to come forward and confront Chief Rector," asked Jackie?

"No. Nor do I think she should. She'd lose her job and accomplish nothing," said Lee. "The good news is that she is mad as hell, has committed to help us in any way possible, so long as we don't put her job at risk."

"It'll be helpful to have an insider at the police department on our team. You guys talk all night if you like," said Jackie, "but this has been a long day and I, for one, am ready to hit the sheets."

"Me, too," said Oscar. "Let's call it a day."

They adjourned to their respective bedrooms. Lee had work to do. He shut the door to his room, dressed for bed and booted up his laptop. He brought up Alamogordo in Otero County and scrolled to vital statistics. He located the marriage record for Tim and Claire Sullivan. Included in that document was Claire's maiden name, Shipley.

He searched Alamogordo White Pages for Shipley, found two he thought to be about the right ages to be Claire's parents, made a note of their address and phone number. He planned to go there in the morning.

His six a.m. departure time made little difference in the amount of traffic. El Paso was a city that never sleeps. Beyond the city limits there was little traffic to slow him down. In spite of the crawling speed limit passing through Oro Grande, New Mexico, he managed to complete the eighty-six mile journey in one hour and twenty minutes.

As he approached Alamogordo, he noticed the opposite lanes had bumper-to-bumper traffic heading west. These were civil service workers and Air Force personnel who lived off-post bound for work at Holloman Air Force Base. It was too early to call upon the Shipley's. His stomach reminded him he'd not yet been fed or had coffee.

It had been no accident that he'd skipped breakfast. He was well acquainted with a local restaurant, Juan's Cactus Café, and knew they served *huevos rancheros*, his favorite breakfast fare. When he passed through Alamogordo, he often stopped there to eat. After he had made his way to the eatery, he found a parking space, bought a paper and enjoyed a breakfast with three cups of coffee. He read just enough newsprint to arrive appropriately at the Shipley's by eight-fifteen.

The Shipley residence on Cuba Street was a modest asphalt-sided single story residence. When he rang the doorbell, a sixty plus balding gentleman with sparse red hair opened the door.

"Morning. What can I do for you?"

"I assume you're Mr. Shipley, I'm looking for your daughter, Claire. I'm hoping to find she's staying here with you and your wife. Here's my business card, I've been retained by an individual who believes that your son-in-law, Tim, was falsely accused of being connected to the burglary of that store in El Paso. My goal is to prove his innocence."

"If Claire is here, I would appreciate having an opportunity to speak with her."

"Excuse me for not inviting you in. Claire is here, but she has an appointment to interview for a job this morning. She needs that job. Give me a minute to see if she has time to speak with you."

"Thank you. I understand the importance of getting a job. However, it's important that I speak with her. I'm quite willing to come back after her appointment."

After speaking with Claire, Mr. Shipley returned to speak with Lee. "Mr. Perkins, she can't see you now. But she'd be happy to meet with you after her meeting. Her appointment is next door to the library. She'll meet you at the library at noon."

"Tell her I'll be there. I appreciate your help. You have a good day," said Perkins.

As he headed back to his car, Lee decided his next move would be to find and talk with an El Paso drug addict with a history of trading cigarettes for drugs. Contrary to the commonly held notion that criminals don't squeal on one another, the opposite is highly predictable. It had been Lee's experience that most criminals, when arrested, immediately tell everything they know, often even without being asked.

Chapter 26

Memorial Park
El Paso, Texas

RAISED LITTLE MORE THAN a stone's throw apart, three no longer *young* men, Glenn Bergmann , Juan Del Bosque and Leo Canales share a common problem: an unshakeable addiction to crack cocaine. All are near the same age, were reared as Catholics and came from middle-class working families. They are scumbags and big-time losers. All have served time in detention.

Their lack of morals, ethics, conscience and remorse is appalling. They squandered their families' resources for lawyers, bail, and the purchase of drugs.

Their neighborhood, Memorial Park, used to have beautifully maintained homes, over the past three decades there had been an evolution of decay. The neighborhood was now characterized by a lack of lawns and landscape.

Population density has tripled. Multiple families of illegal immigrants occupy houses zoned as single unit residences. Crime is rampant. Women aren't safe on the streets. Windows are barred to keep out intruders. Teenage gangs prowl the streets at night.

The three losers now venture into the neighborhood to support their habits. They've become specialists of a sort. They steal only cigarettes.

They've selected Sunset City Food Store as their weekly target of choice. An earlier walk through of the facility confirmed that the cigarette inventory on hand would meet their needs.

The method they normally use to gain entry is a quick break in through the front with a hasty retreat before a response can be organized. At this location, this method won't work, because the front end of the store has a direct line of visibility from the police station.

They have borrowed, without permission, a truck containing a fifty-foot extension ladder and a few tools. They used the ladder to gain access to the store's roof and tools from the truck's assortment to dismantle a section of air conditioning vent.

They entered the vent, then crawled to a grate over an open section of the sales floor and used a knotted rope to descend to the sales floor. After filling plastic garbage bags with carton cigarettes, they hoisted them to the air duct.

They had just up-loaded the last of the cigarettes when the store's manager unlocked the front door at six a.m. to let in the receiving clerk, a bread vendor and the produce manager. He failed to notice the man being hauled up a rope to the ceiling just sixty feet away.

He did, however, notice the store's cigarette inventory was missing, and then spotted the rope hanging from the ceiling. He immediately called the police conveniently located across the street. Four policemen were there in seconds.

By this time the intruders had made their way back to the roof. When they looked over the edge of the roof, they could see that their truck, thoughtlessly parked next to the receiving door as well as their ladder, already had the attention of a policeman.

The ladder leaning on the building left little doubt the intruders were in the building. The policeman laid the ladder on the ground, effectively trapping them, then made a radio call to the policemen inside.

The three policemen who had entered through the front door saw the rope hanging from an air duct at the same time they got the call about the ladder. Realizing they had burglars trapped on the roof, they called for re-enforcements. The store was, in short order, literally crawling with representatives of local law enforcement.

Having been outnumbered and quite efficiently corralled, the three burglars were soon handcuffed, spread eagle, searched for weapons and placed under arrest.

Chapter 27

Noon Friday
Alamogordo Public Library
Alamogordo, New Mexico

AN ATTRACTIVE PERHAPS THIRTY-YEAR-OLD brunette approached a man standing near the library entrance. She looked him up and down, then spoke boldly to his face, "I'm Claire Sullivan, I'm supposed to meet a gentleman here. Would that be you?"

"Yes, I'm Lee Perkins. I appreciate you agreeing to meet with me. Would you like to go inside where we can sit and talk?"

"That's fine with me," Claire said.

"The library opened at eleven," said Lee. "I looked around while I was waiting. They've got a sitting area behind a glass enclosure where we can visit and not be disturbed. If you'll follow me inside, I have the space reserved."

When they were seated he said, "Mrs. Sullivan, I am so sorry about your husband. I've heard he was an exceptionally fine man."

"He was, and thank you for saying that. This whole business has been surreal; I've had a hard time sorting things out. Seems like my life was going along just fine and all of a sudden everything sort of blew up. Mr. Perkins, my Dad told me you're a private detective. Who do you work for and why are you here?"

"Your husband had a friend, Oscar Beasley, who thought very highly of him. He believes Tim had nothing to do with the burglary. He hired me to continue privately with the investigation."

"Oscar," Claire said, "was my friend as well. I'm not surprised he wants to get at the truth."

"You're right. "Oscar wants to clear Tim's good name. He hired me at some considerable risk to his career, so I'm asking that you please keep our meeting confidential."

Lee went on. "I agree with Oscar. Your husband was not complicit to that crime. I'm going to prove it."

"What a nice thing for Mister Beasley to do. Tim thought a lot of him too. My kids need to know that their Dad was the finest man I ever knew. What is it you need from me? How can I help?"

"You have probably already done this a dozen times, but I need for you to tell me everything that happened the night the store had the break in."

"I told the police and the lady detective, Kathy Smith. Tim got home from work about ten pm. The store closed at nine pm. I was still up, but ready for bed."

"I warmed up a bowl of soup and fixed him a sandwich. We talked about our day, what we did, about the kids and what we were going to do the next day. Tim talked a lot about the church building project and the materials he was going to buy the next day when he got paid. He was so excited about the prospect of a new church building, he was almost hyper."

"When did you go to bed? Did you go to bed at the same time?"

"We were both pretty tired, I ironed that day, and it was a big ironing, my back hurt. We went right to bed. Tim rubbed my back for a while, then we both went to sleep."

"Did he ever get up or leave for any reason?"

"No. I'm a light sleeper. If Tim got up, it would have wakened me. He got up once to go to the bathroom, but came right back to bed. That was the only time he got up."

"How about in the morning? Did you both get up at the same time, or did he get up before you did?"

"No, he didn't get up again until the phone rang. It woke both of us. It was Dan Coleman, the store manager, who told Tim there had been a break in and asked him to come to work right away."

"Can you think of anything Tim did or said that evening that you haven't told me?"

"No, that's pretty much all that happened. I think I didn't mention that Tim went in and kissed the kids good night. They were both asleep."

"Mrs. Sullivan, I think that's all I need to know. It's been helpful and I appreciate you giving me this time. I hope everything turns out well for you and your kids."

"Thank you," she said. "Things may be looking up. I just got hired and it's a better paying job than I was expecting to find."

Chapter 28

Saturday Afternoon
El Paso, Texas

LEE'S HANDS-FREE CELL PHONE rang. It was Kathy Smith.

"Hi, Kathy, what's going on?"

"You wanted a call if we got a break in the case. Officially, it's closed. However, something caught my interest this morning."

"Cops in Sunrise City caught three cigarette thieves at 6:00 a.m. this morning. The chief is going to allow me to talk with them."

"I'm on my way back from Alamogordo. When are you going?"

"I'm leaving right now. It's a fifty-minute drive from this station. How about you? Can you meet me?"

"I'm at the North side of Fort Bliss, less than an hour from Sunrise City. I'll meet you in front of their police department."

Sunrise City is located twenty miles from downtown El Paso, has maybe twenty thousand citizens. Its existence is attributable to advertising hype. Land promoters bought the land for little or nothing, cut it up into one-acre lots and dumped them at bargain prices. It's flatter than a pancake, has no trees, the soil is salty; water is scarce, vegetation practically non-existent.

Not one damned thing I know about Sunrise City has any value. It'd help if I knew where to find the darn jail.

Lee remembered seeing a sign reading "El Paso Transitional Center" in Sunrise City the first and only time he had passed that way. Thinking it might be their jail, that's where he went. It turned out to be a private jail built to house up to 200 youth. He was re-directed to the Sunrise City Jail, where he saw Kathy Smith standing near the front entrance.

"Sorry I'm late," he said. "I went to the wrong jail. Have you been waiting long?"

"No, actually, I just barely beat you. I got caught in heavy traffic. You ready to question these scumbags," asked Kathy?

"Sure. You ready?"

"Yeah, but I didn't tell the Chief I'd be bringing a friend."

"Just tell him I'm retired FBI. Most of the time that gets me in the door," said Lee.

"You're pulling my chain. What I hear is most local law enforcement resents FBI interventions," said Kathy.

They found no receptionist at the Sunrise City Jail; the lobby was a cubicle with one window to a secure area beyond and a button to ring for attention. It took three rings to attract someone to their presence. After identifying themselves, an entry door lock was electronically released that permitted them access to the station's work areas.

The person who opened the door addressed Kathy, "I'm Pat Callaway, the jailer, janitor, secretary and general flunky for the Chief. He told me to expect you, Lieutenant. He's not here, but he left instructions that you were to be allowed to interview all three of the prisoners from the burglary." He turned to Lee. "Who're you?"

Kathy answered for Lee. "He's a former FBI agent, now a private investigator working with me on the case. I don't think your Chief will have any objections to him being part of the interviews. If you like, you can call him."

"Naw. That won't be necessary. You can use the first room down the hall on the right. I'll bring them in to you one at a time. Does it make any difference which one you talk to first?"

Kathy looked at Lee, who shook his head no. She gave it some thought and said, "No, but we'd like to read the investigative report of the case before we talk with them. Would that be possible? If you have rap sheets on the prisoners, we'd like to see them as well."

"Sure. I'll make two copies of everything. You need anything else? There's fresh coffee over there in the corner. Make yourselves at home."

Lee and Kathy moved on down the hall to their designated room, each took a chair and waited for the copies.

Pat returned quickly with the paperwork and suggested they read the reports while he fetched the first prisoner.

After Lee read through part of the stack he remarked, "Their Mothers must be proud. All three of these dummies had every opportunity to have the good life and blew it. It's easy enough to understand how the under-privileged go wrong, but it burns my cheeks to see people who had all the perks and opportunities screw up their lives."

Kathy said, "Yeah, gets me too. The truly sad thing is they don't just mess up their own lives; they bring down their folks, siblings and a lot of others with them. Not to mention the costs to society like the legal system and the victims of their addictions."

"What a waste," said Lee. "I've never understood why anyone in his or her right mind would ever take the first blow of crack. I hear we now have over seven million crack users in this country."

"They say that one use is all it takes to hook you forever," said Kathy. "Getting back to why we're here. Do you see a pattern? Do you think they're the guys that did the Better Deal?"

Lee thought about that a second. "If all they'd taken was cigarettes, I'd say it's possible they did both jobs. But it doesn't make sense that they did the safe at one and not the other."

"I see it the same," said Kathy. "Something doesn't mesh. I guess we're just going to have to ask them and see where it takes us. You ready?"

"Yeah and here comes Pat with the first perp. we're going to need one more chair. I'll see if I can find us one," said Lee.

Chapter 29

Sunrise City Jail
Sunrise City, Texas

PAT CALLAWAY SAT THE TALL skinny pock-faced prisoner at the lone table in center of the room. "Okay, Mr. Bergmann. Both hands on the table." Callaway unlocked one cuff, slid it through the steel loop on the table and cuffed the suspect to the table.

"He's all yours. When you're done and I'll bring you another."

"Thanks, Pat," said Kathy. "This may or may not take awhile. It's all up to Mr. Bergmann. "

"Mr. Bergmann, I'm, Detective Smith, I'm an investigator with the El Paso Police Department. This is Lee Perkins. We're investigating the burglary of a Better Deal Supermarket in El Paso. We have reason to believe that you and your companions burglarized that establishment. Before we begin our questioning we want to make sure you're aware of your rights. This interview is being recorded. So we need to establish your identity. Please speak into the microphone and state your full name."

"Ronald B. Bergmann. "

"Are you aware what you say may be held against you and you have a right to have an attorney present," asked Kathy?

"Sure," he said.

"Do you waive your right to have an attorney present?"

"Why should I," asked Bergmann.

"I'm not suggesting that you should or shouldn't," said Kathy. "However, the degree to which you cooperate in our investigation may serve to reduce the severity of your sentence, if you're found guilty.

"I don't need an attorney," he said.

"Note that the prisoner waived his right to have an attorney present. Mr. Bergmann, did you sign a statement that you, Leo Canales and Juan Del Bosque in the early morning hours of November eighth, entered a Sunrise City store to steal cigarettes to trade for drugs?"

"Yes."

"Isn't it also true that you intended to break into the store's safe?"

"No? Don't do safes."

"Isn't it true that when you stole cigarettes from the Central Avenue Better Deal store in El Paso, that you opened the safe and stole the contents?"

"Not true! We only took cigarettes."

"You just admitted you and your friends burglarized the Better Deal Store. Were you aware that the safe was also robbed?"

"I didn't say that! We didn't do a Better Deal store."

"Oh, but you did, Mr. Bergmann, you admitted that on tape. It's now a matter of record."

Bergmann was instantly on his feet. "You tricked me," Bergmann shouted, as he swung a leg at Kathy and missed. "Bitch! I haven't got anything else to say to you."

After returning Bergmann to his cell, the jailer brought in Leo Canales. Lee Perkins read him his rights.

"Leo," he said, "you signed a confession that you and your buddies broke into the store in Sunrise City to steal cigarettes. Is this correct?"

"We admitted we did the store."

"Your buddy, Glenn Bergmann, confessed that the three of you also broke into the Better Deal on Central. Is this correct?"

"He didn't do that. You guys can't hang that on us."

"It appears we can. You want me to play his tape? The store's safe was robbed during that burglary. Where's the money?"

"There isn't any money! All we took was cigarettes. Maybe somebody else took the money. We didn't do it."

"It's hard to believe you didn't take the money when we know you took the cigarettes."

"Look man," said Leo, "I swear to God we didn't rob any safe. That's not what we do. We take cigarettes to trade for our blow and a little hooch. That's it! *Nada mas!*"

"Isn't it true you collaborated with a store employee to gain access to the store safe?"

"Hey, man, where's all this coming from? Don't know anybody there. Didn't make any deal to do a safe job."

The Juan Del Bosque interview was much like the other two. He self-incriminated on the Better Deal break in, denied any knowledge of a safe.

"So what do you think? Did they do the safe?" asked Kathy.

Lee replied, "I don't think so. Which offers the question, who did rob the safe?"

"See any way it could have been Sullivan?" questioned Kathy.

"None. His wife rules him out for me. I think someone went in the store after the druggies took the cigarettes," said Lee.

Kathy mulled that over, then said, "There was plenty of opportunity. The neighbor Beasley talked with said the alarm had been going a couple of hours."

"We can't rule out the security company. Maybe the alarm didn't malfunction. Could be they responded, did the safe and left," said Lee. "I can pursue that and see if it leads anywhere. You got any ideas?" Lee asked.

"I've got one and I don't like it. What if a patrol car happened by, a patrolman spotted the busted window and stopped to investigate? It wouldn't raise any eyebrows to see a cop go inside to check things out. No risk and plenty of opportunity," surmised Kathy.

"Am I hearing you right?" asked Lee. "You're suggesting one of your own patrolmen might be dirty?"

"Actually, not one, but two. They work in pairs. I'd like to think better of our people, but we get a bad apple every now and then," said Kathy.

"If you'll make a list of officers on patrol that night, I'll see if they've come into extra money," said Lee.

"I'll fax you a copy of the duty rooster. The window of opportunity was between one and three in the morning," said Kathy.

"In the meantime, I'll bring up charges on the druggies for the burglary. Everyone is going to think they did the safe too," said Kathy.

Lee asked, "You going to call Rhodes?"

Kathy smiled, "Oh, yeah! He's going to wet his pants."

"I'll let Oscar know," added Lee. "And then I'll call Claire Sullivan."

Chapter 30

Memorial Park
Behind the Library

ELI SANCHEZ WAS WORN-out and tired of looking over his shoulder in fear of getting caught. Six weeks have passed since he and Toby stole the contents of the Better Deal safe. Nothing has happened to cause him to think that anyone suspects he or Toby took the money. He was sure they'd removed any trace of their earlier visit to the store. He wasn't going to tell anyone. The problem was Toby, the compulsive gambler with the big ego and the blabbermouth. Eli was scared his partner was going to give them away.

Tonight he was parked in the turn-around behind the Public Library in Memorial Park, where he had agreed to meet Toby. Eli had realized that Toby was unreliable and high-risk. In fact he'd been following him when he was off duty and he knew he had been playing in a high stakes poker game and losing badly.

The local building contractor who hosted the game was known to have ties to organized crime in New Orleans. The word on the street was that Toby was a big loser being allowed to get in even deeper. Who knows when the syndicate might need a law officer in their pocket?

Toby pulled alongside Eli's cruiser, rolled down his window and said, "Thanks for meeting me. We need to talk."

"Not a good idea, but I'm here. Pull your car over there and get in mine, this may take awhile," said Eli.

Toby parked where he was directed and slid into the right-side front seat.

"What the hell's the matter?" asked Eli. "You're white as a sheet and shaking like a leaf. Calm down. Okay?"

"Eli, I'm not going to beat around the bush. I'm in deep shit. I need twenty-five thousand bucks to settle a gambling debt. Don't you think it's cooled down enough for us to split the cash?"

Eli furrowed his brow as he thought: *you dumbass; they set you up and took you to the cleaners. What'd you expect?* "Toby," Eli said, "Not just no, but hell no! We agreed that we'd wait at least six months before we touched that safety deposit box."

"Eli, this is serious. I've got to have the money. Nobody's looking at us. It won't hurt a thing."

Eli's face flushed with anger. "Toby, you're pissing me off. That's how we get caught. You've got to cool it and stick to our plan."

"Look, I hate to tell you this, but they were going to ice me man. I had to tell them we had the stash, and that I had the money or they would've killed me. I didn't have a choice," sobbed Toby.

Eli suppressed an urge to lash out at Toby. "You didn't mention my name, did you?"

Toby shook his head no. "Hey, no way man, I wouldn't do that to you. They think I did the job by myself."

"Oh yeah! You're lying through your teeth. They know you're too yellow-belly to do it by yourself."

"Eli, I swear, they don't know you had anything to do with it."

"They better not!" said Eli with ice in his eyes, "If I find out you've told them, you're shark bait. *Capsize?* And I've got news for you. We're not going to touch that money until June. That's what we agreed to and you're going to have to stick to your deal. Those cockroaches are not about to do you in. They like having a cop they can screw around. You figure it out. Stall them 'til June. And one more thing: If you tell anyone that I'm involved with that burglary, you won't have to worry about being iced by the bad guys, because I'm going to get there first. Got me?"

"Eli, I'm a dead man," said Toby. "You know it, too. You just want me to get killed so you can have my half. You ought not to treat me like that."

"Don't ask me again," said Eli. "We don't touch the stuff until June. I'm not trying to screw you. I just don't want us to get caught. Now get out. I've got to go."

As he drove away thoughts raced through his mind: *Toby's a loose end. He can tie me to the money from the safe. If he rats me out to the mob, I'm toast. What are my options? I can't go to jail. I've heard what the cons do to cops who get sent to jail.* The thought made him shudder. *That gets me back to Toby. He's the problem. I've got to do something about Toby.*

A plan began to form in Eli's mind. It now looked like El Paso would be adding another suicide to their vital statistics. It makes sense that a cop, with over-whelming gambling debts, might choose to take the easy way out. And, like Toby said, it would be nice to have it all and not have to share.

Chapter 31

Five minutes after eight a.m.
El Paso Regional Offices
Better Deal Supermarkets

WILLARD RHODES WAS A HEARTBEAT away from a state of shock. He had cradled the phone on his desk, but couldn't pull his hand away. His face appeared frozen in a mouth-open expression of stunned disbelief. He was seated in front of his computer screen displaying a dozen e-mail messages, but he had no conscious awareness of what was on the screen. His mind was focused on considering the potential consequences of the message he'd just heard.

Kathy Smith had called. Her message was brief. Three burglars had been caught red-handed stealing cigarettes from a supermarket east of the city. They had admitted to the previous burglary at the store on Central. All had denied any ties to Tim Sullivan or having taken the money from the safe.

Rhodes almost jumped out of his skin as the ringing of his phone jolted him back to reality.

"Hello," he said, as he tried to gather his wits. "This is Willard. How may I help you?"

"Morning, Willard. It's Herman. I've got a heads up for you."

"Yeah! Take a number and get in line. So far today everyone's had a heads up. What's going on?" asked Willard.

"The District Attorney stuck his head in my door a few minutes ago. He told me that some guys got caught over in Sunrise City doing a burglary. One of my detectives went over there and interviewed the twerps, got them to confess to the job at your store on Central. They deny doing the safe or having anything to do with your guy, Sullivan. I hope this thing's not going to come back and bite us."

"You told me you had shut the investigation down. Why was your guy still poking around?"

"It wasn't my guy, it was a gal. It was that female detective, Kathy Smith. I haven't found out why the hell she was over there. I'm going to. The D.A. said she was with a private investigator. I don't know how a private investigator fits in. I'm going to call her in and find out. I thought I better let you know someone was stirring up some stuff. I'll keep you posted."

"I appreciate the call. Actually, I had just hung up after listening to your detective pull my chain. She said she was calling, like you, to keep me informed. I could tell she was getting off by letting me know it wasn't an inside job. This is going to cause some hiccups in the Ivory Tower in Dallas. I'm not looking forward to conveying the message. They'll probably shoot the damned messenger. Look, anything else happens, keep me informed. I especially want to know about this private investigator. Okay?"

"Yeah, sure, I'll call you. And Willard."

"Yeah!"

"Just because the guys that did the break-in weren't working with Sullivan doesn't mean he didn't do the safe. You could still be right. Hang in there," said the Chief.

Nine a.m.
Office of the Company Attorney
Better Deal Supermarkets
Dallas, Texas

"Everett, this is Willard Rhodes. We need to talk; something has come up about the break in at number nine. Can you spare me a few minutes?"

"Not right now. I was headed out the door when the phone rang. I've got to be on a plane to El Paso in forty minutes. I'm running late as hell. It'll be better to meet and talk after I get there anyway. The old man walks in on me here anytime he pleases. My plane," said Everett, "is due there at two. Meet me at the Red Rooster at three."

3:01 p.m.
Red Rooster Restaurant
El Paso

Rhodes walked in the door of the huge Red Rooster bowling alley complex, looked around and spotted the restaurant where he found Everett in a booth.

"Hi, Willard. I haven't had lunch, so I've ordered something. You want lunch?"

"No thanks, I ate something earlier, but I could do with a coffee."

"The waitress will be back with my order. You can order your coffee then."

She appeared with a half sandwich and a cup of soup almost as he was speaking. Rhodes ordered black coffee and a glass of water.

"Let's not get into this," said Everett, "until she gets back with your coffee. We don't need anyone else overhearing what we have going on."

"Okay, so in the meantime, how's business?"

"Business is great. The old man is smiling. That's good, because when that old fart isn't smiling, he's giving me hell. I hope you're not about to tell me something that's going to make him not smile."

The waitress brought Rhodes's coffee and water, asked if there would be anything else, spotted a customer's raised hand and begged their permission to be excused. They nodded their approval, so she scooted off to attend to the customer's need.

"Okay, we can get into it now. What's going on?"

"I got a call from Chief Rector. He's concerned about a call he got from the District Attorney. The Detective that investigated the break-in on Central apparently didn't quit investigating the case when Rector shut it down. He doesn't know why, but he's trying to find out."

Everett's face registered first disbelief, then anger. "What the hell! I thought he was supposed to be running the show. Sounds like his people just do whatever they want. He needs to get a handle on this thing. We dropped a ton of money on that cabin. Put the squeeze on this guy. He can put a lid on it if he wants to."

"There were some arrests out in Sunset City. Some guys broke into a grocery store, not one of ours, and got caught taking cigarettes. Somehow the gal investigating our Central Street Store job heard about the arrest and hustled out there to interrogate the guys that did the job. I'm told they confessed they did the job on Central, but denied breaking into the safe."

"They were all questioned separately, didn't know what the others had said. All of them denied doing the safe. They also denied having any ties to Sullivan."

"That's going to reopen Pandora's Box. Has the media got hold of this yet?"

"No, I don't think so, but there's more. This female detective that's doing the poking around was not alone, she had a private investigator with her out in Sunset City."

"Who the heck would be hiring a private detective?"

"I don't know. Maybe it was Sullivan's wife. Who knows?"

"I think we better find out. Also find a way to shut this down."

"The old man is definitely not going to be smiling."

"Willard, stay close to Chief Rector. See if you can find out why his detective is still poking around. It sounds like Rector needs to shut her down. Is that possible?"

"Don't know. Maybe he can. I'll ask him. You'll know what I know," answered Willard.

"Oh, shit!" Everett exclaimed, as he glanced at his watch. "I've got to run. I didn't plan on this meeting and I have an appointment across town. The company owns the bank in uptown village. The former owner is suing the bank. I'm here to try to settle out of court. You find out who this private detective is and who he's working for."

"Yes, sir."

"And Willard," said Everett. "Stay in touch."

Chapter 32

Better Deal Division Offices
El Paso, Texas

OSCAR BEASLEY MADE AN ENEMY of his boss when he went around him to see Mr. Peterson. Early would nail him if an opportunity came along. It happened sooner than expected.

On the Monday following Oscar's rest and relaxation week in New Mexico he got a call from Jake. "I need to see you in my office right away."

"Be right there," said Oscar as he hung up the phone and headed down the hall. Oscar tapped on the door to Jake's office.

Jake opened the door and said, "Come in. Take a seat."

"Sure. Thanks. Good morning. What's up?"

"Seems to me I recall you told me that everything was in good shape when you asked for last week off, that you expected no problems," said Early.

"Was there a problem?"

"Lots of problems. Your frigging district went to hell while you were gone. All I did last week was put out fires. If you go off and leave me with a mess like that again, I'll fire your ass."

"I left Dan Coleman is charge," he said, "He was to call me if there were problems."

"Did it occur to you that Coleman might be the problem? The majority of the problems I had to deal with happened at his store."

"Dan's my best manager. He's on top of everything going on in his store. What happened?" asked Oscar.

Jake pointed at the door and said, "Get your butt out to number nine and find out, then get back to me with what you plan to do to see it doesn't happen again."

"Oscar went out the door shaking his head with not a clue what the hell Jake was ranting about."

It was probably, a customer complaint. Jake Early doesn't go looking for problems. He's reactionary, raises hell about issues, spends lots of time establishing blame and offers no solutions.

The store's been a problem from the day it opened. It makes lots of money, but the facility is inadequate for the amount of business it handles. Market survey information had indicated a potential for weekly sales of $350,000. It's never had a sales week of less than a million dollars.

The wear and tear of customer traffic was literally wearing out the building and fixtures. Concrete was beginning to show through worn floor tiles, metal refrigeration fixtures looked like refugees from a demolition derby, with dents, scratches and cracks in the glass and mirrors. They didn't have enough parking or an adequate number of check stands.

The City of El Paso had specific building codes that required a parking space ratio to sales area of two to one. From the week the store opened Better Deal's real estate department had been assigned to find room to expand. There was no room to expand to the left or right of the building, because it consumed the entire front half of the block.

To the rear of the store, was a half block of middle-income housing. Most of these folks didn't want to sell and others, seeing an opportunity to make a big return on investment, were holding out for the big bucks. Efforts to find a larger lot in the neighborhood had been futile.

Competitors, seeing Better Deal's success, were beating the bushes trying to find a location to take business away from a competitor unable to defend their turf.

Finally, a strategy had come from the top. Pay the price, do whatever it takes. Buy all the homes behind the store. Offer all of them twice what they originally paid, but only if all of them agree to sell. If they stonewall, authorization was given to go as high as triple the original price.

Instructions were to do the same thing for the adjacent block. Get options to buy the entire block. Then go to the City of El Paso, ask them to close the street between the two blocks, re-plat the two blocks into a single block, rezone it for retail and sell us their street. Offer a million bucks for multi-use land title to the street.

Total projected land cost had been an astonishing five million dollars. More than they'd ever invested in a single store location. They were happy to pay. In less than thirty days construction would began on an 110,000 square foot facility projected to do two million dollars per week in sales and net two million dollars a year in profits.

In the meantime, as the management team awaited the reality of a new facility, the challenges had been daunting. Dan Coleman, in Oscar's opinion, had earned accolades for his accomplishments and the support of top management, not punishing criticism.

Oscar arrived, parked off the lot to leave space for customers and walked to the entrance. Everything on the store's exterior appeared shipshape. When he went inside he spotted Dan walking the sales floor with his grocery department manager. "Dan, when you have a minute, we need to visit," he said.

"Sure. We're about done. Give me five minutes. Where will I find you?"

"I'll be in the break room having a quick cup. See you."

Dan took a bit longer than he'd estimated, but eventually showed. "Get yourself a cup and let's find a place to talk," said Oscar.

"I'm already awash in coffee. Let's go to my office," replied Dan.

The two men made their way two doors down the hall. Oscar closed the door and said, "Take a seat."

"Hey, I'm glad you're back. How was your trip?"

"Fun, interesting and a good bit different than we anticipated. I'll tell you all about it sometime, but first you better fill me in on how things went in my absence," said Oscar. "Jake Early read me the riot act when I walked in the door. What happened?"

"Saver's Center down the street had a fire on Monday. They'll be closed four to six weeks making repairs. Our sales jumped twenty percent. We've had out-of-stock conditions in all departments and customer service has been crappy. It didn't help that I had Jake Early breathing down my neck. Closest I've come to throwing in the towel," complained Dan.

"Don't let him run you off. I know the kind of job you do. I'm sorry I wasn't here to run interference. It was probably my fault. Jake's been looking for an excuse to come after me ever since I went to Peterson about Willard. What have you done to adjust to the spike in business?"

"The main changes have been to hire some folks to pump up the schedule, especially after five o'clock on weekdays and for all day on Saturdays and Sundays, and bump up order quantities. Which reminds me, I do have one need that requires your intervention," said Dan.

"What's that?"

"We need an extra grocery truck delivery early on Saturday night. Our backroom is too small to hold enough goods to re-stock the store."

"I'll see what I can do. The warehouse folks don't like to work weekends even for premium pay, but I don't think they'll have much choice under the circumstances," said Oscar. "Anything else you need from me?"

"Nope. I've got a lot going on. Are we done?"

"Yeah. Thanks for the up-date. Call me if you think of anything else we need," said Oscar.

Chapter 33

TOBY PRESTON HAD PAINTED Eli into a corner that could unravel their plans and compromise Eli. Toby had become an unacceptable liability. There was only one solution. Toby Preston had to go.

His death had to look like an accident to assure it would not lead back to Eli. Toby's route to work was across Franklin Mountain via Scenic Drive, the perfect place for an unfortunate "accident."

The high road above the city and across the mountain was a popular tourist destination with spectacular vistas of the downtown El Paso and Juarez, Cordova Island and the Juarez Mountains.

Over the years, the dangerous twists and turns in the road were responsible for a number of fatalities.

The six percent incline of the west side descent was particularly treacherous and required constant braking. Most of the curves were posted at ten miles per hour. Drop-offs from the curves were hundreds of feet straight down.

Toby's two-phase plan was first to disable the emergency brake on Toby's pick up, then to crimp a brake fluid line just enough to make a crack that would result in loss of brake fluid when more than normal pressure was applied to the brakes.

Eli envisioned that during Toby's eastside ascent of the mountain, he would make only moderate use of the truck brakes. In descending the mountain on the western slope, he would, of necessity, be making high demands upon the brakes in order to slow enough to negotiate the switchbacks.

The heavy foot pressure on the brakes would empty the brake lines and cylinder of fluid, and render the brakes useless. When the brakes failed to work, Toby would apply the emergency brake, which Eli would have disconnected.

The only remaining ability to slow the vehicle would be to "gear it down." That would reduce the speed slightly, but not sufficiently to get around a severe curve. The momentum of his truck would definitely carry Toby off the side of a curve.

Disabling the emergency brake would not be noticed. Eli had observed that Toby never used it. When he stopped, he put the truck in park and never engaged the emergency brake. The more difficult task would be weakening the brake line just enough to cause it to lose all the fluid at the proper moment.

Fortunately for Eli, he was an accomplished auto mechanic; that's how he made his living before he became a cop. The modifications to the vehicle would take little time and only a couple of tools.

Chapter 34

Regional Office
Better Deal Supermarkets
El Paso, Texas

JAKE EARLY SAT ALONE, his back to his door, lost in supposition. *This is driving me nuts. Peterson might as well have tied one arm behind my back.*

Peterson's forbid me to retaliate for Beasley's insubordination. *No one humiliates Jake Early and gets away with it. He'll make a mistake. Like to see Peterson protect him then.*

Suddenly a man wearing a military uniform burst into the room shouting, "Who's in charge here?"

"I am," said Jake. "Who are you, sir?"

"Me? I'm mad as hell. That's who I am. Somebody's head is going to roll," he said.

"Why don't you take a seat," said Jake, "and calm down."

"I'll sit down when I'm good and ready!"

"No. You'll sit down and cool it now or I'll call security and have you thrown out," said Jake. Surprisingly, the man took a seat on the couch.

"Breathe in. Take some deep breaths," said Jake. "Here's some water. Take a drink and try to relax."

The young man was barely out of his teens. The wedding band on his finger indicated he was married. The insignia on his U.S. Army uniform established that he was a corporal in rank.

The red-faced young man turned and faced Jake. "Sorry. Not the way to start a conversation, but you'd be mad too," he said.

"Maybe. We'll see. Now who are you and what's this about?"

I'm Corporal Tony Williams, First Missile Training Battalion, Fort Bliss."

"I'm not going to say I'm glad to meet you Corporal Tony Williams, at least not yet. That was a pretty dramatic way to start a meeting. Next time I'd appreciate a little warning. Why don't you start over and tell me what's got you so upset?" said Jake.

"It's that damned guy that works for you."

"Corporal, you can do this without the name-calling if you want me to listen," said Jake. "Take another deep breath."

The man paused, breathed deeply as instructed then spoke, "It's like this: My wife, Pricilla, she works part-time, or I mean she used to work at your store on Fort Boulevard. Yesterday when she came home from work she was bawling, said she'd quit her job."

Jake interrupted, "Did she say why she quit?"

"She did. She said some guy named Beasley said he saw her steal twenty dollars from her till. He told her they had it on tape, they were going to have her arrested and file charges," said the Corporal.

"That's correct. That's our policy. Was she arrested?" asked Early.

"No!"

"Why not?"

"That's what really pissed me off," said the Corporal, "and why she quit. He told her he'd look the other way if she'd have sex with him. She wasn't about to do that! So she quit. Now what are you going to do about it?"

Jake Early told the Corporal he'd get to the truth of the matter, he'd get back to him should they determine that Mr. Beasley did, in fact, say these things to his wife. He could count on Beasley being held accountable. His wife would likely be reinstated as an employee.

After he'd rid himself of the corporal, Jake basked in the prospects for payback. *Gotcha, Beasley! What goes around comes around. Bet you Peterson says I can fire your butt.*

Almost giddy with excitement, Early called Charles Peterson. "Charlie, this is Jake,"

"Hi, Jake. What's up?"

"We've got a complaint about a wrongful termination by Beasley. He allegedly told a checker he saw her palm a twenty, which she denies. She told her husband Beasley offered to overlook the theft if she gave him sex. She refused and quit. Her husband wants us to fire Beasley, and put his wife back to work."

"Any witnesses?"

"Haven't checked."

"Sounds like you're jumping the gun. What's Oscar's side of the story?"

"Haven't talked with him."

"Well, I'd suggest you have a little chat with Oscar. I suspect he may have a different version of the story. Let me know what you find out.

Chapter 35

Regional Office
Better Deal Supers
El Paso, Texas

OSCAR CHECKED HIS MESSAGES; found he'd missed a call from Jake Early. The message was brief. "Be in my office at eight a.m. in the morning."

The lobby of the Division office was jam packed with vendor representatives waiting to see their direct store delivery buyers. Several were standing for lack of seating.

Division store operations officials shared office space with company buyers and distribution facility managers. Ordinarily the company deliberately separated their operations offices from the buyer offices. The El Paso Division was unique in that they didn't build their facility. It was an acquisition.

Ten years ago Better Deal purchased the Shop Smart Food Chain's seventy-five stores in West Texas and Southern New Mexico along with their distribution facility, milk plant and corporate offices, which were located in the distribution facility.

There were at least a couple good reasons why it would have been best to separate buyer and operations functions. For one thing, buyers have a great many vendors to see and little time to devote to each; as a consequence, the days when they see vendors are hectic. Vendors and buyers alike refer to the lobby on those days as "The Zoo." The chaos was disruptive to the operations department's function.

Another reason they separated the two functions was because vendors are gossips. Operating strategies, marketing and promotional plans were discussed here. If plans are overheard and repeated to a competitor by a vendor, thousands of dollars in advertising dollars could be wasted.

Lastly, the operations offices are where discrete personnel issues are discussed and resolved. The set-up at this office was not ideal, but they own the space and use it in spite of its downsides.

There is no lobby receptionist. Vendors and visitors log into a computer that notifies buyers and others of arrivals. The buyers come to the lobby and summon their next vendor.

Some of the vendors were making subdued comments among themselves and nodding in his direction. He wondered, is it possible they know *more than I do?*

Jake walked into the lobby and asked Oscar to come on back to his office.

"Oscar, we've had an accusation of sexual harassment and wrongful termination from a female checker at the Fort Boulevard store. She claims you accused her of palming a twenty-dollar bill, offered to let her off if she would provide you with sex. Is this true?"

The remarks made his blood boil. "Jake, if you don't mind, I'm going to shut the door." Oscar turned and faced Jake. "Of course it's not true. You know I wouldn't do anything like that."

"Her husband seems to believe her and threatens a law suit if we don't let you go."

"Are you threatening to fire me over this?"

"No, but we have to get to the truth of the matter," said Jake.

"The woman is lying," said Oscar." I'm going to get this resolved quickly. I want you to schedule me for a polygraph, and when the results are in, you and I are going to resolve some issues between us. You're looking for something to zap me with. I'm not going to spend the rest of my career looking over my shoulder to see if you're about to cut my throat."

Chapter 36

ELI TOLD TOBY HE NEEDED to skip their routine of having breakfast to run some errands. What he really needed was time and space to think. That's why he headed to the Rainbow Bar in Juarez. This time of morning he'd have the place to himself.

His problem, of course, was Toby. The best working partner Eli had ever had, but he had one hang up, he gambled.

Toby was as addicted to gambling as addicts are to narcotics. His gambling caused him to break his oath not to tell about the money and the burglary. Unfortunately, his revelation created a trail pointing straight to Eli. No way to avoid it. Toby had to go.

Eli formulated what he viewed as a foolproof plan. Toby would be his own unwitting executioner.

That afternoon Eli went on line, pulled up a manual for the year and model pickup owned by Toby. The manual included schematics of the emergency braking and brake fluid systems. Eli found points of weakness where modifications would cause the brakes to fail.

Eli went by Casa Lincoln-Ford, where he road-tested a pre-owned Ford Ranger almost identical to Toby's. He popped the hood, even crawled under the truck, to become familiar with its mechanics.

There would be some risk he might be noticed when he crawled under the truck and made modifications, so he carefully considered the best time to execute his plan.

Their night shift clock-in time was nine p.m. It was a forty-five minute drive to work. Toby was likely to get into his truck after eight p.m. Eli fabricated an excuse to be around Toby's apartment complex at five-thirty.

It began with a cellphone call: "Hey, Toby, I'm close to your place. I'm on my way out to the Brew House Pub on Gateway. Great burgers and the best onion rings in town. They serve root beer the old-fashioned way, no ice in super cold mugs. You want to go with me? I'll get you back in an hour. You can still get another hour of Z's before you head to work."

"That's a lot better plan than the TV dinner I was going to have."

"I'm only a couple minutes away, but don't come out yet. I need to take a leak. Okay, I use your John?"

"Sure, come on in."

Eli parked on the street just a space away from Toby's truck. As he walked past the truck he stooped down and poured six ounces of dark motor oil under the truck just below the transmission. As he entered the apartment building he trashed the small paper cup he had used for the motor oil.

The Brew House was stacked with people. Every booth and table was occupied. After a short wait they got a booth and ordered a burger and a root beer apiece. They decided one order of onion rings would probably be enough. As they were eating the last of the rings Toby said, "Wish we'd split a burger. They're huge, but I would've liked more onion rings."

When they got back to the apartment complex, a parking space was available next to Toby's truck. Eli walked past Toby's truck and remarked, "Hey, Toby, I meant to tell you earlier. I noticed you have an oil leak. I've got a pin light. I'm going to slide under and see where it's leaking."

"It's not using any oil, it must be something new or maybe it leaked out of another vehicle before I parked here."

While under the truck, Eli used a pair of pliers to remove a nut that held the emergency brake assembly together, totally disabling the emergency brake. Then he crimped a brake fluid line just enough to open a hairline crack. He slid from under the truck and brushed off his trousers.

"It looks like the transmission seal's got a leak. There's a little oil around the connection to the block. It's not bad enough to fix. A leak throws out more oil when the motor's running. When it begins to use too much oil, and it will, you should replace the seal."

"It's been a good set of wheels. I'm counting on it to hold together for a while longer. When we decide to open the deposit box, I'll buy a new truck or maybe a convertible."

"Yeah, well, I've got to go get in uniform. See you at the station."

Chapter 37

7:00 p.m.
North Gate Apartments
El Paso, Texas

TOBY HAD PLANNED time for a thirty-minute power nap and a leisurely drive to work, plus a stop at Starbucks for a caramel latte.

His internal clock let him down. He bolted upright. *Should have set my alarm. Eight-twenty nine, five minutes to dress, leaves twenty-four minutes to get to work. No Starbucks. Hope the traffic is light.*

He ran down the stairs two at a time, sprinted to his truck, almost flattening a poor frog on the sidewalk. He clicked the driver's door open and slid into the seat.

He glanced at the left rear-view mirror, accelerated and pulled into the flow of traffic while managing to hook the driver side seat belt.

Traffic was light. He crossed his fingers as a precaution to avoid getting behind a slow-pokey driver on Scenic Drive.

Darn you, he thought, as a Jeep containing a couple of kids pulled out in front of him from a wide pullover parking spot. *Now I'll be late for sure.*

They negotiated three fifteen-mile-an-hour curves at a snail's pace. Toby hugged the rear bumper of the Jeep, hoping for a stretch of road with no on-coming traffic. A lane cleared, Toby pulled around the Jeep. Its driver deliberately accelerated.

He pushed the gas pedal to the floor. His truck shot ahead of the Jeep, but the momentum required a quick slow-down. Toby hit the brakes, barely negotiated the curve. The Jeep, now to his rear, was burning rubber as its driver struggled to avoid a collision.

Toby had no way to know that brake pressure had leaked half of the truck's fluid through the crack in the line. The now angry Jeep driver was crowding Toby to a reckless pace. As they approached a tight inside curve, Toby braked again. The pedal went to the floor, all remaining fluid escaped through the leak.

Toby tried the emergency brake. It had zero resistance. On reflex, he dropped the transmission into low gear. It slowed momentarily, but quickly regained momentum on the steep decline.

The next curve was marked thirty-five mph limit. The speedometer reading was forty-five. The truck's momentum was such that Toby had to swing all the way out into the on-coming lane to avoid turning the truck over. It sideswiped the two-foot rock wall paralleling the road and bounced the truck back into the right lane where it began to climb the cliff wall. His reaction dropped the front wheels back into the lane.

The truck continued to accelerate as it approached yet another inside curve. Somehow he negotiated the turn without hitting the wall. A very sharp fifteen-mile-per-hour outside curve loomed ominously ahead. He knew the truck would go over the edge. He made a decision to crash the truck into the mountain wall rather than go over the side.

When Toby turned his vehicle toward the wall, he didn't turn sharp enough to crash. Instead, the truck climbed the wall, almost flipped on its back. Toby turned the wheel in the opposite direction, the truck dropped back on all its wheels. Unfortunately, this pointed the truck directly in a path toward the outside edge.

He turned the wheel to the right; it traveled ahead a few feet on two wheels, and then rolled over.

It turned over twice, then flipped three times end over end.

Toby gripped the wheel, fought to stay in his seat. There was a long suspended drop and a sudden awareness this was no accident, that Eli had somehow orchestrated these events.

For a split second Toby felt the jolt of impact, then nothingness. He died instantly. Spilled gasoline on the hot engine block ignited and the truck became a fireball.

The two El Paso High School students in the Jeep ragtop pulled over and parked, got out and stepped as close as they dared to the edge of the cliff. Far below they saw the truck burst into flames.

One had his mouth open, speechless. The other was pointing and screaming. "Did you see that? My God, he's being burned to death."

Words came. "I see it, but I don't believe it. We'd better call 911."

Chapter 38

Human Resource Department
West Texas Division
Better Deal Supermarkets
El Paso, Texas

A PHONE RANG. Myra Coy, recently promoted Manager of Human Resources for the El Paso division answered, "Good morning! This is Myra."

"Myra, this is Jake Early. I believe we've met. I'm the operations manager here in El Paso."

"Yes, sir. We've met. I've been meaning to give you a call. I'd like to make store visits with you," said Myra.

"Be happy to, sometime soon. Right now I have an issue I'd like you to handle. Yesterday I visited with an irate husband of an employee discharged for till tapping. He made some nasty allegations about one of my district managers, Oscar Beasley."

"I've heard good things about Beasley."

"The man told me Beasley confronted his wife, accused her of stealing a twenty-dollar bill. She denied the theft. He had the bookkeeper count down the till, which she confirmed was short twenty dollars. His wife was still in her three-month probationary period and theft is cause for termination, so Oscar let her go."

"I'm familiar with the incident. I received an incident report and termination paperwork on Pricilla Williams from Beasley and the store director. It appears to me everything was handled properly. Is there a problem?"

"There is," said Early. "The young lady told her husband she didn't steal the money, said she resigned to protect her dignity, because Beasley wanted sex to overlook the incident."

"Uh oh," Myra responded, "I haven't heard these accusations. We're likely to be facing some litigation with liability exposure. I don't know Oscar Beasley. Do you think there's credibility to the allegations?"

"Doubtful, but we have to investigate the charges. I've already talked with Beasley. He's insistent the allegations are false, wants a polygraph test to establish his innocence."

"I can set that up, probably for this afternoon. Is there a time preference?"

"Work that out with Beasley. However, I would like to be aware of the schedule for the test and also to receive immediate feedback afterwards."

"I'll call Beasley and get things in motion, copy you the schedule and make sure you get the report."

"Actually, I want a phone call immediately after the test. I'd like to speak to the polygraph operator personally."

"Okay. Is there anything else?"

"Well, yes, as a matter of fact there is. You can work this out with the polygraph operator, but I want to know how you have it planned and sign off on it before you put it in motion."

"Yes, Sir, I understand. What is it you want us to do?"

"Are you familiar with the overnight burglary recently at store number nine?"

"Yes, I've been dealing with a number of human resource issues associated with that incident."

"I would have expected that to be the case. There's another issue that has the potential to become a human resource problem, so I'd like to get you in the boat with me."

"I can't commit to do that without an understanding of the situation. The HR Department walks a line between looking out for company interests and being the employee advocates in the company. We can't do that and report to the operations side of the business," said Myra.

"I'm aware of your position. Please allow me to explain," said Jake. "It has come to our attention that a private investigator is now poking around and making inquiries about some issues connected with that burglary. We don't know why this person or persons unknown would have hired this private investigator, but we very much prefer the appropriate authorities handle the investigation.

"I can see why you'd rather the authorities handle the investigation," said Myra.

"Oscar Beasley," said Jake, "has a previous work history with a now deceased suspect in the burglary. It's possible that Oscar may be the person who hired the private detective. If that were to be the case, it would be a serious matter of disloyalty to the company."

Myra mulled this over a few seconds before responding, "Are you suggesting that we get the polygraph operator to present a line of questions that will reveal if Mr. Beasley is or is not the person who hired the investigator?"

"Exactly! There's one caveat. I'd rather not have Beasley know that this was a planned line of questioning. Do you think you can arrange all this?"

"I may have to put the test off until tomorrow while I work out the details, but I think it's doable."

Chapter 39

Beasley Residence
Mountain Land Subdivision
El Paso, Texas

"**GOOD MORNING, LEE.** You're up and at 'em mighty early. The coffee smells good. Do you need a refill?

"I do. Thanks."

Oscar poured a mug for himself, added his usual liberal pour of half and half with hazelnut and a spoonful of sugar. Then he refilled Lee's cup with black coffee, which he knew to be his preference. To complete the ritual, he lifted the lid on the cookie jar and took out two almond biscotti's.

"I see your luggage by the door. If you're planning to leave, we've probably got some settling up to do. "

"I need to get home. I left a bill for you on your desk. No charge for my time; expenses are on the high side. Not a whole lot to show for it."

"I don't see it that way. The confessions you and Kathy got from the bungling Sunset City burglars helped remove suspicion from Sullivan."

"True, but there're still questions unanswered. Druggies aren't credible witnesses. When someone cashes one of the stolen money orders, we may have an opportunity to find out what really happened. I've been worried about your relationship with your employer. Have there been any repercussions," inquired Lee?

"Oh yeah, "answered Oscar, "I haven't had a chance to tell you, but my boss is being vindictive. I've got to take a polygraph in the morning to prove I didn't sexually harass and unfairly terminate an employee. Jake Early has a big ego. He'll keep zapping me every chance he gets."

"I'm sure you can handle it. It'll all go away in time," offered Lee, "Now, listen, I'm not through with this thing. There's just nothing else I can do right now. If anything comes up at all, let me know."

"Sure will. I've really appreciated what you've done for us. Jackie mentioned that she wants to meet Shirley. Let's try to make that happen. Are you going to hang around long enough to say good bye to Jackie?"

"No, you'll have to tell her for me," said Lee.

"I'm not going to let you get away without something to eat. I make some burritos. Takes two minutes to heat one up."

"Now that sounds like it's worth a two minute wait. You do that while I load up."

Chapter 40

Human Resource Department
Better Deal Supers
El Paso, Texas

"MR. EARLY, THIS IS, Myra McCoy, I wanted to get back to you with about the polygraph test for Oscar Beasley."

"Is everything set to go?" asked Jake.

"Yes," said Myra. "It's set for ten a.m. this morning at World Polygraph Services, the operator will be Warren Betts. He's considered the best, three years as a street cop in New York, twenty years as an Army interrogator, has a BA in Police Science, an MS in Psychology."

"Sounds competent. How about the private investigator question." asked Jake?

"He agreed," said Myra. In addition to questions about the theft, termination, and sexual harassment allegations, Betts plans to check for any association with the investigator."

"I figured he'd fall in line and look out for the interests of the people who pay the tab," said Jake.

"Mr. Early, the test is likely to last at least an hour, perhaps longer. Evaluation of responses to questions takes at least an hour or two, so Betts won't have anything to report until mid-afternoon.

He has your direct phone line number. He'll call you when he has the report finalized. He'll also send you and me hard copies. I believe this addresses all the items in your request."

"Miss McCoy, I asked you to have him call immediately after the test. Why didn't you follow my instructions?"

"I'm sorry, Mr. Early. I should have covered why that didn't happen. I did exactly as you requested. I got a firm refusal. He told me that people have an erroneous perception that polygraph machines can tell if a person is telling the truth or not. A polygraph machine is of some value in determining truthfulness, but it's not an exact science. In fact, it's referred to as a pseudoscience. The reality is that every answer to every question has multiple psychological implications and reactions to questions are highly individual. In fact, some people are so accomplished at lying that they can get false positive reactions to questions."

"There're always going be a few people who figure out how to beat the system," said Jake.

"After I talked with Betts, I did a lot of research on polygraph machines, the operators and results. Scientific studies show the accuracy of polygraph tests to be no better than 61%. I've come to have the opinion that unless someone taking a polygraph test makes and signs an admission of guilt, the report isn't worth the proverbial bucket of spit."

"Miss McCoy, companies all over this country, the FBI, our court system and the military make decisions every day based upon the results of polygraph tests. You hardly have the experience or the credentials to disavow their credibility. I believe I'll make my own judgment call."

"You're in a position to do that if you want. As your HR Representative, I serve as an advisor as to what's in the company's best interest. I think terminating people and making decisions based upon the results of polygraph tests is high risk with a lot of potential for liability exposure."

"Well I've got to do what I have to do. I'm a little surprised to find you seem to be looking more to an employee's interest than to those of the people who pay your salary," said Jake.

"Mr. Early, I assure you I'm very much concerned about doing my job. Apparently you don't know and understand the role of the Human Resource Department in this Company. Among our many responsibilities we are charged with being the employee advocates in the organization."

Chapter 41

9:08 a.m.
World Polygraph Services
Paisano Drive
El Paso, Texas

OSCAR PICKED A PARKING space between the burned out carcass of a tireless Volvo and a chopped and channeled Chevy pickup with a steering wheel of chromium chain links and a crucifix dangling from the mirror.

The GPS says this is the location. Looks more like a crack house than a business, with the steel bars over the windows, the graffiti on the walls, and the beer bottles in the shrubbery.

He stuck his head inside the door. "This the polygraph place?" he asked.

A tubby henna-haired Hispanic receptionist with boobs threatening to overwhelm their harness looked up from her nail file and said, "I'm Bev. You Beasley?"

"That's me. Sorry I'm late. I couldn't find any street signs. Be back. Got to lock up. Will my car be okay here," he asked?

"Maybe, in the day time, it's your tires you've got to watch," Bev said. "Cars they take at night."

"I'm back, had a nine o'clock appointment," said Beasley. "You give up on me?"

"No. I figured you had a problem finding us. The vandals steal the signs. I keep telling Mr. Betts that we ought to move to a better neighborhood. Not likely though, he owns the building."

"I put the address into the GPS," explained Beasley, "which led me to this location. It took a few minutes to discover that your office was actually facing South Yarbrough rather than Paisano."

"Should've warned you. The Post Office says our address is on Pasiano. You're only a few minutes late. Who you scheduled to see?"

"No idea," said Oscar, "They gave me a time and place."

"Let me check our calendar," she said as she simultaneously adjusted a bra strap and pulled up her calendar.

Oscar looked around. *Who's she kidding? From the looks of this place, I bet they don't have more than one operator.*

"Here it is, you're scheduled with, Warren Betts. He's expecting you. I'll let him know you're here."

Moments later a pre-maturely white-haired gentleman approached the lobby. *He must use Rick Perry's barber, not a hair's out of place,* thought Oscar.

Betts was wearing a grey vested pin stripe, accented with a pink and black paisley tie and a matching handkerchief. His shoes were Italian-made black alligator.

"Mr. Impeccable" extended his right hand and flashed a picket fence smile below a handlebar mustache.

"I'm Warren Betts, I assume you're Oscar Beasley. I'm glad to meet you."

A pair of see-right-through-you steel blue eyes, framed by silver-rimmed glasses rested on a long nose. Warren Betts seemed more a corporate CEO than stereotype polygraph operator.

"Excuse me, I'm a little taken a back. You seem out of place, like you don't belong here."

"Oh, I belong here. I own the place. It's unusual for me to run tests these days. Your company asked for me, so why not?"

"Let's go down the hall where we'll be conducting the test."

They entered a small cubicle with no pictures on the walls, bringing to mind, for Oscar, the time he and two of his fraternity pals had spent a night in the Aransas Pass jail on spring break twenty years ago.

The ten-foot space contained two straight-back chairs, a small desk, a table, a briefcase and black metal box with a four by eight inch window of continuous graph paper tape. Six wires protruded from the box to touch the graph paper. There was no connection to a wall plug, so Oscar assumed it was battery powered.

"Please take off your jacket, hang it on the chair at the side of the desk and take a seat. I'm going to connect you to the machine, which will be measuring your respiration, blood pressure and a number of other physical responses to questions. There are four contacts."

"I need to put this strap around your chest, a cuff on your arm and a couple of clips on your fingers. The contacts work fine through a shirt, but won't give a reading through a jacket. You okay with all this?"

"Sure," said Oscar.

"Have you previously taken a polygraph test?" asked Betts.

"Yes, I have. I hate them," said Oscar, "but in this instance, a test is the quickest way to resolve an issue, so I initiated the test. Better Deal used to require polygraph tests in their pre-employment process. They no longer have that requirement."

Betts attached the two fingertip sensors to Beasley. There were three small knobs on the narrow front side of the box and one knob on one of the long sides.

"This is a much smaller piece of equipment than the polygraph machines I recall from my other tests," said Oscar.

"You're right, the newer machines are smaller and print six simultaneous readings on the tape. The older machines took up half the desktop. The new ones are more compact, and do a lot more functions, provide us with more data and they're now portable."

Oscar had a puzzled expression when he asked, "I notice that this machine prints six lines on the graph paper. There are only four contacts. What are the other two readings?"

"The two extra readings are measurements of variances in voice modulation compared to normal. The data comes from a built-in microphone, so it doesn't require contacts to acquire data."

"See the continuous tape with all the wiggly lines? Each of the contacts is creating a line. If we had a straight line, it would mean a contact wasn't secure. They're all working. You ready to get started?" asked Betts.

"Yes, I'm ready."

"The first thing I'm going to do is ask you some questions to get a base line of normal responses. You need to get comfortable and relax," suggested Betts.

"You kidding? How relaxed can anyone be hooked up to all this wiring? I'm as relaxed as an ax murderer strapped to an electric chair."

"Point taken," replied Betts, "Now I need for you to back off the extraneous conversation and focus on answering my questions."

His first series of questions were structured like an interview, with instructions he should answer truthfully. Then he used the data from previous answers to frame questions that required true or false responses. He asked Beasley to deliberately lie after two questions.

Once Betts had a base line of responses, he told Oscar he was about to start the test. He stopped the machine after getting a response to each question and made notes on the tape. His first questions were to determine if Beasley saw the checker steal from her register, then he moved to a line of questions to determine if he'd propositioned the checker.

The machine was programmed to generate a comprehensive report from the data. Betts knew Beasley did, for a fact, see the checker palm a twenty. He was also satisfied he had made no inappropriate suggestions to the checker.

"Mr. Betts, we've been at this an hour. I don't know if we're near done, but I need to make a pit stop soon."

"I'm sorry, that was an over-sight on my part. I should've had you visit the john before we started."

"We do have a bit more to cover, but I'd rather not have you be physically uncomfortable, because it affects the readings. Let's take a break for fifteen minutes. The downside to taking a break is that I have to disconnect you from all this wiring." Betts left the contacts attached to Oscar. Each had a plug he simply disconnected.

"There's a washroom down the hall, out the door and make a left. It'll be the second door on the left. The break room has coffee. It's directly across the hall from the john. You can put your shirt back on if you like."

Betts didn't join Beasley for coffee. He used this opportunity to review Oscar's responses to the control questions he'd asked early on. It was with considerable relief he spotted an opportunity to dig into the private investigator issue.

Oscar walked back into the room already unbuttoning his shirt. "I think my fifteen minutes are up. Are you ready to hook me back up to your toy?"

"Yes, it won't take long to wrap this up. I checked your responses. Two of them ran up red flags. When I asked you if you have ever been dishonest with your employer, your respiration and heartbeat spiked. Also, when I asked if you have always looked out for the interest of your employer. These two questions didn't relate directly to the issue for which you were taking the test, but I have an obligation to resolve why you had a negative reaction to these questions."

"I don't know why I would have had a negative response," said Oscar.

"If you can't think of anything that caused the negative responses, I'll have to keep asking questions until we get this resolved."

"Give me a second to think this through. I'm not sure I'm personally willing to answer more questions. We've already addressed the issues I came here to address."

Oscar sat there, his mind racing through the circumstances and considering potential consequences. Maybe he should just open up and tell the man why he had negative responses to the two questions. He decided to take the risk.

"Mr. Betts, I know exactly what caused my re-actions. I'm reluctant to talk about it because it's going to open up a can of worms. I remember the specific thoughts that came to mind when you raised the issues. I've never been dishonest with my employer," explained Beasley, "nor have I ever failed to look out for their interests. I had a reaction to those questions because I think my immediate superior and our manager of security miss-managed a security situation in a way that led to a suicide of an employee."

"That, by itself," said Betts, "Shouldn't have caused you to feel that you were personally dishonest with the company. Is there more?"

"Yes. This could get me fired, but I believe the employee was falsely accused. The man's family was hung out to dry with this baseless accusation deliberately unresolved. I believe the company tried to cover up their fault in the matter. I hired that man. I've got some ownership and even some guilt about this sorry outcome. My heart is with his family. No one has made any effort to set this situation aright, so I hired a private investigator to find the guilty party."

"Mr. Beasley, I think we ought to end this session at this point. Here, let me get all of the connecting wires off you. You're free to put your jacket on and go if you like. However, I have one last question for you. This is strictly off the record and it's entirely up to you as to whether you want to tell me or not."

"Mr. Betts, I can't promise you I'll answer your question, but I might. What is it you want to know?"

"Is Jake Early the person you feel is responsible for causing the suicide you mentioned"?

"Answering that question puts me in an awkward position. Jake Early already has reason to want to run me off, but I'm going to answer your question. No. Jake did not personally cause the suicide, at least not directly. But he is protecting Willard Rhodes, the Company's West Texas manager of security, who is directly responsible. They're bosom buddies. Unfortunately, it's obvious there are others in higher positions in the company who have gone to a great deal of trouble to sweep this situation under the carpet."

"None of this sounds like the Walter O'Kelly I know."

"It doesn't match up to the high ideals of the company I choose to make a career with either. Honestly, I'm re-thinking what I want to do with the rest of my work life."

Chapter 42

Regional Offices
Better Deal Supermarkets
El Paso, Texas

He was seated at his desk, a sales report in one hand, his favorite mug in the other, when the phone rang. He picked up the intrusive device. "Hello, this is Jake Early."

"Mr. Early, this is Warren Betts with World Polygraph Services. Have you a moment?"

"I do. What's up?"

Yesterday I tested Oscar Beasley. I had instructions to call you when I completed my report."

"That's correct."

"Hard copies are on their way to you, Willard Rhodes and Myra McCoy. What is it you'd like to know?"

"Just need some questions answered."

"What questions?" asked Betts.

"Did the checker take the money?"

Betts hesitated to consider his answer; "I don't have a yes or no answer for you to that question. What I can tell you is Beasley was being truthful when he said he saw your checker pocket twenty dollars."

"That sounds like a yes to me. The checker took the money."

"Mr. Early, you're putting words in my mouth. I have no way of knowing if the checker did or did not take the money. What I said was, Oscar Beasley was being truthful when he said he saw the checker take the money."

"You guys are careful to cover your butts from liability exposure. What about the proposition? Did he ask her for a piece?"

"Again, Mr. Early, I wasn't there, I can't tell you if Oscar Beasley did or did not proposition your employee. I can tell you that our machine readings indicate, and my professional opinion is, Beasley was telling the truth when he told me he didn't make any inappropriate suggestions."

"You're saying that the employee was lying?" questioned Jake.

"No sir, I didn't say that," said Betts. We haven't tested your checker."

"What the hell is it that you are saying?"

"What I'm saying, Mr. Early, is that we can quantify within a narrow degree of confidence, if someone is being truthful or lying. You're going to have to make your own judgment call about what actually happened. I've seen situations where two individuals were questioned about the same incident and each one truthfully believed it occurred differently."

"So what the hell am I supposed to do with this garbage?"

"Like I said, that's entirely up to you," said Betts. "Very honestly, this data is about as good as you'll ever get with a polygraph report. I'm just not the one to tell you what to do."

"All right, I can see you aren't going to let me pin you down. How about the private eye? Did Beasley hire the private investigator?"

"Yes Sir, Mr. Beasley was very forthcoming. "

"No question?"

"Absolutely no question."

"Does he realize it may cost him his job?"

"That's a question you'd have to ask him, sir," replied Betts.

"There you go again dodging the questions."

"Mr. Early, is there anything else?"

"No, I guess not. Send me a bill," shouted a very red-faced Jake

Early.

"Yes, sir. You can count on it. I wish you a good day. Good bye," said Betts.

Chapter 43

Jake Early Office
Better Deal Supers
El Paso, Texas

"**WILLARD, IT'S JAKE.** I just got the polygraph results on Beasley. He admitted he hired the private investigator."

Rhodes asked, "Can't you let him go for that?"

Maybe. Peterson would have to approve. I'm going to run it by him. If he approves, he'll run it by the HR Department."

"What about the till-tapping thing? Did Beasley try to get that gal to go down on him?" asked Rhodes.

"Where did you hear that, asked Jake? The story's different every time I hear it."

"To answer your question, No, the polygraph operator said Beasley did see her steal the twenty and didn't proposition the checker. Beasley's always been straight as an arrow."

"So what happens next?"

"I've got to call Peterson and let him know what happened. Then I'll have to talk to the checker's husband."

"Guess I better let you get on with your rat killing. Thanks for the call. See you later, Jake."

Jake decided to meet with the checker's husband before he

called Peterson. He called Corporal Williams at Fort Bliss.

"Sixth Missile Battalion, Corporal Mariucci, speaking."

"Good morning, Corporal, my name is Jake Early and I'm with Better Deal Supermarkets, I need to speak with Corporal Tony Williams."

"I'm the only one here. The unit is on a training exercise near Oro Grande in New Mexico. They're due back about four p.m."

"That's too bad. I'm sorry I missed him. Is it possible to leave a message for him to call me?"

"Yes, Sir. I can make sure he gets your message."

"Good. He has my number. He'll know what it's about, he's been expecting my call."

"Roger, sir. Consider it done."

At four-thirty p.m., Jake's phone rang. "Hello, Early speaking."

"Mr. Early, this is Tony Williams. I'm returning your call."

"Hi, Tony. Thanks for calling back. We've completed our investigation of your wife's incident. I'd like to meet you to go over that report."

"I'd have to meet either before or after duty hours. I report at eight a.m."

"How about six-thirty tomorrow morning? There's a Denny's in the sixty-six hundred block of Montana Street. I'll buy your breakfast," said Jake.

"Yes, Sir. That'll work for me."

Jake was up early, arrived at Denny's well before Corporal Williams. He picked a table where their conversation would not be over-heard.

Williams was late. Very late! It was forty-five minutes to eight. Not enough time for the meeting to go as planned. Jake was irritated. Williams was apologetic.

"Mr. Early, I'm sorry I'm so late. I got a late start and had fog all the way. I'm going to have to skip breakfast. My Company Commander will have a fit if I'm late. I've got no more than fifteen or twenty minutes before I have to leave."

"We'll just have to make the best of it," said Jake. Let's skip breakfast. Have a seat and I'll tell you what I know. You want some coffee?"

"Coffee would be great."

Jake motioned to the waitress and pointing to his coffee cup then to Tony. The waitress got the message.

When the coffees were served, Jake said, "We better get this going. Tony, when we questioned our district manager about the incident with your wife, he denied having made any overtures about sex to your wife. He immediately volunteered to take a lie detector test to prove he was telling the truth."

"You don't believe that do you?" exclaimed Tony.

"Hear me out! We agreed with him and set up a test. We thought it would be best to use an independent polygraph operator at World Polygraph Services."

"What did you find out?"

"The polygraph test indicated Beasley did see Pricilla take the twenty, also that he didn't make any sexual overtures."

"You're absolutely sure?"

"Tony, I'm sorry. The polygraph operator said there was no doubt."

"That lying witch! I'm going kick her butt. I'm not going to put up with that bull."

"Tony, hold on. She made a mistake. She didn't want to have to admit she stole the money. She took a chance that you wouldn't make a big deal of it. She probably needs some counseling. I hope you won't be too hard on her."

"I can't tolerate a thief or a liar. I wish I'd never married the thieving, lying hussy." He bolted out of the café.

Chapter 44

Hillcrest Apartments
El Paso, Texas

"HELLO, SANCHEZ here."

"You're Eli, right?"

"Yes, who's this?"

"I'm supposed to set up a meeting."

"What kind of meeting?"

"One with my boss."

"I'm gonna hang up."

"I don't think so. You want people to know about your partner's death, or what's in a certain safety deposit box?"

There was a pause in the conversation.

"Cat got your tongue?" asked the mystery voice.

"You have my attention," said Eli. "What do you want?"

"Your partner owed money to my boss. He didn't meet his obligations. My employer explained to him how important it was to pay gambling debts and helped your friend remember he had left some savings in your keeping. You'd be wise not to make this man angry."

"I'm not sure I'm going to do anything. Who's your boss anyway?"

"You need to talk to him. If he wants you to know, he'll tell you. Listen carefully, tonight at eleven p.m., be at Memorial Park Library. Come alone, no guns. You bring a gun, you won't walk away."

"I'll be there."

"He'll meet you in the eastside lot. He's got a black Mercedes. Don't be late."

Eli was literally shaking in his boots. Toby told him he hadn't revealed his name to the gambler. Obviously he lied. *No way do I want to just hand over Toby's share. What's to keep this guy from demanding it all?*

The more he thought about losing Toby's share, the more determined Eli was to keep it. By late afternoon he had a plan. To make it work, he'd have to have a gun.

Clearly, he couldn't risk carrying or concealing a weapon on his person. He'd have to stash one or two. Eli owned two handguns in addition to his EPPD duty weapon, a 38 SUPER Smith and Wesson revolver. He decided to hide all three in the area where he planned to park.

Memorial Park library was closed on Fridays. The library was located adjacent to Crockett Grade School, which lets out at three p.m., so there would be children, parents and teachers around until perhaps four p.m.

Commuters, who don't want to fight the traffic and congestion on Montana Street between five and six, use the road through Memorial Park as a short cut. In addition to being less congested, it's a pretty area with beautiful trees and flowers.

The weather forecast for that evening was cloudy skies, moderate temperatures and winds of five to ten miles per hour. The sun would set about six forty-five p.m. Two halogen pole lights illuminated the library's eastside parking lot after dark.

Eli decided to work under cover of darkness. He arrived at eight p.m., parked on the west side of the library and moved through the trees and shrubbery by touch and feel.

There was a book return box on a circle drive at the rear of the library. Eli planned to park in this circle. Dense forest surrounded the drive and the center median was covered with knockout roses, providing good locations to hide his guns.

Eli found a place for his service revolver waist high in a Hawthorne shrub in the center median. He hid the 9-millimeter Sig Sauer, in the hollow of a tree. His Colt 45 Automatic was concealed under a bucket in a wheelbarrow some worker had left in a small rose garden.

At ten forty-five p.m. Eli arrived at the library from a westerly approach, made a right turn at the north corner of the building, passed across the front of the library, then made a right turn into the parking lot.

The lot was empty. He nursed the car on back to the rear and entered the circle drive. He proceeded around the circle to have a direct view of vehicles entering the lot.

At precisely eleven p.m., a Mercedes-Benz CL Coupe entered the lot. It appeared to have one occupant. A black GMC Yukon containing two additional characters followed it.

The first car entered the circle and confronted Eli's car, the second vehicle entered the circle from the rear, effectively eliminating retreat. The two men got out of the Yukon and advanced to the driver's side door of Eli's car.

Eli could see there'd be no chance to get at his guns.

"Get out, turn round and face the car, hands apart on top of the car."

Eli did as he was told.

"Now spread your legs. We're going to check to see if you're carrying."

While the body search was in progress the driver of the Mercedes joined the conversation.

"Stay turned the way you are. You don't have a need to know who I am. This isn't going to take long. You're either going to cooperate or find yourself in some very deep stuff. Your pal, Toby, he liked to play cards, thought he was a great poker player. He wasn't as good as he thought. To make a long story short, he owes me twenty-five thousand dollars. Here's the marker, as you can see, that's his signature. He told me he had the money, where it is and how the two of you came to have it. He lost the money to me and he signed this marker. That makes it my money.

"I don't know what Toby told you, but he didn't have squat. He lived up every nickel he ever made," said Eli.

"He told us a different story. Seems to me it was pretty convenient that you were holding all the cash when Toby went over the side of the mountain. Too convenient, I think, but then, I don't really care what you did, that's your business. All I want is my twenty-five thousand dollars, plus the interest Toby owes for taking so long to pay up. That happens to be another twenty-five thousand dollars."

"What? That's bullshit. I might give you what Toby owed, but you're sure as hell not getting my share. I didn't get in your damned poker game. That's my money."

"Really? I suppose you earned it. Your buddy ratted you out. You're fair game. I'm reasonably sure you don't have La Tuna Federal Correction Facility on your list of favorite places. You're not in a position to call the shots. So when do I get my money?"

"Look, let's talk about a different arrangement that could be better for you and I don't walk away empty handed."

"I'm listening."

"One of the things we took was an American Express check writer and two bundles of 100 blank money orders. Those money orders can be written up to one thousand dollars each. If you have the organization to cash the money orders, you could net two hundred thousand dollars. What would you say to this: I keep all of the money in the safety deposit box. I give you the check writer and both boxes of blank money orders. You get four times as much."

"When I had my man contact you, all I wanted was the money owed to me by Toby, the twenty-five thousand. Then it occurred to me that your partner's misfortune on the mountain might not have been an accident, that he shouldn't have trusted you, that I'd be a fool to trust you. When you agreed not to bring guns to our meeting did you assume I would trust you?" asked the mystery man.

"Search me. I'm clean," said Eli.

"Oh, I know you're not carrying, but I had you followed. You stashed three guns here."

Eli tried to look insulted. "You got no way to know that."

"The man who followed you saw you hide your three guns. All three guns were removed from their hiding places and are in my possession. It's clear to me that you intended to do me harm. I should have your throat cut. You're fortunate that I hate violence. I'm not going to harm you. However, I'm going to punish you financially. Here's what you're going to do. First, you must pay me twenty-five thousand in cash, to repay Toby's gambling debt. Secondly, you will give me the check writer and all the blank money orders. And lastly, we will return your service revolver. I've decided to keep your other weapons. Do you have any problems with my terms?"

"Do I have any choice?"

"No!"

"Then I accept your terms."

"Good! You're a wise man."

Chapter 45

O'Kelly's Castle
Oak Manors Neighborhood
Dallas, Texas

IT HAD BEEN A TOSS and turn night for Helen. She was finally asleep. Out of consideration, Walter had been careful to keep down the noise.

Up to answer nature's call, he decided not to use the facilities in their master suite. Somehow he'd become disoriented.

Where am I? We need some nightlights in this hall. Somebody could get hurt.

Fearful of the consequences of a fall at his age, Walter dropped to the floor to feel his way.

Ouch! That hurt.

He reached up to feel the object he'd encountered. Sofa table, he decided, heavy. Along the tabletop there was an object, smooth, cold and hard. *A bust. William Shakespeare.*

Now reoriented, Walter got up, moved down the hall, touched the wall and found a doorway, entered, flipped a light switch and used the facility.

He turned off the bathroom light and switched on lights in the stairway to their home's main entrance.

He descended to the entry hall, passed through the dining room and entered the kitchen, searched for and found a bag of Blue Mountain coffee beans and the grinder.

While the coffee brewed, Walter opened their kitchen laptop and checked his mail. He had a message from his life-long friend, Warren Betts.

To: wktoad@amazingfastmail.com
From: wbetts@blazingcomet.org
Hi, Walt.
Heads up. Tested a Better Deal DM today, he's OK. You have some problems with a couple of your guys: Jake Early and Willard Rhodes, maybe more. I suggest you quietly retain a private investigator. Lee Perkins, from Portales is already familiar with the problem.

Interesting e-mail, thought Walter. I wonder what could be going on with Jake Early and Willard Rhodes?

He heard the shuffle of slippers on the stairs. *That would be Helen.* He poured a coffee for her and refilled his own and carried them to the sitting area where they drink their morning coffee.

"Good morning, Honey Bunch," said Helen. How's my lover this morning?"

"I'm good, Sweet Baby. Are you rested?"

"I'm fine. What happened to you," she said? "You've got a bruise on your forehead."

"Someone hit me with a baseball bat," said Walter.

"They did not! What happened?"

"Would you believe I bumped my head on a table?"

"No!"

"It's true," said Walter.

"Explain to me how you managed to hit your head on a table. They're only so high."

"I'd rather not," said Walter. "How about we discuss something else?"

"Okay, what do you want to talk about?"

"I want your opinion about something."

"You make us a fire in the den while I get more coffee. You want a mincemeat cookie with your coffee?"

"Make that two cookies. Your mincemeats are my favorites."

"Here's your coffee and cookies," said Helen. "You owe me a hug."

Helen slid into Walter's lap. He wrapped his arms around her and they enjoyed a long kiss. Helen purred, "Tell me."

"You're rotten. I've spoiled you."

"I know. Now tell me."

"Okay. But you're supposed to wait and let me say it instead of demanding it."

"You take too long. I need it now," she pouted.

"All right, I love you."

"That wasn't so hard. Now what's on your mind?"

"I want to talk about Everett. You're aware I've been giving Everett more decision-making authority, because I need to know if Everett is capable."

"Didn't you tell me you thought Glenn would be a better choice to run the company?"

"I did, Glenn has a better vision. He wants to operate the best-managed company in the business, while Everett wants to manage the largest. I don't think bigger is necessarily better. Glenn has empathy and a better sense of social responsibility."

"I agree with you, so why are you pushing out the perimeters for Everett?"

"Two reasons, Everett has worked hard and earned a shot at running things and I'm not sure the two of them can work together. We may have to push Everett out for Glenn to move in. Does this make any sense?"

"You better decide pretty soon. Glenn will finish his master's at Harvard this semester. He'll be chomping at the bit to come on board," said Helen.

"That's why I'm trying to get a feel for how Everett's going to perform."

"I'm getting more coffee. Do you want some?"

"Only if you bring another cookie."

"Walter, you don't need another."

"Pretty please. They're good!"

"Don't blame me when you have a heart attack."

"I'll split it with you."

"No, you won't. I don't want another cookie. I'm not going to get fat. You'll find some sweet thing to take my place."

Helen, I told you about the burglary of our store in El Paso. I haven't told you some of the details."

"Our security man in El Paso believed an employee worked with the burglars. The accusation became public, the man was also a preacher, his Church fired him and he committed suicide."

"Everett said we should distance ourselves from the suicide to protect our business. The Board supported Everett. I didn't agree. I wanted to help the preacher's family. I could have insisted and had my way, but I wanted to see how Everett handled the situation."

"Today our friend, Warren Betts, sent me an e-mail telling me I need to find out what's going on. He recommended I use a private investigator from Portales, who's familiar with the situation. I'm inclined to go along with Warren's recommendations."

Helen injected, "Warren's a smart man and our friend. If you think we should use the investigator and it upsets Everett, he'll just have to get over it. Walter, you do what you think is best."

"I had decided that's what we should do, but I didn't want to move ahead unless you agreed."

Chapter 46

Early Saturday Afternoon
O'Kelly Castle
El Paso, Texas

"HELEN, I'M UNCOMFORTABLE not knowing what Betts has on his mind. I'm going to call and want you to be in the conversation," asked Walter.

"Fine."

"This a good time for you?"

"Good as any," said Helen.

"Warren, it's Walter O'Kelly. Helen is on the line. We're on speakerphone. Tell us about this polygraph test."

"Hi, Walt, Helen, I didn't expect to hear from you so soon."

"Hello, Warren," said Helen, "How is Betty?"

"Betty's healthy. When she's not working out, she's playing tennis or golf. She's not content that she be alone in her search for the fountain of youth. She's drafted me into her war against fat," said Warren.

"I wish you luck, but I know from experience that you can't win. Chocolate has never known defeat."

"What's chocolate? I've heard of chocolate. It's not allowed in our house."

"Oh, you poor thing. You must come and see us. We'll rescue you. Chocolate is within reach throughout this house."

"All right, you two," said Walter, "We have serious business at hand. Warren, tell us what's going on."

"A bit of a witch hunt, I believe. Your man, Early, arranged a polygraph test, at the request of one of your Managers, Oscar Beasley. Beasley had terminated a checker for theft. When she explained losing her job to her husband, she said she was falsely accused and alleged that Beasley had offered to look the other way for sex. Her husband complained to Early. Beasley insisted on a polygraph test. Early piggybacked on the test to pursue another agenda."

"Did Beasley sexually harass the young lady?"

"Quite the contrary. Beasley's a straight arrow, who has your interests at heart. The woman was not tested, but I have little doubt she's a thief."

"Tell us about Early's hidden agenda," urged O'Kelly.

"Jake had your HR representative, a young lady named, Myra McCoy, include in our work order, a request that I find out if Beasley was responsible for an investigation that Jake thinks might not be in the company's interest."

"Before you tell us your findings, I'm curious what triggered Jake's interest in questioning Beasley's loyalty."

"A couple of reasons: Jake has an ax to grind. Beasley went outside of your chain of command and went to see Charles Peterson, your Executive Vice President about a matter of concern."

"Why would he do that?"

"Largely because he knew Jake had a bias to support one of his friends, a security manager, Willard Rhodes."

"I think I may know what's behind all this. What was it about Rhodes that had Beasley upset?"

"Oscar told me Willard Rhodes is a heavy-handed bully who should have been fired long ago. Because of his long-standing friendship with Early, he's been protected and employees have suffered mistreatment. Beasley contends that Rhodes's ego and ambition led him to falsely accuse an innocent man of a crime. The situation was badly handled and resulted in the man committing suicide."

"And Jake's other reason to go after Beasley was?"

"Jake heard a private investigator was looking into the burglary of your store number nine, trying to exonerate an employee of the crime.

"Jake suspected that it was Beasley who had retained the investigator. Early was hoping to establish Beasley was being both disloyal and insubordinate."

"So, what did you find out? Did Beasley hire the investigator?"

"He was open about that. He did it knowing he could be fired, but felt an injustice had taken place. He was willing to take risks to see justice was done."

"Now tell us what you think and why you have brought this to our attention."

"You probably don't want to hear this and you'll probably see things differently, but I think Early's being vindictive. He's out to get Beasley. His buddy, Willard Rhodes, is a piece of garbage and not your kind of people."

"I wanted you to know Beasley is re-thinking his choice of employers and I don't blame him. You would be a damned fool to let a man with his ability jump ship. Have I pissed you off?"

"Not everyone gets by with telling me I'm a fool. In your case, I asked, I know you're not a butt-kisser. Now why are you recommending I hire this investigator from Portales?"

"I think people tell you what you want to hear, not the truth. You have a situation here that's being mishandled and you need an outsider to bring you facts. You may want to consider getting better acquainted with Beasley. I think it might help your self-objectivity."

Chapter 47

Mid-morning
Better Deal Corporate Headquarters
Dallas, Texas

WALTER O'KELLY HAD his secretary call Charles Peterson into his office.

"Charlie, close the door and sit down. We need to have a little chat."

Peterson reacted quizzically as he closed the door and took a seat to await the hammer to fall.

"I called George and told him to get the plane ready including a couple of bag lunches. We're going to El Paso. Call Oscar Beasley. Have him meet us at 1:45 p.m."

"Okay, but I've got scheduled appointments," said Peterson.

"So cancel them. I want you along on this trip," said Walter.

"What am I supposed to tell these people?" asked Peterson.

"Tell them I didn't give you any choice?"

"I assume you intend to tell me what's going on."

"In due time. Make your calls. We need to get going."

"Do you want me to have Jake Early join us?" asked Charles.

"I don't want Jake to know we're in town and I don't want the people here to know either, especially Everett. You can drive us to the airport. I'll meet you downstairs in fifteen minutes."

Peterson had his secretary cancel his appointments and called Beasley with instructions to be at El Paso International at 1:45 p.m. "Oscar, this is a surprise visit. Alert no one, especially not Jake Early. Mr. O'Kelly wants to make store visits with you. See you shortly."

There was barely time for Oscar to whiff down a What-a-Burger, stow his stuff in the trunk of the Ford, run it through a car wash, and top off the gas.

Oscar arrived at the terminal at 1:30 p.m. *They must have had a tail wind.* The company plane was already on the tarmac.

He parked, and then jogged to get through the terminal and out the gate in time to greet the passengers.

Walter shook his hand and took off toward the terminal. Peterson followed and said, "Don't mind the boss. He needs to get to a bathroom. He hates to use the tiny bathroom on the plane."

"Mr. Peterson, I've never met Mr. O'Kelly. Do I have reason to be concerned?"

"Oscar, I haven't got a clue. Two hours ago he told me to get my coat. I'm sure we'll find out."

They had only moments to wait. O'Kelly was out the bathroom door motioning them to come. "Oscar, I want to go to your store number nine first. We're about to invest a ton of money in that facility. I want to satisfy myself we're doing the right thing. What do you think? Do we need a new store?"

"Yes, sir. We're badly under-stored. If we don't do something soon, our competitors will."

"Why do you think we have done so well in this store?" asked Walter.

"A number of reasons," said Oscar. "The first is the most important: location. We have a good one, easy in and out, convenient access from all directions. Another is the explosive growth caused by being in the best school district in the city.

This is going to sound a bit self-serving, but, very honestly, we've served our customers well. We have good people, top quality perishables, keep a clean store and have very competitive pricing. We've been careful to have the variety these customers want. Our buyers have worked with us to cater to our mix of ethnic shoppers."

"How about discretionary income?" asked Walter?

"Over seventy-five thousand per year per household, the highest in the city. These folks buy what they want. Some blue-collar workers, but mostly young professionals, with families, lots of mouths to feed," said Oscar.

"I'm told you don't think we are moving fast enough," said Walter.

"No sir, I don't," said Oscar. "We've got a good thing going here, but we're vulnerable. If we don't get started on a new facility soon, a competitor is going to build to fill the void."

"Interesting! You may be right. Let's go inside and take a look. Who's your unit director here?" asked Walter.

"Dan Coleman. He's probably the best manager in this district. He's a good trainer who spots and develops winners. I've promoted more people from this store than any other. Dan teaches his folks how to do things right, then gets out of their way and lets them do it. He's also the best customer relation's person in the district. He spends most of his time on the sales floor and knows many of his customers by name."

The trio entered the store and totally surprised Coleman, who handled the situation well. "Welcome to number nine. I hope you find everything shipshape. We weren't expecting company, but we try to be ready for business all the time."

After having Dan give them a quick tour of the store, Walter asked him to walk with them to the car. "Dan, tell me about this assistant manager of yours that killed himself. Do you think he stole the contents of your safe?"

"No way."

"Then why was he accused?"

"You want the truth?"

"Of course I want the truth."

"Accusing Tim Sullivan of being a thief was the most insane, ridiculous, unfair thing I've seen anyone do in this company."

"That's a pretty strong statement. Where did these accusations against Sullivan originate?"

"Willard Rhodes seemed to be convinced Tim was involved. Tim took and passed two polygraphs. Even then, Rhodes stayed on his case. The worst thing was Rhodes's big mouth. Customers heard him blaming Sullivan and people gossip."

"You're telling me you think it's the company's fault that Sullivan committed suicide?"

"No doubt in my mind."

"And what about you, Beasley? What do you think?"

Charles Peterson interrupted, "Let me answer that, Mr. O'Kelly. Oscar came to me about Rhodes's accusations. It bothered me that he was going outside the chain of command, so I included Jake in the meeting."

"Was that a problem?"

"Possibly. As I recall we may have focused more upon Oscar going around Early, than on the issue of Sullivan."

"Sounds to me like the only ones looking out for this company's interest are Coleman and Beasley. What was Rhodes trying to accomplish?"

"I suppose he wanted to solve a mystery and be a hero. The man is obsessed with getting promoted."

"At the cost of a human life? That may be unforgiveable."

"Dan, I'm impressed with you, your people and your store. We're going to accelerate our plans and get you that new store ASAP. Please tell your employees I appreciate the great job they're doing."

"Will do," said Dan. "Thank you for coming by."

"Oscar," said Walter, "I've seen what I came to see. We'll skip going to other stores. Take us back to the airport."

Chapter 48

In the Air
El Paso to Dallas
Better Deal Citation II

THE PLUSH GREY LEATHER passenger seating on the Citation jet included a pair facing forward, a single opposite the exit door and two pair facing in a conversational group. Charlie was seated opposite Walter O'Kelly in the conversational group.

He initiated a discussion. "Walter, what was it we came to see? Were you nervous about plans for number nine?"

"No. I know we need a larger store in that location. I was concerned we were dragging our heels. I want you to break ground and hold a press conference, so our competition and our customers will know we're building a state of the art store.

Charlie, I'm impressed with Oscar Beasley. Is he ready to handle more responsibility?"

"Probably," remarked Peterson. He's capable, but it may be a bit early."

"Why do you say too early?" asked Walter."

"Mostly because he works for Jake. Jake's been down on him since he broke the chain of command. It bothers me as well. "

"Charlie, this isn't the Army. Early is a problem. Get rid of him.

Early retirement, let him go, whatever fits, but I want him gone."

"I'll take care of it, but I'll need a replacement."

"I'm making that decision for you. I want you to promote Beasley. I like people who stand up for their people and for what they believe. Do you have a problem with him?"

"No, sir, it's your company."

"Charlie. I still expect you to tell me if you think I'm wrong."

"I think it's a good decision, but there'll be some ruffled feathers. We have a couple of men with longer service who're going to be disappointed," said Peterson.

"That doesn't mean they're the best choice. Taking all things into consideration, who's the best man for the job?"

"Beasley."

"All right," said Walter, "I want it done right away. Let's talk about Willard Rhodes. I want you to fire him. I can't believe you've allowed that nut to abuse our people. This gets me to you. Charlie, you've done a good job for me up to now. But I want you to know that I'm disappointed you failed to recognize Rhodes' behavior."

Peterson replied, "You're right, I guess I've had my head in the sand."

"Yes, you have. Everyone makes a mistake every now and then, but if something of this magnitude happens again, we'll be talking about your job. Do I make my point?"

Peterson replied, "It won't happen again."

"Enough about that," said O'Kelly, "but we're not through. I have to admit I've had my own head in the sand. I want you to give me your honest assessment of Everett."

"I've been wanting to share some thoughts about Everett, but it's difficult to be forth-coming when family is involved."

"I want to hear the truth. I have a strong sense of family, but the people in this company are like family to Helen and I. If Everett isn't the right man for the future, we'll do something else."

"To be perfectly honest, there are a number of us who are uncomfortable with Everett. He's political and throws his weight around. He's impatient to take over the company even to the point of undermining you."

O'Kelly interrupted, "He can't do that, Helen and I own all the stock."

"That's not all," continued Peterson, "One of the reasons why you have great people is because you're fair and honest with people. You've maintained an environment where employees have the opportunity to fulfill their potential.

Everett doesn't think and operate like you. You're known to be tough, but fair. The thought of Everett running this company is unsettling. He plays favorites, is self-serving and doesn't have your integrity," said Peterson.

"You done? That's my son you're talking about."

"No. This needs to be said. You can be counted on to do what's right. Everett does what benefits him personally. If he ever runs this company, it'll be a different company. I, for one, will probably find new employment. There are others who are already looking."

Clearly alarmed and surprised, O'Kelly said, "Well, I asked you to be honest. Let's keep this between us, but I'm probably going to try to re-direct Everett's career path to something outside the company. It may take a while, but it will get better."

Seeing that his boss wanted action, Peterson laid out his plans. "If the plane is available, I'll return to El Paso first thing in the morning. There's enough time remaining today to work out the severance issues for both Early and Rhodes. I should be able to see Early by nine a.m. and hopefully get Rhodes handled before noon. I'll have lunch with Oscar and outline his new responsibilities."

"You have the option of promoting him to Division Manager or making him the Division Vice President. What do you want to do?" asked O'Kelly.

"I'm comfortable with either. What do you recommend?"

"I'm inclined to put Beasley on a fast track. I see him as possibly being your replacement down the road. I suggest you make him Division Vice President. If he performs as I expect, I'd like to see him as your administrative assistant within a year. When I bump you to my job, he'll be ready to take your place."

"Wow, you're full of surprises today. This is the first time I've had a clue that you would even consider me as a candidate to take your place."

"What sort of reaction do you expect from Beasley?"

"Initially, disbelief. When he realizes I'm not pulling his leg, he'll be elated."

The pilot announced they should buckle their seat beats for a landing.

Walter sighed in relief. "I see we have survived another landing. Rather than go back to the office, I'd like for you to drop me at the house. I have some things to share with Helen."

Chapter 49

O'Kelly's Castle
Oak Manors
Dallas, Texas

WALTER AND HELEN RELAXED under the pergola over-looking the creek that passed through their property. As was his habit, Walter shared his day while enjoying a rum and coke with a twist of lime while Helen sipped at her white wine.

Helen remarked, "You've had a busy day. Tomorrow the world will be buzzing with rumors and speculation as your plans unfold."

"I leave that to Charlie Peterson, that's why we pay him the big bucks. In the meantime, my plans are to arrange to meet this cowboy cop from Portales. I want him to find who really robbed the safe at number nine."

"What have you decided about Everett?"

"I'm considering a number of alternatives. The one certain conclusion I've reached is that Everett, for all our nurturing, is not going to take my place," said Walter.

"Everett is very much his own person and certainly not a yes man," said Helen.

"That he isn't. Nor is he a people person empathetic to the needs of others, or generous and kind. We've somehow raised someone who is arrogant, selfish, unfair and better suited to other pursuits than to the grocery business. He is, nevertheless, our son and I love him. We'll just have to encourage him to point his life in a different direction.

From him," said Walter, "I rather expect we'll have the adult version of a child's tantrum. When he understands that he'll never run the company, I think he'll make his own decisions to turn to other options. How do you predict he'll react?"

"As a child, and even now, I've observed that Everett doesn't get mad, he gets even. I hate to see you the potential focus of his revenge," lamented Helen.

"Do you really think he would try to get even with his own father?" said Walter, in disbelief.

"Oh yes, but I think his revenge will be to try to punish you in some subtle way. I don't see him being confrontational. I think he'll act out his revenge and he'll come to me for support, hoping I will change your mind," said Helen.

"When that fails, what'll he do?" questioned Walter.

"Why try to divide us, of course," said Helen. "He knows how much I value my relationship with his children. Most likely he'll imply he'll have to relocate to some place where I will seldom see them again. They'll be his weapons."

"And what will you do?" asked Walter.

"Support you, silly," said Helen. "We're in this together. I told you I'd support you in your decisions."

"Why is it," asked Walter, "I never saw this side of Everett?"

"You were busy trying to make a living and build a business. I raised the kids. We lived in two different, but parallel worlds. The children viewed you as that man who visited their world from time to time. Trust me. I know them far better than you ever will. We did what we had to do."

"That must have seemed unfair to you," said Walter.

"Not really," said Helen. "I knew you wanted to live your life vicariously through Everett. Every man has that wish for himself and his son. I knew this day was coming. Everett isn't you, nor will he ever be. My heart breaks for you both. You do what you have to do. Everett is an adult. People deal with disappointment every day.

He'll find his way."

"You don't feel we owe him the right to follow in my footsteps?" inquired Walter.

"He hasn't earned that," said Helen, "You and I owe our success to the people who've worked with us to make the business a success. They've invested their lives in a mutual undertaking with us. Our obligation is to see the very best management possible is at the helm of our company. I could never see him in that role."

"We should have had this conversation a long time ago. I thought you expected me to pass the leadership of the company on to one of our children."

"You mentioned you were leaning toward passing the leadership of the company to our other son," said Helen. "I had a phone call we need to discuss. Glenn's application at the University of Texas Medical School has been accepted. He plans to go directly to Galveston from Harvard after he gets his MBA in May."

"I had no knowledge he had any interest in medical school. Glenn's always led me to believe that he would be working in the company after he got his degree," said Walter.

Helen smiled and said, "He was just telling you what you wanted to hear. You should respect and support him in his decision. You have over seventy thousand employees. Don't you think there's someone capable of running this company among them?"

Walter mused over that a moment, smiled and said, "I may have met him today."

Chapter 50

Headquarters Offices
Better Deal Supermarkets
Dallas, Texas

WALTER WAS THE FIRST TO ARRIVE at the Better Deal Operations Center located in uptown Dallas. He made a pot of coffee, booted up his computer, accessed the Internet and did a search for private investigator, Portales, New Mexico. His search brought up two numbers for Perkins Investigations.

"Perkins Investigations, Lee speaking."

"Good morning, Mr. Perkins. I'm glad to find you start your day early. My name is, Walter O'Kelly. You're acquainted with one of my District Managers, Oscar Beasley."

"Yes, Sir. How may I be of service?"

"I've got a job for you, if you're interested. I'll have our plane pick you up at noon; you'll be in Dallas by two. Can you make it?" asked O'Kelly.

"I can," said Perkins, "earlier if you like."

"Noon's fine. Pack clothes for a couple of weeks. You'll be going from Dallas to El Paso. Can the Portales airport accommodate a Citation ll," asked Walter?

"It won't. Our runway's 4500 feet," said Perkins, "that's a

thousand short. The Clovis Airport will work. Meet you there, if you like."

"You know your planes," said Walter. "Are you a pilot?"

"I've got a Cessna Sky Master. It would save you some money if I flew it to Dallas."

"But it'd take more time. We'll come get you," said Walter. "We'll work out our arrangement after you arrive."

"Sounds good to me," said Perkins.

"I look forward to seeing you around two or two-thirty. A car and driver will be waiting for you in Dallas," said Walter.

Perkins Ranch Home
NE of Portales

Lee's wife Shirley, a professor at Eastern New Mexico University, had a three-hour break between classes on Tuesdays. Rather than eat at the cafeteria, she was at home for lunch.

Lee's was surprised to find her at home. "You're supposed to be out making me a living."

"Don't like cafeteria food. What about you? Why are you at home?"

"I'm here to pack a bag. I've got to be at the Clovis airport at noon. I'm going to Dallas, then to El Paso for a couple of weeks. I left you a voice mail," said Lee.

"I never know about you. You're here one minute, gone the next. Have you eaten?"

"No. You might make me a sandwich to go."

"I'll do that. Can I help you with anything else?"

"No. I can pack in five minutes. You having a good day?"

"I am, I've got some good students this semester. Why are you going to El Paso? Is this connected to the case you were working on?"

"Maybe, don't know for sure. By the way, I programmed my office calls to your phone."

"Thanks a lot. I don't have time for that."

"So what's a guy to do? You're too jealous and tight with money to let me have a secretary. There won't be many calls; just make a note about who called. I'll catch up when I get back."

"I'll take your calls. You be careful. Call me when you know where you'll be staying."

Shirley made a ham and cheese on rye, got a diet coke from the fridge, put them in a paper bag.

"I'm about to leave. The sandwich ready?"

"It's in the bag, with a coke and some chips. Give me a kiss before you go. Love you."

When Lee arrived at the Clovis Airport the Citation was on the tarmac, refueled and ready to roll. The pilot, George Seymour, a much-decorated former fighter pilot, was waiting by the steps.

"You Lee? I'm your taxi driver, George Seymour. The guys in the terminal tell me you're a pilot, have a Cessna Sky Master. Great plane. You have any time in jets?"

"Glad to meet you. No. I've never had the opportunity to sit up front in a jet."

"Second seat's open. Sit up front with me. You can take the stick for a while. We're supposed to have light rain, maybe five or ten minutes of turbulence. You ready?"

"I am. All I've got is one bag, a brief case and a bag lunch. Sorry, I didn't pack a sandwich for you."

"Actually, I brought one for you. Let's let her rip."

Lee took the right side seat facing a much larger instrument cluster than on his Sky Master. They strapped in, George did a hasty pre-flight check and got instructions from the tower. He taxied to the end of the runway, revved the two Pratt and Whitney engines and they were off.

"Whoopee! You always take off like that?" asked Lee.

"No. I'm showing off. Just wanted to show you what this baby can do," said George.

Lee flew the aircraft for more than half the flight. George took over when they hit the turbulence.

George made a three-point landing, taxied to the terminal. He turned to Lee and said, "You did good. You'd make a good jet-jockey."

"Too rich for my blood," said Lee. "I can't afford the fuel, much less own one."

"I know what you mean. Uncle Sam paid my learning costs. That's your driver in the Mercedes. Enjoyed having you on board. See you around."

Chapter 51

Better Deal
Corporate Office
Dallas, Texas

WALTER DECIDED NOW was as good a time as any. He went down the hall, walked pass Everett's secretary and stuck his head inside the door. "Got a minute," He asked?

"Hi, Pop. Sure do. What's up? Not often you drop in."

"We need to talk. Are you free?"

"I don't have anything pressing."

"Tell your secretary we're not to be interrupted. What I have to say is not for other ears."

Everett stepped out of the room. "Lisa, hold my calls. No interruptions, please."

"Okay, Pop. What's this all about?"

"This may take awhile. I've made some decisions about the future. I know you've long assumed that when I no longer run the business, it will pass into your hands," said Walter.

"I've never seriously considered doing anything else. Are you telling me something is suddenly different? That it's not going to happen? My whole life, my family's lives are built around that assumption."

"I'm not denying that I may have led you to believe you would someday run the company, but I'm quite sure I've never made a commitment it was a certainty. I believe it's been clear you had to earn it."

"And I have! I've done everything you asked, grades, MBA, law degree. What have I not done to please you?"

"It's not so much what you have or haven't done. You're a bright guy with a special skill set, but I don't see it as being a match to run this company."

"I've got a lot better credentials than you do."

"You're right, but I can see I'm not qualified to run it and surround myself with people who are."

"So what's happening here? Am I fired? Are you giving the company to my little brother?"

"Your brother is not interested. He just enrolled in medical school. And, no, you are not fired, but I do think you should seriously consider doing something outside of the business."

Everett's face turned scarlet and angry. He made a fist and hit the top of his desk. "Why are you doing this? It doesn't make any sense."

"It makes sense to me. We have seventy thousand employees. Many are in for the long haul. They've bet their family's futures on this company. They deserve the best possible leadership.

What are the odds our family will produce the single best candidate? You're competing with a world full of candidates. You're a smart man with a lot of talent, but you don't have the empathy, sensitivity and vision to run this company."

"I damned sure do," said Everett.

"No, Everett. I've watched you. You're political, play favorites, you're self-serving and unfair and you lack compassion and feeling for others. Those are not the qualities needed to manage an organization."

"You are making a big mistake. You're going to be sorry."

"Be careful what you say. Think about it, Everett, you're a wealthy man. Your trust fund is worth millions. Take all the time you need, take some time off, but plan on doing something else. It won't work for you to stay at Better Deal. You have three months.

I'm your Father. I love you. You'll always be part of our family, but business is business. We're done here. Come see me if you have any other questions."

Chapter 52

O'Kelly Castle
Oak Manors
Dallas, Texas

AT PRECISELY TWO-THIRTY Lee was delivered to the front steps of the castle-like O'Kelly home in Dallas. "Thanks for the lift," said Lee.

"My pleasure," smiled the driver, "but I'm not going anywhere. My instructions are to be available to take you to back to the plane. The car will be right here. Hit the horn a couple of times when you're ready to go. I'll come running. I live over the garage."

"Will do. Thanks," said Lee.

He turned. A white-headed gentleman Lee assumed to be Walter O'Kelly was descending the steps. His right arm was extended. In his left he carried what appeared to be a gin and tonic. He pumped Lee's hand vigorously. "I'm Walter. Welcome. Thought you might need something wet."

"Pleased to meet you, Sir. Thank you for the welcome," said Lee.

"Let's go in the house," said Walter. "Helen's about to have a cup of tea and asks we join her before we get down to business."

As they moved into the O'Kelly home, Lee was impressed at

how homey it felt. *Nice place! They must've had a clever decorator. Few larger homes feel this warm and cozy.*

"Honey, meet Lee Perkins, he's the private investigator I told you about."

"Good afternoon, Lee. It's a pleasure to meet you," said Helen as gave him a welcoming hug.

"I'm pleased to meet you, Mrs. O'Kelly," replied Lee.

"Please take a seat. Would you like me to freshen your drink?"

"That would be nice. Maybe a bit less gin and more tonic."

She handed Walter the glass. "You're the master mixer. Would you do the honors," said Helen? "While you're gone, Mr. Perkins can tell me about himself."

Walter stepped away to the wet bar. Lee commented, "Mrs. O'Kelly, I admire your home. It feels warm and inviting. You must have had a good interior decorator," said Lee.

"I'll take that as a complement. I wouldn't feel it was our home if someone else did the decorations."

"Great job. I like it," said Lee.

"We do too. It certainly beats the places we lived when we were trying to open the doors of our first store. Now I'd like to know all about you and your family, but I see from the look on Walter's face I should excuse myself. Walter, you remember I'm not done with this man. I'd like to get to know him better," said Helen. "Lee, perhaps I'll get to see you before you leave. It was a pleasure to meet you."

"The pleasure was all mine, Mrs. O'Kelly. Hope to see you again soon."

Walter interrupted, "We don't have a lot of time. I have the plane on hold to take you to El Paso and I promised the pilot I would have him home in time for parent's night at his daughter's grade school. Lee, I'm aware of the work you've done in collaboration with Oscar Beasley. The police have shut down their investigation of the burglary on Central. I'd like for you to look further into that incident and see if you can determine who robbed our safe. A great many things have been going on in the past few hours. Willard Rhodes is no longer employed by us, nor is Jake Early. The newly appointed Vice President of our West Texas

Division is Oscar Beasley. You'll be working with Oscar and myself. Oscar is in charge. I just need to be kept informed. Oscar is going to have his hands full getting into his new responsibilities, so you will be largely on you own. Oscar's been instructed to provide you any financial resources you require. We need to keep this under wraps until we're ready to bring it to public attention. Agreed?"

"Yes, Sir," Lee injected, "You need to know I always recommend that we let the law take its course. I don't believe in cover-ups."

"Of course, I don't have a problem with that," answered Mr. O'Kelly, then added, "Do I need to sign any sort of a contract?"

"No, that won't be necessary. Do I need to explain how I charge?" said Lee.

"No," said Walter. "I'll leave that between you and Oscar. I don't believe in wasting money, but I'm okay with living well. Just don't put me in the poor house. This card has all my personal contact information. You also need to know our son, Everett, is also leaving, only not immediately. He, Jake Early and Willard Rhodes, have made some poor decisions connected with the death of an employee at number nine. Oscar will meet your plane in El Paso. It's been a pleasure. I'll say your goodbyes to Helen. Have a safe trip."

Chapter 53

Dining Room
Uptown Country Club
Dallas, Texas

EVERETT AND HIS BEST FRIEND, Chuck Davies seldom get together these days. Chuck's three marriages, numerous marital indiscretions and the mysterious death of one spouse have made social interface difficult.

Everett initiated this meeting. Conversation has been small talk, the weather, their families and the view over-looking the eighteenth green.

Everett was struggling with indecision. Was it time to broach the reason he'd suggested they meet? Were the risks worth the gamble?

Most Dallas natives are unaware the Davies wealth is tainted and nasty. Chuck shared with Everett the sources of the family money and power years ago. The Davies are New Orleans Mafioso who own massage parlors, nightclubs, control illegal gambling and run prostitution from Longview to El Paso.

Harry Fletcher, a business partner, manages the shell companies that hide their sleazy investments. He also quietly and ruthlessly deals with bumps in the road caused by Chuck's affairs.

Throughout lunch Everett had directed their conversation mostly to what has been taking place with the Davies. He was surprised to learn that Chuck would soon be moving to New Orleans.

"Why are you moving to the Big Easy?" asked Everett.

Chuck grimaced, "It's not because I want to. I think I'm an embarrassment to my folks. They say it's because my grandfather is getting old and wants me to run things in New Orleans."

"What do you think about it?"

"I've got mixed emotions. I hate to leave all my friends," explained Davies.

"What will you be doing in New Orleans," asked Everett?

"That's up to Gramps. From what he says, I assume I'll be on a fast track to take over the operation. How about you? What's going on at Better Deal?"

Everett had deliberately set up this meeting to talk about his own dilemma. "It sounds like we have somewhat similar problems."

Everett shared how he'd been blind-sided by his parent's decision that he wasn't their choice to run the business, how he'd been told to look for another job. His explanation ended with a declaration. "I can't accept their decision without a fight. Everything I've done has been preparation to run the company."

Davies was familiar with Everett's ambition; the diligence and effort it had required to earn his credentials and shared with him a common belief that owning the company was Everett's birthright.

Everett asked, "What do you think I should do?"

"Not sure. Any chance you could get them to change their minds?" asked Chuck.

"I don't think so," explained Everett.

"What if something happened to them? Are you the beneficiary of their wills?" asked Chuck.

Everett gasped, "Whoa! I didn't have anything quite that drastic in mind."

"You asked me. So answer my question," said Chuck.

"I don't know where you're going with this," said Everett. Yes, they have a will. It specifies I'm to run the business. I'm sure they intend to change it PDQ."

"I don't think you have any choice," said Chuck. "If I were in your shoes, I'd be looking for a hit man. He's screwing you over. That's life. Screw or be screwed. You've got to beat him to the punch."

"You're kidding, of course. I couldn't do anything like that. Besides, that wouldn't solve anything. His will leaves everything to my mom and he wouldn't be doing this if she wasn't in the boat with him."

Chuck shrugs his shoulders and said, "So, snuff them both."

"Come on, Chuck, I'd never get away with it. I don't want to spend the rest of my life in prison," said Everett.

"It happens all the time. You get a professional to do it. Professionals don't get caught. It's just the knee-jerk amateurs who get caught. What are you going to do? You going to let them cut you out or stand up like a man?"

"My folks have been damned good to me," said Everett. "I don't think I can do anything that drastic."

"They're screwing you right? It's an eye for an eye. This is your moment. If you let it slip away, it isn't coming around again. Do it!"

"Chuck, it's too drastic. I'm pissed. I want to do something, but there's got to be a better solution. Help me find something else. Besides, think of the risks, the potential consequences."

"If it bothers you, get someone else to do the dirty work. You know about Harry Fletcher. He has contacts everywhere. He's been Mr. Fix-it for me. I'll tell you what; I'll talk to Harry, get him to meet with you and work out whatever you want."

"I don't think so, but I'll think about it, let you know what I decide." The waiter brought their check. Everett added a generous tip, signed the tab and said, "I've got to go."

"Me too," said Chuck. "I'll be expecting your call."

They rose and embraced. "Good to see you, Chuck," said Everett.

"You, too."

Chapter 54

Business Jet Terminal
El Paso International Airport
El Paso, Texas

THE FLIGHT FROM DALLAS to El Paso was a much happier experience than the pitch and yawl of Lee's earlier in the day flight from Portales. George, the pilot, and now friend, allowed Lee to again sit second seat and fly the jet about half the distance.

George said, "You're ruined forever. Once you've flown a jet, props aren't much fun."

"My prop plane fits my needs. It gets off the ground in a short distance and I can land it on a country road or in a pasture, if necessary."

"What do you fly?" asked Shipley.

"A Cessna Super Skymaster," said Lee.

"Pressurized cabin, twin push-pull, retractable gear?" asked Sullivan.

"That's the one," said Lee.

"Nice rig. The high-mount wing provides great visibility. Hear it'll cruise over three hundred per," said George.

"Close to three-fifty," said Lee.

"See why you like it. I like jets. Different worlds," said George.

At five o'clock sharp, Lee's feet hit the tarmac. He turned to wave, but he was too late. The door was closed. The plane was in motion before Lee reached the gate.

Oscar was asking someone at the desk when the Better Deal Jet was expected. He turned, was surprised to see Lee with bag in hand. "Where in the world did you come from?"

"Scotty beamed me down," said Lee.

"Seriously, how long you been here," asked Oscar?

"Shipley practically threw me out the door. The plane was on the ground less than five minutes.

"We need to get going," said Oscar. "I don't have a lot of time. You're staying at the Wingham Hotel. I'm going to drop you there. There's a car key and a credit card for you at the desk. The car is a white Ford Explorer. It's parked directly in front of the hotel, it's gassed and ready to go. Insurance card is in the glove compartment."

Oscar handed a piece of paper to Lee, "Here's the pin number for the debit card. You can get whatever cash you need from an ATM; cash limit is $300 a day. If you need more, call me and I'll get you what you need. The pad on the seat between us is for keeping track of expenses. Attach the receipts and send them to me weekly. The address is on the form. My cell phone number, office number and so forth are on the backside of the card with the pin number," said Oscar.

"I left on pretty short notice and didn't think to bring a laptop," said Lee.

"There's an Electronics store on Montana," said Oscar. "Use your credit card to buy one. Get a good one. It's okay. The old man said to get you whatever you need."

"I've got some questions," said Lee. "Have you got some time?"

"Not now," said Oscar. "I need to drop you off. I'll meet you for breakfast at six in the hotel's coffee shop."

"See you then," said Lee. "By the way, congratulations on your promotion."

Chapter 55

Better Deal Corporate Offices
Uptown Dallas

EVERETT O'KELLY'S SECRETARY answered his phone. "Good morning. Mr. O'Kelly's office, Lisa speaking."

"Good morning. This is Harry Fletcher. I'd like to speak with Everett O'Kelly. I was referred by Chuck Davies."

"Please hold, I'll see if Mr. O'Kelly is available," said Lisa.

Lisa Morrison, a temporary filling in for Everett's secretary on pregnancy leave rang his intercom. "Mr. O'Kelly, Harry Fletcher is on the phone. Do you want to take the call?"

"Lisa, please call me, Everett. We aren't that formal. His name isn't familiar. Could be for my Dad."

"He asked for Everett O'Kelly and mentioned a referral by Chuck Davies."

The mention of Chuck's name caused the penny to drop. *It's Chuck's Mr. Fixit.* "I'll take the call," said Everett.

"He's on line three," said Lisa.

"Good morning, Mr. Fletcher, this is Everett O'Kelly. Lisa said Chuck Davies asked you to give me a call."

"Chuck Davies said you and I should talk. So I'm calling. What's this about," responded an obviously impatient Harry Fletcher?

Nervous and a bit afraid of being associated with a man with a shady reputation, Everett suggested, "I prefer we talk face to face rather than by phone."

"You want me to come there?"

"No, some place more private," said Everett. *I wonder if my secretary listens in on my calls?*

"Okay, I can do private. Where do you want to meet," asked Fletcher?

"Do you have a suggestion? I'd prefer not to be gone long."

"So, where are you now," asked Fletcher?

"Our offices," responded Everett, "are in Uptown Dallas. Do you know of a place nearby?"

"I do. You know your way around De Soto?" asked Fletcher.

"Fairly well," said Everett.

"We're in the construction business," said Fletcher. "We're building a new regional high school southwest of De Soto out towards Midlothian."

"I'm familiar with the location. Our company just bought a property near there," said Everett.

"We just moved a construction shack onto the site. We can meet there," said Fletcher. "There's nothing there but our shack and a couple of dirt pushers. Is that too far to travel?"

"No. That'll work fine. What time do you want to meet," asked Everett?

"The heavy equipment guys work seven to three. If we meet at three-thirty we'll have the place to ourselves and you can beat the five o'clock rush back to uptown," said Fletcher.

"Okay. I'll see you tomorrow afternoon. Thanks for calling," said Everett, as he ended the call. *Odd that Chuck had Fletcher call me. Wonder how he knew I'd made a decision to do as he's suggested.*

Chapter 56

6:00 a.m.
Breakfast Buffet
Wingham Hotel

LEE PERKINS LOOKED UP from his newspaper, noticed Oscar Beasley taking a seat on the opposite side of the table.

"May I join you?" asked Oscar.

"Been hoping you'd show up. I'm hungry."

"Me, too. I've missed a few meals lately. Too busy to eat."

A waitress poured more coffee for Lee and asked Oscar, "You want coffee?"

"Yes, and keep it coming."

"You want to order from the menu or do you prefer the buffet?"

Both ordered bacon and eggs with hash browns, biscuits, gravy and orange juice.

As their waitress headed toward the kitchen Oscar said, "I'm here to answer your questions."

"You could start by telling me what's going on," said Lee. "I'm confused. Better Deal apparently did everything in its power to shut down an investigation, now the headman is jump-starting it. What's going on?"

"Good question," said Oscar. "He was getting some bad advice.

When he realized he was being misled, he jumped in, got things back on track. Good thing he did, I was about to get the sack. Instead, I got promoted."

"He told me he wants me to stay on it until I find out who robbed the safe. If I find him or them, the company is going to get some backlash," said Lee.

"You do what's right, we'll just have to bear the consequences. It's the stand we should have taken in the first place," explained Oscar.

"You do know it's very doubtful we'll uncover what really happened?"

"It's important to Walter we try. Besides," said Oscar, "I'm pretty sure you wouldn't be here if you didn't think you have a chance to get this resolved."

"I'm not entirely without a sense of where to look," said Lee. "I'm personally satisfied that druggies didn't do the safe. There's only one other possibility; someone robbed the safe after the break-in, before the cops arrived."

"It can be argued it might have been anyone," said Lee, "but in my view, the most likely suspects are either the cops or possibly the security people. I plan to check out the cops first."

"Do you propose to ask for cooperation from the police department's internal affairs people?" asked Oscar.

"No. My experience is that cops close ranks and protect one another. I trust Kathy Smith," said Lee. "She's a straight shooter. I'm going to ask her for help. Otherwise, I don't want to show my hand for a while."

"I leave that to you," said Oscar. "I've got to focus on getting a handle on my new job. You call me if you need help or support. Mr. O'Kelly wants a report at least once a week, so you might establish a routine of calling me on Friday afternoons, so I'll have something to report."

"I'm sorry, but I need to go," said Oscar. "You got anything else?"

"That's all for now."

"Good! Put the ticket on your new credit card. I'll talk to you Friday," said Oscar.

Cody's Electronics
Montana Street
El Paso

At nine o'clock, Cody's Electronics opened for the day, Lee was their first customer. He purchased an HP computer and portable printer, returned to the Wingham, plugged them to a power source and used the hotel code for the wireless Internet connection.

Lee scrolled the two policemen who took the call for the break-in on Central Avenue. He keyed in Eli Sanchez name first. Among the many hits on Eli's name was an El Paso Times newspaper article about the death of Eli's partner, rookie Toby Preston.

Lee read the full article and everything else he could find associated with Toby's career and his death. Toby's address was listed in the article, so Lee decided he'd talk with a few of the neighbors to see if he could pick up additional information.

Northgate Apartments
Fort Bliss Avenue
El Paso, Texas

The Northgate Apartments manager was a very nice sixtyish lady. Preferring to make his inquiry non-sensational, Lee told her he was an investigator for a life insurance company, that the company routinely examines all aspects of the personal lives of policyholders before they settle claims.

His role-play must have resonated with the apartment's manager, because she was very cooperative. From her, Lee gleaned Toby's apartment number and names of his friends within the complex. He learned Toby had off and on again relationships with two roommate nurses who lived on the property.

Not expecting anyone to be at home in the nurse's apartment, Lee was surprised the door was opened by not one, but two attractive young ladies. After explaining his purpose, Lee was invited to come inside.

The two women were nurses at Sisters of Wisdom Memorial

Hospital. Both had the day off. Having just completed the cleaning of their apartment, they were happy to take a break. He accepted a glass of tea. The girls proceeded to tell him everything they knew about Toby Preston.

The shorter of the two, a blonde named Alice Smith, told Lee, "It's a shame. He was a handsome dude. We had a lot of fun when he first moved in. Both of us dated him. I was sweet on him at one time."

"So what happened," asked Lee?

"Lots of things. He was such a leech. He borrowed money and never paid it back. When I realized he was a loser, I quit going out with him."

"How about you, Janie, you dated him too?"

"Oh yeah. I had to learn the hard way. He started hitting on me after Alice dumped him. She warned me, but he was so good looking I had to take a chance. I thought I could straighten him out."

Lee asked, "What changed your mind?"

"Same story as Alice. He borrowed money, never paid it back and told me nothing but lies."

"Toby told stretches to flatter himself all the time," said Alice. Didn't make sense to me, because he was such a hunk without the baloney."

"You do know that he was a high-roller gambler," asked Janie?

"How do you know that," asked Lee?

"Pretty obvious. I could tell if he'd been winning, because he'd throw money around, give me expensive gifts, took me to nice places. The big tip-off was the phone calls. If someone was putting together a game, he'd get a call, leave me to get home on my own," exclaimed Janie. "You want some more tea?"

"Lately, neither of us had been going out with him, but we'd see him at the pool," said Alice. " He told me he'd lost some big-time money in a poker game, he'd had a long winning streak with these same guys, they had set him up by letting him win, then got him in really deep."

"We both knew about his losses and knew he was depressed. We think he might have driven off Scenic Drive on purpose," said

Janie.

After thanking the girls and taking his leave, Lee visited with an older resident who was near the pool. This man told him almost everyone knew and had liked Toby, but most had eventually recognized that he was full of hot air. He also told Lee, Toby owed him money.

Returning that afternoon to his hotel room, Lee considered all the events of the day. Toby's gambling debts might have influenced him to participate in a burglary of convenience. The puzzling question was why would he have gambling debts if he had the money from the burglary?

Lee decided to take a look at Toby's truck to see if there was any evidence that it might have been rigged to have an accident.

Using the computer and on-line resources normally available to officers of the law, Lee found the license number for the truck, called the insurance provider for the name of the wrecking service and from them got its present location. Fortunately, it had not yet been compacted and sold for metals recovery.

The following morning Lee examined the Ranger. The roof was crushed. No one could have survived.

Lee asked the owner of the wrecking company to have the vehicle turned upside down. He checked the brake lines. He found what he had suspected: a brake line had obviously been cut and crimped. He took a picture of the cut in the line.

The Ranger was now evidence in what was obviously a murder. Lee told the owner to make sure the vehicle was not touched. It was now evidence in a criminal investigation.

Detective Division
El Paso Police Headquarters

Kathy Smith answered her phone, "You aren't going to believe what I've found."

"Who is this?"

"It's Lee."

Kathy remarked she was surprised to be hearing from Lee. Naturally curious, she wanted to know if he was working a case.

"Kathy, I really didn't intend to make it known I was in town or working a case. I stumbled onto evidence of a murder, so I've got to bring it to your attention. I'm at El Paso Auto Salvage in Canutillo."

"They're on Interstate Ten towards Las Cruces, I'll be there in twenty, at the most thirty minutes."

"I'll be here."

Kathy arrived forty-five minutes after hanging up her phone. Lee was in the wrecking company garage watching a welder do his magic on an off-road sand buggy. He was adding a cage to the roll bars to protect the passenger seats.

Lee was having a hard time visualizing how a low-slung dune buggy, like this, could be rolled. Then again, who knows where they planned to run this thing.

"Hey, Lee, I'm here. Where's this thing you want me to look at?"

"Oh, hi, Kathy. Good to see you again. Come take a look at this rig first. You ever see anything like this?"

"Sure, lots of people around here have them. This one is cool. Look at that V-8. Bet it'll really zip. I've seen some of those things fifteen feet off the ground flying over a sand dune. Better them than me."

"Different strokes for different folks. I'd kind of like to try it sometime. Come on back. I think you'll find this interesting."

"So, what have you got?"

"Take a look at this Ranger. The brake line's been cut right there. This truck is the one Toby Preston, one of your rookies, drove off the side of Mount Franklin. They called it an accident. You've got a homicide."

"That's going to open a can of worms. I need to get a team out here to see if we can find anything else to add to what you've found. How'd you stumble on this? What are you working on?"

"I'm working a possible connection of Toby and his partner, Eli Sanchez, to that Better Deal safe job you and I were investigating."

"Internal Affairs or Special Investigations should be handling it, Lee. Have you talked to them?"

"Kathy, you know this whole thing got shut down by your boss.

Internal Affairs isn't going to do anything. I'll have to have the whole thing packaged tight and tied with a bow before I can take it to them. Can you look into it personally without taking it to Internal Affairs for a couple of days?" asked Lee.

"The Chief closed the case. He'll explode if he hears I've re-opened without his knowledge," explained Kathy.

"I know it's risky, so it's your call."

"Okay, but not for long, two days, no more."

"I need them," pleaded Lee, "I want to check out Eli, see if I can tie them to the safe. If there's a money trail, I may be able to pin it on them. I may need a court order to look at some bank records. I may be asking for help from you."

"Okay. But you need to move fast, because if you're right, evidence could disappear."

"Better Deal may have pulled some strings to shut us down," said Lee, but they're in our corner this time. Oscar Beasley is the new division vice president."

"Does change things. I thought he was between a rock and a hard place."

"Looks like he's a survivor. I'm out of here. By this time tomorrow I hope to know more about Eli Sanchez than anyone on the planet. I know you've got work to do here, so I'm going to get out of your way. Keep me posted. I'll call you if I come cross anything   interesting."

Chapter 57

Wingham Airport Hotel
El Paso, Texas

LEE SPENT HALF THE NIGHT pulling up everything his computer's multiple search engines could find on Eli Sanchez. No surprises, he grew up in a tough part of town, came from a big family, went to Catholic schools, graduated from Cathedral High School and has an associate degree in criminal justice from El Paso Community College.

Eli's church affiliation was St. Jude's Catholic Church. Lee called and made an appointment to meet his priest. He learned Eli had been an altar boy, got names for two of his friends, found his ex-wife worked as a teacher's aide, they had no children, also he seldom frequents the church these days.

Next stop was El Paso Community College. An associate professor of police science said Eli had been a good student and gave Lee the name of a student known to be his friend.

The friend revealed Eli's past included a few brushes with the law associated with gang affiliations. He'd been arrested twice, no charges stuck, so he had no record. Good thing. A record would have kept him from being a cop.

The buddy knew Eli when Eli wasn't working, he could be

found at Aguilar's Beer Garden on the west side. After lunch, Lee did a swing-by and found Aguilar's had a lot of cars in its lot. Most of them had University of Texas at El Paso window stickers.

Aguilar's reeked of beer and tobacco smoke, which explained why everyone was out on the breezy patio over-looking the Rio Grande harboring a shabby section of Juarez.

A dozen or so guys were seated at the bar. Lee took the open seat next to the space where the serving girls were getting their orders filled and ordered a pilsner tap beer from Mazatlán.

The bars patrons were mostly college kids, about equally mixed Hispanic and Anglo. Lee figured most were cutting classes. There were a few blue-collar guys in the crowd. Probably shift workers or maybe just unemployed.

The tap beer was only a buck, which explained the college kids, there was also a better than average mariachi group with a trumpet player that could be playing in a better league.

From the bartender Lee verified Eli was a regular, loved his beer and spent a fair amount time boozing with his buddies, who were mostly middle-aged guys losing their hair. He also found out Eli chased the college girls with some success.

The bartender pointed across the room, "See the guy at the far table hitting on the two cuties?"

"I see him. What about him?"

"That's Eli, I rest my case."

Lee decided he'd hang around for a while, nursed his beer, chatted up whoever sat the stools beside him and ordered what turned out to be the best jalapeño and cheese nachos this side of Portales. All the while keeping an eye on Eli.

The girls brushed off Eli and took up with some young Anglo dudes who Lee surmised to be frat boys.

Eli decided he was more likely to pick up information if he moved closer to his target. So he cruised around a bit and finally joined some guys about his own age at a big table.

Lee noticed that the seven guys at Eli's table went through six pitchers of beer in the next hour. The volume of the conversation at Eli's table moved up a couple of decibels with each additional pitcher. No one appeared drunk. These guys could hold their beer, a behavior that comes with experience.

Lee suggested to the guys on the stools to each side of his, that they move to a table where the chairs would be more comfortable than the stools at the bar. Each thought that was a good idea. He picked the table next to Eli's noisy companions.

It was by now, well after dark. Eli rose from his chair and announced to his group, "Hey, guys, I got to go to work. You dudes hold down the fort and don't drink all the brews, 'cause I'll want some more tomorrow."

Lee eventually lost his two companions and moved to the empty chair vacated by Eli. When asked who he was and what he did for a living he used a fictitious name and said he was a wine salesman from Houston just passing through. Mostly he just listened and smiled a lot.

It's amazing what you can learn just by listening. No need to ask questions. People tell everything they know in their efforts to be noticed and be interesting. Someone mentioned that Eli was all upset tonight. Someone else said that was because he had someone trying to blackmail him.

When it became obvious there would be no further conversation about Eli, Lee excused himself to hit the John. Afterwards he slipped out the door intending to track down Eli and shadow his activities on the job. He'd be easy enough to find, since Lee was aware of the area he patrolled.

Lee cruised the main avenues around Central Avenue, it wasn't long before he spotted a black and white. This could only be Eli and his partner. Following at a considerable distance, Lee was able to remain unnoticed.

At around eleven thirty, as the patrol car was approaching a motel, it pulled to the curb where a girl in a short skirt was leaning on a street pole. Following a short conversation, the girl turned and walked toward the motel. She went to a door, opened it with a key and left the door open. The patrol car pulled into the driveway in front of the open door.

It didn't take a rocket scientist to figure what was taking place. Eli got out of the black and white, went into the room and closed the door. The cruiser, now driven by his partner, departed. Bingo!

Gotcha! Eli is trading protection for sexual favors. The girl could be a gold mine of "pillow talk" information.

Fifteen minutes later the patrol car reappeared, pulled into the driveway and the driver tapped the horn. A uniformed figure straightening his tie came out the door and got into the black and white. Next came a hasty departure of the vehicle and the girl headed back to her street pole. Wham! Bam! Thank you, Ma'am. That didn't take long.

Giving up the chase, Lee decided to pose as a customer, to interview the girl. He pulled to the curb and was directed to park in front of the same room. In her room, he paid her asking price and a bit more, and then confessed a lack of interest in her offerings. What he wanted was information.

"Look, mister who-ever-you-are, whatever you're doing is none of my business and I wouldn't touch it with a ten-foot pole. Give me one good reason why I should help you."

How about a hundred reasons," said Lee as he handed her a second hundred-dollar bill?

"Not worth it if I'm going to get my brains knocked out."

"What if I promise you that Eli will never know we talked?"

"All right, I've got to be crazy to do this, but I need the money. What is it you want to know?"

She told him that Eli comes by three times per week; he gets a "quickie", seldom tips. In exchange, she works without fear of arrest for solicitation and prostitution. Fair trade. Everybody's happy.

The girl, who looks more like the girl who lives next door in a nice neighborhood than a streetwalker, is a chatterbox and a source of plenty of information. She said Eli likes her, tells her everything. She knows he leads two lives; he gives protection to a lot of girls. He has a lot of money, money over and above his EPPD salary. She also knows someone is blackmailing Eli, that the blackmailer is a heavy hitter. Eli acts tough, but is running scared.

Lee promised the girl Eli would never know she had talked about him behind his back and thanked her with assurances that she had earned her money.

"I know you don't want to hear this, but I owe you something.

You don't have to do this. You are a nice looking woman. You haven't ruined your life, not yet, but you're heading in that direction. There are people out there who'll help you get back on track and have a real life. A decent respectable life."

"It's too late for that. I'm a bad person."

"No you're not. God didn't make any bad people. You've just made some bad choices and maybe you didn't see or know that you had a chance to be good. All of us have to deal with the good and the bad in life. All you have to do is decide being good, like our maker asks us to be, is the best choice."

"I've done the wrong things all my life. I know I'm going straight to hell."

"Bull feathers! You aren't going to hell. Ask God for forgiveness and ask him to show you the way. Now you listen to me. You go find yourself a church, any church. You ask the preacher for help. Tell him that you want to change your life. Do it! You hear me?"

"Yes, Sir, I hear you."

"Promise me you'll go find a church."

"Okay, I promise. You really think I can change?"

"Sure you can."

Back in his car, Lee headed to the Wingham to get some much-needed sleep.

Some people get their lives so screwed up. There's got to be something I can do to get that young lady back on track. First thing in the morning I'm going to call Kathy. I'm going to need her help to put an enabler named Eli Sanchez out of business.

Chapter 58

Wingham Airport Hotel
El Paso, Texas

LEE HAD BREAKFAST in his room. He was on his computer reading the El Paso Times archives account of Toby Preston's accident when his room phone rang.

"Lee Perkins speaking."

"Good morning, Lee! This is Kathy. I thought I'd call and touch base. I had my tech support people check out Toby's Ranger. You were right. It was a homicide. The brake fluid line was deliberately crimped to discharge all the fluid when the brake was operated. The emergency brake had been disabled."

"Any finger prints?" asked Lee.

"No. You told me you were going to check out Eli," said Kathy. "Any surprises?"

"Maybe," said Lee, "Eli had mentioned around that someone was threatening him with blackmail."

"That's interesting, and raises lots of questions. Like, how did you come by this info? What did he do that makes him vulnerable? Who was putting the pressure on Eli? And the zinger, was he paying the black mail," asked Kathy?

"Two sources for the info. The first one was bar talk. I listened to his buddies at Aguilar's, a beer garden, where Eli is a regular. The second came from a streetwalker. I followed Eli on patrol. He's been squeezing the streetwalkers on his streets. One of them told all," said Lee.

"That's going to get him in a lot of trouble. Is he shaking them down for protection?" asked Kathy.

"Sort of. He's taking it out in freebies," said Lee.

Kathy shook her head and said, "What a bum. Any ideas about who might be blackmailing him?" asked Kathy.

"Not yet," said Lee, "but several possibilities come to mind."

"Such as?" asked Kathy.

"It could be someone who knows that Eli was putting the squeeze on the girls, like maybe one of their pimps or even one of the girls. It could also be someone who knows more than we do about how Toby died. It could also be someone who connected the dots and figured Eli for the safe job," said Lee.

"That's a lot of maybes," offered Kathy. "We need to narrow this down."

"Yeah, we do," said Lee. "I'm leaning toward Eli for doing the job on Toby's car. If Eli did the hit on Toby, could be he wanted all the money. Or, consider this, if he did it and someone knows it, they'd have him by the short hairs."

"Did you know Eli used to be a mechanic?" asked Kathy.

"No. Now that's interesting," said Lee. "A mechanic would know how to rig the truck for an accident."

"That's what I was thinking," said Kathy.

"Toby was a gambler. What if he had debts to the wrong people? Gamblers don't put up with customers who don't pay their markers," said Lee. "Maybe it's not blackmail. Could be somebody wanted their money."

"Why would they go after Eli," asked Kathy? "Toby was the gambler."

"Maybe they knew Toby had the money from the safe job. If Toby hadn't paid up, they'd go after Eli," said Lee.

"Makes sense to me," said Kathy. "If they knew or even suspected that Eli and Toby did the safe job, they'd also be thinking Eli did the hit on Toby."

"If they knew he killed Toby," said Lee, "they'd have a policeman in their pocket. He'd have to do anything they wanted him to do. Bad guys would rather own a cop than have the money. Now I'm beginning to see why Eli might be nervous about blackmail."

"Assuming all this is right," mused Kathy, "then all we have to do is find out who's holding Toby's marker."

"Knowing won't prove anything, but it might help us shake something out of a tree," said Lee. "I think I'll take another run at Toby's buddies. See if I can find out where and with whom Toby shuffled cards."

"Oh, I've got something else for you," said Kathy. "It's probably unrelated, but since you're working for Better Deal, you ought to know about it."

"What's that?"

"I was having a chat about a case with the assistant district attorney," said Kathy. "She told me the defendant was asking for a plea bargain. Said he knew about someone trying to hire a hit man. He wanted to trade that info for a reduced sentence."

"So why would that interest me?" asked Lee.

"Because the hit is supposed to be on the guy who owns Better Deal Stores."

"Good Lord! Any idea when this is supposed to happen?" asked Lee. "Did the D.A. allow him to cop a plea?"

"Not yet, they're still working their way through it," said Kathy.

"Kathy, I need to know about this," said Lee. "Can you get more involved?"

"It was my case. You can't get more involved than that, but they usually don't worry about me once the charges are filed. I can talk to my friend in the D.A.'s office and ask her to keep me looped in on the details. I'll relay that info to you," said Kathy.

"Did anyone notify the security people at Better Deal," asked Lee?

"I'm sure they didn't," said Kathy. "Why would they? There's nothing sure about the intel at this point."

"You can't wait on proof positive when something like this is going down," said Lee. "You protect the target and sort it out later.

I've told you that I don't believe in coincidence. Can you see any possible way this rumor could be tied to all this other stuff that's going on?"

"The fog is going to have to lift, because right now I can't see a connection," said Kathy. "Do you?"

"I don't, but I'm going to chase it down, right after I make sure Walter O'Kelly is protected. I'd feel like hell if something happened to that man. Can you get me the name of known associates for this defendant?"

"Unofficially I can," said Kathy. "You need anything else?"

"Is he out on bond?" asked Lee.

"No. No money, no friends with money."

"Okay. If you could question his cellmate, it's possible he might have shared information with him," said Lee.

"I'll call you back about the known associates," said Kathy. "It'll be this afternoon before I can find time to get at his cell buddy."

"Good. Looks like we've got a plan," said Lee. "Oh, there's one other thing. This guy Sanchez, he's a scumbag. After we get the goods on this guy and take him down, I'd appreciate your help to see these street girls have a chance at a real life."

Chapter 59

8:00 a.m. Friday
Wingham Airport Hotel
El Paso, Teas

BEASLEY'S PRIVATE NUMBER rolled over to his answering machine. "Lee here. You wanted a briefing on Friday, but neglected to tell me when and where. Please get back to me ASAP."

Fifteen anxious minutes later the Lee's phone broke the silence. Can you meet me for breakfast in the morning?" asked Oscar.

"Sure. Where." asked Lee?

"Denny's around the corner on Montana. Seven too early?" said Oscar.

"That'll work," said Lee. "See you then."

After ordering breakfast, Oscar was distressed to hear about the possible threat to his bosses' life, but pleased to know Lee was chasing down the rumor.

"Now I have something to share with you," said Oscar. "Yesterday our chief financial officer called to let me know American Express, our money order provider, had reported one hundred and eighty-nine of the two hundred stolen money orders were cashed for the maximum amount on this past Saturday. It's hard to believe, but every one of the banks and retailers had a posted list of the stolen numbers. Eleven attempts to pass the remainder were thwarted and two arrests were made. The FBI is involved, because these transactions were federally insured and took place across state lines in Louisiana."

Lee let the information sink in, then said, "There's no way that could've been pulled off without the assistance and coordination of a large and professional organization."

"I was told the FBI believes it was the organized crime syndicate in New Orleans," said Oscar."

"My speculation." said Lee. "Is that an El Paso poker player got the money orders in settlement for Toby's marker. Our most likely suspect works for EPPD, but the FBI doesn't know what we know. It's going to be awhile before they get around to pointing a finger at Eli. We already know that the building contractor, Fletcher, has ties to the syndicate in New Orleans. I think it's time for me to call some of my buddies with the bureau and bring them up to speed. It occurs to me it may be Fletcher's bunch looking for a hit man for your boss."

"I'd think the FBI would welcome and be interested in any and all possibilities," said Oscar. "Do you have any idea why anyone would want to kill Walter O'Kelly?"

"You work there," said Lee. "I think you're a lot more likely to figure it out than me. Walter O'Kelly might be the person to ask. I know you don't want to do this on a weekend, but I think you better get us an audience with the O'Kelly's, Kathy Smith should be a participant in the conversation."

"I agree," said Oscar.

Oscar called the O'Kelly's. Lee called his FBI friend, Mark Fraga, in Washington, who said he would have the local agent in charge for the El Paso office of the bureau, Luisa Jaramillo, call Lee as soon as possible.

Lee got hold of Kathy Smith, who changed her plans for the weekend. She told Lee she had personally talked with the cellmate of Chester Jackson, the defendant who was trying to trade information in a plea bargain. The roomy had confirmed it was indeed Walter O'Kelly being pegged for a hit.

Chapter 60

Construction Company Office
El Paso, Texas

HARRY FLETCHER WAS STRUGGLING with the selection of an assassin to fulfill the contract on the O'Kelly's. Cost wasn't a problem. Funds were available to hire the best. The problem was the high profile of the targets. Their deaths could trigger a manhunt of epic proportions.

Who would have thought Everett would offer a million dollars from the get go? Sensing more to be had, Harry held out for two million each. Everett had agreed.

He was searching for someone competent, who would do the job for a million or less, leaving three million to split between him and the organization. To distance himself from the hit, Harry was having a second party make the inquiries.

The best professional hit men and women, for the most part, came from Eastern Europe. Each had a specialty with garrotes, knives, pistols and/or sniper rifles, and came at extremely high prices. These people seldom get caught, but none looked right for the job.

Then there were those from Mexico and Guatemala who would sneak into the country and happily cut a throat for as little as a few hundred dollars. The opportunity to make the extra profit was tempting, but he ruled them out, because they were unpredictable and left trails too easily followed. He decided he needed someone who knew how to make a murder appear an accident.

Another possibility crossed his mind. *Why not leverage Eli Sanchez to do the job.* At first he'd discounted the option, because Eli wasn't likely to be a willing participant. There were, however, advantages that appealed to Harry. Eli could be compelled to do whatever Harry wanted. Secondly, Eli had no history as an assassin and wasn't likely to be considered a suspect. *Who would ever suspect a cop?*

One downside to using Eli was, if he got caught, the string could lead the bloodhounds right back to Harry. But then, only two of Harry's men could tie Eli to Harry. Ideally, he'd rather distance himself from the hit by using someone he'd never met, but there are exceptions to all rules. Harry decided to make a proposition to Eli. He'd offer him five hundred thousand dollars to do the job and leave it to him to decide how. A cop should know what works and what doesn't. Let him come up with his own plan and work out the details. Harry believed that Eli would be more careful than anyone else, because cops know what happens when an officer gets sent to the pen.

Harry dialed Eli's number.

"Hello, this is Eli."

"It's me. We need to talk."

Eli recognized the voice. "What do you want now," asked Eli? "I don't think we have anything to discuss."

"And I think you don't have much choice. We need to meet tonight?"

"Why?"

"I'll tell you when I see you. Memorial Park Library, eleven p.m."

Chapter 61

Five-Fifty p.m., Saturday
O'Kelly Castle
River Oaks
Dallas, Texas

THREE CARS ARRIVED near simultaneously, in front of the O'Kelly home in Dallas. First came Oscar Beasley and Lee Perkins, followed by detective Kathy Smith, who came alone. Next was a black Tahoe containing the FBI's top ranking official on the U.S. border, Luisa Jaramillo. All four reached the front door at the same time.

Walter O'Kelly opened the door. "Welcome to our home. I haven't had the pleasure of meeting either of you ladies, but I have a feeling Lee is about to make that happen. I understand all of you've come from El Paso."

"We have come from the pass in the north," said Lee, "and you're right. I get to introduce these two lovely ladies. The lady to your right is, Luisa Jaramillo, special agent in charge for the FBI in El Paso. With her is Kathy Smith, an investigator with the El Paso Police Department."

"I'm pleased to make your acquaintance," said Walter. "And surprised you have come so far to meet us and given up your personal time on a weekend. This meeting must be of great importance.

It's a beautiful day, so we've arranged chairs on the back porch. Oscar, you said we're in some kind of danger. We're anxious to know what this is all about."

"Mr. O'Kelly, Helen will want to be part of this. We've got a lot to cover, so we probably ought to get started," said Oscar,

"Let's move out to the veranda," said Walter. "Please follow me down this hall. If you need a restroom, there's one through this door on the right and another off the porch."

O'Kelly Castle, veranda

"Walter pointed, "We can sit around this table. That door is a restroom. If you need something cold and wet, the drinks are on the serving cart next to the wall, blue glasses are sweet tea, the yellow are unsweetened, clear glasses are lemonade, ice is in the bucket, the coffee is decaf. Helen, come greet and meet our guests. These lovely ladies are Luisa Jaramillo with the FBI and Kathy Smith, with the El Paso police department. You know Lee and Oscar."

"Nice to meet you ladies," said Helen as she shook a hand from each, "and to see you gentlemen again. Walter, why don't you help them with their drinks?"

"I'll do that," said Walter. "Let's get our drinks and move to the table? Oscar seems anxious to start this meeting."

When everyone was seated, Oscar said, "Thank you, Walter, and thank you, Helen, for seeing us on short notice. There's a lot to cover. This meeting was actually initiated, not by me, by Lee Perkins. He asked I pull it together, so I'm going to ask Lee to lead the discussion."

Lee stood and looked pensively around the table. "Each of us has information the others don't have. Some of it's time sensitive, volatile and has become dangerous to the O'Kelly's. It's going to require a coordinated response. I'm going to begin by asking Kathy to bring us up to date on a homicide that's connected to the burglary at number nine."

"Good, Lord!" exclaimed Helen. "Who's been murdered?"

"Helen," said Walter, "Kathy is about to tell us."

Kathy rose as Lee took his seat. "The burglary of your El Paso store has escalated and become a full-blown homicide investigation involving federal authorities. It appears to be connected to a conspiracy targeting both you and Mrs. O'Kelly for death by assassination. We've double-verified our information and feel it to be factual.

Helen was suddenly wide-eyed and scared. She moved her chair closer to Walter and asked, "Who in the world would want to kill us?" she asked.

"Actually, that's a question we want to ask you, but first, we think you need to know some of the other things we've discovered. I doubt that it made the Dallas papers, but one of the two police responders to the break-in at your Central store drove off the side of El Paso's Scenic Drive two weeks ago. We had no reason to connect that event to the burglary, so his death was initially ruled a suicide.

A couple of days ago, Lee was running down a lead in his continuing investigation of the burglary. On a hunch that the victim might have been a perpetrator, Lee decided to check the vehicle he was driving. He discovered the vehicle's brakes had been deliberately disabled, the emergency brake had been disconnected and the brake fluid line had been crimped and cracked to lose all the fluid when the brakes were applied."

Lee rose and said, "Thank you Kathy. The victim, Toby Preston and his partner, Eli Sanchez, were the officers who got the call to respond to the scene at your burglary. They were on patrol in the neighborhood. I have a theory they may have come onto the scene before they got the call to respond. The Preston murder and other information I've uncovered about both these policemen is adding validity to my theory.

I visited with friends and neighbors to this guy Preston. Several people said he was addicted to gambling. Recently, he got into a high-stakes poker game and owed a considerable debt to a gambler named Harry Fletcher. I got a friend to run Fletcher's name through the FBI database and found Fletcher has ties to organized crime in New Orleans.

In the meantime, some other events have been under investigation by the FBI. Luisa is the authority on this situation, so I'm going to ask her to explain how and why her agency became involved."

Luisa picked up some documents and got up to speak. "The FBI is involved because a federal law appears to have been broken. It's illegal to transport a stolen money order across state lines and cash them in another state. This past week, all two hundred blank money orders stolen from your Central Avenue store were either cashed or attempts were made to cash them, in the state of Louisiana. The FBI believes, but can't yet prove, this was an activity planned, organized and executed by organized crime.

When Lee let us know about Toby's gambling debt to Harry Fletcher it hit a hot button with me. Harry Fletcher has long been on our watch list in El Paso, mostly because he has a history tying him to organized crime figures in Louisiana. Up to now, we haven't been able to pin anything directly on Fletcher. He's too smart and careful. We think we're going to nail him for this caper. At this point, everything is circumstantial and not enough to get a prosecution. But we're hoping to be able to establish a proven tie between the stolen money orders and Toby Preston's gambling debt. Or, better yet, prove that Fletcher arranged to have the checks cashed. We're working on both possibilities." Luisa took her seat.

Lee, back on his feet, retook the floor. "There's another piece to this puzzle. We're wondering how Toby's partner, Eli Sanchez may fit into this scenario? If Toby took the money orders from the safe, his partner had to be involved. Kathy and I have been using this theory to look more closely at Eli."

"Have you found out anything?" asked Walter.

"Not much," said Lee. "But it's led to a couple of theories. We haven't found any indication that Eli has come into any extra money. So, we're likely to find if he's stashed money in a safety deposit box or elsewhere. We could use some FBI help, Luisa, to get this accomplished before Sanchez becomes aware he's being investigated."

"Good idea. Happy to do that," said Luisa.

"This brings us," said Lee, "up to why we're here today and concerned about a possible attempt on your lives. In the course of investigating and following Sanchez, I picked up rumors that someone was looking for a hit man to fill a contract. Nothing, however, indicating it was on your lives.

About the same time, Kathy heard from the District Attorney's office that a man she'd arrested was trying to plea bargain information that someone was recruiting to make a hit on you folks in exchange for a reduced sentence. We're now concerned that it may be organized crime that's doing the recruiting. What we don't have, is any idea who or why anyone would be targeting you for a hit.

Our purpose here today is several fold: first, we wanted to let you know this is going on and offer to arrange for personal protection for you. Second, we need for you to point us toward anyone who might wish you harm. Frankly, we can't see a connection between the events on Central Avenue and this activity, though I'm satisfied it's there."

"Walter," said Helen with tears in her eyes, "you have to be thinking what I'm thinking. Should we tell them?"

Walter moved closer to take Helen's hand. "Helen, I'm inclined to share everything we know, but once we do, events are going to be out of our control. I'll honor and support your wishes. What do you want me to do?"

Helen was now crying. "This is awful. It's the most painful decision we've ever had to make, but I agree with you. I don't think we have a choice. Go ahead and tell them."

Walter appeared lost in thought and finally spoke, "I'm wondering where to start. I need to give you a little background. We have two sons. One is considerably older than his brother, who was a surprise born when we were near middle age."

"The older boy Everett was an achiever who gave us every reason to be proud. He was good-looking, academically gifted, very athletic and a natural leader. Everett went to public schools, graduated second in his class in high school, lettered in three sports, and was an eagle scout and president of three clubs, including the national honor society. He was a national merit scholarship finalist and was accepted at both Yale and Harvard."

"He opted to attend Harvard and did well there. He gave up football, track and baseball, but developed an interest in tennis and soccer. He excelled at these sports, still plays tennis and is a par golfer."

"After graduating from Harvard, he went to Cornell University in New York, where he received an MBA degree with focus on retail marketing. Largely at my urging, because I am personally frustrated at my own lack of expertise in dealing with legal interface with business, Everett got a law degree from Northwestern in Chicago."

"When he graduated from law school he married a lovely young lady from a wonderful family. They provided us with four precious grandchildren, including a set of paternal twins. For all appearances, they are the perfect storybook family."

"I failed to mention that along with all the academics, I've made sure that Everett was indoctrinated within the fundamentals of the grocery business. Summers and holidays he worked with the best of our store people. Everett knows, from hands on experience, how every department works. He could easily step in and replace any department manager, store manager, bookkeeper or even a meat cutter without missing a heartbeat."

"Currently Everett serves as a vice president and legal counsel to the board of the company. Over time I gave him an increasingly greater voice in the direction of the business. His performance, though sometimes brilliant, revealed a lack of empathy for others, a management style of playing favorites, and an obvious penchant toward making decidedly self-serving decisions."

"The bottom line is, academically, Everett is much better prepared to run our firm than I am, but some important ingredient isn't there. It took me too long to see it, but eventually I did see it wasn't going to work. It was a huge personal disappointment and cared with it a sense of personal failure, because every man wants to pass something on to his progeny. However, Helen and I both feel our obligations to the employees who made our company successful overrides our hopes for our children. We feel they deserve the best possible leadership to assure the continued success of the company."

"Recently I sat down with Everett and told him he wouldn't be my replacement, and shared he's not the right person for the job; that he needs to plan to do something else with his life. He didn't take it well. I expected disappointment. I wasn't prepared for the unbridled anger or the hate I saw in his eyes. He told me I would be sorry and made some threats I hoped he didn't mean."

"We're dumbfounded to have to consider the possibility that Everett would even think about having us killed, but he is well aware that in the event of our passing, the terms of our will would immediately hand him the total control of the business."

"In a nutshell, as inconceivable as it may seem, Everett is the one and only individual who might in any way have cause to hurt us or who would benefit from our demise."

Lee got back on his feet. "Thank you, Walter. Your information is helpful because it does sound like it could be somehow connected to the search for an assassin. Now it behooves us to put some plans in place to assure positive outcomes."

"Lee," said Helen, "promise me you won't let anybody hurt my boy."

"Mrs. O'Kelly, it's possible Everett and that contract aren't even connected. We're not going to jump to any conclusions. It's by knowing it might be connected that we can better prevent it from happening and reduces the possibility of anything happening to Everett. You've done the right thing. Now we've got to sort out what to do next."

Turning to the rest of the group, Lee went on, "In order to avoid duplication of effort, I think each of us should give an indication of the tactical issues they intend to pursue. Luisa, what is your office going to do with regard to the money orders?"

"To be honest, we've wasted some time by trying to work backwards from the two arrests in Louisiana. That's proven to be a dead end," said Luisa. "Your mention of possible ties to Harry Fletcher opens up new avenues of pursuit. We're well acquainted with, Mr. Fletcher. He and an associate of his, a Mr. Clark Davies, have been on our watch list for some time."

Walter reacted to this comment, "Excuse me, Luisa. Did you say, Clark Davies?"

"I did. He's a person of interest because of his business connections to Harry Fletcher. Do you know him?"

"Sort of, we knew his son Chuck when he was a youngster. His parents were and are our next-door neighbors. When he was growing up, Chuck was frequently in our home. On numerous occasions he was an over-night guest of our son.

Chuck Davies and Everett were friends through their junior high and high school years. We've never had any reason to think anything but the best of Chuck Davies. However, we've had no association with Chuck for a number of years. Nor can I recall Everett having mentioned Chuck for a long time."

Luisa Jaramillo interrupted to comment, "The Davies Family is a much respected family here in Dallas. Few people know that Maria Davies is the daughter of Mickey De Angelino, who we know to be involved in drugs, prostitution and other illegal undertakings from New Orleans to El Paso. We've been unsuccessful in tying the Davies to De Angelino's organization. We believe, however, that it's the source of their income."

"I find this hard to believe," said Walter. "The Davies are members of Coronado Country Club, Clark Davies is active in community affairs and a generous giver to many needy projects. His wife, Maria, is a member of Helen's bridge club. I had always heard that Clark made his money in real estate," said Luisa.

"That's quite right," said Luisa. "The Davies own real estate all over the State of Texas. However, their more seamy investments are held through a second party shell company, a construction company, which owns all the porn shops, strip clubs and liquor store properties. The construction company is a wholly owned subsidiary owned by Davies Investments, LLC."

She continued, "I now believe that Lee is right in his suspicions that Eli Sanchez provided the blank money orders to Harry Fletcher. I'll be happy to commit FBI resources and support to further investigation of Sanchez."

"Would that include checking all area banks to see if Eli has a safety deposit box in his name? Perhaps even getting court orders to open a box, if one is found," asked Lee?

"We'll be happy to do that," said Luisa.

"That would be better than doing it through EPPD, because we'd rather not have this being investigated by their Internal Affairs Department, at least, not yet. The most immediate and pressing issue is how do we best protect the O'Kelly's? Any ideas?"

Mr. O'Kelly suggested, "Lee, why don't you leave that to us? We have a top-flight security department headed up by a former Navy Seal, Barney Oden. He has some good people and can add some more."

"Mr. O'Kelly, if you and Helen are comfortable with that, I'm fine with it," said Lee. "Now that we know that Everett is a loose cannon, I'm thinking we need to have someone keeping track of him. Kathy, can you commit some resources to shadowing his activities?"

"I can and will," said Kathy.

"That leaves me," said Lee. "I haven't shared this, but I'm pretty sure the blackmail threat to Eli is coming from Harry Fletcher. I think Harry is trying to force Eli to do the hit on the O'Kelly's. I can't watch both Eli and Fletcher. I still have good contacts in the Texas Rangers. I'm going to ask them if they will assign a Ranger to give us additional help."

Walter stood and addressed the group. "Helen and I want to thank you for what you do and wish you good luck with these various assignments. We hope you get all of these problems resolved without injury to any of you or your people."

Chapter 62

New Orleans
Friday

THE NEWSPAPER HEADLINES and TV talking points on Friday were about events that occurred the previous Saturday. How, in a highly coordinated act of daring, scores of criminals in Louisiana had violated federal law when they passed near two hundred bogus American Express money orders, victimizing communities and organizations across the state. The checks were stolen from an El Paso supermarket eight weeks ago. A local spokesperson for the Federal Bureau of Investigation was reported to have said this event was evidence of the growing problem with organized crime in Louisiana.

The scope of the act was not apparent until the checks failed to clear the banks this week. The detailed planning, coordination and successful execution of the crime was unprecedented in Louisiana history. Public interest in the event created a media sensation.

Eight a.m.
El Paso

The previous night had been an endless and exhaustive series of heated domestic altercations, bar fights and visits to the scenes of unauthorized entries. Police Sergeant Eli Sanchez had never been so glad to see the end of his shift. He was, in fact, so totally drag assed he choose to skip all his usual after work mischief and went directly to his apartment, where he had languished under a long hot shower, and was now seated alone at the kitchen table in his apartment. He'd made a fresh pot of coffee, unfolded the Friday morning paper and had just finished reading its lead articles:

The El Paso Police Department has been unexpectedly overrun with phone inquiries, out-of-town reporters and journalists, some with cameramen in tow, all wanting background information and details about the theft of the blank money orders taken from the Better Deal Supermarket on Central Avenue.

The El Paso Times and Herald Post newspapers reported Thursday newsprint sales were the first to exceed the Kennedy assassination.

Same as yesterday! Harry Fletcher ought to be happy. He's been repaid Toby Preston's gambling debt several times over. It'd be nice if this was the end of it, more likely it's just the beginning for me.

When Eli and Toby took the money it had seemed safe and simple. They'd planned to sit on their loot until things cooled down. *Boy, were we ever wrong. Murphy's Law: What can go wrong will and did.* It hardly required a rocket scientist to see that all the unwanted attention being given to the money order theft had the potential to bring renewed focus upon the burglary and raise the odds that his involvement might be discovered. *Damn Harry Fletcher and damn Toby Preston!*

Now on top of it all, he was going to be a hit man for Fletcher. No choice about it, but at least Fletcher is going to pay him well. *Maybe it'll work out.*

Eli had two weeks in which to come up with a plan to fulfill the contract. Harry told Eli to make sure it was a foolproof plan. *As if there was such a thing.*

Eli shivered. It wasn't the time pressure. What gave him the jitters was the fear of getting caught. He'd heard what happens to cops who get sent to prison.

His half million-dollar share of the contract fee looked good, felt good. In fact, he'd been fantasizing about how he'd spend the money. But no amount of money was worth taking a risk that could put him in prison. Being an ex-policeman in prison was far worse than being dead. *This caper had to be done right. Failure wasn't an option.*

Eli took a hard look at the realities of his situation. He could see that he had to get a grip on his anxieties, think positive and come up with a plan. He considered and rejected several scenarios.

He ruled out an auto accident as being too similar to Toby's demise and possibly leading back to him. He gave some thought to making a break and enter scenario end in a double homicide and also weighed the possibility of staging a double suicide.

In the end, the only way he could see to make two deaths appear to be accidental was to have a fire, a crime scene-obliterating whopper of a fire. It was no big deal to ignite a fire. There was, however, one tricky detail. Every now and then some lucky dude survived a fire, an unacceptable outcome for this assignment.

The only way to know for certain that the O'Kelly's would perish in a fire would be to hasten their departure to never, never land before the fire was ignited. Simply put, he would have to execute the targets before he set the fire. He decided to name his plan, "Snuff and Puff."

In Eli's experience as a policeman, he had seen that death by poisoning was the simplest, cleanest way to do a murder. No risk of messy blood leaving traces on hands or clothes, no brute force or screams from the victims, and, happily, the most difficult to pin on a perpetrator. He would use poison to assure they were dead before he caused a fire.

His planned sequence of events was to first choose a poison, settle on how to acquire it, then to determine how to best introduce it into the victims' bodies. Then he would have to resolve how to cause a spontaneous fire that would appear accidental and obliterate any evidence pointing to a murder.

At first blush, the plan seemed unnecessarily complicated. However, Eli had seen all of these components carried out successfully in the past. He was confident he could make it happen.

With the outline of his over-all plan firmly in place, Eli began to fill in the blank details. Step one was to make himself an expert in the knowledge and use of poisons.

He spent most of a full day using his computer to study poisons, where they may be found, their toxicity, their trace residue and how they may be administered. He was amazed that the information available on the Internet was virtual direction for how to commit a murder.

He concluded that it was a wonder that murder by poison was not in greater use. Perhaps it was. And was so successful that we weren't aware it was happening.

Chapter 63

Love Field
Dallas, Texas

AFTER THE DALLAS MEETING Luisa Jaramillo hurried to catch a flight to El Paso. Upon arrival, she'd gone directly to her office located in the Federal Building on South Mesa Hills Drive, where she was scheduled to lead an FBI community outreach program to especially qualified and selected citizens of El Paso. The FBI uses these outreach programs to connect their local offices with the communities where they're located. The work was volunteer time donated by FBI personnel.

Although her agenda for this day was exceptionally full, she was also determined to get people assigned, organized and involved in keeping her commitment to aggressively pursue the possibility that Eli Sanchez might have a safe deposit box in a bank or credit union in El Paso or a nearby town or city.

She withdrew two of her top agents from their assigned roles in the Citizens' Academy and redirected their focus to this new assignment. Most of their work would initially be done by phone. If the two-man team got a hit and found Eli had rented a safe deposit box at a specific banking location, it would immediately get more complicated.

Jaramillo wanted to know the date the box was rented, who had access to the box, when it had been accessed and by whom. She also wanted to know the contents of the box, specifically if it contained any of the contents stolen from the safe at the Better Deal store on Central Avenue.

Getting permission to view the contents of an individual's safe deposit box in Texas is no easy assignment. There must first be filed in a district court, a petition to gain access to the box. A district judge may then choose to allow or to deny issuing a court order directing the officials of the institution owning the safe deposit box to allow examination of the contents of the box.

Should a court order to examine a safe deposit box be issued, opening the box may only be done in the presence of an officer of the institution. It becomes even more difficult and complicated if it is deemed necessary to acquire the contents of the box for use as evidence.

Any documents to be removed from a safe deposit box must be copied by an officer of the institution and those copies held by the institution a minimum of four years from the date of their removal. Any contents other than documents must be signed for by a person the judge deems sufficiently qualified to be accountable.

It was well known to the FBI, that banking officials are in most instances, less than enthusiastic at opportunities to be part of these happy occasions. FBI Agents don't really give a hoot whether banking officials like or dislike having to open a box. District judges, on the other hand, can be "show stoppers," so the agents bend over backwards to keep a smile on a Judge's face.

There were just over two hundred and seventy-one banks in El Paso and about a quarter that many credit unions. All but one of these institutions provided an opportunity to rent safe deposit boxes. On the third day of phone calls, the team got a hit. Eli Sanchez was renting a safe deposit box at the Stagecoach Bank on North Mesa Street.

The drafting of the petition to grant a court order to examine the contents of Eli's safe deposit box fell to the female member of the team. Like many FBI agents, she had a law degree. Hers was earned in Texas. She was familiar with Texas law, so she drafted the petition.

Ordinarily Judges do not drop all other of their agenda to immediately respond to requests for court orders. However, it'd been made abundantly clear to the team by Luisa Jaramillo, that she wanted results.

After drawing straws to see who faced the Judge, the agent who drafted the petition went down the hall of the Justice Building to see if she could grease the wheels of justice. She was successful once she got past the Judge's over-protective court secretary and talked with the judge.

Judge Shirley Snider had dealt with this FBI Agent on many occasions, liked her, and admired a woman who could succeed in what is obviously a man's domain. So she instructed her secretary to issue the court order to open the box and signed it upon completion.

With Judge Snider's court order in hand, the two agents departed for the Stagecoach Bank. After finding an accommodating bank officer, they were able to get a look at the contents of Eli's very full safe deposit box.

Not choosing to look over their shoulder as required by law, the bank official retreated to his desk with instructions that the team should signal him on completion of their examination of the contents of the box. It was quickly apparent there was nothing incriminating within the box. Nevertheless, all documents were examined.

Returning to their office in the Justice Building they resumed and completed their calls to the list of El Paso institutions. It seemed timely to report their limited success or, more accurately, their complete lack thereof, to Luisa Jaramillo.

Undaunted, Luisa instructed them to contact the banking institutions in all surrounding communities, including those in Southern New Mexico. On the third day of this effort, they got a hit at The Farmers and Cowhands Bank in Las Cruces, New Mexico.

Since New Mexico laws with respect to access to safe deposit boxes differ slightly from those in Texas, a call was made to an agent with the Albuquerque office of the bureau. His information provided the modest changes needed for a petition to the District Judge in Las Cruces.

The initial rental date for the safe deposit box in Las Cruces was two days following the date of the burglary of the safe at the Better Deal store in El Paso. It had been accessed two times following the first day of rental. On both these occasions, the renter and only person authorized to access the box, Eli Sanchez, had opened the box.

Getting admission to the contents, however, proved to be far more difficult than in Texas. The president of the Las Cruces bank was old school and didn't want the word to get around that they had under any circumstances permitted the invasion of a customer's privacy. A call from District Judge Able Montoya got an assurance of compliance after a threat of jail time.

An inventory of the contents of the safe deposit box included: nineteen thousand four hundred and ninety-seven dollars and two cents in checks, mostly personal checks payable to Better Deal, and a number of payroll checks endorsed by the payees. Also contained therein were eighteen thousand and thirty-one dollars in cash and sixty cents in coins. The last item of note was a double thickness number six brown paper bag containing a pound and a half of assorted old coins.

When the inventory was presented to Luisa, it was accompanied by a question. "Do you want us to get a court order to confiscate the contents of the safe deposit box?"

After a few moments of consideration, Special Agent, Luisa Jaramillo, replied, "No, I think not. Maybe we can catch a bigger fish if we don't reveal we're on to him. However, I want both of you to stay on this. Someone needs to be at that bank during all open hours."

"If Eli shows up and opens the box, arrest him. And I suggest you get the court order, but don't use it. It'll be helpful to have a court order available, because we'll eventually want to have the contents of the box for evidence."

Luisa made a call to Lee Perkins. "Lee, we found the safe deposit box in the Farmers and Cowhands Bank in Las Cruces. I have a list of the contents of the box. I'll fax it to you. It'd be helpful if you can provide me with a list of what was taken from the store's safe, so I can make comparisons."

"Good job!" said Lee. "I'll fax you the list. Have you arrested Sanchez?"

"No," said Luisa, "I want to talk with you, Oscar and Kathy about that. Could you set up a meeting?"

"Sure," said Lee. "May I ask what you've got in mind?"

"I want to catch some bigger fish. If we let the contract unfold," said Luisa, "we have a possibility of tying it to Harry Fletcher. The FBI wants that guy badly. He's associated with half the criminal activity in El Paso County. We might even get a shot at the Davies in Dallas."

"A good idea. I'll make some calls and get back to you."

When Luisa received the inventory of the safe's contents she compared it to the inventory of Eli's safe deposit box. The box was missing twenty-five thousand dollars of the cash and two bundles of the blank money orders. Luisa would love to question Eli about the missing items, but that would have to wait.

Chapter 64

Better Deal Supers
El Paso, Texas

IN HIS NEW ASSIGNMENT as Division Vice President of the West Texas Division of Better Deal Supermarkets, Oscar Beasley, reported to Executive Vice President, Charles Peterson. Until this past year when Alexis Shlanta retired, the four division heads reported to a vice president of store operations.

Peterson had made a bold decision to eliminate an expensive layer of management by making each of his divisions near autonomous entities. He had eliminated the role of operations vice president. Peterson's thinking was that a lean and mean management team with less operating expense would help to maintain a competitive advantage over their competitors.

His plan was to gradually redesign the job descriptions for these positions to make them totally autonomous divisions, each with its own president. In so doing, the decision-making would move closer to the customers they served.

The role of operations VP had largely served to assure that the stores were operated in a similar manner, a sort of "compliance policeman." Peterson called this "cookie cutter" management wherein all the stores looked and operated pretty much the same way.

To an outsider looking in, this different way of doing business might appear to be operational anarchy, with everyone doing his or her own thing. To Peterson it made perfect sense. Every customer would be served by a store that was designed to be uniquely their own, orchestrated to fit their particular wants and needs.

This was the new environment into which Oscar Beasley was newly promoted. He was suddenly almost in business for himself. He could re-invent his stores to make them fit the ethnic mix they served, make them fit the architectural preferences of their area, carry the items customers wanted to buy.

In their first meeting, Peterson had covered all the details of the division VP job description and went on to explain his vision for what he wanted Beasley to accomplish. It was obvious to Beasley that working with Mr. Peterson was going to be a breath-taking experience. Peterson was excited about what he was doing and Beasley found this contagious.

Beasley's first marching orders were to make it a priority to work with the store planning and marketing departments to finalize the plans for a new facility on Central Avenue. Much of the initial planning had already been accomplished, but Beasley would have the opportunity to "tweak" and modify these plans, largely as he saw fit.

The only caveat being a caution not to make so many changes as to significantly delay the project. This warning was hardly necessary because Beasley, more than perhaps anyone else, was very aware of the gross inadequacies of the present facilities.

In the weeks that followed their first meeting, there were many phone calls, as Peterson had made himself available for advice and counsel. Beasley was gaining confidence quickly and had exceeded Peterson' expectations.

In a conversation with Walter O'Kelly, Peterson had shared that he now considered Beasley their best division head and complimented O'Kelly on his good judgment in promoting Beasley.

Progress on the new store on Central moved ahead at a rapid

pace. Plans were quickly finalized and in an amazing feat of construction, a one hundred and twenty thousand square foot building had been completed in one hundred and twenty days. Fixtures were being put in place and merchandise was being delivered to "set" the store.

The new building had been constructed directly behind the old building, so the plans included the gutting and demolition of the existing store. That would be accomplished in four days, during which no business would be conducted.

As illogical as the timeline may seem, the plan was to literally dump all the merchandise from the old store into plastic totes and transport the goods to other stores and in a single day. On the following day all of the old store's fixtures would be removed. The third day they'd use bulldozers to tear down the old building and haul it to a dump. The location formerly occupied by the old store building would be paved for the new store's parking lot on the fourth day. A grand opening of the new store would take place the following day.

The planning and logistics for this project were extensive and would be over-seen personally by Oscar Beasley. It would require a small army and perfect coordination.

When asked why the big rush? Oscar's explanation was simple, "The profits lost from closing a facility that generates sales of near two million dollars a week more than justify the extra expense and planning to re-open it quickly."

Chapter 65

Tularosa, New Mexico

CLAIRE SULLIVAN HAD ALWAYS believed she would be a homemaker, a wife and a mom. It never occurred to her she might someday have to be the provider for her family. Even though she had earned a high school diploma, she was ill prepared to be the bread-earner following the tragic death of her husband. She didn't know how to type or use a computer and had no work experience other than having been a homemaker.

Despite the holes in her education, she was smart, tenacious and determined. These qualities and a pleasant disposition eventually landed a job for her in Tularosa, New Mexico. The starting wage was only slightly more than minimum wage. So she and her children had to continue to live with her parents in Alamogordo until her earnings improved.

Transportation was a problem. She found she didn't know enough about cars to keep their old clunker running. With no work history or credit rating she couldn't buy another car. The problem was solved when her father co-signed a note to help her buy a better car.

Claire felt guilty for having to impose upon her parents, but she had no choice. She gave most of the money she made to her parents to help them off-set the burden of three added members to their household, keeping only enough to pay for gasoline and a car payment.

She applied for and received food stamps and a modest amount of financial assistance from state welfare, which she also gave to her Mom. She owed money for the cost of Tim's funeral and had no money to make the payments.

She realized without her parent's help, she would be living on the streets, homeless, and her children would be in foster homes. She thanked God for his blessings every day.

After less time than she believed possible, she received a generous raise in pay for her work as a file clerk at the abstract company in Tularosa. The raise just about equaled the cost of day care for the children.

She became friends with Jane Day, the daughter of a New Mexico State Representative, who held the franchise to sell the racing program magazine featuring the schedules for thoroughbred and quarter horse races at the Ruidoso Downs Race Track at Ruidoso Downs, New Mexico.

Jane worked for her Dad selling programs at the track on weekends. She persuaded him to hire Claire to work for him as well. The work paid well and Claire did it in addition to her job at the abstract company.

The combined workweek and weekend job incomes was enough to allow Claire to rent an apartment in Tularosa after she had saved enough money to pay her first month's rent and deposits.

The downside to this arrangement was Claire would have practically no time to spend with her two children. The children would have to spend their day in childcare.

She felt that she had already imposed upon her parents for too long. When she saved what she needed, she and her children moved into an apartment in Tularosa.

Claire had not yet found a new church home. The population of Tularosa was predominantly Hispanic Catholic. She found them to be lovely people. She was twice invited and twice attended Catholic services. However, she did not go back.

Her friend Jane, a Methodist, asked her to consider attending church with her in Alamogordo. She was barely getting by financially and decided they could not afford the additional travel costs. If she went to church, it would be in Tularosa or not at all.

The truth was Claire was not motivated to get back in church. She was disappointed with her church and its members for the way they treated Tim and blamed them for his death.

For most people, church was a twice a week activity. Claire's church and family life had always been as one, the center of her activities. Now she had lost her husband and felt she had lost her church as well.

Her friend Jane saw that Claire had no life outside of her work and her children. She encouraged her to begin going out with some of the young men they were meeting at Ruidoso Downs.

Jane and Claire were both good-looking women. Each of them had opportunities to date and have a good time. Jane had been taking advantage of these offers, and led a very active social life.

Claire, on the other hand, declined these attentions and kept her focus on being a good Mom. She couldn't find closure for Tim Sullivan's death and considered herself still in mourning.

She didn't want her children to forget their Father, so she spoke about him often, reminding them what a kind, generous and caring man he had been and how he had loved his family. She told them how hard he worked and how he loved and served God. She told them his spirit would be with them always.

It disturbed Claire greatly that Tim's life had ended under a black cloud of unresolved charges of dishonest behavior. She yearned and prayed for the day when Tim would be exonerated of these unjust allegations.

Chapter 66

IN RECENT WEEKS, Eli Sanchez had been working an average of about ten hours a week of overtime as a patrol officer. Most of the time he was happy to have the additional income. Not so this week. He was under the gun to complete the plan for the demise of the O'Kelly's.

He needed every spare minute to research and select a poison to do the job. It was difficult to select the one best suited. He had two criteria, fast acting and very lethal.

In addition to being an efficient killing agent, he wanted one difficult to detect. This wasn't absolutely necessary, since his plan was to dispose of the bodies using fire.

Toxicologists have a way of rating a poison's lethality called LD-50, or 50% lethal dose – the amount on average that kills half of the targeted subject animal or person. Because no government would permit testing on humans, the ratings were determined in tests using lab animals.

Human metabolism works differently from animals, so tests for effectiveness in humans included, of necessity, a certain amount of guesswork. The guesswork combined with a minute sample of actual historical experience from situations where it was known a particular poisonous agent had been employed, provided some insight into the effectiveness of certain poisons.

There are three sources for poisons: from animals, others from plants and those that have been formulated in laboratories. Eli systematically conducted his research by category, beginning with poisons derived from animals.

One of the most potent land animal poisons was thought to be from the Inland Taipan, a central Australian snake. Using a 150-pound subject human, the lethal dose, or LD-50, of this poison was calculated to be two milligrams, about the weight of five dandelion seeds.

The two most toxic poisons that can be acquired from marine animals come from the hook-nosed sea snake and the box jellyfish. Both of these venoms are treatable, if one is lucky enough to have the antidote on hand. If you are bitten by a blue-nosed octopus or eat too much inexpertly prepared puffer fish, no antidote can save you.

Absolutely the most poisonous animal substance is batrachotoxin, which comes from the poison arrow frog from South America. As little as the weight of two grains of table salt will turn off your lights for good.

Ricin, which comes from castor beans, causes your arteries to clog up. Injected or inhaled, a quantity the size of a pinhead will kill you. At the moment, there is no known antidote.

One of the most common and easiest to acquire poisons is the botulin toxin that causes botulism, which is encountered in contaminated food such as home-canned foods. Botulin is tasteless and odorless. You probably wouldn't know you had consumed the LD-50 of 0.4 billionth of a gram per kilogram of body weight before paralysis sets in.

There are also some really chilling lab produced toxins. Take dimethyl mercury, for instance. A drop of this stuff can be readily absorbed through the skin, even if you were wearing latex gloves. It would take awhile, but you are good as dead. This one was tough to beat for lethality.

Then there were the nerve gases, like Sarin, Soman and VX. These babies can kill you in sixty seconds or less.

Next, he got to polonium. This one was extra potent: with an LD-50 of 10 to 50 billionths of a gram per kilogram of body weight, one vaporized gram of this stuff can kill nearly 1.5 million people.

Finally, he considered the least detectable of all poisons, deuterium oxide, aka heavy water, which he ruled out because it was almost impossible to acquire and required too much of it to do its' job.

After considering these and a multitude of others, Eli realized the solution was really dictated by the accessibility of the poison. Some poisons couldn't be acquired by any means, legal or otherwise, others required a license.

He was drawn to potassium cyanide mixed with sulfuric acid because he figured out how to get the ingredients, but he couldn't figure out how to use them short of tying up his victims and putting them in a closet where the gas would kill them.

In the end, he picked cyanide powder. He chose it primarily because it was a really sneaky poison. It was clear and had very little taste and just a hint of the smell of Almonds. It worked by stopping the cells from absorbing oxygen. The body asphyxiates itself. In most cases, the heart muscle just stops working.

Eli was more than a little influenced by his favorite mystery author, Ian Fleming, whose famous agent extraordinaire, James Bond, was known for administering cyanide capsules in the ominous plots of several novels.

Then, too, there were a number of Hitler's cohorts, as well as Hitler himself and his mistress Eva Braun, who chose to use cyanide capsules to hasten their departure from this life.

Eli felt sure Harry Fletcher, with all his ties to the underworld, could find a source of supply. Once acquired, he'd figure out a way to get the tablets mixed with the victim's food.

Now all he had left to plan was how to make a fire look accidental.

Chapter 67

El Paso

LEE CALLED HIS FRIEND Ranger Captain Jose Lopez, and explained his need for assistance from the Rangers. Such requests usually go through the Governor's office, but a friendship spanning more than twenty-five years cut through the red tape.

The Texas Rangers don't have a large contingent of officers. They get involved in special instances when it appears local law enforcement can't handle a situation without assistance or at the specific direction of the Governor of Texas.

Jose had to be careful to make sure Lee's need matched up with the criteria to commit Ranger resources. When Lee explained the prime suspect in this case had apparently tampered with evidence and shutdown an investigation, the matter was resolved favorably. Rangers are often used to investigate maleficence of public office. Jose agreed to assign one Ranger.

Lee had hoped for more help, but knew the Ranger policy was, "one riot, one Ranger."

Jose had one stipulation. The Ranger was free to work with Lee, but forbidden to report to Lee or any other officer or organization. Ranger authority supersedes local law enforcement and no Ranger reports to a private detective.

Ranger Sam Vaquera was dispatched from Waco to El Paso where he was to meet Perkins at the Windham Hotel.

Perkins is an imposing figure. He's six foot six inches tall. Add to that, the high crown of his John B. Stetson white hat and the height of his Justin boots and he's intimidating.

Sam Vaquera, at five foot five inches tall, is the most diminutive ranger in the history of the organization. Lee was startled at his size and uncharacteristically remarked, "That damned, Jose! I asked for a Ranger and he sent me half a Ranger!"

Vaquera made no comment to this insult, but chose instead to clamp down on Lee's hand in an unbearable vice-like grip. He allowed Lee's obviously extreme discomfort to continue until he saw tears in the man's blue eyes.

Having made the unspoken point that powerful things can come in small packages, he released his grip, smiled broadly and said, "I'm pleased to meet you."

After massaging the feeling back into his hand and pushing the bones more comfortably in line with their normal position, Lee remarked, "Damn that hurt! But I sure as hell had it coming. I'm pleased to meet you too."

It took Lee almost three hours to bring Ranger Vaquera up to speed. Despite their shaky initiation, the two men bonded in the special way that lawmen do. It was apparent they'd work well together.

"Now I know what's going on," said Sam, "I'm wondering what it is you want me to do?"

"We have divided things up between the FBI, Kathy Smith's EPPD detectives and myself," Lee said. "I'm keeping an eye on a couple of loose cannons and need your help to keep the O'Kelly's alive.

Everett O'Kelly," said Lee, "is a disturbed and angry man. I don't think he's going to act out his threats to his parents, but I may be wrong. I need your help to keep an eye on him.

Eli Sanchez, as you're also aware, may already be a killer. We suspect he may be the assassin under contract to kill the O'Kelly's. It appears to us that he's being manipulated and blackmailed by some very serious people with connections to the mafia."

You and I are going to be working at least twelve hours a day to make sure we stay a step or two ahead of these guys."

"If I'm reading this correctly," said Sam, "things are just about ripe to start playing out. Everett O'Kelly knows he has a very tight window of opportunity in which to make his move on his folks. Someone will make an attempt to take the O'Kelly's lives in the next few days. We need to be ready to react and make our move first."

Chapter 68

LUISA JARAMILLO HAD been looking for hard evidence that would persuade a federal judge to issue a court order to approve eavesdropping on Harry Fletcher. The Agency had long thought Fletcher and his associates were part of an organized crime syndicate centered in New Orleans, Louisiana.

After making a presentation of the combined investigations by Perkins, the EPPD and the FBI and pointing out two lives were now at stake, a federal judge signed a court order authorizing the wiretaps. He agreed there was now sufficient probability that Fletcher was involved in arranging murder for hire across state lines, also it was likely he was associated with the cashing of federally insured money orders.

That same day federal agents clandestinely tapped Fletcher's business and home landline phones as well as his Internet provider connection. Equipment was put in place with the ability to eavesdrop upon and record room conversations using landline phones not in use even while hung up in their cradles. These connections were made off-site in co-operation with Fletcher's service providers.

His cellphone calls were being monitored and recorded using a wireless interceptor housed in a van parked about nine hundred feet from Fletcher's office. A Parabolic listening device mounted on the roof of the van and directed toward a window of Fletcher's office was amplifying minute window vibrations allowing agents in the van to listen to conversations in the office.

Six technical specialists and two agents were assigned to provide around the clock monitoring of the equipment. Two of the technical specialists made a late-night break-in to Fletcher's garage where they installed tracking devices on his vehicles, leaving no trace of their entry.

Two days after these arrangements had been made, Eli Sanchez called Harry Fletcher to advise him he had a plan. Fletcher asked Eli to come to his office rather than discuss it over the phone.

They had no idea their conversation was being monitored by the Federal Bureau of Investigation. Nor did they give pause to the possibility the meeting they scheduled would include eavesdroppers affiliated with the same agency.

When Eli asked Harry for assistance with the acquisition of cyanide powder, Fletcher told him, no problem. He could and would provide the substance needed.

Included in the details of the plan was the involvement of Everett O'Kelly in helping to co-ordinate the application of the cyanide powder into food for the O'Kelly's. Fletcher expected Everett would decline to be involved, but agreed to approach him anyway. It would facilitate and make easier the task.

Fletcher asked Eli to explain in detail how he envisioned starting the fire and how he intended to make it appear to be accidental. He knew the Dallas Fire Department would investigate to determine if the fire was arson. They have a reputation for excellence in determining the nature of a fire. He wanted assurance their investigation would lead to a dead-end.

Eli explained a number of years ago he had been on the scene of a fire where a pile of oily rags left in the sun had ignited by spontaneous combustion. Eli's plan was to leave a stack of oily rags in a position on a workbench where the light from the window reached the rags.

"Show me," said Harry.

"I need a location to place these rags in sunlight," Eli said.

"You can use this windowsill," said Harry.

He placed the rags in the sunlight. "This cotton ball has been soaked in super glue," he said, as he placed the ball among the rags. "The glue will combust spontaneously in fifteen to twenty minutes. I've done some trial and error experimentation with numerous combinations and quantities of ingredients and know this works every time. Arson inspectors can't easily determine if fire accelerants have been used at a fire scene, but it can be done by laboratory analysis. All ignitable accelerants leave a residue called ILRs. The trick is to leave only residue that would be present under normal circumstances," said Eli.

"Is this going to leave bread crumbs that'll lead back to us?" asked Fletcher.

"No," said Eli. "Like I told you, the exact right amount of super glue in a cotton ball will self-ignite in fifteen minutes. Arson inspectors will find only the residue from the oily rags, because a single cotton ball won't leave enough ILR to be detected. Even if it did, super glue and cotton balls are standard household items. The plan is fool proof."

In exactly fourteen minutes the cotton ball ignited and the oily rags became an inferno.

"Sweet Jesus! Put out the fire before this place goes up in flames," said Harry.

Following the demonstration, Harry was satisfied that Eli's plan would work. He told him he would be presenting it to Everett O'Kelly for approval.

Later, when he presented the plan to Everett, he was surprised that Everett agreed to assist in getting the cyanide into his parent's food. He provided additional assistance by recommending a specific window above a workbench in the garage, a location he thought would be the best spot for the pile of oily rags.

Everett was anxious to make sure the plan was executed without a hitch; he provided information about where shop towels were kept, as well as where they kept small engine oil for lawn equipment, and oil to lubricate squeaky door hinges, ceiling fans and household appliances. All that remained was to set a date for the "accident."

As a result of the FBI's surveillance efforts they were now privy to almost every detail of a planned double murder. It remained to determine how to intervene to save two lives, prevent arson, bring down a branch of the Mafia and to bring the perpetrators to justice.

Chapter 69

SAM VAQUERA HAD BEEN following Eli Sanchez since eight in the morning. Lee and Sam had agreed to work twelve-hour shifts. Sam got the long straw and the day shift.

At nine-fifteen Eli walked into an office building located at Piedras and Montana Streets. Sam plugged the address in his laptop. It belonged to Horizons Unlimited, President and CEO, being one Harry Fletcher. *How interesting!*

Eli's business at this location didn't take long. At nine-nineteen he was back out the door and headed to his EPPD cruiser. Hard on his heels was a tall bald man in a three-piece suit. The man paused to lock the front door, was now starting a black Mercedes. Sam assumed he was Harry Fletcher.

This posed an interesting dilemma: should Sam continue to track Eli's activities or take a chance the new player was Fletcher and follow him instead. Sam chose to follow Fletcher.

The Mercedes headed west on Montana with total disregard for the posted speed limits. Suddenly, it braked hard and pulled into the drive-thru of a Starbucks. His order filled, the driver re-kindled his sense of urgency and laid a peel of rubber as he pulled back out onto Montana Street. On North Mesa, he turned right, kept up his pace until he spotted a black and white hiding on a side street next to a school zone.

The black and white must have had him, because its driver pulled in behind the Mercedes. For the next couple of miles up Mesa the Mercedes driver watched his odometer needle, the rearview mirror and behaved.

When the Mercedes reached the west exit for the University of Texas at El Paso Sun Bowl Stadium, its driver turned left uttering a prayer the black and white would continue north. It did!

Once he reached the stadium, the Mercedes driver hooked another right, passed the stadium and pulled into the north parking lot next to the lone car in the lot, a light blue Cadillac SUV. He parked the Mercedes, got out and opened the right front door of the Caddie, shook hands with the driver and settled into the seat.

Sam parked on the ridge road overlooking the parking lot and zoomed in with his binoculars. He wrote down the license numbers for both the Cadillac and the Mercedes, used the computer in his vehicle to check for the owner of the Cadillac. It was registered to Everett O'Kelly. Next he checked to see who owned the Mercedes. He wasn't surprised to find it belonged to Harry Fletcher.

Unknown to Sam, the watcher was being watched. An FBI agent had been following Everett O'Kelly's Cadillac. He, too, had determined that the black Mercedes belonged to Harry Fletcher. At the moment the agent was double tasking: recording the voice transmissions from the Cadillac and entering the tag number of Sam's pickup in an auto registry inquiry. He came up with zilch, but, no matter, they'd soon be getting acquainted and comparing notes.

Following a thirty-minute meeting between Harry Fletcher and Everett O'Kelly, Sam deemed their meeting sufficiently important he should call, wake up Lee and report. He found someone had beaten him to the punch. Lee had been awakened by a call from Special Agent Luisa Jaramillo, who told him that she had some recordings she thought Lee ought to hear.

Lee, after hearing Sam's report, told Sam he thought it would be a good idea for the two of them to drop by Luisa's office. Sam was in agreement and offered to pick up Lee. He declined, because

Sam was already on the right end of town. "No point," he said, "in doubling back." On the way they called Kathy Smith with the EPPD and arranged for her to also attend.

By three p.m., Lee Perkins, Sam Vaquera, Kathy Johnson, Luisa Jaramillo and two of her field agents were seated in a small conference room of the Justice Building on North Mesa Street.

Special Agent Jaramillo, who was seated at the head of the table, took the floor, "Earlier in the day we were able to record a conversation between Eli Sanchez and Harry Fletcher confirming Eli Sanchez was hired to plan and execute the deaths of both Walter and Helen O'Kelly."

"How was it you were able to record what was said?" asked Lee.

Luisa smiled. "Trade secret! You think we broke the law, don't you? We didn't. We made an uninvited visit to Fletcher's garage in the middle of the night and bugged his cars. But we had our ducks lined up. A judge approved a court order," said Luisa. "From the same conversation, we confirmed the hit contract was initiated by Everett O'Kelly, also he would be involved and providing assistance in the implementation of the plan. It was interesting to find Everett O'Kelly was paying the contract fee for killing his folks to Harry Fletcher. Sanchez was being leveraged, actually blackmailed, by Fletcher using the knowledge Sanchez caused the death of his patrol partner, Toby Preston. However, Sanchez was also in line to be paid a considerable sum, a sort of sub-contract fee.

We also found out from the recording, how the contract was going to be fulfilled," said Luisa. "Fletcher has agreed to provide Sanchez a quantity of cyanide powder that will be used to poison the O'Kelly's food."

"Why would they use a poison?" asked Kathy. "It leaves residue that can be discovered in an autopsy."

"After the O'Kelly's are poisoned," said Luisa, "the plan is to stage a spontaneous combustion fire. The purpose of the fire is to cover evidence of the poisoning and make the fire appear to be the cause of the death."

"I'm surprised Everett would agree to torch a multi-million dollar estate to cover their tracks," said Lee. "Have they set a timetable for all this to take place?"

"The date for the implementation of the contract isn't set. We know it'll be soon. Everett O'Kelly is supposed to let Harry Fletcher know if a day occurs when household help won't be on duty in the O'Kelly household," said Luisa. "In the meantime, we now have enough information in hand to work out an action plan to take down these bad guys."

Lee interrupted with a question, "Luisa, I'm wondering, now that you have all this information, do we really need to put the O'Kelly's at risk? It seems to me, you have all you need to get prosecutions of all parties."

"Not necessarily," said Luisa, "we are much more likely to get a conviction if we intervene in an attempted homicide, than if we made arrests for conspiracy to commit a homicide. I want to catch these folks red-handed, but I don't want to put the O'Kelly's at risk. That's why you're here. We need a plan. So, how about it guys, you ready to put together a joint operation?"

Chapter 70

Better Deal old store #9
El Paso

CONSTRUCTION OF BETTER DEAL'S new number nine-replacement store was almost complete. All of the new fixtures were in place; the non-perishable merchandise was stocked and ready for sale. It remained only to tear down the existing store, to pave the parking lot and to set up the perishables items.

The old store was no longer open for business, all merchandise had been removed from the building and a three hundred-man crew was busy removing fixtures in preparation for the demolition of the old store building.

Oscar Beasley was on site in the front lobby of the old store visiting with the job foreman assigned to oversee the teardown operation. A workman interrupted their conversation with a question. "Is there someone available who can open the safe? It's tied to the floor from the inside. We need someone to open the safe so we can take it loose from the floor."

"Mr. Beasley, please excuse me for a few minutes. This is a showstopper and I need to keep things moving. It would save time if one of your people would open the safe for us. Do you have someone on hand who has the combination?"

"Dan Coleman is next door in the new building. He knows the combination. I'll call and ask him to run over here. I'm kind of curious to see how a safe is secured myself. I think I'll just hang around and see what you do to remove it."

"You'll be disappointed. Most of the time all we have to do is remove four bolts from the inside of the safe to free it from the floor."

Dan Coleman was available and came immediately to open the safe.

When the door was opened, Robert Whitehead, the demolition foreman, took a look inside the safe. "Uh Oh! There's nothing simple about this one. The safe is bolted and welded to steel anchors set in the floor. I'll need someone with a cutting torch to cut it free."

There was a ten-minute delay until a welder arrived with equipment to cut the steel securing the safe. After the steel was cut and anchor bolts removed, the safe was secured with a heavy chain and a hydraulic lift was brought in to remove it from the floor.

As it was raised from the floor, previously hidden debris was exposed behind the safe. Oscar noticed broken fragments of what appeared to be a quart size glass jar.

He immediately made a connection between the broken jar fragments and the robbery of the store safe earlier in the year. Dan Coleman's missing coins had been in a Mason jar. There was a better than good chance the debris was fragments of that jar.

Oscar shouted a command with alarm on his face, "Hey! Hold up there! Don't touch the glass behind the safe. It may be evidence from a robbery. The fragments need to be checked for fingerprints. I realize this is going to slow you down, but I'll get an investigator out here right away to gather the pieces."

Oscar used his cellular phone to call Luisa Jaramillo. "Luisa, it's Oscar Beasley. I'm in our old store on Central. We're in the process of demolishing the old building to make room for parking. I just watched the removal of the safe from the old office. There are broken Mason jar fragments behind the safe. It occurs to me the glass may be from the container for the coin collection taken in the burglary."

Luisa replied, "Bet you're right. Has it been touched?"

"No," said Oscar, "but they want to get it out of their way. They're in a hell of a hurry to demolish the building."

"Don't let them touch a thing," she said. "I'm on my way."

Oscar's call had caught Luisa in a meeting with Lee Perkins and her agents. It was about over, so they cut it short. Luisa briefed Lee about the jar. She said, "I'm going to send a couple of techies over there to check for prints. I'm thinking about going along to make sure it doesn't get screwed up. You want to tag along?"

"Sure. Why not," said Lee?

A three-car caravan lead by Luisa's black Yukon SUV, its' siren blaring and lights flashing, hurled toward Central Avenue. The location was less than halfway across El Paso. They covered the seven miles in ten minutes.

Luisa's technical people carefully collected and processed the jar fragments for prints, allowing a very frustrated Robert Whitehead to try to regain the momentum lost from his tightly orchestrated demolition project.

Luisa questioned the tech that dusted for prints, "Did you get any clear prints?"

"Sure did! Got some good ones. There's one very clear print in what looks to be blood. I'd say someone must have cut himself picking up the glass. What's this all about anyway?"

Luisa suddenly realized that she hadn't given an explanation for the sudden run to the Better Deal store. She filled in the gaps for her people, and then turned to Oscar and Lee. "I'll put a priority on getting the fingerprint results back to you. If there's a hit or an ID, I'll give you a call. I think we should have answers in three to four days. I'll bet we get a hit on your boy Eli or his partner, Toby. Are we through here? I think it's time for a beer. We've earned one. I just happen to know of a good place with Bud Light on tap."

Chapter 71

EVERETT O'KELLY HAD BEEN playing nice with his folks. In fact, he apologized for his "you'll be sorry remarks" and told his Dad that he was right. He would be better suited to practice law or perhaps enter politics.

Walter acknowledged the apology and said, "It's in the past. Forget it."

Everett told his Dad he was looking into possibilities in both law and politics and was sure he'd be resigning from his position at Better Deal within the three-month deadline imposed by his Dad.

As Helen had predicted, he intimated that thus far his best offers had come from cities some considerable distance from Dallas.

Everett's wife and children were blissfully unaware there were any issues between Everett and his folks, so they continued in their happy interface and involvement with Nana Helen.

Conversely, it was not a happy time for Nana. She knew these could be her last days with Everett, and soon to unfold events would put her relationship with his wife and children at risk.

She knew Everett was fabricating every word of his conversation and had a hidden agenda connected to his visit. She found it incredibly difficult to smile and make small talk when she knew he was there to plot and plan their demise. She marveled at how well Walter was carrying on.

Finding a window of opportunity to kill the O'Kelly's had proven a bit more difficult than Everett and Eli had anticipated. One key element of the plan was to implement it when no non-family members were in the house.

The O'Kelly's didn't use a lot of domestic household help. Helen cooked most of their meals and Walter liked to grill and loved to make the salads. Only on rare occasions did they use help in the kitchen. Their residence was a large one, so Helen did have two ladies who cleaned house twice weekly. They came on Mondays and Thursdays.

Yard maintenance was a different situation. The yard was huge and required lots of attention. Old Sam Sheppard had taken care of the yard for years. He and his wife Ann lived over the five-car garage or "Carriage House" as the architect had described it. Sam used to hand wash the O'Kelly's three cars, but lately he had been taking them to a carwash.

The additional two bays of the garage were used to store lawn maintenance equipment and to house the car provided for the Sheppard's by the O'Kelly's.

Sam has two helpers, who both live off-site. One was his son, Jeff who, like Sam, worked full-time for the O'Kelly's and was married and had no children. The other was a single young Hispanic guy who was a student at UTEP working part-time to pay his way through school.

Sam's wife had a small studio in their apartment, where she wrote children's books and did her own illustrations. She actually made greater earnings than Sam, which didn't bother him in the least. Between them, they were accumulating a nice "nest-egg" that would soon allow them to retire in comfort.

Everett had been going nuts trying to keep his commitment to find an opportunity to implement "Snuff and Puff." In the past, it seemed to Everett, his parents were often home alone, so this was an unanticipated problem.

Everett was not the only frustrated party. Several hundred miles to the west, Luisa Jaramillo had been wringing her hands and pacing the floor. Decidedly proactive in all matters, she decided to take the situation in hand. She called Walter from El Paso and set a date for him to make sure all the help were off duty.

It was decided that this next weekend the Sheppard's would all attend a make-believe family wedding in, of all places, Falfurrias, Texas. The part-time Hispanic UTEP student employee would have the weekend off.

Walter agreed to mention to Everett they would be at home alone all weekend. This, Luisa thought, should get things moving. It was expensive to maintain a "holding pattern."

Chapter 72

HIS HONOR, THOMAS FOLEY, the Mayor of El Paso, and El Paso City Manager, Patricia "Pat" Spier, had only a short distance to travel in the city-owned Ford Taurus sedan. They had just left El Paso's City Hall on Durango and Franklin Streets just south of Interstate Ten to attend a meeting in the offices of the El Paso Federal Bureau of Investigation located in the Federal Justice Center on South Mesa Drive.

The salary for the Office of Mayor of El Paso was forty-five thousand dollars per year, a token salary that was far less than was paid to career subordinates. Foley resented the disparity, even though his was a part time position and the others were fulltime.

Matters were made even worse, when the El Paso City Council recently downgraded the role of mayor in favor of a strong city manager government. The new arrangement made Thomas Foley a titular head of city government relegated to greeting visitors and passing out "keys to the city." Nevertheless, Foley never missed an opportunity to "grand stand" and act out being "in charge."

Pat parked the Ford in the building's underground garage, locked the vehicle and both she and Mayor Foley headed to the elevator that would take them to the FBI Offices. Pat was surprised to be confronted at the elevator door by Marisol Chavez, a well-known reporter for the El Paso Times Newspaper with a photographer in tow.

"Good afternoon Patricia, Mayor Foley. We're here as requested. I hope you have a moment to fill us in before the meeting."

Spier said, "Marisol, I am not quite sure how you happen to be here, but the meeting we're about to attend is not a public event and the press were specifically excluded. How is it you happen to be here?"

"My editor told me the mayor had called and requested a reporter and photographer for an important meeting with Luisa Jaramillo."

"Well, Mayor Foley was told this would be a private meeting. He must have misunderstood. Mayor, I suggest that you apologize to Marisol, because she will not be attending this meeting. Now please excuse us, we need to get on to the assembly."

The Mayor shrugged his shoulders, mouthing that he was sorry, as they entered the elevator and closed the door.

"Thomas, your grandstanding is so predictable," said Pat. "Marisol is not going to forget that you caused her this inconvenience. It will be a cold day in hell before I will ever invite you to anything. You're an embarrassment to the voters you represent."

Just as the elevator door was about to open to the third floor, Patricia again turned to Mayor Foley, "Thomas, I need to make something very clear between us before we go into this meeting. You have zero authority to make any commitments on behalf of the City of El Paso. I suggest you keep your mouth shut."

Foley shook his head in the affirmative.

"That won't do. Tell me."

"Okay, I'll keep my mouth shut."

"You'd better."

They made a left turn when exiting the elevator and proceeded down the hall to Special Agent Jaramillo's office. When they entered the office foyer, a secretary rose to escort them to a small conference room.

Louisa stood at the head of the table addressing a seated group of five. She interrupted what she was saying to acknowledge the last of the expected attendees.

"Good afternoon Mr. Mayor and City Manager Spier. Please come in, take a seat and I'll make introductions.

To my left is, Lee Perkins, a private investigator working on behalf of Better Deal."

Lee rose to greet and shake hands with the mayor and city manager.

The Mayor commented, "I recognize you. You're the FBI agent who took a bullet when you arrested the drug lord that killed the federal judge in San Diego. The tabloids all said you saved other lives that day, that you're a bigger than life hero. I'm pleased to meet you."

Luisa continued with the introductions, "Next to Lee is Jesus Dominguez, who heads up EPPD Internal Affairs Investigations.

The lady to Officer Jesus' left is detective Kathy Smith, also with the El Paso Police Department.

To my right is Senior Ranger Captain, Jose Lopez, with the Texas Rangers.

Seated next to Captain Lopez, is Texas Ranger Investigator, Samuel Vaquera."

She paused, looked around. "I don't think I missed anyone. Now that we have the introductions out of the way, I'd like to get directly into the purpose of our meeting. Ranger Vaquera, is responsible for the part of the investigation that has led us to invite you to join us, so I'm going to turn the meeting over to him at this time."

"Thank you Luisa," said Sam. "On behalf of the Texas Rangers, I want to recognize you for the valuable assistance we've had from your people in this investigation.

A number of weeks ago The Texas Rangers received a request to look into a charge that El Paso Police Department Chief Herman Rector, accepted a bribe to deliberately close an investigation. I was assigned to investigate the allegation. I have completed my investigation and have copies for your consideration," said Sam.

"As you can see, it's a lengthy report. I have no intention of going through it in detail. You may do that at your own leisure. I will, however, summarize the key points of my findings.

I was able to establish a series of phone calls and personal visits took place between Willard Rhodes, the Better Deal West Texas Director of Corporate Security and Chief Rector. Following this series of phone calls and meetings, Chief Rector did, in fact, instruct investigators to terminate their investigation of all aspects of the burglary of the Better Deal store on Central Avenue, including further investigation of a suicide of an employee possibly connected to the burglary.

On the day following the termination of the investigation, Chief Rector was in Ruidoso, New Mexico, where he made an acquisition from the Real Estate Department of Better Deal. He purchased from them a riverside cabin with an appraised value of $365,000. A representative of Better Deal had purchased the cabin the previous day for $369,500.

Chief Rector paid fifty thousand dollars cash to Better Deal for a totally free and clear title to the cabin in Ruidoso. All of these transactions are carefully documented. There is no question that Chief Rector is guilty of misuse of the authority of his public office," said the Ranger.

"Unfortunately, there's more," said Sam. There's a tampering with State's evidence charge. An item of evidence connected with the investigation of the burglary disappeared. In fact, Chief Rector denies it ever existed. That item was a suicide note left by the store employee accused of being involved in the burglary.

Included in my report are two sworn depositions, one establishing the existence of the suicide note and a testimony that the suicide note was in Chief Rector's personal possession at the time it disappeared. That pretty much sums up my findings, so Luisa, I'll turn it back to you."

"Thank you, Ranger Vaquera," said Luisa. "Anyone have any questions?"

Mayor Foley raised his hand.

"Mr. Mayor," asked Luisa, "do you have a question?"

"Yes," said Mayor Foley. "What is it you plan to do with this report?"

"Actually, that's a question we have for the City of El Paso. We're giving the report to you along with some suggestions," said

Luisa. "But before we share our thoughts, we want to make you aware that we are presently involved in another related investigation. There are individuals involved who are exposed to considerable personal risks.

The full cooperation of the El Paso Police Department is a critical issue in protecting these individuals and also to bringing some very bad characters to justice. The Federal Bureau of Investigation considers Chief Rector a significant roadblock to accomplishing these goals.

This brings us to our recommendations," said Luisa, as she put down her notes and assumed a dead serious expression. "We strongly recommend that the City of El Paso remove and replace Herman Rector as Chief of Police. We also suggest that you file charges of malfeasance of public office with the additional charge of tampering with state's evidence."

"Excuse me, Agent Jaramillo," asked City Manager Spier, "Do I understand that you are recommending we fire Chief Rector?"

"Pat, this is largely a courtesy to the City of El Paso," said Luisa. "If you and the City Council deal with this issue behind closed doors, it's going to be far less embarrassing than if you have to respond to it as a public issue. I'm confident you'll take the appropriate action.

This pretty well wraps up our presentation. Let me know what you decide to do," said Luisa.

Bill Taylor, one of the three assistant special agents assigned to the El Paso Division of the FBI, rapped on the door and stuck his head inside. "We just received a report from the lab in Virginia. You might want to look at it before you let these people leave," said Taylor, as he handed her the report.

Luisa held up her hand. "Hold on for a minute while I see what this is about."

She shook her head and pursed her lips as she read. "Bill," she said, "I'd like for you to make copies of this report for Lee Perkins, Lieutenant Smith and Ranger Vaquera. What we have here is the fingerprint report from the broken glass found behind the safe at the Better Deal burglary. There is a one hundred percent certainty the prints belong to deceased EPPD officer Toby Preston. The glass fragments are from a quart Mason jar.

The report serves to connect the dotted lines, exonerates Tim Sullivan and certainly points to his partner, Eli Sanchez, as being a likely partner in the robbery of the safe. While it won't get us a conviction, it certainly points us in the right direction. I'm going to ask all of you to keep this information confidential until we have more damning evidence to convict Sanchez."

Chapter 73

CLARK DAVIES' LOVELY WIFE Maria wears the pants in the Davies family. Before she was married, she was, Maria De Angelino, the daughter of New Orleans Boss of Bosses, Mickey De Angelino. Her Father, Mickey, spoiled her rotten and made sure she had everything she wanted, including her husband, Clark.

When she was a freshman at the University of Texas, she had spotted Clark Davies and decided she had to have him. He was definitely the trophy hunk of his then junior class. Maria was "pick of the litter" herself. She had the best of classic Italian good looks, tall in stature, with clear olive skin, beautiful wavy black hair, and a gorgeous smile complemented by a sparkling personality.

No doubt Maria could have reeled Clark in without assistance, but her Daddy tried to make certain she got her man. Mickey made it clear to Clark using carefully veiled, but threatening remarks, that he would be well advised to marry Maria. Clark hardly noticed. He was already hooked and head over heels in love.

Their June wedding the following year took place shortly after Clark graduated from the University of Texas with a business management degree. It was the social event of the year in New Orleans.

It was common knowledge in New Orleans that the De Angelinos were associated with unsavory activities. Mickey wanted more than anything that his daughter Maria and his grandchildren would have an opportunity to lead more normal lives and be more socially accepted. To assure his family was distanced from his criminal and other more unsavory operations he had long ago separated his legitimate investments from his criminal enterprises.

The key management people in the legitimate enterprises had no idea their financial backing came from criminal activities. Maria's choice of Clark Davies as a husband matched nicely with Mickey's grand plan for Maria's future. He arranged that Clark be hired for a mid-management role in the organization from which he was rapidly advanced and ultimately became the CEO.

In time, Mickey made Clark aware of the nature of his other sources of income and was pleased that it didn't seem to make any difference to Clark. Clark knew how his bread was buttered, had tasted the good life, and was not about to give it up or muddy the waters.

Surprisingly Clark wasn't scared or intimidated by Mickey. Under his leadership the legitimate enterprises had prospered and grown so that Mickey considered Clark a vital and essential part of the organization. Clark's only fear was the future. He could see, at some point down the line, he and Marie would be in contention with Harry Fletcher to lead the total organization in the event of Mickey's death.

The legitimate businesses consisted of shopping centers, apartment complexes, several automobile dealerships, a winery and two beer distributorships geographically dispersed from Longview to El Paso and Amarillo to Brownsville. All of these investments were now clustered, controlled and operated under the umbrella of a single business entity, Davies Enterprises, LLC, located in Dallas, Texas. The CEO of Davies Enterprises was Clark Davies who knew well that behind the scenes he answered first to Maria Davies and ultimately to Mickey De Angelino.

There were, to be sure, also De Angelino investments across the same geographical area in more risky, shady and more profitable undertakings like, titty bars, nightclubs, massage parlors, prostitution, extortion, gambling, money-laundering, a chop-shop in El Paso that did a brisk business supplying auto parts stolen in the United States to Mexican mechanics and a large construction company.

Harry Fletcher was CEO of Horizons Unlimited, Inc. And the sole employee of another named Border Investments, LLC, a shell company called Texas Diversified Industries, whose stock was owned entirely by four individuals, Mickey De Angelino, Maria De Angelino Davies and Mike Smith, a Chicago investor, in turn, owned Border Construction, Inc. as well as Border Investments.

The Dallas location for Davies Enterprises was sufficiently distant to assure that few people, if any at all, made the connection between the Clark's and the New Orleans De Angelino money and influence.

Nearly half of the return from the illegitimate investments in Texas was funneled directly to Clark and Maria. This cash flow had long provided the means for Clark and Maria and their children to live exceptionally well.

Harry Fletcher also benefitted nicely from a ten percent share from his operations with the balance going to Texas Diversified Industries. While Harry's income ran into the millions per year, he felt he should be allowed partner status in Texas Diversified. He also aspired and was conspiring to ultimately replace Mickey.

The Davies enjoyed the money and their high-flying life-style, and their social position in Dallas. Mickey was comfortable that he had arranged his business affairs to allow Maria the life he wanted for her and her family. He failed to see that the stage was set for conflict.

Maria did not personally want to take her father's place. She wanted Clark to have that opportunity. She and Clark agreed, that somehow they had to be positioned to thwart any attempt by Harry Fletcher to orchestrate a take-over.

Clark had already proven to Mickey, that he could be successful on his own. She knew there was jealous contention between Clark and Harry Fletcher. In her view, there was a need to somehow elevate Clark's position now, while her father was in control, rather than wait for matters to be resolved.

Chapter 74

FROM TIME TO TIME Maria shared some of what is going on inside the businesses operated by Harry Fletcher with her husband Clark. Clark and Maria were neighbors to the O'Kelly's in Dallas, so Mickey thought it was appropriate to keep Clark in the loop about the contract with Everett O'Kelly and how Harry planned to use an El Paso policeman to execute the contract.

Clark found this whole scenario extremely fascinating and pointed out to Maria that this was a very big deal with huge unexplored opportunities. "Better Deal Supers is the largest privately-owned business enterprise in Texas. Everett O'Kelly has allowed himself to become compromised and is now vulnerable to blackmail and extortion."

Since Harry had not pointed out anything along these lines, Maria decided she'd like to hear more. "Okay. You have my attention. What are you suggesting?"

"Consider this, assuming the plan to eliminate his parents goes as planned, Everett will become the sole-owner of Better Deal Supers. Knowing his involvement in their death is worth untold millions, because exposure could ruin him. If we threatened to unmask him, he would have to give us anything we want. It's possible we could wind up owning the company, but that would probably be pushing too hard and be too visible to withstand scrutiny. At the very least, we could insist that Everett share an ownership position in Better Deal."

Maria could see that Clark was right. It was a huge opportunity. An opportunity that could go beyond increasing their wealth, it could also be the means she has been looking for to move her husband beyond the reach of Harry Fletcher.

Together Clark and Maria formulated a plan that would leverage Everett into having to give them half of his company stock, a position as Vice Chairman of Better Deal's board of directors for Clark and a board seat for herself.

Maria practically salivated as she considered their potential for greater income and higher status on the social ladder. She was pleased to see Clark show some initiative, but cautious as she considered the possibilities that their lives might not withstand closer scrutiny.

A plan of this magnitude would have to have the approval of her dad, Mickey De Angelino. And because it infringed upon an operation being run by Harry Fletcher, it had the potential to ruffle his feathers. She was going to need Mickey to keep Harry in line.

This whole matter was far too sensitive to handle over a phone, so Clark made an appointment to see Mickey that same afternoon and made air flight reservations to depart late morning.

The plan was extremely well received by Mickey. He had all manner of advice as to how Clark should approach Everett. He recommended to Clark that he and Maria should use their leverage to acquire 51% ownership position for themselves in Better Deal. Additionally, he suggested that Clark's son should also be given a board seat, perhaps even a key management position in the company. Clark could see he had gained some new respect from his father-in-law.

The only personal request from Mickey had to do with a freight company subsidiary owned by Better Deal. Their drivers were not members of the Freight Hauler's Union of Texas. Mickey's organization gets a considerable rake-off from union dues in Texas. He said assistance in getting Better Deal's drivers to join the union would strengthen his position and leverage with the union and be financially rewarding for him.

Clark's same-day return flight was a red-eye flight departing at midnight. Mickey insisted that Clark stay for dinner and a toddy or two afterwards. By the time Mickey had him delivered to the International Terminal, Clark was feeling no pain.

Chapter 75

WALTER O'KELLY ENCOUNTERED Everett in the hallway at the headquarters offices of Better Deal Supers, and asked, "How are things going?"

"We're all fine. Liz and the kids are going to be in Longview this weekend to help celebrate her Mom's birthday. I'm going to be at loose ends. I'll probably burn some ribs and just watch the playoffs on the tube."

"We're kind of at loose ends ourselves. All the hired help will be gone. Why don't you come over and cook the ribs on my Japanese smoker? That thing does a phenomenal job on pork ribs. You'll need to get an early start, it takes 10-12 hours to cook them to perfection, but it's worth the wait. I plan on watching the two play-off games myself. I'd enjoy the company."

"Sounds like a plan. I'll be over about seven to get the charcoal going. Would it be all right to bring a friend? I have a houseguest coming. He's a cop and friend who lives in El Paso."

"Sure! Bring him along too! The more the merrier. I assume you'll do enough ribs to share with your mom and me. I'll mention to Helen what we'll be having for an entrée, so she can make a side dish or two. I think all you need to bring is your ribs. We have charcoal, starter, matches, and most anything you may want to drink except beer. Helen says I'm putting on extra pounds. She blames my weight on the beer, if you and your friend want beer, you'll have to bring your own.

Later in the morning, when Everett called Fletcher in El Paso, an FBI communications specialist wirelessly monitored the call. He saw where the call originated and switched on a recording device.

"Harry, this is Everett O'Kelly in Dallas. We finally have a break and will have a window of opportunity this weekend to put the "Snuff and Puff" plan in motion. All employees at my folks place will be off duty. I've been invited over to smoke some ribs and watch the play-offs. I told my dad I'd be bringing a houseguest, a policeman friend from El Paso."

Harry took a moment to mull over this turn of events and responded, "I'll contact Eli Sanchez to see if his schedule has the flexibility to spend a day in Dallas.

"I doubt this opportunity will present itself again. I think you ought not to give him a choice. Timing is critical. I'm certain my folks plan to change their wills. I'm anxious to get this done quickly. If they change their wills, there'll be no point in our arrangement. It's now or never," said Everett.

"Okay, I understand," said Fletcher. "We've got Eli between a rock and a hard place, so we can insist he do it now. I'll get hold of him and let him know it's not negotiable. He'll just have to work it out. I'll get back to you to confirm our ducks are in a row."

"If you don't mind, I'd rather that I call you. You might catch me when I can't talk. I'll call you this afternoon between work and home."

When Harry ended the call he speed-dialed Eli Sanchez.

"Eli, Harry Fletcher. Can you talk?"

"No, not right now," said Eli.

This is pretty important," said Fletcher, "so don't fail to call back. Okay?"

"Yeah. I'll call you," said Eli.

Eli wasn't working when he got Harry's call. He worked at night. He was with a female friend, definitely not a lady. A friend for whom he would look the other way expecting her favors in return. She considered it a small price to pay to avoid time in jail and the expense of an attorney.

It took little time to complete his arrangement with the streetwalker. He gave her a small tip and made an exit from her fleabag motel room.

As soon as he was alone, he made the call to Harry. Harry and the same agent who had previously listened in on his calls picked up the phone simultaneously. Harry spoke. The agent did not. He flipped on the recording device.

"Harry, what's up?"

"We have that opportunity you've been waiting for. You need to get yourself over to Dallas by Friday evening. You'll be at the O'Kelly place all day. The hired help is off. Their son is cooking ribs and watching ball games with the old man and his wife. He told his folks that you're his friend, so they think you're his houseguest."

"I've got the weekend off, so the timing is right. But I don't have the pills or powder you promised. I can't pull this off without it," said Eli.

"I've got it here," said Fletcher. "You need to drop by to pick it up and we can walk through how this is going to go down one more time. Can you come by my office now?"

"Come on Harry! You know I can't go there! I'll be burned. Meet me behind the Memorial Park Library in half an hour. They're only open a half-day on weekdays, so we'll have the place to ourselves. How about bringing my two guns back? It's about time you gave the damned things back to me."

"Maybe! I'll think about it," said Harry.

As foretold by Eli, the area behind the Library was deserted. Harry got out of his Mercedes and slipped into the passenger seat of Eli's Chevy. "You have a room reserved and paid for at the Crescent Hotel in uptown Dallas. Be in the hotel lobby at 6:30 a.m., checked out and ready to go. Everett will pick you up. Act like you're greeting an old friend when you see him walk in. Here's a photo, so you'll recognize him."

"Oh! Give me a minute!" Harry went back to his car and reached into the glove box, then hurried back. "I've got your guns and the powder you wanted. You come after me with a gun again and you're a dead man. Understand?"

"I hear you. That was a stupid mistake," said Eli. 'It won't happen again. Thanks. I'm glad to get them back. I'm not about to play John Wayne again."

"You're not the first one to do something stupid," said Harry. "Let's talk about this job. You up for this?"

"Yeah! Other than feeling like I just had my last meal?"

"You've just got the jitters. Everybody gets them. I get them, too. You'll do fine," said Harry. "Think about what five hundred thousand dollars will buy. Put that together with what you've got in that safety deposit box and you'll be in tall cotton. Besides that, you'll be off the hook with us."

"Sounds good, but don't kid me, I'll never be off the hook with you guys. You get a cop with his pants down and you are going to milk it for all it's worth. It's just a matter of when and where, I know it will be sooner rather than later."

Harry just smiled.

Chapter 76

9:00 a.m.
Tuesday
Office of the City Manager
El Paso

AFTER A NEAR SLEEPLESS night of considering her options, City Manager Pat Spier had reached some conclusions. She'd decided that her best alternative was to move swiftly and decisively to get all the issues resolved before they hit the fan.

She'd been in her office since eight. So far, there've been no calls from the press. She told Mayor Foley after the meeting in the FBI conference room that if a single word about the meeting passed his lips, the office of mayor would be abolished.

Her office staff worked nine to five. At nine sharp her administrative assistant tapped once, entered with a paper cup in hand, "Stopped at Starbucks. Got you a caramel latte. Anything special going to happen today?"

"Good morning. Bless your heart. What kind of day are we going to have? One you'll remember for sure, because you're a key player.

Trisha, I need for you to set up a meeting in my office in one hour. Call Jim Baker and William Foster. Let them know it's very important that they be here at ten o'clock. Apologize for the short notice.

If they ask what the meeting is about, tell them I can't tell them until we talk. Ask them not to mention they're meeting with me. They're going to be upset. You hang tough. Oh, and Trisha? Get me confirmation the minute you know it's going to happen, okay?"

Trisha made her calls and, as expected, both men bristled at being given short notice. When they'd finished venting, each indicated he'd be at the meeting under protest.

Like a lot of men, these two haven't accepted women as equals, much less accepting them in positions of authority. Trisha privately enjoyed hearing them grovel. It was a hoot to get to work for a tough old gal like Patricia Spier.

Trisha tapped on Patricia's door.

"Come on in."

"Ms. Spier, the meeting is set for ten. Both parties indicated they would be present, all-be-it under protest."

"I take it they took a few shots at the messenger?"

"Oh yeah, they let me have it big time! Made me proud to work here. They know you don't put up with BS. I enjoyed stuffing it in their ears."

"I should've called them myself. I owe you one. Sorry to put you in the line of fire.

There are some things I need for you to do before they get here: Set up the small conference room for the meeting. This meeting may run a bit long, so we'll need coffee and water. Both these guys drink their coffee black. And I'll need two copies of this report for pass-outs. Be sure to stamp them as "Confidential."

I'm going to need to have you take notes. Every word of this meeting needs to be documented exactly as spoken. I know you take shorthand, but it would be a good idea to have a recorder to make sure you don't miss anything."

"Will do," said Trisha. "Is there anything else I need to know or do before the meeting?"

"Yes, a couple more items," said Patricia. "I don't want any interruptions. Everyone is going to want to know what's going on. You keep it under your hat. No gossip! No rumors! What is said in that room stays in that room! There will be more meetings today. Everything remains private until we're done."

"Mums the word," said Trisha.

"Okay," said Patricia. "Let me know when the first one arrives."

Five minutes to ten
First Floor Lobby
City Hall
El Paso

Jim Baker and William Foster entered the elevator to Spier's floor at the same time. When the door closed William Foster growled, "Did that pompous witch summon your too?"

"She did," said Jim. "She must think we don't have anything to do but kiss her fat bottom. I hope this is short and sweet. I've got a load of stuff to do."

They exited at the executive floor; found they were face to face with Trisha. "Right on time."

Foster spoke, "We're here. Where's this mandatory meeting taking place?"

Trisha smiled, suppressed a snicker and said, "Small conference room down the hall on the right. I'll let her know you're here."

Trisha tapped twice, poked her head in the doorway, "The Bulls are in the corral. I hope you have on your steel panties."

"Not to fear," said Patricia. "I can handle these sissies. Let's rumble."

Both ladies moved down the hall and entered the conference room, "Good morning gentlemen. I appreciate you coming. Trisha will be taking notes. Our conversation will be recorded."

Trisha offered the pouting men coffee and water, which both declined. While the others were taking their seats Pat put the "Do Not Disturb" sign in the holder on the door to the conference room.

Seated at the head of the table Pat began, "Gentlemen, the document in front of you is a lengthy report of an investigation of malfeasance of public office and tampering with state's evidence. A Texas Ranger assigned to the case did the investigation. The report was reviewed and turned over to us with the understanding that we have an opportunity to deal with our own problems. If we don't resolve them, they'll do it for us. They want it done now.

I've taken the time to read it in its entirety. I urge you to do the same," said Patricia. "For now, I'll attempt to summarize: You're probably familiar with the report in the El Paso Times and the accounts on television about a Baptist minister who committed suicide. He was a part time employee-manager at the Better Deal on Central Ave. It's been broadly publicized that the man took his life in remorse because of his assumed complicity in a burglary and theft from the store safe.

This investigation has revealed that it was rather a bit more complicated. Someone with the Better Deal organization persuaded our Chief of Police to terminate the investigation and make the suicide note disappear.

I've got a stack of evidence," said Patricia, "that proves that following the termination of the EPPD investigation and the convenient misplacement of the suicide note, Chief Rector purchased a cabin in Ruidoso for a mere fraction of its market value.

Were it not for a very bright young city detective named Kathy Smith, who had the courage to do the right thing, this city would have egg dripping from ear to ear and down our chin."

Foster couldn't contain himself, "Jesus, Pat, our liability exposure here is huge. Rector knows better than to pull a stunt like that."

"You think so? Sit tight! There's more," said Pat. "To make matters worse, it turns out two EPPD patrolmen were the perpetrators of the burglary on Central. You'll recall one of our patrolmen recently drove off a cliff on Mount Franklin. That was no accident. He was murdered, most likely by his partner and fellow accomplice to the burglary and theft."

Patricia continued, "Why was he murdered? Probably because he had loose lips and told the underworld figures holding markers for his gambling debts he had the money from the burglary to pay his gambling debt or maybe his partner wanted all the money. Who knows?

Included among the items stolen from the safe at Better Deal were two hundred blank money orders and a check writer. Following the death of Toby Preston, the officer whose pickup did the swan dive off Scenic Drive, the gamblers holding Toby's note put the strong arm on the other officer, Eli Sanchez, who talked them into taking the blank money orders and the check writer in lieu of cash.

The money orders have a maximum amount per check of one thousand dollars. Two weeks ago in a single day one hundred and ninety-seven of them were cashed almost simultaneously for max amount in one hundred and ninety-seven out-of-state locations. Logistically, this required a large organization and probably had the assistance of a major crime organization. As you might well imagine, this caught the attention of our friends over at the Federal Bureau of Investigation."

Jim Baker did the math, "That's almost two hundred thousand bucks. That kind of money attracts lots of flies. This is a very big deal."

Patricia tried to keep things on track, "I think I failed to mention that there are some things going on in the internal affairs at Better Deal. Walter O'Kelly's son Everett, their company attorney, has been doing this cover-up stuff behind his Dad's back. The old man is trying to get at the truth of the matter. He hired a private detective named Lee Perkins, to do some snooping around. It has largely been Perkins, with some support from Kathy Smith and a Texas Ranger named Samuel Vaquera, who has brought the facts out into the open.

The FBI, the Texas Rangers, Lee Perkins and Kathy Smith have all been working together to bring these events to some kind of closure. They recently got court orders for wire taps and have a fairly large task force doing surveillance activities. The FBI thinks they can take down the local, as well as the New Orleans mob when they try to murder the O'Kelly's.

Is this getting too complicated to keep up?" Patricia asked. "I hope not. About a week ago O'Kelly confronted his son and told him that he had pretty well ripped his britches and would no longer be the heir apparent to take over his business. Everett didn't take this news well. He was familiar with the language of his parents wills, knew he was designated to run the company upon their deaths. To make sure he got the job, he contracted to have them murdered before they could change their wills.

Ironically, the mob is using their leverage on Eli Sanchez to force him to snuff the O'Kelly's," said Patricia. "Incredibly, they intend to pay him a five hundred thousand dollar contract fee. How bizarre is that? It's all scheduled to go down this Saturday."

Jim interrupted, "If I were Sanchez, I don't think I'd count on being left around as a potential witness."

"Can't see he has a choice," said Bill. "They have him between a rock and a hard place."

Patricia suggested, "I think that's his problem. We need to address our own problems. The task force is very concerned that Chief Rector needs to be removed from the loop because they're afraid he'll screw up their operation. That, gentlemen, is why they met with me, which brings me to why you're here.

Bill," she continued, "I agree with you that this mess reeks of potential law suits. I'm about to call Chief Rector in here and fire his ass. The one thing we don't need is a wrongful termination suit and the other is a bunch of bad publicity for the City of El Paso. So, I need to cover my ass. Tell me, can I fire Herman Rector?"

She looked at Foster, "Let's start with you, Jim. You wrote the Employee Handbook. Did Rector break enough rules for me to terminate him? What are your concerns if I do?"

"Pat, from a personnel department standpoint, my primary concerns are first, what policies and procedures apply? Can we prove we covered them in orientation training? Did the man follow them or break them? Then, do we have the documentation to prove that he broke them? It'll take me a few minutes to confirm we have a record he attended orientation training. I came on board before he did, so I think it's likely we can prove he attended orientation."

Jim continued, "Page ten in the employee handbook gives us the authority to take corrective action, including termination, when there is evidence of fraud or an illegal act.

The top ten percent of employees, those in the top income

brackets, have historically been treated somewhat differently than line jobs in this one respect: most of our terminated employees may be considered at some later date for re-employment. The handbook states that terminated key employees are not eligible for re-hire."

"We don't want this guy coming back," said Patricia.

"That depends on how consistently we've dealt with other terminated key employees. I believe our history will show we've always terminated employees for dishonest and/or illegal acts," said Jim. "But I'm not entirely sure, without doing some research, that we've never made an exception in re-hiring one. And lastly, the city employee handbook requires the personnel department conduct an exit interview. If you'll allow me one quick phone call, I can confirm if he was documented for attending orientation."

"Sure, go ahead," said Patricia.

Jim dialed his office, and confirmed Rector did attend orientation.

Jim turned his attention back to the meeting and said, "Okay, Here's my assessment: we can prove he knew the rules. Since we have the proof that he violated the law, I say we have every right to terminate him as not eligible for re-hire. I think it's possible we may have made an exception or two and re-hired a terminated ex-key employee. I don't see that as a roadblock. My recommendation is to move ahead. Fire him, just don't forget the exit interview."

Patricia responded, "Good, I want to make sure we have our act together before we jump into this. The Chief has lots of friends who're going to raise hell if they think he has been shafted.

"Bill, from a legal perspective, what are your concerns?" asked Pat.

"I think you're in pretty good shape as far as termination is concerned. But I didn't hear you address the question of what happens to his employee retirement pay, benefits package, or termination pay if he is fired for "cause."

He paused briefly and assumed a very serious look of concern, "Unfortunately the city has been inconsistent in how we've dealt with this issue. There was a time when we paid a severance even when an individual was fired for "cause," but in more recent years

I believe Jim has consistently denied severance, retirement participation and benefits if someone is fired for dishonesty. Am I correct?"

Jim answered, "You're right."

Bill continued, "That being the case, we have to be consistent. We can't fire him and give him his retirement package. I think you're aware that we have more lawsuits on this one issue than any other. There are a number of attorneys in El Paso who make a good living specializing in wrongful termination suits. Even when we have all our ducks in a row, a judge may rule in the employee's favor."

Patricia asked, "Bill, Chief Rector has been in that office for over twenty years. He's been with the police department almost thirty. If I fire him is it likely he would pursue and win a wrongful termination suit?"

"No. But it is likely he would pursue and win a suit to be allowed to have his retirement benefits."

"As much as I want to fire him, I sure don't want to get us into a lawsuit, especially if it's likely a judge would give him his benefits package anyway." said Patricia.

Jim raised a question, "What if you gave him a choice? What if you tell him he's fired or he can choose to resign? If he resigns, with his years of service, he's eligible for early retirement and keeps his benefits package."

Patricia scowled deeply, gritted her teeth and said, "Damn it, I don't believe in rewarding crappy behavior, but it appears I don't have much choice. What if he takes the option of being fired?"

William Foster was momentarily lost in thought, then said, "Pat, that's not likely, but he might because he would be eligible for unemployment compensation. He'll have to make that decision himself. No judge will be sympathetic to his position thereafter."

"Let me see if I understand. You're saying I can call him in, fire him, tell him all the reasons he's being let go and exactly what I think of his behavior, then offer him the option of being fired or resigning?"

Bill said, "That pretty much sums it up."

"Well at least that's something," said Patricia. "Win a few! Lose a few! It's all part of the job. Gentlemen, thank you for your time. I'm glad we talked because I'm sure as hell going to fire his butt. I think we're done here. Thank you for coming."

Both men rose and took their leave. On the way down the elevator Baker spoke first, "Well, what did you think of our City Manager's performance?"

"Me? I think she's a gutsy old gal," said Bill. "We're lucky to have her, even if she does chap my ass from time to time. What about you?"

"I hate to admit it," said Jim. "But she's a winner. If we still had Foley and the city council running things it'd take six months to get this resolved. I'll make you a bet. Rector will be gone before quitting time."

"No taker here, because I think you're right," said Bill.

Chapter 77

Office of the Chief of Police
Civic Center Plaza
El Paso

CHIEF RECTOR WAS IN A HUDDLE with his young protégée, Assistant Chief of Police, Bill Shelton. They'd been discussing several detectives on their promotion list as possible candidates for chief of detectives. Shelton had just made a strong case for Kathy Smith, who he felt was far and away their best detective.

Chief Rector voiced a concern that the department has never had a female in that role and he was very concerned about how a woman would be accepted.

"Chief, you know as well as I do we can't even take that into consideration these days. Besides, this gal is tough as nails and can handle herself as well as any man. Better than most! I stand behind Kathy one hundred percent," said Bill.

"If she's your pick, I'll go with your judgment. You got anything else," asked Rector?

"That's all. Thanks for your time. I appreciate your support. Kathy will do a good job. See you later," said Bill.

Office of the City Manager

Civic Center Plaza
El Paso

Following the departure of the city attorney and personnel director, Patricia Spier called Trisha into her office. She said, "I told you this was going to be a busy day. Now we're ready for the main event. I need for you to track down Chief Rector and get him on the phone with me."

"Will do," said Trisha. When she was again seated at her desk, she dialed Rector's number. He answered on first ring.

"Ms. Spier," said Trisha. "I have Chief Rector on the line."

"Got it! Thanks," said Patricia.

"Chief, good morning. This is Patricia Spier. I need you in my office right away. Are you available?"

"Actually, I'm pretty busy. Can we put this off?" *Oh my God! I wonder if she found out about the cabin?*

"No, this is important. How long will it take to wrap up what you're doing and get up here?" asked Patricia.

"Give me five minutes to finish what I'm doing and I can be in your office in ten. What's this about?" asked Rector.

Chief Rector's office was only one floor removed from the city manager, so he was a minute or so early.

"Howdy, Trisha. I think your boss is expecting me," said Rector.

"She is, go on in," said Trisha.

"Good afternoon, Pat. How you been?"

"Busy as usual. This job is never boring," said Patricia. "Sit down, Chief, while I shut the door."

Rather than sit down behind her desk, Patricia chose to sit on the opposite side next to Rector. "Chief," she said. "I'm going to cut to the chase. You don't know it, but you've been the subject of an investigation by the Texas Rangers, the FBI, your own Department of Internal Affairs and Lord knows whom else. They've come to me with evidence showing you've been guilty of malfeasance of public office and of tampering with state's evidence."

"Those are pretty serious charges. I doubt very much they can prove them," said Rector.

"They convinced me and I believe they can. My first inclination was to fire you on the spot. It's certainly what you deserve, but first I want to hear what you've got to say for yourself. I find it very hard to believe that anyone in his or her right mind, with your years of service and as close as you are to retirement would risk it all for a damned cabin."

"Pat," he squirmed in his seat, then answered with a quiver in his voice, "I'm not sure I really know. I wanted it. I couldn't afford it. After all the years of putting up with all the pressure, of not being appreciated, I guess I convinced myself I'd earned it."

"No, Herman, you didn't earn it. All of us have to put up with lack of appreciation. It comes with our jobs."

"I thought we did the transaction in a way that wouldn't be criticized, that it was technically legal. What exactly are they charging?"

They haven't charged you yet, but trust me, they will. What they want first is to get you removed from office so things can work like they're supposed to work. They have documentation that shows the sweet deal you got on the Ruidoso cabin from Better Deal and sworn affidavits that you had in hand a suicide note that you say never existed. I'd say they have you by the short hairs. You may even wind up doing some time for some of this," said Patricia.

"I was ready and wanting to fire your ass. You can thank Bill Foster for recommending that I give you an opportunity to take early retirement. Your choice is either you resign effective immediately or I fire you now. What do you want to do?"

"Jesus, Pat, can't we work this out? I really need some time to think this through. There's got to be a better way," he pleaded.

"No, it can't be put off," said Patricia. "Make a choice now."

"You're sure as hell one insensitive old cow. I guess I'll resign. Do I get my retirement and benefits?"

"If I fire you, you won't. If you resign, you get your retirement and your insurance. You made the right choice. So here's the deal: you're retired as of right now. Get yourself over to Jim Baker's office. He's got your retirement paperwork. Then clean out your desk and turn in any city property including your car, gun, badge and anything else that belongs to the city. I want you out of here today. Understand?"

"Yeah, I hear you," said Rector. "I can't believe you're coming down on me like this. I thought we were friends. Don't the good things I've done for the department count? Does one mistake erase everything?"

"Chief, you have no idea how disappointed I am in you. You betrayed the public's trust. In my view that's contemptible. By destroying that man's suicide note, you left that man's family thinking he was a low-life thief. Completing that investigation would have exonerated him. Anyone who would do that to another person is no friend of mine. Now get your sorry ass out of my office."

Patricia made a call to Bill Shelton asking him to come to her office right away.

"Bill, have a seat. I'm afraid I have both good news and bad news. The bad news is that Chief Rector has decided to take early retirement effect today. He'll be gone before the day is done. The good news is that for now, you'll be the acting Chief. A bulletin to that effect will be sent to all department heads before the day is done. I plan to put your name forward as my recommendation to be the new Chief of Police. That will have to be brought to the City Council for approval.

I'd like for you to give some thought as to whom you will recommend to be your replacement if you are approved. I assume you want the job. Is that correct?"

"Well sure, I want the job," said Bill, "but what brought this on so suddenly? Chief Rector has been nothing but a straight shooter with me. I feel badly about taking his job."

"You don't need to feel guilty," said Patricia. "The man deserved to lose his job. Chief Rector screwed up big time; took a bribe, also made some other bad decisions. I gave him a choice: early retirement or get fired. He decided to retire. I know you hold him in high regard. I did as well. Big disappointment, but he did it to himself."

"When does all this become effective," asked Bill.

"Today. When you walk out of this office, you're in charge," said Shirley. "There're also some things going on this weekend that you need to know about. A task force including the Texas Rangers, the FBI and one of your detectives, Kathy Smith, are involved in a sting operation that may require additional EPPD resources. This is a big deal. I want you to give Kathy any help she requests."

"Sure. Kathy has already given me a heads up. I told her I'd see she gets what she needs," said Bill.

"I think that's it for now. We'll talk about pay adjustment and other related issues as soon as we get beyond the council vote. If you get the nod, I'll make pay retro to now. Any questions?" said Patricia.

"Just one. Chief Rector and I had decided to promote Kathy Smith to Chief of Detectives," said Bill. "Will that decision still stand?"

"Absolutely! Send me the paperwork. That's it for now. I wish you good luck. You've earned the promotion. Call me if you need any help," said Patricia.

After Bill Shelton was out the door, Patricia picked up her cell phone and dialed Luisa Jaramillo.

"Luisa, Patricia Spier. Thought I should let you know, Chief Rector was given a choice of early retirement or termination. He opted for early retirement. He's gone effective today. Bill Shelton, the assistant chief is now acting chief and has been recommended to be permanent. What's going on with your task force?"

"It's a relief to know we'll be dealing with Shelton," said Luisa. "He's a good man. It looks like everything goes down this Saturday. We have a Task Force meeting early tomorrow morning to make sure we have all the bases covered to protect the O'Kelly's and to make the planned arrests of guilty parties. One of the arrests will be an EPPD police sergeant. "

"If he deserves it, that's his problem," said Patricia. "You might suggest to Kathy that she ought to share that with Bill Shelton. By the way, Kathy is about to be promoted to Chief of Detectives."

"Kathy's a good choice," said Luisa.

I guess I'd better wish you good luck this weekend. All of you have a lot on your plate. You guys be careful and stay safe," said Patricia.

Chapter 78

Friday morning
FBI Offices
One Justice Way
Dallas, Texas

LUISA JARAMILLO HATED to give up control of the task force, but she had no authority in the Dallas Metroplex. Mark Jennings, the Special Agent in Charge for Dallas, had the jurisdiction. They were acquainted, but hadn't worked together previously. The tall handsome black man had a reputation for being one of the Bureau's best agents.

Mark earned his spurs with the FBI and other organizations. His roots were as a much-decorated United States Marine Corps Captain, who served in Baghdad, then as a Sheriff's Deputy in Missouri and a stint with the Los Angeles Police Department, where he took the fight to the gangs in the Watts area. He'd come up through the ranks of the FBI, with assignments that included oversight and training of bio-nuclear response teams, crisis management of both domestic and foreign terrorists situations and dealing with organized crime activity. Somehow along the way he acquired a Juris Doctorate degree.

Luisa opened the meeting. "I get to open the meeting this

morning, but I won't be up here long. Dallas is Mark Jennings's turf, so I'll be turning the meeting over to him shortly. But first, I want to thank everyone who's served on this committee for his or her support and contributions and I want to thank everyone for being here this morning with special thanks to all of you with the Dallas office for making us West Texas hillbillies feel welcome. Whoever brought the maple donuts probably doesn't know they're my favorite. I just want you to know you hit a homerun with me.

For those of you who haven't met him, I want you to meet Mark Jennings, the Special Agent-in-Charge for the Dallas Division who is now officially the lead in this investigation," said Luisa.

Jennings rose to take the floor, "Thank you, Luisa. I've been trying to get up to speed on all the facets of this investigation. Looks like you folks have had your hands full. I've taken the liberty of including the Dallas Chief of Police Bob Brandt, as well and the Dallas Fire Chief Jeff Jones, at our meeting this morning, since it's likely we'll need some support from them to handle tomorrow's activities."

"Additionally, as you look around the room you'll notice a number of new players. They're members of my team who've been added to the task force," said Mark. "They've already been briefed on the background of this case. How it began as an investigation of a burglary, caused a suicide, escalated to murder, forgeries and organized criminal activities.

Now it appears we have a conspiracy to murder two of our most respected citizens using poison and hiding the act with arson.

Well, that isn't going to happen on my watch. We're going to nip that plan in the bud, but we want to be careful how we do it, because we have an opportunity that we don't want to slip through our hands," said Mark.

"If we handle this right, we'll not only be protecting the O'Kelly's, we can bring down the organized crime family that controls most of the criminal activity in two states. This kind of moment happens once in a lifetime. Let's not screw this up," said Mark.

After he gave his remarks time to sink in, he said, "The best place to start this morning is to bring everyone up to speed on what has been learned from our wire taps. Luisa has been receiving and reviewing transcripts of the wire taps, so she's best suited to give us a summary."

Luisa, who had just been seated, rose again and said, "I think most of you know for the past couple of weeks we've been working together monitoring cellular and landlines calls and e-mails in Dallas, Fort Worth and El Paso. You're probably not aware we're also tapping some Louisiana lines as well. The key subjects of interest in this case are: Eli Sanchez and Harry Fletcher in El Paso, Everett O'Kelly in Dallas, as well as Mickey De Angelino, in New Orleans. We have not shared with you that we added to this list, the home and business traffic for Clark and Maria Davies in Dallas. Mark and his people have been handling that for us," said Luisa.

"We have gleaned incriminating information from these wire taps establishing the stolen blank money orders and check writer from the Better Deal Store in El Paso were obtained from Eli Sanchez by Harry Fletcher to settle a gambling debt owed by Toby Preston, Eli's partner, in the burglary. We have reason to believe that Eli Sanchez murdered Toby Preston," said Luisa.

"Fletcher arranged to send the blank money orders and American Express check writer to Mickey De Angelino, in New Orleans, who we suspect arranged for the forging and cashing of the stolen money orders. At this point we have only circumstantial evidence that De Angelino organized the money order scam," said Luisa. "But we're confident we'll be able to pull these loose ends together."

"Additionally," said Luisa, "we've been able to establish that Mickey De Angelino, his daughter Maria Davies, and a Chicago personality as yet unidentified own and control all of the considerable enterprises managed by Harry Fletcher.

Where we felt they would be secure, we also had Mark and his people covertly install video feeds and recorders which have been instrumental in giving us evidence that will allow us to successfully prosecute all these individuals."

The Davies wiretap also revealed a new twist in events," said Luisa. "There are now plans by the Davies to use blackmail and extortion to leverage themselves into an ownership position in O'Kelly Investments, Inc., if Everett is successful in eliminating his parents," said Luisa.

Luisa had completed her update, so Mark rose to take her place. "My first order of business is to make sure everyone understands the number one priority tomorrow is to protect the lives of the O'Kelly's," said Mark. "Our second priority is to gather enough evidence on Eli Sanchez and Everett O'Kelly in the act of attempted murder and arson to get convictions and to take them down along with the organized crime kingpins in El Paso, Dallas and New Orleans.

Now I'd like to talk through the plan to protect the O'Kelly's," said Mark. "Our two concerns are we need to make sure Eli doesn't poison the O'Kelly's, and no one gets hurt arresting Eli. There's a concern about safety, because we know Eli will be armed. He owns three registered pistols. Obviously, we'll have boots on the floor to prevent Eli from having an opportunity to harm anyone or to flee. It's not a foolproof plan. There'll be some risks."

"I've met personally with the O'Kelly's to instruct them under no circumstance are they to consume anything unless they personally open the container and it's been handled by no one other than themselves," said Mark. "They're also aware of the risk that bullets could fly when we make the arrests."

"The FBI has installed video and audio feeds in the kitchen, pantry, butler's pantry, by the bar, the outdoor kitchen, in the den and in the media room where they'll be watching television. Oh, and I forgot, also in the location where they plan to start the fire. Luckily that was a discussion item gleaned from a wiretap. There'll be a van parked near the O'Kelly residence containing three men who'll be monitoring eight monitors. These operators will all be looped to our communications network. There are also monitors upstairs in the carriage house and in an attic storage place for us to see what's going on," said Mark.

Jennings looked at Kathy and said, "Kathy, the Dallas PD has provided us with a ten-man swat team. I'd like for you to lead them. It would be a good idea for you to meet with them this afternoon. I'd like to suggest that you plan to place four of them in the carriage house; two near the front gate and four hidden in the attic of the house. All of us, including the swat team, should wear wireless headphone communications equipment to monitor the hearing devices placed around the house," said Mark.

Kathy raised her hand, "Mark, the swat team wears helmets with wireless Bluetooth communications. The half dozen of us that came in from El Paso don't have that equipment. Will you have it available for us as well?"

Mark responded, "We have a tactical support team that's bringing communications equipment for everyone. They have your cell number and will be getting in touch with you today to discuss your needs. You might want to pull together a list of what you need in anticipation of their call. They have a lot on their plate. Your list would be a big help."

"We'll need someone to show us how to use it," said Kathy. "In case it's different from any we've used in the past."

"They'll show you how to use it when they deliver."

"Thanks, Mark," said Kathy. "I don't think we've told you, but we have a backup plan in case things fall apart on us. Lee and Sam acquired a Federal Express uniform that fits Sam. The plan is to have Sam ring the doorbell with Lee hiding to one side. When the door opens they'd barge in. Are you okay with this part of the plan?"

"Sounds risky. Hope we don't get to that, but it's okay as a backup," said Mark. "I'm concerned that it's a possibility a fire might actually get started. That's why I've included the fire department in our meeting. They plan to have two fire trucks parked on quiet back streets within two blocks of the O'Kelly home.

The trigger for everyone is going to be from what happens on video. When Eli and Everett put the cyanide powder into a food product, we hold steady until Everett attempts to get his folks to consume it," said Mark. "That's when we move in. The key is the poison has to actually be in the food or beverage."

"What's the plan to deal with the Davies, Fletcher and the bunch in New Orleans," asked Luisa?

"Our plan," said Mark, "is to simultaneously move to arrest the

Davies here in Dallas, Mickey De Angelino in New Orleans and Harry Fletcher in El Paso.

For those of you who will be boots down on the O'Kelly property, I want you in the house and quiet as a statue in a park by five o'clock. A bird poops on your shoulder, it's okay to smile, but don't say a word or make a move that makes a noise," said Mark.

Lee Perkins raised his hand. "I have a concern. The Davies live next door to the O'Kelly's. They're aware of what Everett and Eli plan for today. If they see swat teams, police activity, fire trucks or anything out of the ordinary, I would expect them to take action to scuttle the plan, maybe even bolt. Don't you think we should arrive more discreetly from a direction not visible to the Davies and try to use as few vehicles as possible?"

"You're right! That's an oversight. The Davies are neighbors to the O'Kelly's and I've got folks planning to converge on them after we take down Eli and Everett. Thanks for bringing it up. We could've blown the whole effort," said Mark.

"Luisa, call Helen O'Kelly's number and ask if there's a side to her house that isn't visible from the Davies place?" suggested Mark.

Helen answered, first ring, "Helen O'Kelly."

"Hi, Helen. Luisa Jaramillo. We're in a meeting talking through our game plan for tomorrow. Lee pointed out that the Davies might notice our activity. Is there an entryway we may use and an area where we can park our vehicles that isn't in the Davies' line-of-sight?"

"Yes," said Helen. "There's a walk-through gate on the west side. We keep it padlocked because it's seldom used. I can remove the lock. That side street is a dead end cul-de-sac and heavily treed. You can park your vehicles there without being noticed."

"Perfect," said Luisa. If you'll remove the lock on the gate, we'll use that entrance. Is there an entrance to the house from the west side?"

"Well, sort of. There isn't an entrance to the house, but there's a lift door for an old coal shoot to a coal storage room used when the house was heated with a coal-fired furnace. That room's empty and the lift door's locked. There's a door inside the basement that has access to the rest of the house. We keep it locked with a bar across the door. I'll unlock both those doors and remove the bar," said Helen. "You'll need a ladder to enter using the coal shoot."

Luisa shared Helen's response with Mark. "Perfect," he said. "Tell her she solved a big problem for us. We'll count on her to unlock the doors and we'll bring a ladder. Ask her one last question. Is there a Westside entrance to the carriage house?"

When Luisa put the question to Helen, she said, "No, there isn't, but I can have Walter leave a garage door open at the far south end of the carriage house and all you will have to do is take one or two steps around the corner to get in the garage. There are steps from the garage that'll take your men upstairs."

"Mark, this is getting ridiculous I don't belong in this conversation." She handed the phone to Mark. "You and Helen need to talk with each other."

"Helen, this is Mark. Luisa's right. It's better for me to talk with you. I hate to ask you to repeat yourself, but, if you don't mind, I'd like for you to tell me about how to get in the carriage house."

She repeated what she had told Luisa.

"That'll work. Are you and Walter ready for tomorrow?"

"We are, but we aren't looking forward to it because we know it's going to go badly for Everett."

"We understand. Thank you for your help. You be careful tomorrow. Everything is going to be fine. See you in the morning."

Mark turned to Luisa. "Sorry. I didn't intend to get you caught in the middle. It looks like all our bases are covered."

Then he turned back to address the group, "Anybody have any more questions or concerns?" No hands went into the air. "Anybody thinks of anything, call me. See you all at five a.m.; be sure to wear your Kevlar vests. I don't want anyone to get hurt."

Chapter 79

O'Kelly Residence
Fairfield Ave
Country Club Estates
University Park
Dallas

UNIVERSITY PARK, THE SITE of the O'Kelly home, was one of the older neighborhoods of downtown Dallas. Its twenty-three thousand plus residents include primarily the wealthy, middle-class professionals and educators, apartment dwellers and students. All lived within a little less than four square miles.

Because the area was handy to downtown offices, the restaurant district, the ballet, the symphony, the Dallas Mavericks and, of course, SMU and the Country Club, it was one of the more desirable places to live in Dallas. An average residence sold for upwards of a million dollars.

It wasn't unusual to find a home had been purchased for millions, then torn to the ground and replaced by a more up-to-date edifice.

Large parcels of land, like the ten-plus acre track whereupon sat the O'Kelly home, were hard to come by. It was because of the larger lot that the O'Kelly place had come to be called the "O'Kelly Castle".

Their home was a mixture of Colonial and early American architecture dominated by huge live and post oaks surrounded by a high wrought-iron fence and dense foliage. The interior was less pretentious than one might expect, but made quite nice by the little things: the accent pieces, the comfort of the furnishings, and the eye-pleasing colors. It was elegant, comfortable, functional, and maybe a little dated.

Even though the O'Kelly's were awash in money, they didn't believe in wasting it. Helen did her own housekeeping for years, because others didn't clean to suit her. Lately she'd conceded to delegating it to others at Walter's insistence.

Five a.m.

Kathy Smith had been designated to run the Swat Team. She was first to arrive at 4:55 a.m. Lights were on in the kitchen. She entered the coal-bin chute, having brought a ladder as instructed. The door to enter the house was unlocked and open. She went up the stairs, entered the kitchen and found Walter making a pot of coffee.

"Good morning, Walter. You're looking beat. You must not be an early riser."

"Oh, I'm an early riser. In fact, we're both early risers. To be honest, neither of us got much sleep last night. Made some coffee. Want some?"

"I brought my own and you need to be careful about offering it to others. Everett and Eli don't need to be wondering why there are extra cups around when they get here at 7:00 a.m."

"Good thinking. I suppose that's why you brought your own?"

"Exactly. Besides, I need to get busy. I'm going up to the attic and get the lay of the setup and then over to the carriage house to look around. Anything I can do for you?"

"No, guess not."

"Okay, see you in a bit."

At this moment, ten swat team experts in firearms and hand-to-hand combat arrived. They were dressed in black, including their bulletproof vests and handcuffs. A glimmer of reflected light could give away their presence.

Each carried blackened Bushmaster M-4 .223 caliber assault rifles with 16" barrels. Additionally, they were armed with 9mm Smith and Wesson Military Pistols for which they have two spare clips. Their faces have been smudged to deny reflection.

Kathy was at the gate to direct each team member to his assigned location, sending them on their way with an admonition to speak only in low tones.

Kathy was similarly attired in black, but she didn't carry an assault rifle, preferring a pistol for close quarters operations.

By 5:05 everyone had arrived and been sent to their assigned posts. Kathy noticed a Federal Express delivery truck parked on the side street, no doubt containing both Vaquera and Perkins. She was amazed they had been able to obtain the use of a Federal Express van.

At 7:15 a.m. a black 4-door Mercedes sedan entered the front drive and parked immediately at the steps leading to the front door. Two casually dressed men in short pants and sandals approached the house. Each had a coffee mug in one hand and a grocery bag in the other.

Everett rang the bell. His Dad opened the door. In the attic, the carriage house, a nearby van and other listening posts, a bevy of police swat team members, FBI agents, a police detective, a Texas Ranger and a private detective had observed their arrival.

"Morning, Everett. You must be the friend from El Paso. I'm Walter O'Kelly."

"Dad, this is Eli Sanchez. I appreciate you letting him tag along," said Everett.

"Mister O'Kelly, I'm pleased to meet you."

"Eli, I'm pleased to meet you as well. Please call me, Walter. Come on in? It's already getting hot out here. Everett, you can introduce Eli to your mom while I freshen your coffees."

"Dad, if you don't mind, I think we need to fire up some charcoal and get the ribs going. I want to cook them eight hours at a low temperature, so they'll be tender."

"Sure, you do whatever you need to do. The charcoal is under the outdoor sink. The matches and starter cubes are in the top drawer. Mesquite chips are under the sink with the charcoal."

"The first playoff game starts at noon. Are you and mom going to watch," asked Everett?

"Planning to. If it's a good game we watch it all. If it's no contest, we'll find better things to do. These teams are supposed to be an even match. We're going to watch it in the media room. You're welcome to join us."

"We probably will," said Everett, "In the meantime, we need to get our fire going and the meat on the grill."

Everett lit the charcoal. It took about thirty minutes for the charcoal chunks to burn down to glowing hot coals and another ten minutes of messing with the airflow to get the temperature to hold at 220 degrees. Eli and Everett used the time to discuss which food to use with the cyanide powder.

"My dad likes something to munch on during a game. I'll offer to fix some sandwiches and something to drink. Both he and mom like pimiento cheese on toast," said Everett.

"I'm thinking, their drinks are the way to go, because the powder will dissolve," said Eli.

"It seems to me the powder might stick to the ice and not fully dissolve," said Everett. "Maybe we ought to mix the powder in the drinks before we add the ice."

The outdoor kitchen conversation was overheard clearly by ten of the response team members: Lee Perkins, Kathy Smith, Sam Vaquera, Mark Jennings, four firemen in the two fire trucks and three FBI agents setting in the monitor van. Mark told everyone this was no call for alarm. He was confident the O'Kelly's wouldn't take the drink offer.

When Everett offered to get cold drinks for his parents, his dad said he thought he'd just have a cold can of diet coke, which he'd fetch from the refrigerator. He asked Helen if she wanted one. She indicated she would.

Back at the grill to check on the ribs, Everett told Eli he was surprised by the canned drink orders. Both of his folks usually have ice in their drinks. By now it was getting close to noon and the start of the ball game. Eli asked Everett if he thought they'd go for the sandwich idea. Everett seemed sure they would. They always have something to nibble on while they watch a game. Sandwiches are normally included.

Back in the house, they fixed fresh pimento cheese sandwiches with a liberal addition of cyanide powder. They made two without the additive for themselves. When the sandwiches were offered, Walter said, "I've been thinking about pizza all morning. Sweetie, would you like a pizza?" A pizza was ordered.

Eli and Everett ate their own sandwiches. There were no takers for the others. At the next check on the ribs, Eli mentioned, "I think something's wrong here. Do you think they're on to us?"

"I haven't seen anything to indicate they are. I know we aren't having luck so far. We need to be patient. We'll have an opportunity before the day is done, maybe when we serve the ribs."

"Eli didn't take long to respond, "To hell with that! I'm ready to get this show on the road. I'm going to use my weapon. The fire will destroy the evidence."

"I'd rather you didn't do that."

"To hell with you. I'm tired of screwing around."

Eli's comment caused an immediate reaction. Sam and Lee were already moving at a dead run to the front door and didn't hear Kathy's order to do just that. Lee said, "Ring the bell! Tell them you're the pizza guy!"

"But I don't have a pizza."

"By the time they notice, we'll be inside. Draw your weapon and hold it behind your back. I'll be covering you."

In the attic, Kathy ordered the four black boots swat members to quietly descend the attic stairs and head for the media room to protect the O'Kelly's.

The doorbell rang. Walter opened the door; Sam pushed Walter aside and rushed in just in time to take a hit to the shoulder from Eli's automatic. Lee was a step behind Sam and popped off two shots from his single action 44 in Eli's direction.

Eli took both shots in the chest. He was dead before he hit the floor. A 44 Magnum is what folks in Alaska carry to stop a bear. The hollow point cartridges leave a small entry hole and a basket-size exit hole.

Everett was not armed and simply stood there with his mouth agape. After picking himself up from the floor, Walter turned to Everett, shook his head and shouted. "Are you out of your damned mind? You have a wife and family. We're the people that care for you most. Why in hell would you try to kill us?"

"Because you were going to screw me. I knew I had to do it before you could change your wills."

"Everett, we changed our wills before I told you to find another job. You wouldn't have gotten the company."

The sandwiches Eli and Everett had prepared were still on the platter next to where Everett stood. He grabbed one he knew was tainted and took a large bite, which he quickly swallowed. Cyanide is a very fast acting poison and nearly painless poison. There would be no time to prevent his death.

Most poisoning is an ugly way to die. Knowing this, Kathy quickly hustled both Walter and Helen into an adjoining room to spare them the exposure to Everett's demise and agony.

Mark Jennings had been in the carriage house and made an appearance on the scene just as Everett drew his last breath. He quickly surveyed the scene and realized what had taken place. He pulled out his cell phone and speed dialed into a conference call. He said three words "Do it now."

Chapter 80

MARK JENNINGS LEFT the O'Kelly home as soon as everything was under control. He told Kathy he and Luisa had some big fish to fry next door and counted on her and the local police to wrap up all the issues at the O'Kelly house.

He and Luisa walked around to the side street where he tapped on the door of a Chevy van that appeared to belong to the TV-US Network. It was, in fact, an FBI surveillance monitor van packed with high tech electronics. A side door slid open.

"Okay, Guys, your surveillance job's done. I need you for back up for an arrest, we don't expect any resistance, but you never know. Better safe than sorry."

He instructed them to follow him in their van. He and Luisa walked to the black GMC Tahoe parked a few steps away. After he located the federal arrest warrant, they drove past the O'Kelly residence to enter the circle drive of the Davie's Residence and parked at the walkway to the front door.

When he rang the doorbell, both Clark Davies and his wife Maria, answered it.

"Mr. and Mrs. Davies, I'm Mark Jennings, special agent with the Federal Bureau of Investigation. This is special agent Luisa Jaramillo. We have a federal warrant for your arrest."

"Clark was taken aback, "What are the charges?"

Jennings responded, "Sir, both you and your wife have been charged with conspiracy to commit two murders, participation in an organized crime and money laundering scheme. Please turn around and put your hands behind your backs."

"I want to call our attorney," said Davies.

"You can call him after you've been booked," said agent Jaramillo.

Both Davies did as ordered; afterwards they were read their rights and hustled into the backseat of Mark Jennings Tahoe.

Luisa told Mark that she was going to take her rented car, because she needed to check out of her hotel room, get to the airport and get back to El Paso. She thanked Mark for all his assistance.

While she was in route to her hotel, she called one of the agents she had assigned to arrest Harry Fletcher.

"Jim, how did it go with the Fletcher arrest?"

"A little hairy, no pun intended," said the agent. "We thought he was going to put up a fight, but he must have reconsidered. He wouldn't have had a prayer, too many of us and we had him pretty well covered."

"That's good. Nobody hurt. Have you heard how it went in New Orleans?"

"No. I haven't had time to check, have you?"

"No, but I'm about to call. Good job. See you."

Luisa had the cellular number for, Chester Farris, the Agent-in-Charge for New Orleans in her speed dial.

"Chester, how did it go with Mickey De Angelino?"

"Not good. He had three big guys for bodyguards. They put up a fight. One of them took a slug through a hand before they decided to give up. None of our guys got hurt. Would you believe we found the check writer they used to forge the money orders in De Angelo's office? Mickey is finally going to do some time. He's been a hard bird to stick with anything, but we got him today," said Chester. "How'd it go in Dallas?"

"The Fletcher and Davies arrests were no problem," said Luisa. "But the arrest in Dallas had some bad guys go down. One was shot dead by a private detective and a Texas Ranger took a hit in his shoulder. One of the perpetrators we had planned to arrest, committed suicide before we could stop it."

"Sounds like we got all the bad guys. Should put a big crimp in criminal activity for a good while."

"Let's hope so. We appreciate all the help," said Luisa.

Chapter 81

NO ONE, NOT A SINGLE SOUL, monitoring the video feeds, had noticed that Eli had carried a paper sack back into the house after he and Everett made their last inspection of the ribs on the Green Egg. Everyone was busy reacting to his comment about shooting the O'Kelly's. Had they been paying closer attention, they would have wondered why he set the sack down on a bench by a window and why he lingered there for a moment with his hands in the bag.

The sack contained cotton balls, a tube of super glue and oily rags, the ingredients he planned to use to start a fire by spontaneous combustion. In the last few seconds the bag was in his possession he emptied the tube of super glue into the center of three cotton balls and left them in the paper sack. His research had established that super glue in a cotton ball, if exposed to direct sunlight, would spontaneously ignite in a matter of minutes. What he didn't know was that it would also ignite in a paper bag if it remained in the sun.

It had required over two hours to deal with the Dallas Coroner, have Eli's body transported to the morgue and Everett's to a private funeral home, to have Emergency Medical Service do a temporary fix for Sam's gunshot wound, then to transport him to the Methodist Hospital Emergency Room.

The day's events were emotionally and physically devastating for the O'Kelly's. Helen had required a sedative to calm her down. Walter did his best to contain his pain, so he could comfort Helen.

By four o'clock most of the task force had left the scene. The swat team, FBI agents and their technical support people had removed all their equipment and said goodbye. The two fire trucks were long gone. Remaining were Lee Perkins and Kathy Smith, who had volunteered to stay the night at the O'Kelly's, largely to provide moral support and consolation for the O'Kelly's.

Additionally, they could see that they were needed as buffers to protect the O'Kelly's from the media, all of who were anxious to know what events had taken place at the O'Kelly Castle and the Davie's place earlier in the day.

The carefully orchestrated takedown of the Mickey De Angelino Organization in New Orleans, Harry Fletcher's operation in West Texas and the Dallas Metroplex dominated the next day's headlines across the country.

At just short of five o'clock, a fire detector began to screech toward the rear of the O'Kelly house. Lee and Walter hurried to investigate. They found a room and part of a hallway in flames. Walter ran to the phone to call 911. He told Lee there was a fire extinguisher in the pantry and shouted to Kathy to get Helen out of the house, which she did.

The Dallas Fire Department arrived and quickly extinguished the fire. They did a good job of cleaning up after the fire. The room and hallway would have to be replaced. The smoke damage, however, was another issue. The odor of smoke and the tar-like residue of smoke were throughout the house.

Although Lee and Walter had done their best to extinguish the flames, the fire extinguisher was too little and too late, but it probably saved the rest of the house. By the time the fire department had arrived, the room and hallway were fully engulfed in flames.

Arson investigators were on the scene before the fire was under control. As Eli had predicted, there was no clear evidence to suggest the fire had been deliberately set.

The O'Kelly's chose to ignore the Fire Captain's suggestion that they spend the night elsewhere. Both Kathy and Lee, out of concern for the O'Kelly's, volunteered to stay overnight. It was six-thirty before the Fire Captain gave the all clear and permission to use the house.

It occurred to Lee that there were ribs being smoked on Walter's Green Egg. He checked mainly out of concern that another fire might need to be extinguished. He discovered two racks of pork ribs done to perfection. The evening meal was no longer a matter of concern.

It was not a pleasant night. The smell of smoke was almost overwhelming. That smell just never goes away. Eventually the O'Kelly's would replace carpets, drapes, some furniture and much of their clothing. Even expensive paintings would forever retain the odor of smoke in their pigment. Many items and surfaces can be scrubbed fresh and repainted, but the home was forever altered.

In spite of all their efforts to be a buffer to assure the privacy of the O'Kelly's, a Dallas Morning News reporter's phone call was answered directly by Helen. He was a smooth talker and persuaded Helen to give him an audience.

On Monday morning his interview with Helen appeared in the newspaper. It was a reasonably accurate account of the events of the weekend. The article was kind in its references to the Better Deal organization, the O'Kelly's and even Everett, but the truth was all there and it would take a toll on the Companies' good will. The reporter remarked on the O'Kelly's resilience in the tragic loss of a son and their home in the same day.

The big surprise for readers was the involvement of the socially prominent Davies family and their association with the mob. It was their involvement and the takedown of organized crime in three major cities that made the lead copy and headlines.

Both Helen and Walter knew they had been fortunate not to be crucified in the press. This crisis having been resolved, they had to get on with the rest of their lives. They agreed they needed to reassess their priorities and set some matters aright. Their most immediate concern was for their daughter-in-law and her children and for Everett's funeral service and burial.

Chapter 82

OVERNIGHT THE O'KELLY'S had somehow managed to compartmentalize their grief. Walter O'Kelly called Charles Peterson to say he wouldn't be coming in on Monday. He briefed him on all that had transpired on Saturday and told him that he had confidence in his judgment, to call him only if absolutely necessary.

The house was a smelly, disorganized mess. It was decided they would have breakfast at Hillstone Restaurant. Walter requested a private dining room.

The previous night Walter and Helen made decisions about how they would like to go about settling matters for Claire Sullivan and for her children.

Walter asked for breakfast to be served family style; that they bring scrambled eggs, bacon, sausage and ham, pancakes, syrup, biscuits and gravy. They would serve themselves.

Helen said, "Yesterday was the worst day of our lives. Somehow we went wrong in preparing Everett for life. We know Everett chose his own destiny. He's not the first person who allowed selfish greed to take precedence over doing what's right, but in our hearts we share the guilt."

"Last night we realized that we were not alone. Others have been affected by these events, especially Claire Sullivan and her children. While we can't do anything for Tim, we're positioned to do much for Claire. We intend to do everything we can to see Claire has a good life and her children have opportunities to fulfill their potentials."

"We know little about Claire, her life and her needs. Lee, we know you've met her and assume you're able to give us some idea how we might help her and her children."

"Mrs. O'Kelly, I've spent time with Claire. She's a lovely young woman, but she's having a tough time. When I met her, she was staying with her folks and looking for a job. I understand she now has a job in New Mexico and lives in a rented apartment."

Walter asked, "Do you think she would be interested in pursuing an education?"

"She's obviously bright and could probably do well in school, particularly if she didn't have to work while attending. But I have no idea if she'd want to go back to school. Since she has no resources, I'm doubt if she has even considered it," said Lee.

"We think it might be best if you talk with her for us," said Walter.

"I'll do that. Is there anything else you want me to ask her?" said Lee.

Helen spoke up, "Yes, there is. We're going to set up trust funds for her children. We need their ages and names. We decided to put a million dollars in each fund; a trust manager will oversee the investment of the funds, which will go to each child when they graduate from high school."

Walter added, "We're also setting up an income trust for Claire to assure she can raise her children and be a stay-at-home mom. We'll buy her a nice home when she knows where she wants to settle down. If she wants to go back to school, we'll pay the cost of her education."

Helen chimed in, "We'd also like to do one other thing, if it's still a need. We'd like to build a church. Her husband was working for us because he wanted to help his congregation build a church. Do you know if they went ahead with their project or what happened to his church when he died?"

"I have no idea. Kathy, do you know anything about his church?"

"Not much. I interviewed some of his members following his death, so I have some contacts."

Walter asked, "Would you talk with them and find out the status of their project?"

"Sure. I'll do it today and get back to you," said Kathy.

"We'd be very grateful," said Walter.

Back at O'Kelly Castle

When Kathy and Lee took the O'Kelly's back to their home, Walter thanked Kathy for all she'd done.

"Mr. O'Kelly, thank you, but I was just doing my job. I need to get back to my office and find out what I need to be doing in my new position. I'll make some connection with Sullivan's Church members and get back to you this afternoon."

As she drove away Walter asked Lee to come inside. He and Helen had a few additional things to discuss with him.

"Lee, you've done a commendable job in resolving all the issues connected with the burglary. It hasn't all been happy endings, but now we know the truth and have the opportunity to make amends to some degree.

You've been very good to see this investigation through with us. Both Helen and I feel we'd like to continue our business relationship into the future. How would you feel about being Vice President of Security for O'Kelly Enterprises?"

"Walter, I'm seventy years old. My work-life career is way behind me. I just do this part time investigator stuff for fun. Going back to work full time is the last thing I want to do, but I'm flattered at your offer. My wife is about ready to retire from Eastern New Mexico University. She wants to run and play."

"We know you've missed being with your wife. I expected you would turn us down, so I have another proposal. How would you feel about a part-time arrangement? We'd pay the equivalent of three months' salary annually and give you a spot on the Better

Deal Board? You'd be advising us on security matters. You can keep the company car you're driving, and we'll pay your expenses. You'd have to make quarterly meetings and maybe an occasional special Board meeting," said Walter.

"I like your second proposal," said Lee.

"Good. Now there's one other thing. You told me you like Colorado and go there to fly fish. Helen and I own a log cabin on the Rio Grande River near South Fork. The cabin is located on gold medal trout waters. We have other plans for this summer, we'd like for you and Shirley to use the cabin. All you have to take is your clothes and your food."

"I'm afraid I'd feel like a mooch if I took advantage of your offer," said Lee.

"Lee, you're certainly not a mooch. It's something we want to do. Please do us a favor and allow us to do this for you and Shirley," said Walter.

"In those terms I don't see how I can turn you down. We'll use your cabin. I plan to call Shirley shortly; she'll be excited to hear about Colorado.

Walter asked, "When do you plan to go see Claire?"

"I need to head back to El Paso to pick up my belongings, then head toward Portales. I could make it a point to see Claire when I go through Tularosa, then call you after I get home. If it's okay with you?"

Chapter 83

KATHY HAD WORKED the previous week with no day off. She was energy depleted from an action-filled weekend and desperate for a normal workday.

She exited the elevator of the Regional Command Center and noticed the floor was packed with people.

Someone shouted, "She's here."

They began to clap. Someone shouted, "Speech!"

Her eyes filled with tears. She raised her arms. It got deathly quiet.

"This is nice. Thank you. I hope you're this pleased after I've had the job a while. I'm not big on speeches, but I'll try," said Kathy.

"I imagine you'd like to know what it'll be like to get your marching orders from me.

First of all, we've got tough duty and don't get much appreciation. It's hard to be upbeat when we are dealing with the dredges of society, the losers who make poor choices, and those anti-social and violent people who get into one jam after another. Our work schedules are crappy, we're too often confronted with dangerous situations and the pay isn't all that good.

Maybe it'll help to know I appreciate what you do. Keeping

people safe is a huge responsibility. If we don't do it right, someone gets hurt, maybe even dead. I believe in doing good work.

On the other hand, the bad guys are people with feelings, hopes and aspirations. Unfortunately, they probably didn't have much chance for a good life. These people have rights. I'll be making sure we treat these people with dignity and respect.

There's a balance between these two perspectives. It's a hard line to walk, but it's the road we're going to take," said Kathy.

I should warn you I call it like I see it. If you're screwing up, I'm going to tell you, but I'll also give you credit as earned. I'll do my best to be fair," said Kathy.

"You're probably wondering what kind of boss I'll be. I'm not going to tell you how to do your jobs. You can't be me. I can't be you. There are lots of ways to get things done. Just get it done. My door will always be open as a resource for you, not a roadblock.

We are entitled to a life outside of work. I'll try to keep things in balance so your personal life has a chance to be a happy experience. Work should be fun. Let's all look for humor in what we do and maintain a good outlook. I look forward to working with all of you. You've made my day. Thanks," said Kathy.

Most people stayed long enough for coffee, cake, to offer their congratulations and wish her well, then hurried back to work.

Once the lobby was cleared, Kathy looked for and found her desk. On it was a summons from Bill Shelton. His office was on the next floor. The door was open. She walked right in.

Shelton rose, smiling, "Good morning, Kathy. Congratulations on the promotion. Sorry I missed the cake and punch, too much on my plate. You've had a busy weekend. When did you get back?"

"Sunday evening, a long weekend."

"I'd appreciate a quick summary of how it went," said Bill.

"Sure, but I have a question," said Kathy. "Any word from the council on your promotion?"

"Yes, I got the job."

"I hoped you would. Congratulations. As far as a report is concerned, the newspaper accounts are pretty accurate. We were lucky it went as well as it did. Too many issues had to be dealt with on the spot."

"Like what," asked Bill?

"When Eli Sanchez realized he couldn't work his plan to poison the O'Kelly's, he decided to improvise and shoot his targets. Lee Perkins and Sam Vaquera eliminated the threat, but Sam took a slug in his shoulder. He'll recover, but the O'Kelly's son Everett, won't. He deliberately took a bite of a sandwich laced with cyanide and died instantly."

"Awful way to die," said Bill.

"Mark Jennings, Luisa Jaramillo and their agents moved in on organized crime in El Paso, Dallas, and New Orleans. I haven't had a chance to talk with them to find out how it went," said Kathy.

"That's about it, except a commitment I made to the O'Kelly's, they're going to help Claire Sullivan, the widow of the preacher who committed suicide and maybe do some things for his church. I told them I'd get some information from his congregation, which may result in the gift of a building.

I know I need to get things organized here, but I have promises to keep. If you don't mind, I'd like to get those commitments out of the way first," said Kathy.

"Sounds like everyone did a good job. Is the Ranger in the hospital?"

"No, he headed back to Waco on Sunday morning. Do you want more?"

"I'll wait for the written report. You get on with your plan. You got a nice raise. It'll show up on your next check. My routine is going to include a staff meeting on Mondays at one. You can skip today, take care of your promise to the O'Kelly's. Call me, door's always open."

Chapter 84

AL LANDRY SPOTTED KATHY coming up the walk and met her at his door.

"Good morning, Kathy. It's nice to see you again. Come on in. Carol has a pot of coffee and chocolate chip cookies."

"Exactly what I don't need. I'm getting big as a horse," said Kathy.

"You look pretty slim and trim to me. Come on in," said Al.

"This visit, like my last, is connected with the Sullivan suicide. If you've been reading the papers, you must be aware we've established Sullivan had nothing to do with the burglary at Better Deal."

"I haven't read today's paper! That's wonderful." Suddenly he looked shocked and became speechless. Tears began to flow. "Oh my God! We drove that man to take his own life. That's horrible! Claire must hate us," said Al.

"You weren't alone in causing Tim to take his life. There's no doubt you participated and made a tragic mistake. That's a burden you'll have to confront. I know it wasn't intentional, but it was awful. God teaches forgiveness. Maybe you need to ask him how to forgive yourselves," said Kathy.

"You aren't the only ones who'll have to deal with guilt. The

O'Kelly's son could have exonerated Tim Sullivan, but chose to hide the facts. He's dead, took his own life. His parents know they can't bring Tim back, but want to set things right. They sent me to ask you some questions."

Carol asked, "What can they possibly want from us?"

"Before Tim's death, your church was meeting in a facility belonging to another church. Do you still meet there? Does your church still exist?"

"Yes. We do. Same place. Mike Jones, a retired pastor took Tim's place temporarily. Unfortunately, Mike doesn't have the kind of oomph and energy Tim had, so the church hasn't been doing well financially. He's filled our pulpit far longer than he intended and wants us to find another pastor. We've been unable to find one the church can afford."

"How do you think it would be received, if the O'Kelly's offered to build a new church building?"

"It'd be nice," said Carol, "but what good would it do if we don't have a pastor? I doubt we could handle the up keep and utility cost."

"There's something else that bothers me," said Al, "What we did to Tim. We really don't deserve a new church. When the word gets out, we may lose what few members we have."

Kathy looked Al in the eye. "A new church wouldn't be a monument to your guilt or to the O'Kelly's. It would be exactly what Tim Sullivan prayed for and wanted: a place where Christians can come to worship. It would be God's Church."

"You sound like Tim. Tell you what," said Al, "Report what we told you and get back to me if the O'Kelly's want to make a serious proposal. I can take whatever they offer to do to the five-member Board of Deacons and we'll see if they can make it work."

"I have one last question. If they were to build you a church, have you given any serious thought to what you would want to build?"

"More than a little thought actually. Tim and our Facilities Committee had plans for three stages of construction. One of our church members is an architect who donated his time. Phase one is a five thousand square foot sanctuary with a nice entry, a storeroom, kitchen, a business office, a pastor's study and restrooms.

Phase two is another five thousand square foot addition with a fellowship hall and four classrooms. Phase three is smaller with a nursery and more classrooms," said Al.

"Would it be possible to borrow or make a copy of those plans?"

"Al replied, "I have a key to the church. We have several copies of the plans. I don't think it'll hurt to give you a copy. If you'll follow me to the church, I'll get you a copy."

"Perfect. You need to understand there's no assurance anything will come of this."

Chapter 85

AFTER SUNDAY BREAKFAST with the O'Kelly's and Kathy, Lee said his goodbyes and returned to his hotel to call Shirley. She feigned anger because he hadn't called. He apologized, hoping she was just giving him a bad time to make him squirm. He explained about making a part-time job commitment and how he had accepted the use of the O'Kelly cabin for the summer. He mentioned he had one last thing to do before he headed home.

He'd been able to go home most weekends. It had been four weeks since he'd seen Shirley. This was the longest time they'd ever been apart. She said, "Lee Perkins, I don't like this one bit. You're making decisions without discussing them with me. You need to get home ASAP, so we can talk."

"Uh oh! You're mad. Honey, I want to come home, but I can't. I'll be home before the weekend. I want to see you and sleep in my own bed. The board member job isn't time-consuming. They meet every three months. I thought you won't mind and the pay is terrific. If you don't want to use the cabin in Colorado, just say so," said Lee."

"I don't like it when you're gone. I'm tired of doing your yard work and there's guy stuff that needs to get fixed like changing faucet washers and repairing running toilets."

"I understand. Bye now. I'll see you in three or four days."

Lee had so much on his mind he hardly noticed the ten-hour trip back to El Paso. He stopped by the Wingham Hotel, gathered up his belongings, checked out and instructed the desk clerk to send the final bill to Better Deal. On his way out of town he stopped briefly by the Beasley residence to say his goodbyes.

The eighty-six mile trip to Alamogordo was uneventful. Years ago it was more entertaining. Jackrabbits and cottontails, a few coyotes and lots of large tarantulas crossed the road. They were so plentiful; the drive was an obstacle course. It wasn't at all unusual to see up to a hundred or so of the little guys on one trip. It was difficult to avoid driving over one that had failed to complete the crossing.

Nowadays no more than maybe one or two rabbits cross the road, the coyotes are still around, but the tarantulas have vanished. No one knew what had decimated the varmint population. The dominant theory was that hunters had killed them off. Lee thought this unlikely, because much of the countryside was in the military reservation and inaccessible to hunters. Almost certainly it was caused by a change in food or water availability. Whatever the cause, he missed seeing the rabbits.

Much of this area was secured in long-term leases held by the U.S. Army for use as a missile test range and for military training exercises. Their property began just north of El Paso and ran north for about two hundred and fifty miles. It was originally acquired for a B-29 Bombing Range during WW ll. The upper end of the range was used to test the first two Atomic Bombs at a location called the Trinity Site.

Lee stopped for a cold drink and nature's call at one of the only two pit stops available on the trip. They were both in Oro Grande. The one he picked reeked of beer and urine. *Next time I'll try the other. This one's a disgrace.*

The memory of the stench lingered in his mind. He tried to think of other more pleasant things and decided to focus to how he was going to approach Claire Sullivan. *I forgot to call. It's possible she might not even be in Tularosa. It's too late now. Hopefully this won't be a wasted trip.*

Up ahead he saw an overpass high above a railroad. This meant he had almost reached Alamogordo. A quick look at his watch reminded Lee it was time for a bite to eat. He decided to eat before he called.

Almost all of the fast food places in Alamogordo were located just a few blocks past the overpass on Highway 70. Hi-D-Ho Drive In was definitely not a "fast food" restaurant, but Lee remembered that they made a Green Chili Burger to die for; it was worth the extra time. He whipped the Ford into Hi-D-Ho.

The burger was juicy and good. When he finished, he asked if they had a Tularosa phone book. They did. In it he found Claire's phone number. It was not a match for her previous number. It was Sunday afternoon. Good chance he would catch her at home. He did.

"Claire, this is Lee Perkins. I'm in Alamogordo, where I stopped for lunch. I have an issue I'd like to discuss. Would it be at all possible to visit with you this afternoon?"

"I remember you well. You're the private investigator Mr. Beasley hired to look into the possibility of proving Tim didn't aid in the burglary in El Paso."

"That's right, from your remarks I'm assuming you're unaware of what took place this past weekend in El Paso. I think you're going to be very, very pleased when you hear what I have to report. May I stop by to see you now?"

"I don't see why not. I usually iron on Sunday afternoons, so don't plan to stay too long. I won't get another chance until next weekend."

"I understand. I'll try to get right to the point. Where are you located?"

"We live in the Vista Grande Apartments on the far northeast side of town."

"I remember seeing them the last time I was in Tularosa. They're on the HI way to Ruidoso."

"We're in apartment 132. How long do you think it will take you to get here?"

"I'm at the Hi-D-Ho in Alamogordo, maybe thirty minutes. I'll see you shortly."

Claire probably doesn't subscribe to an El Paso paper. He mentally chastised himself for not calling her. He owed it to her more than anyone to let her know it had been established Tim had nothing to do with the burglary.

When Claire opened her door, Lee couldn't help feeling sorry for her. The apartment complex was rundown. No doubt all she could afford. It was, however, clean and neat, as were her well-mannered kids. From all appearances Claire was a good mother.

"It's nice to see you again, Mr. Perkins. Please come in and tell me what I may do for you," said Claire.

"Actually, Claire, today it's more what I may do for you. I have some good news."

"How nice. Please sit down. May I offer you a cold drink"?

"No. Thank you. I just had a burger and a coke, but I will sit down. With your permission I'll get right to it, so you can finish your ironing."

"That'll be fine. I appreciate your consideration," said Claire.

"Saturday was a very busy day in El Paso. The FBI, The Texas Rangers, the El Paso Police Department and others were involved in a sting operation resulting in the arrest of some organized crime figures and the death of an official of Better Deal, the Company Attorney, and a son of the owners. A Texas Ranger was shot, but he'll recover," said Lee. "The good news I mentioned is information from these arrests absolutely proves your husband had nothing to do with the burglary of the Better Deal store."

"The O'Kelly's are extremely remorseful about how this has affected your life and about Tim's death. They've indicated they'd like to do some things to make life better for you and your children, which brings me to why I'm here," said Lee.

They want to set up education trust funds for your children in the amount of one million dollars each, as well as an income trust to assist you in providing for your children.

They've also offered to pay for further education for you, if you so desire. To make all this happen, I need some information. I need dates of birth and full names of your children, the same from you, as well as your social security number and how you get your mail or your bank account number, and bank routing number, if you prefer direct deposit for the income trust money," said Lee.

"You don't necessarily have to give me an answer to the education question now, but if you want to go back to school, I can get things in motion. I'm sure you don't know where or how you'd want it built at this time, but they also want to build you a home."

"There's one other issue. The O'Kelly's asked Kathy Smith to find out if New Hope Church still exists and if there's a continuing need for a new facility. The O'Kelly's are going to offer to build them a building," said Lee. "I promised you I'd be brief. I think I've covered everything. Do you have any questions?"

Lee had failed to notice that Claire was both smiling and crying.

"I have been praying the day would come when Tim would be exonerated. Our children deserve to know their father was a fine and decent man. I'm pleased for them. It proves prayer really works. God is good!"

"All the time," said Lee.

"I'll give you the information you requested," said Claire. "It'll take only a minute to write out the children's information and my social security number. I prefer direct deposit. I'll just give you one of my blank checks. They can pick up my account number and the bank routing number from the blank check. I'm having a hard time believing this is really happening."

"It's real. Believe it!!" said Lee.

"Building the church Tim envisioned would be a wonderful tribute to Tim's memory. He'd be pleased. That is, if they still have the need. I hope that works out," said Claire.

She turned suddenly serious and concerned, "It occurs to me that the church members who were so quick to convict and condemn Tim are going to feel some remorse. I know they didn't do what they did on purpose. They acted impulsively on bad information. I was initially bitter towards them, but I've come to realize it wasn't done maliciously. They did what they thought was right. I don't want them to think I blame them. Tim believed in forgiveness. It would dishonor his memory not to forgive," said Claire. "Please let them know I harbor no bad feelings."

"You are far kinder than I would be. They're a bunch of gossips that destroyed an innocent man's life and screwed up yours as well. Not to mention how all this affected innocent children who'll not have a father," said Lee.

"That may not be entirely true. I now have another man in my life. At this point he's just a friend, but he wants to be more. In time, they may have another man for a father, we'll just have to see," said Claire.

Lee, thank you for coming. You've no idea how much your visit meant to me. All this began because Mr. Beasley had the courage to stand up for Tim. He's a wonderful man. Please tell him how much I appreciate him and all he has done for us."

"I will," said Lee. "Now if you'll excuse me, I'll let you get back to your ironing and I'll head back to El Paso. It was nice to see you again. Goodbye."

Chapter 86

Between Oro Grande, NM and El Paso, Texas

AS HE WAS RETURNING to El Paso, Lee remembered he owed it to Oscar to bring him up to speed and he needed to arrange a final meeting with the O'Kelly's about the visit with Claire. He also had some questions for Oscar about the car and other expenses he needed to get resolved before he left town.

It was late afternoon. He was almost back to El Paso. There was time to squeeze in some of his agenda before the day was done. He dialed the number for Oscar's Mountain Park home. Jackie Beasley answered.

"Hi, Lee," said Jackie. "My phone says it's you. You want Oscar. Right?"

"Correct. Is he handy?" asked Lee.

"Depends on how the play-off game is going. The best answer is, maybe," said Jackie.

"I've no idea who's playing. I've been too busy to keep up," said Lee.

"Me either," said Jackie. "Besides, I don't do football. I'd rather read a book. Hold on."

"I can't believe you don't like football. Everybody likes football," said Lee.

"I didn't say I didn't _like_ football. I said I don't do football. The game's interesting, but totally devoid of value. I'd rather learn or do something. I've got better ways to spend my time than sit on my rump, eat hot dogs and yell 'til I get laryngitis. Oscar mentioned the game has been pretty one-sided, so I'm sure he'll talk with you. I'll tell him you're on the phone," said Jackie.

She carried the phone to the den and said, "Lee's on the line."

"Lee." said Oscar. "How are you buddy? You in Portales?"

"No. I'm less than an hour from your place. I've been in Alamogordo visiting with Claire Sullivan," said Lee.

"You ought to go home weekends. Shirley's going to break your plate," said Oscar.

"Sounds like you've been talking to Shirley. I didn't call her last night," said Lee. "I was on an errand for the O'Kelly's and lost all track of time."

"Yeah, I know. The old man talked to Charles, who shared with me. How'd it go?" asked Oscar.

"If you'll invite me to stop by. I'll fill you in. I'm going to try to wrap all this up by tomorrow morning and head home," said Lee.

"Come on by," said Oscar. "The game will be over before you get here."

The Beasley home was in the deep shadow of the mountain by the time Lee arrived. On the lower slope and flats below, streetlights and house lights were coming on like twinkling stars. No view of the sunset on this side of the mountain, but a beautiful view nonetheless.

Jackie responded to the doorbell. After a hug, she handed Lee a cold bottle of Corona.

"Oscar is in the den. The score is tied; time is running out, so it may run into overtime. You may have to wait to get his attention," said Jackie.

Lee walked into the den. Oscar was on the edge of the couch leaning toward the tube. He didn't glance Lee's way. "Have a seat! This is about over. If the Jets make this field goal, they win," said Oscar. "That's it, good kick. Game's over! It was a lousy game until the last quarter. The Cowboys scored twelve points in the last five minutes and tied it up. I thought this might be their year to take a seventh title, but they just couldn't get it together."

As he turned off the TV he turned to face Lee. "Hey, the Corona's a good idea. Give me a minute to get one, then you can fill me in," said Oscar.

When he returned, Jackie was at his side. "Do you mind if I listen in? Claire has been on my mind for a long time."

"Not at all," said Lee. "We all have a stake in this. I assume you're up-to-date on Saturday's events?"

"We read what was in the Sunday morning El Paso Times and on the evening news on KTSM. I also had a phone call from Charles Peterson, who shared the O'Kelly's plans."

"Actually, those reports are spot on, so I won't repeat what you already know," said Lee.

"When I talked with Claire this afternoon, she was okay about the trusts for her kids and the income for herself. She's going to give going back to school some thought and she's not in a position to know where she'd want to have a home at this time. She's pleased to hear Tim's plan for a church might become a reality," said Lee. "The high point in the conversation was when she heard that Tim had been exonerated. There were some tears and some smiles. What's going on with you guys?"

"I've made some pretty sweeping changes in how we do business, eliminated some positions, cut some costs and lowered a lot of prices. They may decide to run me off," said Oscar.

"I hope not," said Lee. "Well, that's all I've got. In the morning, I'm going to report by phone to the O'Kelly's and head home. You guys flew me up here and I've been driving a company car. Did I understand Mr. O'Kelly correctly about keeping the car?" asked Lee.

"If he said you'll get one, I'm sure you will. It may not be the one you're driving. That one is the division backup vehicle for breakdowns. My guess is you'll get a new one. You'll be reporting to Peterson. He's on the Board and knows all about it," said Oscar. "The next board meeting is in April. They'll probably order you a car and swap out for this one in April. By the way, congratulations are in order for the board position. That's a sweet deal."

"If you think of anything else you need to know about the visit with Claire, let me know. It's been a long day, so I'm going to head to the hotel. Good night," said Lee.

In route to his hotel from the Beasley home, Lee called Walter O'Kelly, "Good evening."

"Hi, Lee. How'd it go?"

"You want all of it over the phone tonight, or do you want me to call you in the morning?"

"How about a taste of it? The short version tonight and the whole tamale in the morning?" said Walter.

"I was hoping you'd say that. I'm pretty wiped out. It's been a long day," said Lee. "To put it a nutshell, she liked the trust plans for the kids and will accept the income trust money. She wants to give school some thought, and thinks now is not the time to build a house," said Lee. "She hadn't heard the news about Saturday, so it put her on cloud nine when I told her about Tim's exoneration. There were tears and there were smiles. I'm glad I got to give her the news.

She's living in a dump, but it's clean and neat. She's a good mom. You're doing the right thing. She deserves better."

Walter asked, "Did you say anything about the church?"

"I did," said Lee. "Have you heard anything from Kathy about her visit with the church?"

"Yes. They aren't doing very well, but they still exist and still meet in the old building. They're about to lose their temporary pastor and don't have the money to replace him," said Walter.

"Have you decided what you want to do?" asked Lee.

"We think so. We were waiting to hear from you about how Claire reacted to the possibility," said Walter.

"I thought I saw her eyes light up when I mentioned you were considering the possibility of a building. She said Tim would be pleased. You won't believe this, but she was very concerned about the people in the church. She doesn't want them to feel guilty about Tim. Said she forgives them. She's quite a lady," said Lee.

Walter ended the conversation by suggesting that Lee call about nine in the morning, to which Lee agreed.

Chapter 87

EARLY MONDAY MORNING Lee packed his bags, and checked out of the Wyndham. He found they'd already been asked to send the bill to Better Deal. He poured a coffee to go and snared a couple of their donuts. By nine a.m. he was close to Roswell and pulled over to make the call to the O'Kelly's.

Following his report, Walter told him they'd made some decisions. Several choices required his participation.

An attorney was drafting the trust documents for the children and Claire. El Paso's First National Bank was going to deposit $10,000 a month to Claire Sullivan's account.

They wanted Lee to be a liaison between the O'Kelly's and Claire. His first assignment was to fill Claire in on these details. If and when Claire went back to school or wanted a house, Lee was to make the arrangements.

While he was at it, he may as well fill her in on what they decided about the church. They were going to build and pay for phase 1 of Tim's church plans, a 5000 square foot building. While it was under construction, they wanted to do some things to assure it was a healthy church financially.

They were going to foot the salary and expenses for a new pastor and a minister of music. It wouldn't take more than six months to build a building. The church could use this grace period to grow the congregation and get finances on firmer footing.

They had assigned Oscar Beasley as coordinator for fulfilling the commitments to the church, their pastor and church leaders.

Additionally, to assure the church membership had healthy growth, Oscar would make available an advertising budget and provide Better Deal's marketing expertise at no expense to the church.

Lee arrived in Portales late morning. He went directly to her classroom at Eastern New Mexico University. Her class was in session, but he walked right in. When Silvia saw him she excused herself, ran to his arms. One long kiss later, she turned to the applause of her class and said; "I haven't seen my husband in over a month. I can see we're not going to get anything productive done today. You have a walk for the balance of today's class. Enjoy."

Chapter 88

DURING THE MONTHS that followed, Claire decided she would go back to school. At Walter O'Kelly's suggestion, she took a vocational interest and aptitude test to match up her skill set with her choice of careers. The test results indicated her best potential for career success would be in social work practice.

She applied for and was accepted as a student at the University of Texas at El Paso, where she planned to earn both undergraduate and master's degrees in social work practice. Lee arranged and facilitated her relocation. Her income was more than sufficient to provide a lovely apartment near the campus and childcare as needed.

Oscar became an ex-officio member of the New Hope facilities committee. The committee took advantage of Oscar's access to the expertise of Better Deal's real estate department, resulting in the acquisition of seven beautiful treed acres in a high visibility location.

Completion date for construction of the church was estimated to be about June first.

A Pastor search committee located a dynamic young man who had recently graduated from Baylor University with a divinity degree, to whom they offered their pastor position. He accepted and the church was showing significant growth under his leadership.

A much-experienced music leader from Trinity Baptist Church in Kerrville, who wanted to relocate to El Paso, noticed the posting for a music leader in El Paso. He applied and was called to serve. He gratefully accepted the position.

Shirley Perkins planned to retire at the end of May. She and Lee decided to take full advantage of the O'Kelly offer of the use of their Colorado cabin for the summer. They purchased a yellow four-wheel drive Jeep Wrangler, two yellow Honda ATV's, a trailer to transport the ATV's, two complete fly-fishing outfits, plus walking sticks and hiking shoes for each of themselves.

In September it was announced that Charles Peterson would be taking Walter's place as chairman and chief operating officer of O'Kelly Enterprises. Oscar Beasley, because of his stellar performance as division vice president in El Paso, was given Peterson's position as executive vice president to be effective in six months. As soon as the El Paso church project was completed, Oscar, Jackie and their children would be moved to Dallas, where he would be Peterson's administrative assistant and understudy for six months.

Beasley chose for his replacement as division manager in El Paso, Dan Coleman, who had been filling Beasley's old slot as district manager.

Chapter 89

ON SUNDAY OF JUNE 2012 three hundred members and guests attended the dedication of the new sanctuary of New Hope Baptist Church. Seated together were Luisa Jaramillo, Kathy Smith, Lee and Shirley Perkins, Oscar and Jackie Beasley, Walter and Helen O'Kelly.

Claire Sullivan gave the dedication speech. "I appreciate you asking me to speak on this occasion. Tim would be pleased to see his dream fulfilled.

Tim would want us to dedicate this church to be a beacon of light to draw others to God, spread the good news of his love and forgiveness, asking only we believe in him and love one another.

He'd also tell you he was wrong to take his own life. God has a plan. When we are in despair, we're to call upon him to get us beyond our troubles.

I worry that some of you feel a burden of guilt for what happened to Tim. Neither Tim nor I want you to carry that yoke around your necks. We all make and learn from our mistakes.

God loves us, forgives us when we make mistakes. We need to learn to forgive one another, even to forgive ourselves. God bless you."

———————

About the Author

AUTHOR, BERRY HAWKINS, AND HIS WIFE, LA RUE

Berry Hawkins owned and operated a supermarket, was district manager for a grocery chain, then managed domestic and international sales for a spice and extract company. He retired, got bored with fishing, golf and travel. A friend invited him to join a writer's club. It was love from the first meeting.

Deadly Outcome is the first of three thrillers whose events occur in and around El Paso, the Dallas Metroplex, and southern New Mexico, and feature the synergy of a female police lieutenant, a grocer and a retired Texas Ranger.

To learn more about Berry Hawkins visit:
BerryHawkins.com

39650777R00214

Made in the USA
Columbia, SC
11 December 2018